T0113465

A Fistful
of Fig Newtons

ALSO BY JEAN SHEPHERD

A Christmas Story

In God We Trust, All Others Pay Cash

*Wanda Hickey's Night of Golden Memories,
and Other Disasters*

The Ferrari in the Bedroom

A FISTFUL OF FIG NEWTONS

By Jean Shepherd

*Illustrated by
the Author*

Broadway Books
New York

First Broadway trade paperback edition published in 1987.

A FISTFUL OF FIG NEWTONS. Copyright © 1981 by Snow Pond Productions, Inc. All rights reserved. No part of this book may be reproduced or transmitted in any form or by any means, electronic or mechanical, including photocopying, recording, or by any information storage and retrieval system, without written permission from the publisher. For information, address Broadway Books, a division of Random House, Inc.

"A Fistful of Fig Newtons"–originally appeared in *Playboy* magazine, Copyright © 1981 by Playboy Enterprises, Inc.
"The Light at the End of the Tunnel"–reprinted with permission from *New Jersey Bell* magazine, number 3, 1980, Copyright © 1980, New Jersey Bell.
"The Mole People Battle the Forces of Darkness"–originally appeared in *Playboy* magazine, Copyright © 1971 by Playboy Enterprises, Inc.
"Marcel Proust Meets the New Jersey Tailgater, and Survives"–originally appeared in *Car and Driver,* Copyright © 1975 by Ziff Davis Publishing Company.
"The Lost Civilization of Deli"–originally appeared in *Omni,* Copyright © 1979 by Omni Publications International, Ltd.
"The Whole Fun Catalog of 1929"–Copyright © 1978 by Chelsea House, Reprinted from THE WHOLE FUN CATALOG, Chelsea House Publishers, New York.
"Lost at C"–originally appeared in *Playboy* magazine, Copyright © 1973 by Playboy Enterprises, Inc.
The lyrics from "Why Don't You Do Right" by Joe McCoy by courtesy of Moreley Music Co.
The lyrics from "It Was a Very Good Year" by Ervin Drake– Copyright © 1961 & 1965 by Dolfi Music, Inc. All rights controlled by Chappell & Co., Inc. (Intersong Music, Publisher). International Copyright Secured. All Rights Reserved. Used by permission.

BROADWAY BOOKS and its logo, a letter B bisected on the diagonal, are trademarks of Random House, Inc.

Visit our website at www.broadwaybooks.com

Book design by Michael Collica

Illustrated by the author

Library of Congress Catalog Card Number: 80-2872

ISBN 0-385-18843-9

This book is a work of the imagination. However, some essays are observation and conclusion. The characters depicted in the short stories are fictional. They do not represent any actual individuals, living or dead.

JEAN SHEPHERD

To Leigh and Daphne–
Who share my bed, my board,
and walks along the sea.
May they never regret it.

"I am not a crook."

      . . . Richard M. Nixon

        ex-government employee

"Only the centipede recognizes

      the five thousand footsteps of his

        Grandfather . . ."

          . . . Banacek

Contents

A FISTFUL
OF FIG NEWTONS

You let other women make a fool of you...

I banged on the steering wheel as Peggy Lee belted it out in her mean, silky, snotty, "get me some money" voice.

"YEAH, YEAH!" I hollered stupidly as Billy Butterfield's trumpet rasped out the bridge.

You sit there won'drin' what it's all about...

Stuck in rush-hour traffic, the maniac in you takes over. The mouth of the Lincoln Tunnel was four blocks and two thousand cars away.

My radio was tuned to WNEW, the only station that the bastard can get in midtown Manhattan. In a way, that curious misfortune might have been one cause of what was to follow. WNEW is an instant time warp leap into the past. A flick of the knob and you're magically back in the 1940s and '50s of Peggy Lee, Dinah Shore, Ella Fitzgerald, and a lot of singers who haven't made a record since Eisenhower retired to Gettysburg.

My mind ticked over idly. I hummed, I whistled, I spit out the window.

You sit there won'drin' what it's all about...

The radio buzzed obscenely, a rank, juicy Bronx cheer of a buzz, and quit. God dammit! I thumped my fist on the plastic dashboard, sending up motes of cigarette ashes from the ashtray, but the radio remained as silent as a dime-store Buddha incense-burner. If there is ever a time when you need a car radio to keep you company, it's in a long line of creeping traffic.

I thumped the dash. No luck. All the while my eyes were darting back and forth over the traffic; left, right, rear mirror, right, left, rear mirror, clickety-click-click, in the style of the true urban driver. There's always a yellow cab or a Puerto Rican in a battered van, marked *ACE PLUMBING SUPPLIES*, ready to beat you out for every precious inch. Nerves is what it takes, nerves of steel; cobalt steel. Fighting your way to the mouth of the Lincoln Tunnel at rush hour is no place for lady drivers with blue hair or frail stock-brokers with rimless bifocals.

An airport bus sent a blast of diesel fumes that caught me fair and square, a clean shot.

"Braak, braaak"—my city cough rattled my ribs. "BORK!"

Suddenly there was a brief opening ahead. I shot forward, skittered through the line like an NFL halfback and gained a full car length on a cursing Connecticut driver who got caught lighting his cigar. I cackled. I could see him in my rear mirror mouthing evil words. I threw him a quick finger and whipped up next to a looming tractor-trailer. I was grateful for a moment or two of shade. I was actually within striking distance of the tunnel mouth itself, at last.

The streams of traffic, in five or six lines, edged into the evil black mouth. Theoretically, there is supposed to be a system for alternate cars to go forward into the tunnel, each in his turn, but like everything else in the urban jungle of today, that system is an outmoded joke, like taking off your hat in an elevator or opening doors for women.

I had a brief image of a hulking giant trying to put toothpaste

*back into a Colgate tube as I hunched over my wheel, deep in bat-
tle. I saw my chance. A tiny opening between a big, blue clunker of
a Buick Riviera and a puttering Valiant. I slammed the transmis-
sion into LOW-LOW, floored the accelerator.*

ZZZzziiiPP! I made it, I made it! Whoopee! I was in the tunnel!

*Two snakelike lines of traffic inched through this gloomy tile-
and-concrete alimentary canal, the lower colon of the city of New
York spewing its waste out into New Jersey.*

*The tunnel jogged slightly to the left. The entrance behind me
disappeared. I was now far below the sinister, sludgy waters of the
mighty Hudson. God only knows what indescribable obscenities
lay above me, protected only by a thin shield of rusting steel and
crumbling concrete. Hardly a soul alive today remembers when the
ancient tunnel was built. Dimly lit by yellow bulbs, the tunnel lives
in a perpetual basement gloom. No dawn, no sunset, no spring or
summer, fall or winter; only Man and the rats inhabit this man-
made wonder of nature.*

*It affects people in many ways. I once knew a man who was in
every way a civilized creature, the product of centuries of Western
culture—Yale, Skull & Bones, a reader of John Updike, a subscriber
to the opera—who had one fatal flaw. The instant he entered the
tunnel he reverted to his ancient Paleolithic forebears. Deep fears
gripped him. He saw lurking carnivores with yellow eyes in the
shadows. Perspiration gushed from his every pore. Each minute in
the tunnel was sheer hell. It finally got so bad that he sold his elegant ancestral home in Princeton, moved to a cockroach-infested,
furnished flat in Manhattan, where he remains today, a prisoner
of the Island.*

*Other victims of tunnel madness have an uncontrollable urge to
blow their horns, apparently in the feeble hope that the echoing din
will reassure them that they are still alive. I've always thought that
a deep study of the effect of long, sinister tunnels on the mind of
commuters would be a valuable one, perhaps giving us a clue to
the rising incidence of madness, breakdowns, and broken mar-
riages among ex-urbanites.*

I crept forward. Overhead, little yellow lights blinked, indicating some poor bastard was in trouble ahead.

Purgatory. That's what the tunnel is. I'm suspended between heaven and hell; no time, no seasons, accompanied only by my sins and fears. My personal tunnel defense has evolved over years of driving. I let my mind roam free as a bird, shutting out the gloomy Now.

Ahead of me in a heavily souped-up Dodge Charger (a true Kid car), a crowd of male college students swilled cans of Budweiser. A peeling decal on the rear window read RUTGERS SCARLET KNIGHTS GO! I could see a hulking undergraduate in the rear seat, blowing large pink bubbles of the finest Fleers. He wore a scarlet-and-black Rutgers T-shirt with the numerals 69 obscenely emblazoned for the world to see. The bubble burst, draping his nose with pink, rubbery chewing gum.

"Ah," I muttered, "the cream of our youth, the future hope of America."

A can flew out of the window and bounced off the tile walls of the tunnel, ricocheting onto my hood where it dug a neat gouge in the expensive paint.

"Hey, Sixty-nine, you slob!" I yelled into the echoing din; fruitlessly, of course. My tunnel-loosened mind darted nimbly to another T-shirt, another university many states away.

Old Number 76, where is he today? My mind savored his Armageddon, his defeat, his disgrace.

A Fistful of Fig Newtons or the Shoot-Out in Room 303

The squat, chunky glass nestled chill and reassuring in my hand. It was one of my treasured set of matched old-fashioned glasses celebrating the long-past Bicentennial of our blessed land. Each tumbler bore in magnificent cut-glass bas-relief a portrait of a Founding Father. Thomas Jefferson, his face stern and yet patriotically inspiring, sweated slightly on the side of my icy glass. Under his portrait, etched with authority, was a quote from the Great Democrat himself:

I believe in The People.

I stood at the window of my fourteenth-story apartment and stared listlessly out into the gathering gloom. Far below me were hordes of wandering picketers, their signs waving in the dusk, distance muting their hoarse obscenities. Occasionally a siren wailed, accompanied by the distant wink of red flashers. The apartment lights dimmed momentarily but struggled bravely back on, narrowly averting the third blackout of the week. The Jack Daniels glowed deep in my interior. Going about its therapeutic work, it warmed me.

I glanced down at Jefferson, whose ear was just under my right thumb.

"Tom, I'm not sure it's working out."

Another muttering wave of distant protest filtered through my dusty venetian blinds. One of the problems of living fourteen stories above the city is that you tend to see things too clearly, especially after a jot or two of bourbon. Down on the street, amid the pitched battles for survival, you get caught up in the fray. In the continuous pinball game of life, shouldering old ladies aside for a vacant cab, thumping children in the ribs for a seat on the subway, kneeing a nun in the groin for the last remaining hot pretzel engrosses you and you fail to see, ultimately, that the whole damn thing is falling apart. But high over the city, after a desperate Friday at the office and the final flurry of insulting memos to cap the day, the vision sharpens; the mind tears aside the veil of wishful thinking, and there it is.

Incidentally, you can call me Dave if you like. That's not my real name, but I prefer to remain anonymous, for reasons that will become obvious.

I sipped more bourbon and, struck by a sudden transient urge, ripped the cover off the current issue of *New York* with its gleaming white headline reading: 101 Free FUN Things to Do in the City! With smooth, adept, practiced skill I quickly folded the cover into a paper airplane. It was an art which I had not used in many years, and one which I had perfected grade after grade at the Warren G. Harding School. I fished around in one of the rickety, creaky drawers of my Swedish Moderne Finish-It-Yourself desk and found a red felt-tip marker which had insolently leaked over a pile of unpaid bills. I quickly scrawled on one wing of my airplane:

Look out–I'm coming to get all of you.

On the other wing, I signed: GOD.

It looked good. Inching my window open a crack so as not to let in too much soot and noxious carbon compounds, I launched the plane out into the darkened canyon. It rose swiftly on an updraft, banked to the left, and began gracefully volplaning down, bearing with it my hopes for a better world. Down, down it drifted until, finally lost from view, it disappeared into the mob. A few white faces suddenly peered up at me. It might have been imagination, but they seemed frightened. One face, however, mouthed a foul word.

"And the same to you, Jack, with bells on it."

I smiled my carefully cultivated Dick Cavett smirk and settled squashily into my amazingly uncomfortable bean-bag loveseat. A distant phone tinkled and I knew that the elderly maiden lady who lived in the next apartment was getting the first of her nightly obscene phone calls. Even chaos and barbaric anarchy have their routines.

The morning's *Times* lay scattered about my feet. ALL THE NEWS THAT'S FIT TO PRINT: hostages, wars, perversions, the crossword puzzle, which had lately itself begun to reflect the age; an occasional shocking four-letter word creeping in here and there: Reston's calm voice daily chastising the world for its follies.

I flipped the switch on my TV set, the Cassandra of our days.

Mayor Koch's face appeared, his white shirt rumpled with sweat, his tie hanging at half-mast. Flashbulbs popped. His eyes rolled wildly in the glare.

I muttered: "By God, he still looks like Frank Perdue, the Chicken King."

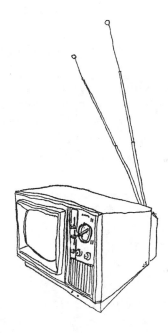

"I have informed the strikers' representatives that this city can no longer tolerate . . ."

I flipped the channel. Koch again. Another flip; another Koch. On all the channels nothing but Koches. If Karl Marx were alive today, he would have written: ABC is the opiate of The Masses.

Then I knew what I had to do. Desperation has its limits. My hand turned the channel selector to that one island of total, tranquil, heart-warming escapism: Public Television. Where else can you relive the entire Victorian era in endless reruns, a world peopled with simple, honest maids and butlers, and square-jawed English squires? Occasionally the fare shifts even further back in time and Shakespeare's Henry V rides out again into battle, but such fun, poetic battles. French chefs eternally prepare arcane treats featuring fish available only off the coast of Normandy and then for only a fortnight out of the year, when they are running. I settled back, prepared to enjoy an hour or two of total, heavily endowed Culture.

"The following PBS program was made possible by a grant from the Mobil Corporation."

"Aha," I hissed, "the Petroleum Broadcasting System is still greasing the ways."

A blast of atonal, formless electronic music consisting of a series of a-rhythmic beeps and assorted transistorized hooting, the kind of fanfare that always precedes a "serious" program on PBS, filled the room. The credits unrolled endlessly, a series of tricky little exploding letters, where most of the rich endowments go. Jazzy titles ain't cheap.

" 'America . . . [Pause. Another blast of beeps] the Aesthetics of Transition . . .' [Pause. Assorted hoots] the sixth program in a series of twenty-four . . . [More credits exploded into multicolored space] moderated by Alistair Cooke."

I settled back deeper into my bean bag, wondering briefly why every program about America is hosted by an Englishman and knowing damn well that the reverse certainly wasn't true, that the BBC would never use Jack Lemmon to discuss the Plantagenet line.

Mr. Cooke's calm face appeared. In the background, an imposing wall of heavy leather-bound volumes gave the scene weight and depth. As his cultured tones, cool, calm, unemotional, droned, I reached down to the floor for my Jack Daniels bottle. Several cockroaches retreated hastily. More sirens wailed, punctuated by the furious klaxons bearing the wounded to Bellevue.

"Our guest tonight is the distinguished visiting lecturer at the University of Chicago . . ."

Another face appeared on the screen, smiling with well-bred diffidence, a face clearly at home amid the dusty stacks, a face obviously prepared to hold its own in the highest literary soirees in the land. I leaned forward, the expensive lima beans beneath my rump rattling and tinkling as they sought other positions of discomfort.

By God, I knew that face, that cool smile, that drooping left eye, that rumpled tweed jacket with its faint but heavy growth of moss. I knew that face! Was it the bourbon? Was it another symptom of my approaching madness?

"Dr. Umbaugh, we are pleased and honored to have the privilege of discussing the aesthetics of frontier courage and the emergence of . . ."

Good Christ Almighty! Umbaugh! UMBAUGH! Good God! I clutched the Great Democrat tightly and took a mighty swig, followed immediately by an uncontrolled belch.

". . . why yes, Mr. Cooke, the unique talent and attitude bred on the frontier of barbarian America were the result of many factors. Chief among them, I must say, was cosmic Boredom, and . . ."

I struggled to my feet. Umbaugh, you son of a bitch! Tell 'em, you bastard, tell 'em!

I threw a pair of ice cubes into my glass, eager to listen to the words of the most talented, fiercely, nay, ferociously courageous man I had ever known.

Doctor Umbaugh. Of course. That was inevitable, at the very least. Umbaugh was one of those to whom the academic atmosphere was akin to milk and honey, the Promised Land. He fed on academia the way a whale inhales plankton, whereas I and most of my comrades back in those days when my life briefly impinged on Umbaugh's struggled ceaselessly against it, alternating between the stark terror of imminent failure and crashing, utter boredom, boredom of a mind-numbing nature so palpable and real that you could almost see it growing up the walls of our poured-concrete prison.

The midwestern university that I had recklessly elected to attend on the GI Bill of Rights, a charitable outpouring of public monies which has led to the psychic downfall of multitudes of erstwhile worthy garage mechanics and plumber's helpers, had been designed by one of those architects of the French school known, in translation, as: Art is Truth, Ugliness is always honest; hence Art is ugly, and there are few materials in the world as ugly as poured concrete. Attending the university was much like living in a vast, glass-enclosed concrete viaduct. It was the concrete more than anything else, I suspect now, that set the wheels in motion which catapulted Umbaugh into the realm of Legend.

It was 2 A.M. of a rainy, dreary fall night that it happened, a Friday in fact. I paced restlessly about my poured-concrete cell in a dormitory ironically named after one of America's more sickeningly romantic early poets. We, the inmates, referred to it as "U. S. Gypsum Hall." The twin dormitory next to us was called "The Portland Cement Arms" by its natives. The rain splashed against the pitted aluminum window casement forever sealed against outside reality by modern design. Either that, or some prudent administrator had had the windows protected against the threat, always present, of suicide. I paced as much as an eight-by-six-foot room would allow, a room with its poured-concrete desk, its poured-concrete bureau with its endearing little poured-concrete knobs. I wore only a pair of sagging Jockey shorts, my Fruit of the Looms being at the laundry. I had $2.82 between me and the bottom of my financial tank. I was running on the fumes. It was ten days before my next GI check was due from Uncle Sugar. Any student who could get up the scratch had long since fled this vast concrete carbuncle in the midst of the cornfields for weekend solace in the nearest big city. Not me. Not with $2.82 in my Levi's and an Organic Chemistry exam coming up first period Monday morning. The only citizens left on campus were the destitute, the about-to-be-failed, and the truly zealous.

I peered out of the window into the sleety rain. Far below, a coed struggled against the storm, dimly lit by one of the "colorful" fake turn-of-the-century gas lamps that had been installed in the Quad to counteract, theoretically, the plastic ivy which was attached to the exterior walls of our dorm. Real ivy does not grow in that climate, so the alumni of an earlier class had contributed the plastic variety to our well-being. It came from Montgomery Ward and was the best quality plastic ivy obtainable. It, at least, enabled the university to legally get away with the line: The restful, ivy-covered walls of tradition-laden . . .

The starlings loved it, yelling and honking amid the rattling leaves at all hours of the night, carrying on the obscene activities that set starlings apart from the rest of the more civilized bird world. The coed moved through the dim light below. I listlessly peered down at her. About five feet tall, going maybe a hundred and eighty pounds, she wore skin-tight toreador pants which showed off her vast hams to best advantage. Her head covered with pink plastic barrels, she was typical of the campus queens the school specialized in: corn-fed, gum-chewing Home Ec majors. No wonder *Playboy* was passed from sweaty hand to sweaty hand until its pages were limp and ragged. It was the only port in a storm.

I moodily squatted on the edge of my poured-concrete bed with its meager foam rubber cushion. Mere inches from my nose, *Principles of Organic Chemistry*, a hated volume of arcane, useless, stupid lore lay open on my desk amid a few scattered notebook pages bearing my pitiful notes. Chemistry was my Moby Dick. I had a brooding, certain knowledge that it would get me in the end. Subsequent events were to bear this out, but that is another story.

Suddenly, out of the blue, a happy thought struck me. "Yeah," I muttered, leaped to my feet and dove into the minute niche in the concrete wall that the college handbook called: Spacious, walk-in closets. I pawed through the pile of accumulated junk: my old combat boots, a pair of galoshes my mother had sent me, four pairs of mismatched Japanese shower clogs, limp-stringed tennis racquets, clothes hangers. Aha!

Weeks before I had hidden away from the avid, hungry eyes of my dorm mates a two-pound Family Size Parti-Pak of Fig Newtons. I retrieved my treasure from amid the rubble and sat happily on the bed, contemplating the virgin, pristine beauty of the

unopened package. I freely admit that I am a depraved Fig Newton freak. There aren't many of us, but there is a bond between
the lovers of the noble Fig Newton that transcends all. The Fig
Newton itself is one of the most glorious creations of Man, its subtle, soft, sand-hued crust of a sensual shade, its dark, rich, tart filling of the ancient figs from the sun-drenched shores of Greece
redolent of the earth's bounties. There are those who actually enjoy such obscenities as cherry Fig Newtons, strawberry Fig Newtons, and even, God forbid, chocolate Fig Newtons.

What blasphemy! The very name Fig Newton describes beautifully this classic pearl of the baker's art. Legend has it that Isaac
Newton himself concocted this paragon while contemplating the
laws of motion. There are those who maintain that his discovery
of the Fig Newton was vastly more important than that business
about gravity, which any fool could have come up with.

I hefted the package in my hand, with its provocative invita-
tion: Cut along dotted line. The rain drummed monotonously.
The dormitory was deathly still, except for the occasional shuddering moan of distant plumbing. With my right thumbnail, I
carefully split the dotted line, savoring every moment to the full.

Believe me, any break in the soft, muzzy, stifling boredom is
manna to the prisoner. I have always felt that it was no coinci-
dence that Hitler wrote *Mein Kampf* while in the slammer. If he
had had a couple of pounds of Fig Newtons to play with, maybe
the world would have been spared WWII.

Carefully, I eased the flap upward and outward, laying bare the
two compact rows of magnificent beauties. Immediately the
musty concrete smell of my room was drowned in the incomparable fragrance, the subtle, haunting perfume that is characteristic of vintage Fig Newtons. I breathed deeply. Beads of perspiration
covered my nose, the sweat of sensual anticipation. I placed the
package carefully on my desk and arose, to steady my nerves.

I stepped to the window to prolong this moment of ecstasy.
Down below, a solitary cyclist splashed through the puddles, his

soggy field jacket identifying him as another ex-GI in pursuit of government-funded knowledge. He still wore the patches of his old division, the 9th Infantry.

I turned, and carefully extracted a Fig Newton from the company of its fellows. The drama was about to begin, although naturally I was not aware of it at the time. Umbaugh was about to become Legend.

I sniffed the full-packed beauty and took a tentative nibble, savoring the rich yet somehow poignant flavor, hinting as it does of the overtones of Greek tragedy; the fig of Elektra, Orestes, and even Oedipus himself. A few crumbs trickled down my wrist. I finished off the first with lip-smacking gusto; a second, a third. As I settled down to my fourth Fig Newton, I became aware of a heavy clumping outside my door.

"Christ Almighty, God dammit!" I muttered, frantically attempting to hide my treasure under the pillow. Our dormitory was peopled entirely by beings whose sense of smell surpassed that of the timber wolf's. Any hint of food, anywhere, was sure to bring the ravenous parasites.

My door slammed open and there stood Goldberg, his hulking blubbery form almost filling the room, clad in the standard sagging Jockeys and shapeless T-shirt. He wore pink, rubber-thonged sandals and a two-day growth of smarmy beard.

"Fig Newtons! I smell Fig Newtons. Y'got Fig Newtons!" he wheezed hoarsely.

What a kick in the ass, I thought. Goldberg, whose appetite was rivaled only by the giant garbage disposal trucks which lurched daily about the campus, gobbling up anything in their paths, was the last one I wanted to see this night. Known as "Pig-out" to his friends and "the Slob" to all others, Goldberg was born to eat.

"Hey, Pig-out, I thought you went to town." I struggled to appear civil and welcoming.

"Nah. I'm broke. Gimme a Fig Newton."

There was no way around it. The iron-clad law of the dormitory mandated that we share and share alike; a stupid law, but there it was.

I extended the package to Goldberg. He scooped up three at one swoop, the poor little Fig Newtons hopelessly clinging to each other for companionship in their last moments on earth. He stuffed all three into his garbage chute.

"Mmmmff, mmmffffph," he grunted like a rooting hippo.

What the hell, I thought, it's every man for himself now. I grabbed a couple of Fig Newtons, barely avoiding his grasp, and chewed happily. A feeling of comradeship filled the room; peace, tranquillity. It would not last long.

The silence of the room was broken only by the sound of our steadily chomping jaws and occasional grunts of animal pleasure.

"Been saving these," I said between chomps.

"What for?"

"A night like this, Goldberg. A night like this."

The rain drummed relentlessly outside. The faint red glow of a distant neon sign transformed the drops rolling down the pane into rubies. Off and on the sign went. It was a distant neon arrow pointing down through the night to JACK'S GOLDEN DOME TURNPIKE DINER. EAT . . . EAT . . . EAT . . . EAT . . . it endlessly intoned, beckoning the drivers of K-Whoppers, Macks, and Peterbilts to come and graze at the all-night trough.

EAT . . . EAT . . . EAT . . . And so we did, for a few blissful moments. Again, the steady clomp of shower clogs approaching my door. Goldberg glanced up, his chin dribbling crumbs.

"Whozzat?"

"Hide 'em!" I muttered.

Too late. Blotting out the light entirely from the outside hallway was the immense, looming, mountainous form of Big Al Dagellio, the recognized terror of the Big Ten gridirons for the past three seasons. Football players in that neck of the woods are not students, or even human beings, in the ordinary meaning of the term. They are bred for the purpose. It is rumored that there is a Lineman Stud Farm hidden in the remote fastnesses of the state where these monsters are carefully nurtured from birth, destined only to execute bone-crushing tackles and shattering blocks on their way to the Rose Bowl. Rarely seen outside the confines of their special athletes compound, these killers can be dangerous when loose. What Big Al, known familiarly to sportswriters as "Old 76," was doing in our dorm, I'll never know.

Naturally, we were both awed and flattered to be in the presence of such a demigod; two hundred and eighty-seven pounds, six feet five and a quarter, with a size twenty-two neck and a thirty-inch waistline, Big Al was wedge-shaped; pure sinew, gristle, and covered with a thick, bristly mat of primitive fur. Numerous broken noses had reduced his nostrils to blow-holes. Enveloping him was a distinctive animal aroma, the scent that great snuffling dinosaurs of the Reptile Age must have carried, redolent of primal swamps and ancient fens. He was as imposing as a bull rhino in heat, and about as lovable.

He extended his immense paw toward me. I had the fleeting impression that his palms were covered with hair.

"Gimme cookie," he grunted.

There's nothing a Fig Newton aficionado loathes more than hearing a Fig Newton called a "cookie," but I let it pass.

"Of course. Heh heh, of course. Have all you want, Big Al."

"T'anks."

And Old 76 joined me and Goldberg in our contented chomping. My tiny cell was getting crowded, but the evening was yet young and the pieces were falling into place of a historical event that is still recounted on the campus these many years later. At least three folk songs have been written about it.

About half the box of Fig Newtons had gone to that Great Cookie Jar in the Sky when the star of the evening made his entrance. I, personally, believe that he had somehow set the whole thing up. But we'll never know. A light tapping was heard; polite, discreet. I creaked to my feet and opened the door. There stood the tall, lanky figure of one of the least-known members of our dormitory clan. He had the clammy sluglike pallor of the true scholar, one obviously born to live only for footnotes, cross references, and bibliographies, a natural writer of treatises.

"Hi." His voice was soft and diffident. "I'm Umbaugh. Schuyler Umbaugh from the first floor, and it is rumored that there are Fig Newtons available. I could scarcely credit my senses when I heard of it, but..."

Big Al, glancing up from his fistful of Fig Newtons, rasped, "Give 'im some."

"My name's Dave, and this is Goldberg, and..."

Umbaugh, with a casual wave of his long, thin, cello player's hand, said, "Of course. Everyone knows Mr. Big Al. Indeed."

He edged into the room, he too dressed in the uniform of the day, T-shirt, shorts, and shower clogs.

"Yes, sir, the Fig Newton is one of my favorite vices, and I have brought with me something which makes the Fig Newton truly sing."

He produced a heavy, pregnant twelve-pack of Pabst Blue Ribbon beer. He went on in his soft, precise voice:

"Fig Newtons and Pabst, a combination rivaled only by vodka and caviar. Here, have a brew."

We quickly dove in. Within seconds, all four of us were inhaling cooling suds, washing down the Fig Newtons, creating a taste combination that is truly indescribable. At first thought it sounds grotesque, but no, there is something about the fermented hops mingled with the crushed fig that is dynamite.

"You guys are awright," Old 76 muttered as he unleashed a shuddering burp that rattled the casements. Goldberg punctuated the conversation with an appreciative fart. Dormitory life was being lived to the fullest in Room 303.

Goldberg suddenly lurched to his feet, a can of beer in one hand and a Fig Newton in the other, and announced:

"What the hell ... I'll be right back."

His room was two doors down the hall, and seconds later he reappeared, the Fig Newton gone but still bearing his beer. In his now empty hand he carried, its string encircling his index finger, a three-foot-long, magnificent, richly gleaming salami.

"My aunt Bella sent it to me for my birthday. I been savin' it for a celebration."

Goldberg handed the salami to 76, who promptly bit four inches off the end. He passed it to me. I bit off a luscious, garlic-laden mouthful and on it went to Umbaugh.

"The history of salami is an interesting one . . ." He addressed us in the well-modulated tones of a born teacher. "The name derives from the tiny island of Salama off the southern coast of Sicily. The early eighth century saw the emergence of the first sausage of this type. Its fame quickly spread. The sausage took its name from its homeland, salami being the plural of Salama, which is the more proper–"

"Fer Chrissake, gimme another beer."

Big Al was clearly not interested in theory, being purely a man of action.

Umbaugh continued: "St. Pietro Salami, one of the early Christian martyrs, according to legend added the garlic as the result of a Divine revelation. His subsequent canonization in nine hundred and thirty-two led to . . . Oh yes, of course. Have a beer, Mr. Seventy-six."

And so a happy hour was spent in my yeasty, fetid concrete room. Worries of carbon compounds and the halogen series had been banished for the moment. The gray wolves of boredom were held at bay and they skulked uneasily in the rainy outside world. A huge bite of garlicky salami, a quick slug of beer, and a nibble of Fig Newton, in that order, was the routine.

Salami, Fig Newtons, and beer passed from hand to hand. Occasionally low, gurgling stomach rumbles added a fitting obbligato to our debauch.

Umbaugh, his mind ranging widely over the whole panoply of human experience, entertained us with arcane facts.

"Are you gentlemen aware that the fig stands unique in the tangled world of nature's flora? It has a deep-throated blossom which must be fertilized by a tiny insect which, flying from male blossom to female blossom, carries the minute fertilization cell which makes this luscious Fig Newton possible."

"No kiddin'?" Goldberg, always eager for more Sex news, listened intently.

"Yes, Goldberg, but it is essentially a sad story, since this tiny insect, Latin name *Blastophaga psenes*, dies the very instant the eggs are laid. The blossom closes over it, and each fig absorbs the tiny body of a departed insect heroine. The Great Fig Blight, which struck Turkey in eighteen-oh-seven, due to . . ."

"Y' mean there's goddamn dead BUGS in these things?" Old 76 looked up from his Pabst, his eyes glowing with menace.

"Yeggkk!" Goldberg glanced nervously at his half-eaten Fig Newton.

"I wouldn't put it exactly that way, Mr. Seventy-six. However, in a manner of speaking that is true, but . . ."

At the time I thought that under the influence of the beer and the bonhomie of the moment, Umbaugh was putting us on. Later, I was astounded to find that he was telling the truth. There is a tiny dead insect in every fig in the world.

But by then it was too late. The Fig Newtons had disappeared and we were on our last beer, with only maybe six inches of salami left to go. It was close to 4 A.M. and, if anything, the rain was drumming down harder than ever. At this moment Umbaugh began to spring his trap. Big Al, who later went on to glory in the NFL after a spectacular career in the Big Ten, was about to learn a lesson.

"Big Al." Umbaugh tilted his string-bean six-foot, six-inch, one-hundred-and-five-pound frame forward slightly, bending in the middle like some intellectual praying mantis, a faint sardonic smile playing over his sallow features. "It must be truly satisfying, in a deep primal way, to smash the Iowa line to smithereens, to crush Ohio State's vaunted All-American halfback into the dust of the gridiron, to be a modern gladiator: fearless, indestructible, impervious to defeat."

A flicker of confusion clouded Big Al's tiny bb eyes.

"Uh . . . yeah. Well, the bastard give me the knee in the first quarter, so I hadda get the son of a bitch."

Both Goldberg and I listened to this exchange with rapt attention. Umbaugh could be on dangerous ground. One treads softly around a rutting mastodon.

"Well, you certainly did get the, as you say, bastard. I happened to be passing through the student lounge on my way to the library at the very moment the TV set was displaying the scene of his vainglorious departure from the game, on a stretcher borne by four of his humiliated teammates. The roar of the crowd as the ambulance left the arena was certainly thrilling and, I might add, not a bit too soon. Ohio State tends to get a bit cheeky, eh?"

Big Al moodily chewed the butt end of the salami, its string hanging forlornly out of his mouth and into the rough stubble of his granite jaw.

"Yeah, well, he shouldna tried comin' through me after givin' me that knee. Them dumb fuckers never learn."

"By George, that was well put." Umbaugh smiled admiringly at Big Al's clever mot. "I'll have to remember that. I was rather relieved, though, that after the operation they announced that he would probably walk again. In time." Umbaugh smiled benevolently.

"Yeah, well, I figured since he was only a sophomore, the dumb jerk didn't know no better, so I went easy on him."

"I, for one, admire you, Big Al, for letting that fool Snake Hips off so easily. True charity. Even he must be grateful that you let him off with only a cracked pelvis, a few shattered ribs, and maybe a crushed spleen."

Big Al's steel-blue bbs flickered as he appeared to study Umbaugh intently. My God, I thought, if Big Al senses that he is being put down, all three of us could go the way of that Ohio halfback in an instant.

"Hey, Big Al . . ." I asked bravely, trying to change the subject, "do you always wear your jersey with the number and everything around like that?"

"Nah. Only around the dorm. I can't get no T-shirts that fit. They all rip down the back."

His grass-stained red-and-white jersey with its spectacular "76" had been cut off to give breathing room to his hairy, bare midriff.

But Big Al was not about to be put off by any clever conversational feint from the likes of me. His ball-bearing eyes continued to stare steadily at Umbaugh.

"What you say your name is, huh?" He leaned forward, his cordlike muscles rippling, playing like sleek dolphins over his shoulders and mighty back.

"Ah . . . Umbaugh is the name. Umbaugh. The name has an interesting derivation. Back in the early twelfth century—"

Big Al cut him off in mid-prattle with a furious animal snort. "Umbaugh! I t'ought I knew that name. Yeah. You're the horse's patoot that wrote that dumb fuckin' letter to that stupid newspaper."

A spasm of mortal fear gripped my guts. Of course, it was Umbaugh who had written that sardonic blast which had appeared in *The Crimson Bugle*, our despised student newspaper. Entitled "Athletics—Boobs' Paradise," it had rocked the campus:

> *These loutish oafs thudding into one another with all the human qualities crushed underfoot . . . I demand that the English Department go on strike against this further, indeed highly applauded display of human depravity. The name "Jane Austen" is known to barely 1% of the student body of this so-called Institution of Higher Learning, but 99% of my alleged fellow students can give you the name, weight, and record of every third-rate substitute lineman in the entire Big Ten. How long will this barbaric . . .*

Big Al stood, his crew cut lightly brushing the ceiling of my cell, his steady gaze, unblinking, bored deep into Umbaugh. My God, he's gonna charge, I thought wildly.

Goldberg cringed next to my bureau. He appeared to be counting the knobs studiously. Umbaugh cleared his throat.

"I confess, Big Al. It was indeed I. However, I meant it only in jest. As an exercise in Swiftian humor and satire, I . . ."

"Can the crap." Big Al certainly had a way with words. "That Jane what-the-fucks-'er-name, she some broad yer shackin' up with?"

For a fleeting instant I had a brief vision of the prim, virginal authoress of *Pride and Prejudice* sneaking off into the night with Umbaugh for a little hanky-panky.

"Or more likely you're a friggin' fag." Big Al sucked sullenly at his beer can.

"Jane? Oh, of course, you mean Jane Austen. I suppose one could say, metaphorically, we have been 'shacking up,' immersed as I have been in her work for three years now, preparing for my doctoral thesis, entitled 'Irony—the Last Bastion of the Beleaguered Mind.' I suppose you might say that . . ."

Struck by a sudden thought, he paused.

"By George, that is good. 'Shacking up.' I must tell Dr. Bloombuster that one, he'll—"

"You goddamned eggheads are a royal pain in the butt. The trouble with you dumb shitheads is that not one of you ever could beat nobody at nothin', and you can't stand nobody who can so you go around blowin' off."

A river of sweat poured down my back. The evening had taken a nasty turn.

It must have been just about then that Umbaugh decided to close the trap. It's hard to tell. All I know for sure is that Umbaugh said nothing for a long, tense moment. The rain drummed steadily on my window. Goldberg appeared to be trying to draw a cloak of invisibility around his blubbery hulk.

Finally, in a low voice, Umbaugh answered Big Al's charge:

"That theory perhaps has some validity, Big Al, but then, on the other hand, there are those who believe that deadly combat is the very soul of Man and that we all have it."

Under my breath I hissed, "Careful, Umbaugh, careful . . ."

"Every man," Umbaugh continued in an even voice, "has his own game, where he is a killer, and . . ."

"What the fuck do you know about games, you skinny piss-ant?" It was then that Umbaugh struck.

He casually extracted a large, flat blue-and-white box from his T-shirt breast pocket. With cool deliberation he removed a silver-wrapped lozenge from the box, unwrapped it, and popped its contents into his mouth.

Goldberg, obviously trying to ease the tension in the room, squealed nervously, "Hey, Umbaugh, you got candy!"

"Not exactly, Goldberg. I am merely indulging in a Boomo-Lax tablet."

Boomo-Lax, the legendary laxative that billed itself as: Tastes like a fine French bonbon; yet has the action of a Hand Grenade.

Goldberg, the human garbage disposal, could not pass this up.

"Hey, gimme one. They taste like chocolate, don't they?"

"I believe the phrase is 'a fine French bonbon,' " Umbaugh answered, licking his lips appreciatively. "Say, would you gentlemen care to join me in a bit of a contest? A game, if you will."

Big Al immediately rose to the challenge. Since tot-hood he had won everything in sight, bashing and thundering over countless opponents throughout the years. He could not allow Umbaugh's challenge to pass.

"What kinda game? You wanna arm wrassle or somepin?" His eyes suddenly blazed with the fierce hot light that had withered the soul of many a defensive back.

The thought of Umbaugh's matchstick arms cracking merrily under the onslaught of 76's concrete biceps made even Umbaugh laugh.

"Oh goodness gracious, no! The contest I propose involves true intestinal fortitude."

"You mean guts?" Al snorted. "You mean guts, you skinny twerp?"

"You could say that," Umbaugh answered calmly.

I was to find out, shortly, how truly he spoke.

Goldberg, who had been busily licking the interior of the Fig Newton box for any odd crumbs, asked, "What kind of game?"

Umbaugh drew himself to his full height, his thin milky body with its knobby knees and sunken chest looking a bit like a hat rack wearing a too-large T-shirt.

"It's quite simple, actually. I have forty-nine tablets of this delicious Boomo-Lax left in this package, having already eaten one, which I will throw in as a handicap. We will pass the package from hand to hand, eating Boomo-Lax tablets in turn, and the last man left in the room wins. It is as simple as that. Of course, we will allow three minutes between tablets, under the international rules."

"Of course," I said, "rules are rules."

"You tryin' to say, you skinny bastard, that you can eat more of them dinky chocolates than I can? Me?"

Al, who had never refused a challenge in his life, was not about to begin now. Goldberg, on the other hand, had motives far simpler. He never turned down the chance to eat anything, unless it had hair on it and crawled. I, however, was like one of those poor yaps who gets sucked into a bar fight and begins swinging wildly at everything in sight, only to wind up with a broken hand from hitting the gum machine and thirty days in the can. Not only that, but I thought I saw a way out of what looked like was going to develop into a truly bad scene.

"Fifty dollars, Big Al. To make the game more sporting. I propose a gentlemen's wager of fifty dollars each, the winner takes all."

Big Al, his face suddenly wreathed in the same smile of

Christian charity that had once graced the visage of Mighty Casey at the bat, chuckled evilly.

"You're on, sucker."

Numerous alumni had seen to it that Big Al never had to worry where his next supply of cash was coming from. It was said that twice monthly a Brinks truck delivered his "incidental expenses," with two armed guards carrying heavy sacks. Linemen of his ilk don't come cheap in the Big Ten.

Goldberg, sure of victory, recklessly joined the fray: "Count me in."

Well, what could I do? A man has his honor, and after all, I can eat chocolate with the best of them.

"Okay, deal the cards," I barked with the assurance of Henry Fonda sitting in on a poker game with Jack Palance. "I'll bet fifty bucks out of my next GI check, which I get in ten days."

"The game is afoot, men. I now declare Time is in." Umbaugh's manner had become formal, almost Victorian. He consulted his watch carefully and then passed the box of Boomo-Lax to Big Al.

"Take one tablet, pass it on to the next contestant, and then finally around to me, the dealer."

Big Al grabbed a silver cube and popped it into his maw, chomping ferociously. He spit out the wrapping defiantly.

"What a stupid game. Jee-zus!"

Goldberg took his hungrily, and I followed suit. By God, they did taste like a fine French bonbon. Umbaugh, with great delicacy, unwrapped his tablet and began sucking daintily.

"One round, players, has been completed."

"Hey, they're good. Hey, they're really good. Can I have two on the next round?" the Human Garbage Can asked happily. I could see that he, too, was relieved that combat had been averted.

"Now, now, we must have rules. One per round." A minute passed in silence as the tension rose in the arena.

"Round two."

Umbaugh passed the box to Big Al, and it quickly made the circuit.

"Hey, this is dumb. I could eat the whole goddamn box. What kinda dumb game is this?"

Big Al was chafing at the bit. He wanted more action. He was about to get it.

After the third round I noticed that a crowd had begun to gather at the door, which had been left ajar by Umbaugh, for reasons we were about to learn.

"Get 'em, Big Al!" a freshman wearing a red-and-white beanie yelled.

"Courage, Schuyler. Steady on." A willowy English major in a chartreuse silk robe cheered on his favorite.

Umbaugh passed the box on its fourth trip. The crowd grew. Rumors had spread throughout the dormitory that a thrilling athletic contest was going on in 303 and that Big Al Dagellio was being challenged by a nerd from *The Literary Quarterly*. Hoarse shouts of encouragement, bursts of applause echoed in the hall. Catcalls; huzzahs. Betting between spectators had broken out. Partisanship was rampant. I was pleased to note that I had my share of backers, no doubt the result of the time that I had eaten an entire meatloaf in the campus cafeteria on a dare. I was not without qualifications.

Naturally, the heavy favorite was Old 76. It was known via the sports pages that he daily breakfasted on two three-pound sirloins and a dozen and a half eggs (sunny side), seven yards of country link sausage, and two gallons of homogenized milk. We all remembered vividly a photograph which had appeared the year before in the Chicago *Tribune* showing Old 76 at the Festive Board. The caption had read: Athlete devours entire turkey for Thanksgiving.

Of course, Goldberg's sickening gustatorial adventures were well known. I must admit that few put their money on Umbaugh. Unfortunately, the crowd usually backs favorites, often to its sorrow.

Eighteen minutes into the game, just after our sixth Boomo-Lax, Goldberg, suddenly and with no prior symptoms of distress, lurched to his feet, swayed for a moment like an elephant in a hurricane, let go a mighty, quavering belch, and made a staggering leap for the door. The crowd roared, and parted like the Red Sea. Goldberg thundered down the hallway, his shower clogs making a mighty clatter. As he ran, a high thin moan accompanied him.

The sanitary facilities for the third floor were at the far end of the hall. The crowd bellowed a mighty cheer as Goldberg just made the door, in a skidding turn, and hurled himself from sight.

"Many are called; few are chosen," Umbaugh smiled thinly. "One down, three to go."

Big Al snorted. "I know'd plenty of blubbery guys like that before. They never last. Gimme another one a'them little bastards. They ain't bad."

"Round seven." Umbaugh passed the box to Big Al. He swallowed his tablet, after a quick chew.

"Umbaugh, y'better quit while yer ahead," he rasped.

The crowd sensing his malevolent competitive nature, fell silent. He handed the box to me, and to this day I can't clearly remember what happened. Maybe it was the excitement; maybe I just didn't have it. I don't know.

Just as I reached for the Boomo-Lax I had the uncontrollable sensation of becoming suddenly inflated, as though someone had cruelly blown me up like a helium weather balloon. I felt my Jockey shorts stretching and cutting into my middle. They were so tight that there was an audible thrumming sound. My arms stuck out at right angles from my distended body. I felt like a Macy's Thanksgiving parade Donald Duck float in a high wind. I caught a fleeting glimpse of Umbaugh's lip, curled in disdain. I was beyond caring.

"Yes, with the action of a hand grenade," he hissed.

I bounced and skittered to the door. Through the buzzing sound in my ears I could hear the crowd faintly, as from a long distance, as they cheered and hooted. The seventy-five feet or so down the corridor seemed to grow longer and longer as I wildly waddled, my teeth clenched, trying to hold back the molten lava which boiled inside me, a human volcano about to erupt, slaying thousands in its devastation.

At last I crashed through the door marked MEN and, moaning weakly, I hurled myself into one of the blessed booths. Even in my feverish panic I saw Goldberg's foot extending out from under the third booth down, his pitiful shower clog resting forlornly fifteen feet away. I heard him rumbling and crying piteously for help. I was busy with my own troubles.

It was as though a runaway Roto-Rooter had gone berserk in my gut. Bits of chewed salami spurted from my ears. Never before, or since, had I had such a horrendous experience.

"Ooohh, I'm gonna die . . ." Goldberg moaned.

I envied him, since it was obvious that I had already passed into the Great Beyond and was paying for my sins. Was I in hell? Was Satan himself squeezing me dry like a human washrag?

What seemed hours later I tottered weakly out into the hallway, a wraith of my former self. The crowd had doubled in front of my room. They were still at it!

I edged through the mob, my body sore and aching. Umbaugh still stood as he had all evening. Big Al was casually leaning against the concrete wall next to the casement. They were eyeball to eyeball. It was the age-old confrontation; mano a mano, High Noon. The Intellectual, the Man of Ideas versus the Beast.

"Round twelve," Umbaugh barked. Spectators murmured. There was a scattered burst of applause. Umbaugh, with the maddening air of the intellectual who firmly believes that he is one of the very few who holds the key to the mystery of the Universe, downed his deadly bit of chocolate.

The greatest defensive tackle the Big Ten had yet produced followed suit, a sneer creasing his naugahyde features.

"You dumb fuckers never learn," he muttered.

A voice in the crowd murmured, "That's just the way he looked before he nailed Snake Hips Leroy Johnson in the Ohio game. Oh, God, I can't watch."

Umbaugh casually waved a limp-wristed salute to his few supporters, who were mainly from the staff of *The Literary Quarterly* and *The Barbaric Yawp*, the campus poetry rag.

"Courage, Schuyler," one of them piped.

Another, a short wartish person in a Samoan toga, lisped:

"It's Ape Man Sweeney versus Daedalus."

Umbaugh turned and withered him with a glance. "I presume you mean Icarus, you oaf. However, the thought was well meant."

The Wart scrunched deeper into his toga, his acne reddening. Old 76's face darkened.

"Who the hell does Ape Man Sweeney play for? Never heard of him."

Umbaugh smiled benignly. "I never heard of him either, noble foe. Shall we continue?"

I had edged my way through the crowd and back into my room and was now busily mopping up the gushing perspiration that ran into my eyes and dripped off my nose. Something told me that I would soon be making another trip down the hall.

Umbaugh, noticing me at last, acknowledged my presence.

"You fought gamely and well. Feel no shame."

"Thanks."

"Round thirteen."

In silence, the gladiators put away their deadly potions. Somehow the crowd sensed that we had reached the turning point. Tension was so thick that it hung like a fine blue haze in the room. The rain had finally ceased and the first faint silver fingers of dawn had touched the ancient oaks of the Quad. Saturday was beginning to happen, the biggest Saturday of the season, in fact. We were playing Michigan today for the Big Ten championship, the winner, of course, to go to the Rose Bowl.

Umbaugh leaned forward, his washed-out gray eyes peering unblinkingly into Big Al's bbs. He whispered, barely audible to any outside the room, drawing out the syllables of his words to underline their import.

"Rounnnnd . . . [long pregnant pause] four . . . teee . . ."

Before he could complete his announcement, Big Al stiffened. An inchoate bellow of animal intensity shook the concrete walls. "UUUUUOOOOOONNNNNKKKKKK!"

He lurched forward and then began to topple slowly, like a great redwood felled in the forest. Umbaugh, moving backward, with snakelike agility, his voice lashing out, warned:

"Move back. This could be dangerous."

With a muffled thud that rocked our immense dormitory building, Big Al hit the floor, his red-and-white jersey darkened with sweat. The "6" of his famous number curled weakly under his bushy armpit.

Umbaugh casually hoisted up his drooping shorts as he coolly stood over his fallen foe.

"Jane Austen lives."

It was all over. My room was never the same again, even after hosing it down repeatedly and soaking the walls and floor and, yes, even the ceiling with powerful disinfectants. Big Al lay prone, his immense bulk quivering as giant spasms shook his frame. His followers, white-faced and stricken, rallied to his aid. They tugged and pulled his almost lifeless hulk down the hall, trailing noxious fumes. It was then that Umbaugh displayed the style of a true champion.

"Well, boys." He stretched luxuriously and scratched his ribs with satisfaction. "It's been an exciting evening. And as a nameless Phoenician captain once wrote: When the ship sinks, you've lost the battle."

His followers, their eyes glowing with admiration, applauded their hero. I kept my silence. After all, he had disemboweled me.

From far down the hall came the sounds of rushing water and the rumble of an expiring beast.

Walking to the casement window, Umbaugh squinted out into the dawn, the faint red glow of Jack's neon sign playing over his ascetic, chiseled features.

"I feel like a spot of breakfast. A healthy hunger or, as the English would say, I'm a bit peckish. A stack of blueberry buckwheats drenched with maple syrup and a scoop of butter would just hit the spot. And since I am now somewhat flush this morning, I'll treat the gang to what the old Golden Dome Diner has to offer. What do you say?"

I lay back limply on my monk's slab. Within moments the room was empty. The arena was silenced. Only the ghost of the heroic struggle remained.

Later that fateful day our Alma Mater went down to humiliating defeat. Michigan, a decided underdog, had pulled off an upset. I still have a clipping that reads:

LOSS OF ALL-AMERICAN COSTLY TO STATE

(State Campus, AP) Missing his first game in three years of All-American play, Big Al Dagellio, State's brilliant All-American tackle, was the probable cause of Saturday's defeat. State's losing 26–20 cost the home team a trip to the Rose Bowl and the league championship.

The head coach refused to be interviewed after the game as to the cause of Dagellio's failure to play, stating only: "The bum lost a lot of weight." He would not elaborate.

Dagellio himself was unavailable for comment and remained in seclusion today. Rumors that Dagellio had been suspended from the team were neither confirmed nor denied by officials, leading to further speculation.

I shifted uneasily on that goddamn bean-bag loveseat, which I have hated since the day I bought it. Taking a deep, inhaling suck at my bourbon, I squinted closely at Umbaugh's triumphant face on the screen.

"I hope that some of our viewers today, Mr. Cooke, have come to appreciate the role Boredom has played in the world's history. As a little-known Phoenician captain once inscribed: 'When the ship sinks, you've lost the battle.' Yes, Mr. Cooke, it is never wise to put your bets on the favorite. As the legend of Icarus shows . . ."

The truth, after all these years, hit me. With a hoarse cry I top-

pled forward, knocking my precious Thomas Jefferson tumbler
to the floor with a crash, his stony visage shattering into slivery
shards, the rich amber bourbon staining the *Times* editorial page,
thoroughly soaking a Tom Wicker column entitled: "The Intellectual; America's Most Precious Asset."

You Benedict Arnold. You crummy, rotten Quisling. Selling out
State to Michigan. You son of a bitch. For the first time I truly understood why the Archie Bunkers of the world, the slobs of the
universe, instinctively distrusted the Intellectual. They were right
all along!

I moaned weakly in my shame. I had been cruelly used by this
smarmy, poetry-quoting wimp. My simple, innocent lust for Fig
Newtons had led to the defeat of my beloved State by the hated
Wolverines. Oh, God, if the *Alumni Journal* ever gets wind of this!

I took a deep swig of Jack Daniels straight from the bottle for
sustenance, courage in my hour of self-revelation. I knew then
with a deadly certainty that guilt would pursue me the rest of
my life.

THE BASTARD HAD LAID A BIG BET ON MICHIGAN!

Me, and Goldberg, and poor dumb Big Al Dagellio were just
pawns, shills if you will, in Umbaugh's sinister game. No wonder
he had all that dough to pay for those postgraduate credit hours,
that convertible, that vintage Beaujolais, those stupid imported
Egyptian cigarettes. Oh, Lord, will perfidy never end?

A line from Tennessee Williams' *Cat on a Hot Tin Roof* came
back to me in that moment of fevered illumination, Big Daddy
bellowing, "Mendacity, my boy. Mendacity is what life is about!"

I shook my head in rueful admiration, the kind of admiration
that you feel for John Dean of Watergate fame, the little pimple
pulling off the Big Steal and coming out of it rich. Umbaugh, you
son of a bitch. Few people in the world know what your true talent is. The greatest Boomo-Lax hustler who ever lived. You hus-
tled us, you talented horse's ass!

Once again I felt the terrible panging clutch in my vitals

known to the trade as "Boomo-Lax Backlash." I staggered toward the john, flipping off the TV just as Alistair Cooke said:

"This has been a highly enlightening program. We would like to take this opportunity to thank Dr. Umbaugh for . . ."

I gasped out, "Them dumb fuckers never learn!" as I barely made the blessed sanctuary.

Sad but true, they don't. Learn, that is. But did you note that the victim was heading for the right place to soothe his soul?

So much of my best solid contemplation is done in the john. If venerated ancient thinkers hung around in ivory towers, it certainly follows that today's pundits do a lot of serious work in tiled sanctuaries far from the madding throng. And no wonder, with the price of ivory.

Archimedes hollered out "Eureka!" in his bathtub. No mention of his study or library. How many cosmic concepts came to Benjamin Franklin while in the privacy of what passed for a john in his day? Come to think of it, they had outhouses, didn't they? Two-holers. Somehow, it's a little unnerving to picture George Washington heading out into the rain, carrying a corn cob, while contemplating various profundities that would affect free men for centuries.

Just where was Edison when the idea for the light bulb struck him? It would be easy to say, "The laboratory, stupid," but is that true? Did he merely execute his idea in the laboratory?

The fathead behind me gave out a loud blast on his air horns, jarring me out of my restless inner debate. That's one of the things

I find myself doing more and more, debating with myself. George Washington contemplating democracy while in the outhouse? No, you fool. He sat in his eighteenth-century study, scratching away with a quill pen on parchment, while wearing a powdered wig. Come on, you dummy, you know better than that.

I noticed that the temperature gauge in my car was creeping up to around 200 degrees. Jesus Christ, overheating! Am I going to be the next yellow light? When was the last time I checked my radiator level?

Ahead, the Rutgers crowd appeared to be singing. I glanced in the mirror. The Horn Creep was right on my rear bumper. Is that his tongue lolling out or is he sucking a popsicle? When will this ever end?

My mind seized that thought like a rat terrier grabbing a chicken bone.

After all this torture in purgatory, you end up in Jersey. Jersey, for Chrissake!

The Light at the End
of the Tunnel

The moment that I peered out to sea through the unblinking eye of the magnificent Margate Elephant, I sensed that somehow I was in the spiritual heart of New Jersey. A gigantic wooden pachyderm of distinctly irritated mien, the Margate Elephant, constructed–if that is the proper word–about a century ago on a sandy remote beach, was an instant success among the stylish toffs of the period. New Jerseyites wearing beaver hats and sequined bustles jostled for reservations to spend a weekend, or perhaps a honeymoon, in its rooms, finished in polished teak and a curious combination of nautical and pseudo-Bombay décor.

The Margate Elephant still stands, distinctly Jersey, radiating elephantine vitality; dignified in the W. C. Fields manner, yet slightly mad, a true Jersey work of art rivaled only by the Flagship, which decade after decade has sailed bravely upstream against the traffic on Route 22, its steel flanks rakishly cutting the potholed concrete, forever heading toward the Lincoln Tunnel bound on its own sinister voyage, currently carrying its cargo of cut-rate furniture.

The Flagship could very well be the Margate Elephant of the twenty-first century, with committees of earnest, fluttery ladies circulating petitions for its preservation as a "historical monument."

There is something different about New Jersey. What it is, is difficult to define, but as a student of Jerseyana I can only describe some of its vague outlines. Jersey, we all know, has replaced Brooklyn as the subject of stand-up comedians' gags, everywhere. A comic in a nightclub in Zagreb, Yugoslavia, can get an instant laugh by just belting out, "New Jerseyanski!" and rolling his eyes. The audience collapses, most of all any New Jerseyites that are in the crowd.

It has been said by official pundits that you can take a man out of New Jersey but you can never take New Jersey out of the man. How can you best describe this mythical Jerseyite?

First of all, there's his driving. Sullenly reckless, lacking the kamikaze verve of the Californian, he is the world's most dogged and dedicated tailgater. Any time I am a thousand miles from the state, driving along innocently, and a rusting Plymouth Fury lurches out of the blackness and clings tenaciously to my rear bumper, threatening to climb up over the trunk, I know without even seeing him that a Jerseyite is on his way to Disneyland.

He has learned his New Jersey driving eccentricities negotiating that distinctive automotive hell known as the New Jersey Traffic Circle. Totally unknown to most of the civilized world, New Jersey's traffic circles stand alone in their Margate Elephant–like craziness. The first time I saw one I couldn't believe what I was looking at. After a lifetime of driving in other parts of the country, with conventional staid overpasses, viaducts, crossroads, stop-lights, etc., etc., suddenly I found myself going madly round and round, surrounded by hordes of blue-haired ladies piloting violet-colored Gremlins. In and out they wove. I passed my turnoff four times before I got control of my mind and was hurled out of the traffic circle by centrifugal force, back in the direction I had come. Good grief!

But now, after years of New Jersey life I have become a master of the Hackensack Hesitation, the Clifton Carom, the Lyndhurst Lurch, the Camden Creep, the Vineland Veer, and, of course, the Fort Lee Finger; all necessary maneuvers for a skilled pilot in the gay, mad world of Jersey driving.

Then, of course, there are other indelible Garden State characteristics. There is something truly lovable about summer at the New Jersey shore. Millions of sweltering Jerseyites packed chock-a-block into tiny wooden cubicles in a physical intimacy with one another that is rivaled only by the more densely packed districts of Calcutta. I once saw a happy New Jerseyite, clutching in his fist a can of Piels Real Draft Style beer, suddenly seized by a fit of sneezing in his Jersey shore cottage. In the next cottage the top of his innocent neighbor's tuna salad sandwich flew off violently and lodged in the curtain rod amid the summer cottage cobwebs. That slab of Arnold Stone-ground Wheat bread caused much friendly snickering in the neigborhood and a lot of talk down at the local gin mill, which, of course, is decorated with plastic anchors, fake fish net, and for some reason a portrait of Woodrow Wilson done in needlepoint.

Don't get the idea that I don't like Jersey. On the contrary, I love it. And why not? Life there is never dull. It can be many other things: irritating, terrifying, but dull—no.

Take a friend of mine, an elegant, very social, much-monied doctor residing in a very lovely suburb in the Watchung Hills. For months he and his wife planned a summer gala; barbecued pheasant, cheese dips flown in from Switzerland, liveried batmen dispensing canapés from the kitchens of Maxim's of Paris, the works.

The guests assembled on his lush estate, the rich New Jersey grass cropped to putting-green silkiness. Women were never lovelier, nor men more handsome. The Japanese lanterns flickered in the soft summer air, when suddenly, with no warning, what at first had appeared to be an approaching curtain of smoke struck, and within an instant the elegant party had disintegrated into a whooping, hollering, slapping mob. A vast formation of New Jersey mosquitoes, flying in echelon, had attacked with the deadly efficiency of a squadron of P-51s strafing Berlin.

Within moments the bedraggled mob, covered with lumps and scratching unashamedly, huddled in the living room, myself among them, taking solace in the obvious fact that Mother Nature bites and stings all men, rich and poor alike, especially in Jersey.

And there is something distinctly real about a phenomenon which I have observed and which I call here New Jersey Nostalgia. One night in a remote college town in Colorado (and no state could be more different from New Jersey than Colorado, believe me), I was wandering along a darkening frontier street when suddenly my nose detected the sharp, poignant fragrance of Home. My nose began to sweat in excitement as I dashed down the street, following the scent. I rounded a corner and there it was–BIG VINNIE'S NEW JERSEY PIZZERIA. There, nestled amid the taco parlors, the chili joints, and the alfalfa sprout dispensaries (Colorado abounds in health nuts) was the Real Thing; a pizzeria straight out of Camden or Lodi, or Jersey City for that matter.

An instant later I was inside, had ordered a rich slab of the Mother Food of New Jersey. Known to the pizza aficionado as a "Full-tilt Boogie," it had everything: anchovies, sausage, green peppers, double cheese, onions, and the greasy thumbprints of Vinnie himself.

I was back home. Two sweating former Jerseyites manned the place for expatriots, their accents redolent of the Meadowlands. One shouted at me over the hullabaloo:

"Y'wanna bee-yah to go with it?"

"Yeah!" I hollered over the din.

"How 'bout a Rheingold?" he yelled back. "Real bee-yah, not like this Coors sissy stuff they drink out here."

"They used to sponsor the Mets games," I contributed at the top of my voice.

"Them were the days." Vinnie smiled benignly as he shoved the beer toward me and nodded to a fading photograph of Bud Harrelson which hung over the cash register. It was signed To Vinnie, from a Pizza nut—Bud.

For a few moments I was back in the land of the Margate Elephant, the Flagship, the Leaning Tower of Pizza, Two Guys from Harrison, Route One on Saturday night—in short, the homeland.

Yes, there are times when I head west out of Manhattan at 4 A.M., hurtling through the deserted, spooky Lincoln Tunnel for an eternity, and then with a feeling of relief I spot the Light at the End of the Tunnel, and it hits me again. Yep, the Light at the End of the Tunnel that everyone is always talking about is New Jersey!

The light at the end of the Tunnel—New Jersey?

Awful thought! But then, maybe the Ship of State which Presidents are always threatening to pilot at last into A Safe Harbor could be the Staten Island Ferry, plowing through the murky waters of the bay amid orange peelings, 7-Up cans, and the occasional deceased Mafioso come loose from his concrete moorings at the bottom of the sea.

Good Lord! Right above me a couple of those gunsels wearing cement sneakers could be stuck in the mud, looking down at me. Oh, ugh.

I glanced to my right. Why the hell do I always manage to land in the slow lane? My lane had come to a complete halt. The temperature gauge crept over 200. Oh, God.

I deliberately forced my imagination to rescue me from this dismal trap. Think uplifting thoughts, that's the ticket. Truth. Beauty. Liberty. The one thing you don't get in a tunnel—Liberty. A mental picture of the great statue flashed in my brain.

Yes, the Statue of Liberty, as awesome a piece of Slob Art as the Margate Elephant ever was, also stares out over the dark ocean's waters. Was it the Statue of Liberty herself that set the whole

pattern for American tourism, culminating in Disneyland with its incredible transistorized Abe Lincoln?

Disneyland could only have been created in America. My country 'tis of thee, of thee I sing. What is it in our national psyche that makes us create Raggedy Ann and Raggedy Andy; the Emerald City and Fantasyland, U.S.A.? Nowhere else in the world do they build fake rivers filled with plastic crocodiles and mechanical natives hurling dummy spears at rubber rhinos, complete with little orange-and-yellow signs reading PICTURE TAKING SPOT so that this curious adventure can be recorded for those poor souls left at home.

No wonder every Russian dictator who comes to our shores has an insane desire to visit Disneyland. They believe in Utopias too.

The Utopia Complex has afflicted us from the day that the first American stubbed his buckled shoe on Plymouth Rock. A sad, hopeless dream very much like inventors ceaselessly trying for Perpetual Motion. It seems so simple. The wistful little slogans: WAR IS NOT GOOD FOR LITTLE CHILDREN AND OTHER GROWING THINGS: HONK IF YOU LOVE JESUS, are all by-products of Utopianism.

Maybe that's why Disney hit the double jackpot. He created one, in real, vibrant, living styrene and for a few hours, for a price (even Utopia has gate receipts), you are back in the world of good witches, ukulele-playing bears, and "real authentic" Penny Candy stores where the prices start at forty cents per jawbreaker.

We can even imagine a Utopia for gaffers, where they have toy stock markets that always go up, transistorized octogenarians that play Vincent Lopez hits.

No, Childhood itself is a Utopia to Americans. Childhood, in fact, is an actual place. Like any other place, it is wide open to the cruel jibes of we buffoons. If Jersey can take it without crying, why not Childhood?

Camp Nobba-WaWa-Nockee. Of course! I had not thought of it in years. I settled deeper into my worn naugahyde seat. The horn blasted again behind me.

Camp Nobba-WaWa-Nockee...

The Mole People
Battle the Forces
of Darkness

"Camp Nobba-WaWa-Nockee. Boy, what a great name!" said Schwartz as we squatted down, tying sheepshank knots at a scout meeting. Troop 41 was scattered around the church basement.

"Camp what?" Flick asked, snapping his rope at Kissel's bottom, causing Kissel to kick him on the knee.

"Nobba-WaWa-Nockee," Schwartz answered. "Didn't you see that sign on the bulletin board? Take a look. Tells you all about it."

Flick, Kissel, and I read the notice:

CAMP NOBBA-WAWA-NOCKEE, A BOY'S CAMP IN THE SYLVAN MICHIGAN WILDERNESS. BOATING, LEATHER-CRAFT, AND A WELL-BALANCED, HEALTHFUL DIET. UNDER THE PERSONAL DIRECTION OF COL. D. G. BULLARD, U. S. ARMY (RET.), CAMP DIRECTOR. SPECIAL RATES TO BOY SCOUTS.

There was a penciled note at the bottom: "See me. Mr. Gordon."

Mr. Gordon was our scoutmaster. He drove a truck for the Silvercup Bread Company, the official bread of all us kids, because they sponsored "The Lone Ranger." Somehow, because Mr. Gordon worked for Silvercup, he seemed to have a direct connection with the Lone Ranger and Tonto, and he never denied it. We clumped over to Mr. Gordon, who was instructing two kids in artificial respiration. One lay flat on the concrete with his tongue hanging out, pretending he had drowned, while the other kid, Scut Farkas, sat on his back—Scut's favorite position—gouging away rhythmically at his rib cage.

"You count to yourself: 'One first-aid, two first-aid, three first-aid . . .' " Mr. Gordon stood over them calling strokes, while the kid underneath turned purple trying not to laugh.

"Mr. Gordon, what about Camp Nobba-whatever-it-is?" Flick asked.

"Oh yes." Mr. Gordon peered at us blandly through his thick glasses. "Camp Nobba-WaWa-Nockee is a truly splendid experience. I went there as a boy. You'll gain much from Colonel Bullard. Since I am an old Chipmunk myself, they have offered to give special rates to any boys in Troop 41."

I thought, What's a Chipmunk? I should have asked. It would have saved a lot of trouble later.

That night half the troop went home with brochures extolling the glories of Camp Nobba-WaWa-Nockee on the shores of Lake Paddachungacong. All over the neighborhood, skirmishes broke out as members of Troop 41 hurled themselves onto the floor and threw tantrums to be sent to camp. Ours was not a summer-camp neighborhood. In fact, summer was considered a time of glorious freedom, when we eddied up and down alleys, through vacant lots, and over infields with no more sense of purpose than a school of minnows. Now, in our innocence, we were clamoring to be enlisted in Colonel Bullard's legions, where we would learn indelibly that there are other kinds of summers.

Camp began on the tenth of June, which was a week after school let out, and you could sign up for a four-week or an eight-week period.

"You'll have to talk to your father about it." My mother sounded a bit uncertain as I tore around the house waving the brochure, already—in my mind's eye—paddling a birchbarck canoe down the rapids in classic Indian fashion. It was bowling night and there was no telling how the old man would be when he got home. It all depended on how he rolled. Some nights, when his hook wasn't breaking and he wasn't picking up any wood, he'd come home sullen and smelling ripely of beer. He'd slam his bowling ball into the closet along with his shoes, and go

stomping around the kitchen, muttering. On those nights, nobody said a word.

My kid brother Randy, upon hearing about Camp Nobba-WaWa-Nockee, had run cheering around the dining-room table about five times, until he found out that kids under ten weren't allowed, after which he threw a fit, falling onto the floor, kicking off his shoes, and crawling under the daybed, where he lay sobbing and punching the wall.

While I was throwing stuff all around my room, digging in my closet among the socks and baseball cards for my boy-scout ax, there was a roar in the driveway that meant the old man was home from bowling. Our Oldsmobile made a distinctive, loose-limbed, gurgling racket that came from 120,000 hard miles and gallons of cheap oil.

"YER LOOKIN' AT A GUY THAT JUST ROLLED A SIX-HUNDRED SERIES! My God, was I pickin' off them spares! You never saw nothin' like it!" He strode across the kitchen ten feet tall, smelling of Pabst Blue Ribbon and success. "You wouldn't believe it. I picked up a seven-ten split tonight that was like somethin' outa this world!"

He opened the refrigerator and grabbed a couple of cans of beer. "On the second game, I had six strikes in a row before I spared. Wound up with a two forty-eight. Even Zudock had to admit I was really layin' em in."

"Dad," I said, "I–"

"Ya know, kid, I'm gonna start givin' ya bowlin' lessons. If I'd a started at your age, lemme tell ya, I'd have a two-twenty average at least and–"

"He has something he wants to ask you," my mother broke in, setting a clean glass down in front of the old man. She was always trying to break him of the habit of sucking up his beer out of the can. He opened the Pabst, took a long swig from the can, and wiped his mouth.

"Hey, what the hell's this?" He was looking at the Camp Nobba-WaWa-Nockee folder on the table.

"That's what he was going to ask you about," said my mother nervously. I could tell she was on my side. "You see, he wants to go to camp this summer."

"CAMP!" The old man set his beer down hard. "Camp!"

"Yes!" I leaped into the breach. "Mr. Gordon, our scoutmaster, told us all about Camp Nobba-whatever-its-name-is and Schwartz and Flick and Kissel are going and a lot of other kids from the troop and . . ."

My father peered at the brochure intently, looking at a picture of a bunch of kids sitting around the campfire.

"Camp? Well, I'll be damned. I never went to no camp when I was a kid." Then he read aloud: "Indian lore and leathercraft with . . . hey, how the hell much is this gonna cost?"

I knew it was time for me to be quiet.

"It's on the back." My mother sounded cheerful as she poured the rest of the beer into the glass.

My father scanned the figures on the back. "Holy Christ!"

"They give boy scouts special rates," my mother said hopefully.

"They'd better, at those prices." He started flipping the pages. "Hey, what's this?" He looked closer at the brochure. "What's this archery stuff?"

"That's bows and arrows," I squeaked.

"Bows and arrows!" The old man chortled. "Boy, you could'na paid me to shoot bows and arrows in the summertime when I was a kid."

"And they have birchbark canoes, and they have this lifesaving badge with—"

The old man drained his beer. "Listen," he said, "you shoulda seen what I did on the third game. I started out with an open frame and it looked like I was gonna blow it, but then the old hook started to work and—"

"Don't you think just this once we might be able—" My mother hung in there.

"Camp? Sure, why the hell not? If the kid wants to mess around with bows and arrows, I guess you gotta get that kinda stuff out of your system."

At this, there was a sudden hysterical bleat from under the daybed.

"What the hell's eatin' him?" asked the old man.

"Kids under ten can't go to camp," I stated with deep-felt satisfaction. There were more muffled sobs and thumpings as Randy kicked the wall.

"KNOCK IT OFF!" the old man hollered. "You'll get your turn. You're too little to be messin' around with bows and arrows."

There was another shriek from under the daybed, but you could tell he didn't have his heart in it. I guess he knew it wouldn't do him any good to yell and holler any more, and he might even wind up getting a swat on the behind if he kept it up.

I lay in bed that night stiff with excitement, even then aware that a new era had begun. Camp Nobba-WaWa-Nockee—with its dancing waters, its zestful program of outdoor sports and recreational activities under the personal supervision of Colonel D. G. Bullard, U. S. Army (Ret.)—lay just ahead, glittering in the golden sunlight like the Emerald City at the end of the Yellow Brick Road of springtime.

The next night, at the kitchen table, my mother filled out the application—signing me up for a month—stuck it in an envelope, slapped a stamp on it, and handed it to me.

"Here. Take this down to the mailbox before your father changes his mind."

I tore out of the house and flew down the street to the mailbox. It clanged shut. The die was cast! Though I didn't know it at the time, I was about to enter the sacred rolls of Camp Nobba-WaWa-Nockee, my name for all time inscribed on the birchbark scroll that was kept under glass in the Longlodge, the camp's main wigwam.

A week later, a message arrived for my mother on camp stationery, which featured a bright yellow arrowhead and the silhouette of an Indian paddling a canoe in the moonlight.

Dear Madam:

We take pleasure to inform you that your son has been elected to the Chipmunk tribe of Camp Nobba-WaWa-Nockee. The Chipmunk tribe are the first-year boys, and I'm sure your son will enjoy being one. The following items must be brought to camp by your Chipmunk:

1. Single-bed-size muslin mattress cover.

2. Camping clothes, including shorts and hiking shoes.

3. Necessary accessories such as underwear, socks, and toilet articles.

4. Writing equipment, as letter writing to home is mandatory.

Please be sure that every item of clothing, etc., is clearly marked with your Chipmunk's name.

Your Chipmunk will appear at the downtown bus terminal in Chicago at 7 A.M. June 10th to assemble with the other campers in order to be driven by the camp bus to Camp Nobba-WaWa-Nockee. Your son will be in good hands and I give you my personal assurance that we will return a more manly boy to you. Our methods have borne fruit over the years.

> *Sincerely,*
> *Colonel D. G. Bullard,*
> *U. S. Army (Ret.)*
> *Camp Director*

She read it over a couple of times and passed it to my father, who was studying the sports page—in vain—for the merest hint of good news about the White Sox. He read it and turned to me.

"Well, Chipmunk, you all set for a big summer?"

"Yeah." It was about all I could think of to say. For some reason, I was beginning to feel a little scared.

The next couple of weeks were nothing but running around

buying new shorts, T-shirts, and underwear without holes. My mother toiled night after night with the name tapes, attaching them to every sock and handkerchief. My brother had become permanently sullen and spent a lot of time in the bathroom with the door locked, or under the porch.

Now that we were Chipmunks, Schwartz, Flick, Kissel, and I drifted off from the kids who weren't going to camp. Already we were becoming part of the special world of Camp Nobba-WaWa-Nockee. On the way to the store at night, I would practice walking like an Indian, so that I could sneak up silently in the woods when I was hunting deer. I had read about it in Uncle Dan Beard's column in *Boy's Life*. I began to feel lean and sinewy as I moved like a shadow past the poolroom, a lone hunter in search of game.

The days crawled by with maddening slowness. The close of school, which usually ranked second only to Christmas in sheer ecstasy, passed almost without my noticing. Even bigger things were in store. Little did I suspect how big.

On the night before the big day, it took forever for me to go to sleep, and it seemed like five minutes later I was awake again. It was already four-fifteen. The alarm was set to go off in an hour. I lay there in the dark, listening to the old man snore. Outside, the rain was pouring down in sheets.

By five forty-five we were in the Olds, my huge suitcase piled in the back seat between me and my kid brother, who appeared to be glad that it was raining for my first day in camp.

"Jesus," said the old man, "I haven't been up this early since the Bumpus mob's white-lightning still blew up."

My mother, who was huddled in the front seat, bundled against the chill, with her hair all done up in aluminum rheostats, kept saying, "Now, you write. And you be careful, you hear? I don't want you getting drowned." Like all mothers, she had a thing about drowning.

We pulled up at the bus terminal at precisely six-fifty. Already a milling mob of kids, with associated parents and sisters and a raggle-taggle crowd of kid brothers, all of whom looked mad, had formed in the main lobby under a canvas banner that read CAMP NOBBA-WAWA-NOCKEE. A short, round-faced man wearing a khaki uniform with a yellow arrowhead on the sleeve stood on a folding chair amid the mob.

"I'm Captain Crabtree," he shrilled. "Now, all you campers, listen carefully."

The excitement was electric. I spotted Schwartz in the crowd, lugging a steamer trunk. Flick and Kissel were over on the other side. Mrs. Kissel was sniffling.

"HEY, SCHWARTZ!" I hollered.

"I said LISTEN!" Captain Crabtree stared balefully through his glasses at me. I had made my first false move.

"Say all of your good-bys and make it snappy. We move out at 0700. Convey all your baggage over there to that platform. All Chipmunks raise your hands."

I stuck my hand proudly in the air along with about a third of the rest of the kids.

"This is your first year, and you are not aware of the tradition of the Chipmunk cap. My assistant, Lieutenant Hubert Kneecamp, will pass them out. You will wear your Chipmunk cap at all times, so that you can be readily identified as a Chipmunk."

Oh boy! A Chipmunk cap! It has often been noted that lambs go eagerly to the slaughter. So it was with Chipmunks. Lieutenant Hubert Kneecamp, who doubled as the bus driver, stumbled out onto the platform carrying a huge cardboard box. He was tall, very thin, and had a sad expression that reminded me of Pluto in the Mickey Mouse cartoons.

The lieutenant opened the box and began to pass out bright green beanies with a yellow arrowhead on the front. I pressed forward, so as not to miss my cap. Lieutenant Kneecamp shoved one into my waiting mitt. I quickly jammed it onto my head. It came down over my ears and I could barely see out from under the brim.

"They're all the same size," Lieutenant Kneecamp said over

and over as he passed them out. I noticed Schwartz's beanie sat on the top of his head like a half of a green tennis ball.

"NOW, ALL YOU CHIPMUNKS," Captain Crabtree shouted, "LINE UP ON THE PLATFORM. You will sit in a group at the rear of the bus. A Chipmunk does not speak unless spoken to."

The non-Chipmunks were a head taller and a foot wider than any of us. They had the kind of faces that kids who smoke have. They hit each other in the ribs, laughed back and forth, and a few threw wadded-up balls of paper at us Chipmunks. They wore identical blue jackets and Captain Crabtree called them Beavers.

"O.K., kid. Give 'em hell and hang in there." That was all my old man had to say to me.

My mother patted my hat down over my ears and whispered, "Don't forget what I said about your underwear. And you be careful, you hear me now?"

"ALL RIGHT, CHIPMUNKS, ONTO THE BUS. SINGLE FILE, THERE. MOVE OUT."

The captain herded us onto the bus. We surged to the rear, battling for seats next to the windows. I squatted down in the back between Flick and Schwartz. Kissel sat a few rows up, next to a big fat Chipmunk who looked scared and was sobbing quietly. Then the Beavers whooped and trampled aboard, and Captain Crabtree stood in the aisle.

"Now, I don't want any trouble on the trip, because if there is, I'm gonna start handing out demerits. Y'hear me? You play ball with me and I'll play ball with you." This was a phrase I was to hear many times in future life.

The parents stood on the platform outside the bus, waving and tapping on the windows, making signs to the various kids. Up front, Lieutenant Kneecamp started the engine with a roar. As it bellowed out, the fat Chipmunk next to Kissel wailed and began sobbing uncontrollably. Captain Crabtree stood up and glared angrily around the bus until he spotted Fatso.

"I DON'T WANNA GO!! WAAAAAAAA!! WAAAAAAAAAA!!!"

Lieutenant Kneecamp peered wearily around from the driver's

seat with the expression of one who had witnessed this scene many times before. A couple of the grizzled Beavers laughed raucously and one gave a juicy Bronx cheer.

"WAAAAAAAAAA! I AIN'T GONNA GO!!"

The fat Chipmunk had hurled himself onto the floor of the bus and was crawling toward the door. Captain Crabtree, with the practiced quickness of a man who had seen it all, grabbed him by the scruff of the neck and said in a cold, level voice:

"Chipmunks do not cry. We will have no crying."

The fat Chipmunk instantly stopped bawling and retreated slightly, his eyes round and staring.

"Put that hat back on, Chipmunk. NOW!" The fat Chipmunk quickly jammed his hat back onto his head.

"Lieutenant Kneecamp, will you please proceed?" Captain Crabtree had the situation well in hand. Pale and shaken, the fat Chipmunk slumped down next to Kissel. He had a wad of gum stuck on his knee. The lieutenant threw the bus into gear and we slowly pulled out of the terminal, amid frenzied waving and cheering among the assembled parentage. We rumbled out into the gray, rainy street, and the last sight I had of my family was the familiar image of my old man holding my kid brother by one ear and swatting him on the rump.

Captain Crabtree stood swaying in the aisle. "In three hours we will arrive at camp. We will make one stop, in precisely ninety minutes. If you have to go to the toilet, you will hold it until then."

I had already felt faint stirrings. Now that he mentioned it, they flared up badly. I had been so excited that I'd forgotten to go after breakfast.

"We will now sing the 'Camp Nobba-WaWa-Nockee Loyalty Song,'" Captain Crabtree shouted over the roar of the engine. "Here, pass these songbooks back. I have counted them. I want every one of them returned at the conclusion of the trip." He needn't have worried.

He handed out mimeographed blue pamphlets. There were mutterings here and there. The fat Chipmunk had closed his eyes and appeared to be holding his breath. I was handed a songbook. The lettering on the front read *Nobba-WaWa-Nockee True-blue Trail Songs.*

"All right, men. The 'Camp Nobba-WaWa-Nockee Loyalty Song' is the first song in the book. It is sung to the tune of 'Old MacDonald Had a Farm.' You all know it. Ladadeedeedadadum," Captain Crabtree sang tonelessly. I opened the book. Schwartz and Flick, their hats jammed down on their heads, had their books open, too. Life at Camp Nobba-WaWa-Nockee had officially begun.

The captain produced a pitch pipe that looked like a little harmonica. He blew briskly into it, producing a wavering note that was barely audible over the bellow of the worn Dodge motor.

"Now, sing it out. All together. I want to hear some life in it." He blew into his pitch pipe again. Led by the Beavers, we began to sing the "Loyalty Song":

> *"Nobba Nobba-WaWa-Nockee . . .*
> *EeeIiiEEEEEiii OHHH . . .*
> *With a weenie roast here . . . and a snipe hunt there . . .*
> *EeeeIiiiiEEEEEEEIiii OHHHH*
> *With a leathercraft here . . . and a volleyball there . . .*
> *EeeeeIiiiiEEEEEEiiii OHHHHH."*

There were thirty-seven verses, which made reference to pillow fights, totem poles, Indian trails, and the like, with the concluding blast:

> *"Colonel Bullard is our chief . . .*
> *We love him, yes we do.*
> *Nobba Nobba-WaWa-Nockee*
> *EeeeIiiiEEEEEEIiii OHHHHH."*

Again the bus exploded in a roar of cheers and stompings, with a few hisses and a couple of raspberries from the Beaver contingent. The rain drummed on the sides of the bus as we hurtled toward our gala summer.

"Boy, lookit those great jackets all the big kids have," said Schwartz enviously.

"Yeah," said Flick. "And what's that yellow thing on the front?" Over each boy's heart was a golden emblem.

Kissel, who overheard us, squinted closely at the Beaver sitting in front of him. "I dunno," he stage-whispered. "It looks like a picture of a rat holding an ice cream cone."

The Beaver turned savagely, baring yellow teeth, his bull-like neck bulging red with rage. "That's the Sacred Golden Tomahawk of Chief Chungacong, you stupid little freak!" he snarled. "Hey, Jake! You hear what this stupid little kid called the Sacred Beaver?"

"Yeah, I heard. I think we gotta teach 'im a lesson, eh, Dan?"

Dan Baxter, as we were later to find out to our sorrow, believed we should *all* be taught a lesson.

The fat Chipmunk, without warning, again hurled himself to the floor of the bus. A skinny Chipmunk yelled out, "HEY! He's doin' it AGAIN!"

Captain Crabtree rose ominously from his seat, staring back into the swaying bus. The fat Chipmunk lay sprawled in the aisle, kicking his feet like a grounded frog, his eyes clamped shut, his arms held rigidly to his sides. I had seen that move many times before. My cousin Buddy was famous for his spectacularly creative tantrums. One of his specialties was the very same catatonic beauty that the fat Chipmunk was now performing surpassingly well. If anything, he was even better than Buddy at his peak. The bus slowed to a crawl as Captain Crabtree lurched down the aisle.

"GET UP!" he barked, his voice crisp and cutting. The fat Chipmunk just lay there, quivering. One of his feet flicked upward, neatly disengaging his shoe, which bounced off the captain's chest. It was a nice touch. The entire busload of kids, all of whom from time to time had themselves practiced tantrum throwing, recognized a tour-de-force performance.

"I SAID GET UP!" The fat Chipmunk quivered again, this time producing a venomous hissing sound—an interesting detail.

"What was that?" The captain's voice was menacing. "What did you say?"

The hissing continued, now accompanied by a curious sideways writhing of the body that produced a rhythmic thumping as his plump buttocks drubbed on the bus floor.

"O.K.," Captain Crabtree barked. Reaching down with a quick, swooping motion, he hauled the fat Chipmunk to his feet. Instantly, Fatso's legs turned to rubber in counterattack.

"I've had about enough out of you," the captain muttered, his glasses sliding down his nose from the exertion of holding the fat Chipmunk erect.

"This guy's great!" Flick whispered, more to himself than to any of us. It was obvious we were witnessing a confrontation that could go either way.

"I'll give you one more chance to sit down and behave."

Captain Crabtree steered the blubbery, quivering mass toward his seat. The fat Chipmunk seemed to swell up like a toad, his face turning beet-red. Just as the captain was about to lower him to his seat, he let fly his ultimate crusher, a master stroke of the tantrum thrower's art.

"BRRRAAAUUUUGGGGGHHHHH, BRAAAAAHHHHKKKKK!"

For a moment, none of us could comprehend what was happening. It was done so quickly, so cleanly, so deliberately. The captain staggered back, bellowing incoherently. A pungent aroma filled the rear of the bus. The captain reeled, dripping from his necktie down to his brass belt buckle. The fat Chipmunk seemed to have shrunk two sizes as he squatted on his seat, exuding malevolent satisfaction at a job well done.

"STOP THE BUS!" the captain hollered brokenly. "NOW!"

His crisp suntans were completely soaked by a deluge of vomit. The bus careened to a halt. The captain rushed up the aisle and out the front door. He disappeared into the weeds at the side of the road.

Immediately, the crowd broke into an uproar, with a few scattered bursts of applause coming from the Beavers up front. The fat Chipmunk had won instant respect. Schwartz, his voice rising in excitement, asked, "Hey, kid, how'd ya do that?" There was no reply.

Flick, who was the naturalist among us, since he raised rabbits and hamsters, put the event in perspective. "He's like a human skunk. When he's trapped, he just lets 'em have it."

The fat Chipmunk had opened his right eye and fixed Flick with a piercing glare. From that instant, he was known as Skunk. It was not in any sense a term of derision. He had clearly demonstrated that he could handle himself exceedingly well and was, in fact, lethal.

The captain, drenched to the skin from the driving rain, with bits of residual vomit staining his tie, but once again in charge, reentered the bus.

"All right. Let's move out," he ordered in a voice still shaking with rage. "One more incident and the colonel will get a full report."

Comparative peace settled over the mob, which was now somehow changed as we rolled on through the rain. There was a brief stop at a gas station with an adjoining diner. We lined up outside the john.

"Hey, take a look at Skunk," Flick said to me. Skunk was on a stool in the diner, taking on more ammunition in case there was further trouble.

We moved out again in a haze of drowsiness. It had been a long trip. The country had turned to farms, Bull Durham signs, and occasional run-down vegetable stands that all seemed to be closed. Old, gray, sagging farmhouses with hand-lettered signs reading FRESH EGGS and HANDMADE QUILTS FOR SALE rolled past. We were in Michigan. It wouldn't be long now.

Finally the bus slowed at a crossroad. A rutted gravel road wound off to the north. A swaying yellow arrowhead attached to a tree trunk read CAMP NOBBA-WAWA-NOCKEE 2 MI. The bus exploded in a tidal wave of cheers as it wheeled onto the gravel road. We were almost there. I felt a wild tightening in the pit of my stomach. In just a few minutes I would be at camp. Camp!

It was raining even harder now. The ditches on the side of the road were rushing torrents of muddy water. We were among heavy, dripping trees, and the branches intertwined over the road until we were rolling forward through a dark, green-black tunnel. Anxious and subdued, the Chipmunks peered out the windows into the passing gloom. We lurched around a bend and headed down a slope.

Schwartz hit me sharply on the shoulder. "Hey, look!" He half-rose from his seat, pointing toward the front of the bus. I stared ahead. The windshield wipers slapped back and forth. Then I saw it–a gray, flat gleam through the tangled trees ahead.

"What is it?" Flick asked, squinting. A tall, sandy-haired Beaver turned a scornful glance in our directions. "What does it look like, stupe?" He nudged the bullet-headed Beaver next to him and said loudly, for our benefit:

"Jee-zus. They're getting worse every year. Guys like that wouldna lasted five minutes when we were Chipmunks. Right, Jake?"

Jake, the bullet-headed Beaver, laughed a grating cackle that boded ill for any Chipmunk who crossed his path.

"It's the lake!" I shouted. "Holy smokes, it's Lake Paddaclunka-whatever-they-call-it!!"

An expanse of choppy water lay ahead. The short, broad Beaver turned at this remark, his red neck straining again at his T-shirt.

"Hey, Jake!" he barked. "They don't even know Old Pisshole when they see it."

At this, five or six Beavers began poking each other and making incomprehensible cracks. Jake turned and grinned mirthlessly in our direction. He was missing three lower teeth and one of his ears appeared to be badly chewed.

"Y'mean none a'you know what Paddachungacong means?"

He waited for an answer. All we could do was stare dumbly back. "Well, I'll tell ya. It means Sacred Place Where Big Chief Took a Leak."

Again the Beavers roared in appreciation of Jake's cutting wit. We later found out he was telling the truth. That's exactly what Paddachungacong means.

By this time, the bus had rolled onto a broad clearing that sloped down to the lake. A row of stubby square log cabins with green tar-paper roofs straggled off toward the woods. The bus lurched to a halt in front of a long, flat, low building with a dark, screen-enclosed porch.

"All right, men, let's move out." Captain Crabtree again stood in the aisle, directing the troops. "Watch out for the puddles. And move up onto the porch."

The yelling, scrambling mass of Beavers up front charged out the door and onto the porch, slamming the screen doors. We followed quietly, not knowing quite what to expect. The rain had let up, but the mud was two inches deep. My shoes had grown four sizes by the time I had walked a yard.

"Quit splashing, Schwartz!" hollered Flick as Schwartz kicked up sheets of muddy water behind him. A chill wind blew off the lake. Just before I reached the steps, a sharp sting hit me on the back of the neck. Instinctively, I swatted at it. Already a huge welt was rising next to my left ear. I could see several other Chipmunks swatting at invisible attackers.

"I see why they got screens all around that porch," muttered Flick as he scratched frantically at his ribs.

Inside the building, which was a big empty hall with a lot of long wooden tables pushed together at one end and a row of naked light bulbs hanging from the ceiling, the Beavers milled around as though they owned the place, with the cool, on-top-of-it air of battle-scarred veterans. Captain Crabtree climbed up onto a chair and clapped his hands for attention.

"All right, men. Let's quiet down here. Colonel Bullard will be along shortly. He wants to greet you personally and will perform the initiation rites."

The rain, which had picked up again, drummed heavily on the roof. Here and there, a few puddles soaked into the wood of the floor under dripping leaks. I stared out the windows to my right. A few kids who had arrived earlier in other buses trudged back and forth wearing raincoats. Somewhere off in the distance, I heard the sound of a Ping-Pong ball being batted back and forth.

"When the colonel arrives I want all of you to stand up straight and be quiet, y'understand?"

The crowd shifted restlessly. Outside I spotted a tall figure wearing a trench coat rounding the corner of the building. There was a loud clumping on the steps, the screen door swung open, and Captain Crabtree snapped to attention.

"Ten-HUT!" he shouted. "COLONEL BULLARD!"

The colonel, his face deeply tanned and seamed, as though carved from rich mahogany, strode to the center of the room.

"Jesus," said Flick, "he must be seven feet tall!"

The colonel was wearing a peaked military cap with a large gold eagle. He wore gleaming black boots and carried a whiplike swagger stick, the first I had ever seen, which he slapped smartly against his dripping trench coat. The room fell silent, except for the steady patter of rain on the roof. He towered above Captain Crabtree, who was standing at attention atop his chair.

"At ease." His voice was deep, resonant, official. "This looks like a fine body of men. We'll soon whip them into shape, eh, Crabtree?"

Captain Crabtree nodded briskly four or five times and descended from his chair. Colonel Bullard cracked his face into a huge grin, his teeth gleaming brightly in the gloom. For the first time, I noticed he had a thin mustache, like Smilin' Jack.

"Fellows," he boomed, "we run a tight ship here." He slapped his swagger stick hard against his whipcord puttees. "But a happy one. Right, Beavers?"

It was a rhetorical question, since none of the Beavers answered.

"But happiness, fellows, must be earned. A good workout in the morning, a few hours of honest labor, and then we have fun. Now, all you Chipmunks raise your right hand. So." His gloved first shot up nearly to the ceiling. "And repeat after me the Sacred Oath of Chief Chungacong."

He extended his forefinger and thumb at right angles, his fore-finger pointing at the ceiling, his thumb jutting out sharply. "This is the secret sign of the Brotherhood of Nobba-WaWa-Nockee. Now," his voice grew richer and fuller, "repeat after me: 'Oh, Great Spirit of the Woods, Oh, Giver of Life . . .' "

Our forefingers pointed like a forest of toothpicks at the leaky roof.

" 'We shall work hard and play hard, with clean minds and clean bodies, to thy greater glory.' "

Together we shouted out the creed. The colonel paused dra-matically. "And now, for the most important part of our cere-mony—the Secret Wolf Call of Camp Nobba-WaWa-Nockee. Captain Crabtree, perform the call."

The captain, eyes closed, tilted his head back and from deep inside his khaki tunic came a high, rising, spine-tingling wolf call. It echoed from floor to ceiling, from jukebox to screen door. The colonel, his face solemn after the last note died, said in a low voice: "Men, once you have joined your brothers in the sacred Nobba-WaWa-Nockee wolf cry, you will be bound together for-ever." A hush fell over the mob. Even the grizzled Beavers were caught up in the occasion. "Together, men. Let's hear it."

The colonel waved his swagger stick like a wand over the crowd. Slowly at first, but then with gathering momentum, a great collective howl rose to the rainy heavens. I found my eye-balls popping, my neck bulging as some strange primitive beast deep within me rose to greet the rolling storm clouds. Schwartz, sweat pouring down his nose, seemed to be rising from the floor. The fat Chipmunk, his glasses steamed up in excitement, yowled in the corner. The colonel, his face impassive, loomed like a great oak amid the banshees. Just as the wail reached its peak, he slapped his swagger stick hard against his trench coat. Instantly, as if a switch had been thrown, the howling ceased, leaving a ringing silence. The colonel stared slowly around the hall, his gaze direct and level, taking in all of us.

"Men, we are now brothers." He turned and strode from the hall without as much as a backward glance.

"HOORAY! YAY! YAY! HOORAY!" A ragged cheer broke out.

Captain Crabtree was back on his chair. "All right, you guys. Let's get cracking. We've got to move into the lodges before noon chow. Let's go."

Led by the Beavers, we charged out of the hall back into the rain. Lieutenant Kneecamp had unloaded all the baggage, which was piled up in five neat pyramids with signs on each one. He shouted into the hubbub: "Whatever pile your bag is in is what lodge you're assigned to. I don't want no arguments. That one over there is Eagle Lodge, that one's Grizzly Bear Lodge, that one's Hawk Lodge, that one over there is Polar Bear Lodge, and that one on the end is Mole Lodge."

We finally found our stuff, after a lot of rooting around, in the Mole pile. It figured. I hoisted my suitcase, which felt twenty pounds heavier, since it was now soaked with Michigan rain water. Three or four new counselors had appeared, dressed in khaki jackets with yellow arrowheads on the sleeves.

"All right, you guys from Mole Lodge, follow me," one of them called out listlessly. We fell in behind him as we struggled up a slippery clay slope toward the long line of log cabins.

A motley collection of kids squatted in cabin doors or lurked about in slickers and ponchos, watching the new shipment check in. A couple hollered: "You'll be sorr-reee!"–an ancient cry that must have echoed around recruiting camps in the days of Attila the Hun.

The counselor glared in the direction of a pimply kid who ducked behind a cabin after chucking an apple core at Schwartz.

The counselor scooped up the apple core on the first bounce and winged it back at the retreating figure. It caught him neatly between the shoulder blades, splattering wetly as it hit.

"That'll be three Big D's, Klooberman."

"Sir?" asked Flick as he staggered along under his huge steamer trunk. "What's a Big D?"

The counselor glanced at Flick. "A Big D, kid, is a big fat *dee-merit*. You get more'n five and they cut off your ice cream. More'n ten and forget the swimming. After fifteen, y'go on bread and water. Klooberman just went over twenty."

"What's gonna happen to him?" Schwartz asked, looking scared.

"Wait and see." That was all he said as he swung open the creaking door of our little log-cabin home, standing aside for three startled squirrels to vacate the premises before walking in.

"Here it is, you guys, and you better keep it shipshape or you're gonna answer to me, Morey Partridge, personally. Y'got it?"

We got it.

"And another thing," he went on. "Once you pick your bunks, I don't want no movin' around, because of bed check. You pick yer bunks, y'stay there."

We clumped into the dim little cabin. The walls were lined with bunks stacked three high, making six in all. The far wall had a tiny window that looked out into the black forest. Schwartz, Flick, and I were the first in. Behind us toiled three other Chipmunks, lugging their heavy baggage. The one at the end of the line was the fat Chipmunk. He dragged a monstrous steamer trunk over the threshold and without a word collapsed on the low bunk nearest the door. I don't think he could have gotten any farther. He took off his glasses, which were round and metal-framed, with white tape holding one earpiece together.

"I wanna top one!" Schwartz said excitedly as he clambered up the narrow ladder to the highest bunk near the eaves. I shoved my suitcase onto the middle one. Within five minutes, we all had our individual territories staked out and we were ready for business.

"What's your name?" I asked the strange Chipmunk in the bunk opposite me. He was unpacking a pair of water wings from his suitcase.

"Calvin Quackenbush," he said over his shoulder, somewhat defensively.

The fat Chipmunk snorted nastily. Quackenbush glared at him. "What's so funny, fatso?"

Life in Mole Lodge was already hardening into the pattern it would follow in the weeks to come.

From somewhere out in the rain a bell clanged–immediately followed by the thunder of hundreds of galloping hoofs.

"What the heck is that?" Flick hollered, rushing to the window and peering into the woods–the only point on the compass from which the sound wasn't coming. The thunder grew. Schwartz threw the front door open. Kids hurtled by, kicking up muddy water, yipping and yelling as they ran, hundreds of them pouring out of the lodges, from every building, all rushing down the slippery slope that we had just struggled up. There's something about a rushing crowd of people that sort of sucks you in. In a moment, I found myself out the door and running with the crowd, sloshing through puddles, Schwartz panting beside me. Flick brought up the rear, falling down and getting up and falling down again. We must have run 100 yards amid the ravening mob when Schwartz, gasping and wheezing, shouted at a tall Beaver who was going past us like a freight train, his knees snapping high, his arms flailing.

"HEY! What's going ON?"

Without looking aside, the Beaver tossed back, "It's Hamburger Day!"

We had arrived at Nobba-WaWa-Nockee a few minutes before the absolute pinnacle of the week: Saturday lunch.

From all directions, streaming hordes of kids surged toward the mess hall. Some raced up from the lake, carrying paddles; others dropped tools and Indian beads as they ran, fresh from leathercraft. I saw a counselor, attempting to slow the mad dash, engulfed and overrun by the mob. Up the steps we ran, spraying mud and gravel. Inside the mess hall, most of the tables were already filled with hardened campers who knew the ropes. The meal, served by fat ladies in white uniforms, turned out to be light gray hamburgers, soggy French fries, cole slaw, and pitchers of cherry Kool-Aid, a true kid meal. The uproar was deafening as pieces of bun flew through the air and counselors battled the

barbarian hordes, attempting to maintain some semblance of civilization.

"NOW, SIDDOWN! YOU CAME IN HERE TO EAT, NOT
THROW POTATOES AROUND!" Captain Crabtree, in a momentarily clean uniform, shoved at writhing bodies amid the turmoil.
It was all over in a couple of minutes. Stuffed with hamburgers
and soggy with Kool-Aid, we followed the crowd back out into
the rain.

"Hey, you guys!" It was Morey Partridge. "You better not be late
for forestcraft. Down at the rec hall in ten minutes. Y'get two Big
D's for every minute you're late, so get your rumps in gear." He
scurried off into the drizzle to break up a wrestling match that
had broken out in the mud.

Out of breath, faces red, clothes clammy, we squeezed into the
crowded rec hall, which was already filled with Beavers and fellow Chipmunks. Another counselor stood on a platform next to a
blackboard, peering at his wristwatch. At the stroke of one, the
lecture began:

"Forestcraft consists of learning to live off the land in the
wilderness. The Indians . . ."

Behind us the screen door slammed noisily and three Chipmunks attempted to skulk in unnoticed. The lieutenant at the
board rapped his pointer sharply on the floor.

"Sergeant, get those men's names and lodges. We'll deal with
them later."

A chunky counselor wearing a Nobba-WaWa-Nockee T-shirt
and a businesslike crew cut closed in on the cowering malefac-
tors. There was a brief session of muttering in the corner and the
lecture continued. It was all about how you could tell what direction north was by looking at the moss on trees and how, if you
knew where north was, everything was O.K., for some reason.
The moist atmosphere of the rec hall slowly approached that of
the Amazon jungles as 100 tightly packed bodies exuded noxious
gases and the flat voice of the lecturer twanged on. Schwartz
dozed off and limply slumped sideways against the leg of the pool

table. Immediately, the sergeant rapped him sharply across the neck with a rolled-up copy of *Field & Stream.*

Schwartz started violently, his eyeballs round and glassy. "It's got my foot!" he blurted incoherently. Apparently he'd been trapped in the middle of a nightmare. Chipmunks snickered for yards around.

"What's your name, Chipmunk?" The sergeant peered into Schwartz's face.

"Uh . . . Schwartz."

"What lodge are you in?"

"Mole." Schwartz had yet to learn that no enlisted man ever gives his right name or serial number to an MP.

"That'll be two big ones for interrupting the lecture." The sergeant scribbled something in a notebook.

"The direction that vines and creepers grow on the trunks of trees is important. When lost, a woodsman . . ."

After what seemed like several days, the lecture was over. The wilted mob surged out with relief into the driving rain.

"Boy, this is fun," Flick said earnestly to no one in particular. "If we ever get lost, now we can find where north is."

"Yeah." It was all I could come up with, since I was too busy keeping an eye out for the sergeant, who was picking kids out of the line ahead of us. He got the three of us with a single scoop of his hand.

"You guys are on cleanup detail. Let's move."

We joined a clump of Chipmunks who were cowering next to a battered pickup truck. For the next couple of hours, we hopped in and out of the truck, picking up candy wrappers and stray twigs around the grounds. Between the trees, I could occasionally glimpse groups of campers in ragged formation, on mysterious missions. And from somewhere in the distance, the sound of a Ping-Pong ball continued, as it would day and night for the weeks to come. Though expeditions were formed to find the table and those who were playing on it, no one ever did.

"Get that cigarette butt over there. By that big rock." The sergeant, whose name was Biggie Clagg, a second-year defensive guard at the University of Iowa (first string) didn't miss a thing.

"If I ever catch the little crumb who was smokin' that, he'll be sorry he ever heard a' cigarettes. They stunt yer growth and they wreck yer wind. I don't wanna catch none a' you guys puffin' on a butt, y'hear?"

So it went as we drove in the rattly truck back and forth through the trees and over the trails.

"You guys are really lucky getting the cleanup detail today," said the sergeant from behind the steering wheel. "Now you got it over with. You won't catch it for another week." We all agreed that we were lucky indeed. If we hadn't been on this great detail, we might have been wasting our time playing ball or puffing on butts. We looked out at the other campers as they marched about, with honest sympathy for their having missed the chance to be with us.

"Maybe you guys don't know what good work does for ya, but one day you'll realize it's the best thing for ya. Keeps ya sharp. Cuts the fat off ya. Good for yer wind." Biggie continually flexed his muscles as we scurried among the weeds, carrying burlap sacks and searching for bits of paper.

"Hey! I found a dead turtle!" Flick hollered excitedly.

"In the sack," Biggie barked. "We don't want no dead turtles clutterin' up the trails."

Flick poked the turtle with a stick. It lurched forward. In a single motion, it snapped the stick cleanly in two. Flick leaped back wildly with a cry of mortal fear. The turtle, in high dudgeon, lumbered off into the undergrowth.

"Boy, what a chickenshit!" sneered Schwartz, flailing a branch about and looking for another turtle.

"YIKES!" he screamed a moment later, leaping upward, his feet churning to keep him off the ground. "HELP! A SNAKE!!"

The entire detail of Chipmunks scrambled onto the truck in

about two tenths of a second. A tiny green garter snake slithered away unconcernedly. A garter snake's life in a boys' camp is a hectic one.

We drove on. "I don't know what you guys would do if ya ever saw a rattler," Biggie rumbled in his raspy voice. "What a buncha pantywaists."

The rain had petered out. From time to time, the sun broke through the overcast. Out on the lake, a fleet of green canoes milled about on the choppy waters.

"Look at those guys out in those rowboats," said a Chipmunk near the front of the truck.

"You'll get your turn tomorrow," Biggie said. "And they're not rowboats, stupid. Those are canoes."

They were the first canoes any of us had ever seen in the flesh. They looked great. Occasionally, from the lake, we could hear muffled shouting followed by wild splashing, but we were too busy picking up candy wrappers to watch.

Our first day in camp ended with supper in the mess hall— corned-beef hash, canned peas, dill pickles, and grape Kool-Aid, followed by watery Jell-O and Nabisco wafers. My mother would have had a fit at our diet, but we thought it was great.

As we were finishing, Morey Partridge came over to our table to announce: "Since this is the first day in camp for you Chip- munks, there won't be a sing-song tonight, so's you can get set- tled in your cabins. You get the night off."

We wandered out of the mess hall into the twilight. The second shift of mosquitoes had come on duty. A great swirling cloud drifted over us from the lake. We swatted and scratched.

"Boy, do I have to go to the toilet!" said Flick uneasily, shifting from foot to foot as he slapped. I was with him on that. We hadn't gone since the diner back on the road. The time had come.

"I think it's over there." Schwartz pointed up a path that wound behind the rec hall. We joined a long caravan of fellow campers winding up the dim trail. A wooden shed with a swinging door lit by a yellow light bulb stood at the head of the line. From time to time, a kid would come out, ashen-faced, with an apologetic air. As each appeared, a cheer went up.

The line inched forward painfully. It was getting more serious moment by moment.

"Jeez, I'm goin' in the bushes," Flick finally said after a quarter of an hour.

"Y'better not," said Schwartz between clenched teeth. He already had two demerits. "If Biggie found *that* on cleanup detail, he'd really get sore."

After an eternity, and just in the nick of time, Flick and I finally got inside the shed. It was lit brilliantly. There were four holes cut in an elevated wooden platform. Two other Chipmunks were hard at work. Furtively, we got down to business. The four of us squatted in embarrassed silence. Three frantic-looking Chipmunks who stood in the doorway formed an impatient and ribald audience. Somehow I had never thought of this side of camp life. It was my first experience with mass facilities, and it had a curiously inhibiting effect. I found that I didn't have to go as much as I thought I had. As a matter of fact, nothing happened at all.

"Come on, you guys! Yer just sittin' there!" One of the audience banged his fist on the wall in desperation.

Still nothing happened.

The kid on the end hole stood up, buckled his belt, and scurried out with the air of a man who had done nothing but had taken a long time doing it.

"Oh, wow!" The loud Chipmunk beat another kid to the hole, ripped his pants down, and squatted with obvious relief. Three other Chipmunks entered and began pacing and observing. The new kid on the end hole, who'd been so anxious, fell silent. He, too, was having problems.

"I guess I didn't have to go," Flick whispered and left with his face to the floor. I followed shortly. It was the beginning, although we did not yet know it, of a mysterious ailment known as the

Nobba-WaWa-Nockee Block, or Camper's Cramp. Many a kid went for two weeks or more before finally giving in.

Back at Mole Lodge, we prepared to spend our first night in the woods. You've never seen a dark night till you've spent a night in the Michigan woods. We were glad to be indoors. There were great shadows on the walls as I climbed up into my bunk. The fat Chipmunk already lay in his bunk, reading a thick paperback, holding it close to his nose in order to make out the print.

A face appeared in the screened doorway: "Lights out in half an hour, at nine-thirty." It disappeared.

Schwartz's head peeked over the edge of his bunk. "Ain't this great, you guys?"

From somewhere in the gloom, Flick answered, "Yeah. Sure is."

I lay dead tired from the long day, the bus ride, the lecture, Captain Crabtree, the rain, the cleanup detail, Biggie; all of it was like some endless dream. I had been away from home only since morning, and already I could hardly remember my kid brother, my mother, and the old man. The lights went out. After a brisk flurry of whispering, silence.

I shifted restlessly on my muslin mattress cover. The mattress seemed to be filled with fingernail parings. Constellations of prickly things jabbed me everywhere. Finally, I slipped off into a troubled sleep.

"What's that?" It seemed like I wasn't asleep for five minutes when Flick's voice, trembling with fear, made me start straight up. I hit my head a reeling crack against the bunk above and fell back stunned.

"There's something out there!" Flick's voice ended with a slight sob. Mole Lodge was in a turmoil. From the window, the dim-gray light of early dawn fell on the board floor. I heard Schwartz mutter, "Look out and see what it is!"

There was a pause. Another voice answered, "Oh yeah? Do it yourself. It ain't gonna get me!"

It was the dreaded Thing in the Woods syndrome that afflicts all denizens of every kid camp everywhere. We lay petrified until the sun came up and reveille was blown. Only the fat Chipmunk slept through it all. He was the first person I ever saw who slept with his glasses on.

It was a sharp, brisk, sunny day. Camp Nobba-WaWa-Nockee swung into action. After breakfast—oatmeal, milk, raspberry jam, burnt toast—Morey Partridge announced:

"Wolves, Eagles, Polar Bears, Jaguars, and, oh yeah, Moles—it's time for leathercraft. Let's go. On the double."

Leathercraft! There are few among us who have not felt the pain of a needle piercing a thumb, the inexpressible boredom of toiling over a wampum belt or a lumpy wallet bearing the like-ness of Roy Acuff done in colored Indian beads. For the next cou-ple of hours, we fumbled with pieces of leather, hacking and chopping away. A tall, reedy counselor who called himself Cliffie moved among us in his tight pants and furry shoes, clucking sweetly.

"Yes, boys, we certainly love to make things, don't we? My, just think how pleased your mommies and daddies are going to be with the wonderful leatherwork you'll bring them from camp. Made by your very own little hands!"

I decided on a spectacular creation featuring the silhouette of *The End of the Trail*, which was a picture of an Indian on a horse looking down sadly at the sunset. I had admired it on a calendar my old man had gotten from the Shell station. I figured I would do it with beads and copper rivets.

"That's very nice," said Cliffie, peering over my shoulder. I could smell a faint whiff of perfume. "What is it?" I told him. "My, my, your mother will love that," he commented in a somewhat stunned voice, maybe because it was more than four feet square. That was the only way I could figure out how to get all those beads and rivets into the picture. "Well, keep up the good work." He patted me affectionately on the behind and strolled off.

Kissel was bent over a shoulder holster with a fringe for his father's bourbon bottle, and Flick was deeply involved in a grotesque catcher's mitt that already looked like a dead octopus. We toiled away happily until Jake, the muscular Beaver, barged in.

"What the hell is that silly thing?" he sneered, poking at Kissel's creation. Kissel said nothing, his face crimson. We sensed trouble.

"Jee-zus, is that supposed to be an Indian?" Jake snarled at my laboriously penciled outline. "Looks like a scarecrow takin' a crap on some kind of a goat." He cackled at his own rotten humor. I peered down at my drawing. He was right. It did look like a scarecrow taking a crap on a goat.

"Oh yeah?" I answered with my famous slashing wit. Jake ignored me. He turned his attention to Flick.

"Hey, kid!" Flick looked up from his monstrosity. "Wait'll Cliffie boy sees yer makin' a jockstrap for your pet elephant."

The fat Chipmunk, who was silently working away on some obscure object at the other end of our table, glanced up, his tiny eyes expressionless behind his thick glasses.

"Who ya lookin' at, fatso?" Jake glared at him. The fat Chipmunk sniffed quietly and returned to work. "Boy, Chipmunks are gettin' worse every year." Jake went back to his crowd of Beavers over in the corner.

That afternoon we set off on a hike, led by Captain Crabtree, wearing shorts and a baseball cap. "Now, boys, a hike is not just a walk. A woodsman is alert. He knows the meaning of every broken twig. He can identify every leaf in the forest. I want you to examine things and learn. Off we go now, follow me."

At a rapid pace, the captain charged off into the woods. We followed, grunting and scrambling.

"Look around you, boys. Nature is kind," the captain sang out. We looked.

Ten minutes later, an uproar broke out as a Chipmunk near the rear yipped frantically past us–pursued by 12 million angry hornets. Chipmunks flew in all directions, yelling and screaming.

The captain stood in the middle of the trail. "STAND STILL,

BOYS. THEY WON'T STING IF YOU STAND STILL! THEY'RE MORE AFRAID OF YOU THAN YOU ARE OF THEM!"

I burrowed deep in a thick growth of shiny green leaves that I wasn't to learn until my second nature lesson—too late—were called *Toxicodendron*, commonly known as poison ivy. I caught a glimpse of a cloud of hornets settling on the captain, who stood like a statue. Foraging patrols of free-lance hornets ranged up and down the path, searching for scurrying Chipmunks.

The captain suddenly bellowed hoarsely and took off in the direction of the camp. An angry wedge-shaped formation of hornets streamed after him. We didn't see the captain again until three days later when he snuck in the back door of the mess hall. We didn't recognize him at first. Once again, the notorious Stand Still and They Won't Hurt You theory had failed. But the captain, a true nature lover, didn't give up on it until the following year, when he tried it on a bull grazing in a meadow.

In those three days, meanwhile, the lines had been drawn clearly. Being a Chipmunk, we learned, consisted mostly of attending lectures, making wallets, and fighting off Beavers, who could spot you a mile off wearing that damned Chipmunk cap. The only time you didn't have to wear your cap was when you were sleeping, which wasn't often—between being scared every night by the Thing in the Woods and having to get up at 3 A.M. and wait in line to go to the toilet. We quickly fell into the rhythm of life at Nobba-WaWa-Nockee.

A few days later, Biggie Clagg gave us a swimming lesson, but not before we had been warned by two Beavers in the mess hall to beware of the monster that lived in the lake.

"Y'gotta watch it," one said. "Y'remember Marty?" he said to his friend, who had a pinched face and a worried look. "It grabbed him right over there by that big rock. He barely got out alive. It's got some kinda spines that sting ya, and it's got suckers on its feet, and if it ever gets ya, it'll drag ya right down to the bottom and eatcha."

I stood quivering in six inches of icy lake water—but not

because it was cold. If there's anything I don't like, it's suckers and things with spines.

"Let's go. Come on." Biggie, his massive thighs working like pistons, charged into the water, huffing and blowing as he thrashed about. A few Chipmunks waded in gingerly after him.

"What's the matter with you guys? Let's get pumpin' here!" shouted Biggie, his voice echoing across the lake.

The news about the suckers and the spines had swept like wildfire through the Chipmunks. We cringed together in a craven knot with the water up to our ankles. A foolhardy few had ventured out to where the water lapped at their kneecaps.

"Now, I'm gonna show you the dog paddle. That's the first thing you gotta learn." Biggie apparently hadn't heard about the monster. He swam briskly twice around the rock where it lurked and headed back for shore, his huge feet splashing out behind him.

"EEEEEEEEEEE! IT'S GOT ME!!" The Chipmunk farthest out in the water—a kid named Elrod from Monon, Indiana—struggled wildly toward shore. Instantly, panic surged through the crowd. We fled screaming toward the beach.

"WHAAAAAAAAAAAAAA!"

"IT'S AFTER ME!"

"HELLLP!"

As I struggled over the jagged rocks toward the shore—through four inches of water—I felt slippery things clutching at my ankles, suckers grabbing at my heels.

"EEEEEEEEE! IT'S BITING ME!"

"FER CHRISSAKE, WHAT THE HELL'S GOIN' ON HERE?" Biggie boomed out as the squealing horde scampered up the beach. Biggie followed, his hair dripping. We huddled together on the sand.

"There's nothin' out there but sunfish. Don't tell me I got a buncha girls on my hands. Get back in that water!"

Reluctantly, we waded back out into the lake. For an hour we practiced the dog paddle, but the terror never left us. Nobody got within fifty yards of the rock.

That was the night of our first weenie roast. We sat around the sputtering campfire by the tennis court as a tidal wave of mosquitoes enveloped us in a humming black fog. Moving closer to the fire to escape them, we roasted the entire front of our bodies– leaving our rear flanks completely exposed. It created an interesting pattern of skin irritations. And, as things turned out, the mosquitoes ate better than we did.

"My tongue! It's burning up! It's on fire!" Schwartz cried out in pain after he had bitten into a smoldering charcoal weenie. For a week afterward, his tongue looked like a barrage balloon.

At least he got to taste his. I held a weenie in the flames for a couple of seconds until my green twig, which wasn't supposed to burn, flared into a raging inferno. Waving the stick to put out the fire, I knocked fifty-seven other kids' weenies into the flames. I wouldn't be here to tell the tale if we hadn't been issued two weenies apiece. I didn't want to take any chances on the second one, so I gulped it down raw, following it up with fifteen or twenty of the marshmallows that Beavers hadn't heated into boiling white balls of pitch and then dropped down Chipmunks' backs. It wasn't until later that we discovered the raw weenies really were raw weenies, and the action that night at the latrine was spectacular.

As we milled around the fire, batting at mosquito squadrons, scuffles broke out in the dark as Beavers waylaid Chipmunks who had foolishly strayed too far from the firelight. Then Colonel Bullard made a sudden and dramatic appearance, his face lit by the flames.

"This is the stuff, eh, boys? Cooking your own food under the heavens! Living the clean outdoor life! I am reminded of my own youth, spent in the clean air of God's own prairies. Now, all together, boys, let's sing our beloved 'Nobba-WaWa-Nockee Loyalty Song.' "

With the fervor of a Methodist choirmaster, he led us in a droning, endless performance, punctuated by the obbligato of slapping and scratching at the fringes of the circle. Schwartz's tongue was so thick by now that you couldn't understand what he was singing. I looked up at the deep ebony arch of Michigan sky, luminous with millions of stars, and all the travails of the day were forgotten. What fools we mortals be.

After the weenie roast, we trooped up to the rec hall. It was letter-writing night. Every three days, it was compulsory to write home. We hunched over the pool table and every other writing surface in the place, racking our brains for something to say to the home folks. I struggled over the blue-lined tablet my mother had bought for me. It had a cover with a red Indian head on it.

> *Dear Mom & Dad & Randy,*
> *I am at camp.*

I pondered long and hard, trying to think of something else to say. But nothing came, so I printed my name at the bottom and put it in the envelope. Just as I was about to seal it, I remembered something else. I took the letter out and wrote under my signature:

> *P.S. Schwartz burned his tonge. It is really fat. There is a funny thing in the lake that has suckers on it.*

I ran out of gas again. Cliffie, who was in charge of letter writing, swooped from kid to kid, making sure they were saying good things about the camp. He glanced at my letter.

"My, my. This is very good." His eyes narrowed a bit at my reference to the thing with suckers, but he let it pass.

Kissel licked the stub of a pencil and started on the third page of his meticulous description of the shoulder holster he was making in leathercraft. Flick hid what he was writing.

As I lay in bed that night, my stomach rumbling ominously with fermented weenies, Schwartz sprawled above me, whimpering over his bulging tongue. Flick, who had gotten a half-dozen strategic hornet stings, writhed in his sack. The kid who had the bunk above the fat Chipmunk had been picked up during the day by a gleaming Cadillac and swept out of our lives forever. For the time he was with us, he had said nothing, but he cried a lot at night. Mole Lodge was shaking down into a tight unit. Little did we realize, however, that there was a hero among us.

"The canoe paddle is held thusly. It's all in the wrist. Y'gotta have a steady, even stroke, like this."

At last! All my *Boy's Life* fantasies were about to come true. They just didn't have canoes on the south side of Chicago. A canoe was something you read about that Indians paddled around on Lake Gitchee-Goomie. We converged on seven or eight or so canoes that were pulled up on shore—long, imperially slim, forest green, each emblazoned with the proud yellow arrowhead of Nobba-WaWa-Nockee. Canoes are so beautiful that even the dullest clod of a Chipmunk got excited at the sight of them. Like most things of beauty, they are also highly dangerous.

An unfamiliar counselor, who wore a black cowboy hat, green swimming trunks, and an orange life jacket over his camp T-shirt, neatly flicked the canoe paddle, demonstrating the stroke.

"Y'gotta have a beat. One . . . two . . . three . . . DIG. One . . . two . . . three . . . DIG. Steady. Even. Got that, gang?"

We had it, or thought we had.

"The bow paddle gives you the power, while the stern paddle gives you power and steers."

Schwartz whispered to Beakie Humbert, another kid from Troop 41. "Which one's the bow?"

"The one in the back, jerk. Boy, you don't know nothin'." Beakie was famous in the troop for his knot tying and for his merit badge for wood carving, which he got for chopping out a totem pole from a railroad tie.

"Now, you guys over on this end go first." The counselor pulled his cowboy hat down over his eyes. "Two to a canoe—but put them life jackets on first."

Mine was already on; I leaped forward eagerly. The next thirty seconds were a blur. I remember stepping into the front of the canoe from the little pier, with Schwartz right behind me in the back, then shoving off into the water just the way he had told us. A split second later, I found myself deep underwater, having caught a brief glimpse of the gleaming bottom of our canoe flashing in the sunlight. Wildly afraid that the thing with suckers would get me, I flailed to the surface, my life jacket jabbing me in the armpits. Weeds streamed from my hair. A frog and a small bullhead skittered out of my path. Schwartz, blowing frantically, arms flapping like a windmill, stood hip-deep in the mud a few feet away. Waves of raucous horselaughs rolled out over the water.

I struggled up onto the pier, scraping my knee as I did. Schwartz continued to flounder helplessly in the weeds. The counselor paddled his canoe expertly to the wreckage.

"All you guys just saw how not to do it, right?" More catcalls. "Now, let's try it again."

This time I clung desperately to the pier while I put first one foot, then the other, and finally my whole weight into the canoe. Schwartz, who had sworn off canoes for the rest of his life, had retired to the shore and was hiding behind a stump. Flick eased himself into the stern, his face looking like poured concrete. We were in and still upright.

"Now, push off and paddle like I showed you."

I gave the pier a tiny shove, and immediately the canoe, seemingly propelled by hidden forces, glided across the water, heading rapidly for the opposite shore, two miles away. I dug my paddle into the waves to keep from cracking up on the other side. We spun rapidly counterclockwise.

"Hey, Flick, paddle, willya?" I hollered, looking back over my shoulder and seeing that Flick was sitting low in the stern, his hands clamped like vises on both sides of the canoe. His paddle floated some thirty or forty feet behind us.

"I don't like this," he squeaked. We were drifting out to sea. My life started flashing before my eyes. I dug in again. We spun faster.

We probably would have spent the next week corkscrewing around the lake if the counselor hadn't paddled out and towed us to shore.

"All right, you guys. Give somebody else a chance."

We joined Schwartz behind his stump.

"Boy, I never knew paddling a canoe was so hard," said Flick as we watched two other Chipmunks flip over, their paddles flying high in the air.

"Whaddaya mean, paddle?" I answered. "You didn't do nothin' but sit there."

Flick thought about this for a bit, then answered, sounding bugged: "Whaddaya expect. This was the first time I was out. You were out with Schwartz before." That was true, so there was no point arguing.

The gulf between the Chipmunks and the Beavers widened as the weeks went by. Rumors swept the mess hall that five Beavers, led by Jake, had pulled off a daring panty raid in the night on the girls' camp across the lake, that Jake and his mob were planning to burn down Eagle Lodge and Jaguar Lodge, and would mop up Mole Lodge just for laughs. One Chipmunk had fled screaming into the night when he discovered that he was sleeping with a woodchuck. Jake and his cronies immediately claimed credit and threatened reprisals against any Chipmunk who reported the incident to Crabtree. It was even rumored that Crabtree himself was an undercover agent working for Jake's mob. Morale among the green-beanie wearers sank rapidly. Even Cliffie, in self-defense, was trying to curry favor with Jake and his truculent toady Dan Baxter, the short, broad Beaver with the red neck who had bedeviled us on the bus ride to camp, ten years ago.

One quiet Tuesday, Mole Lodge was struggling fruitlessly to win a volleyball game from the Chipmunks of Jaguar Lodge, which had two six-foot-six-inch monsters who kept hammering the ball down our throats, since the rest of us averaged about four foot six. Suddenly, in the middle of the game, a rumpus broke out in the woods back of one of the Beaver cabins.

Biggie had trapped Baxter red-handed with a freshly lit Lucky Strike clamped in his jaw.

"O.K., Baxter, I got you at last! You're the one that's been throwin' them butts around. Hand over that package."

We crowded around in a big circle as Baxter, his face a rich crimson, his stubbly neck bulging with anger, hauled out a freshly opened pack of Luckies from the pocket of his shorts and handed them over.

"You like cigarettes, Baxter? O.K., buddy boy, you're gonna get cigarettes. You keep puffin' until I tell you to stop. You're gonna smoke every one a' these coffin nails one after the other. Now, get puffin'. One a' you guys go get me a bucket from the latrine."

A Beaver behind me who had obviously been around hissed in a low tone, "My God, it's the bucket treatment!"

Baxter puffed away sneeringly on the Lucky, while Biggie stood over him. Jake and his scurvy crew mumbled in the crowd, giving bad looks to any Chipmunk who dared to smile. Someone came running back with the mop bucket.

"O.K., Baxter." Biggie grabbed the bucket and lowered it upside down over Baxter's head. A murmur swept through the audience. "Now, you puff on that Lucky, y'hear me in there?"

Biggie knocked on the top of the bucket with his knuckles, making a hollow donging sound. Smoke billowed out from under Baxter's helmet. "Keep puffin', Baxter. That smoke is gettin' thin." Biggie knocked again on the bucket. More smoke billowed out.

"How long can he keep it up?" said the Beaver behind me in an awed voice.

We found out. Baxter cracked at a little over six minutes. A hollow gurgling sound came from under the bucket.

"Had enough, Baxter?" Biggie lifted the bucket. Baxter, his face the color of a rotten cantaloupe, lurched into the weeds, retching violently.

"Watch it there, Baxter. You're gonna have to police that up." Biggie rubbed it in. "Hey, Baxter!" he yelled. "What you need is a nice Lucky to calm your nerves."

There was another storm of retching, then silence.

"All right, you men. Get back to what you were doin'. This ain't no show."

We scattered. Another Nobba-WaWa-Nockee legend was born. Naturally, there were repercussions. A Chipmunk who had laughed openly at Baxter's humilation was mysteriously set upon in the dark one night, depantsed, and found in the latrine, his head protruding from the second hole. He was rescued just in time. Cross-examined for hours in relays by various counselors, he wisely refused to say who had perpetrated the deed. Every Chipmunk in camp knew that Jake Brannigan and Dan Baxter had struck again.

"Come on, you guys, quit screwin' around. I gotta find my sweater! You heard what old Fartridge said. We got ten minutes to get out by that crummy flagpole before they start this crummy treasure hunt." Flick was rooting around in his laundry bag as Schwartz and a couple of other guys rolled on the floor, battling over a bag of malted-milk balls they had found cleverly concealed under the fat Chipmunk's mattress.

"Fartridge," of course, was Morey Partridge. Because of his complexion, he was also known as "Birdshit" among the Chipmunks. Historically, prisoners of war have always given deserving names to their jailers. Cliffie, for example, was better known as "Violet" or "That Fag" among the green-beanie crowd. It was reported that even Mrs. Bullard herself called the colonel "Old Leather Ass." Biggie had become "the Tank" or "Lard Butt" and Crabtree had evolved to "Craptree" and finally to "Crappo." He was even, among the Beavers, known affectionately as "Crabs" in commemoration of a legendary invasion that had occurred the year before at Nobba-WaWa-Nockee after Crappo had spent a big weekend in town. The resultant furor culminated with every camper's being doused with DDT, green lime, and Dr. Pilcher's Magic Ointment, but all to no avail. The scourge was finally defeated by marinating everyone, including Mrs. Bullard, in drums of kerosene. There was even talk among the state authorities of burning the camp down. Mercifully, the crabs took the hint and departed for the girls' camp across the lake.

The treasure hunt was the traditional high point, the crowning event in the panoply of camp life. By now, we were scarred, mosquito-bitten, smoke-blackened veterans of almost four weeks on the shores of Lake Paddachungacong. The hunt began with everybody in camp—Beavers and Chipmunks alike—gathered in a huge circle around the flagpole. A tremendous campfire lit up the ring of faces with a flickering orange light. For the past week, the treasure hunt had been the number-one topic of conversation. Now, here it was—zero hour. The heat from the roaring flames blossomed the festering blotch of poison ivy under the thick coating of calamine lotion on my back. It was the darkest night we'd had since coming to camp. No stars, no moon, just the pitch black of the Michigan woods. The lake had disappeared with nightfall and become a black, sinister void.

At the base of the flagpole, in the center of the ring, Colonel Bullard swept us all with the gaze of imperious command. Across the circle, I could barely make out the stolid bulk of Dan Baxter skulking behind Jake Brannigan, who was whispering to his circle of veteran Beavers. The light glinted on their golden badges of rank. I adjusted my Chipmunk cap, setting it squarely on my head. It was going to be a long night. I heard Schwartz chomping nervously on a malted-milk ball next to me in the darkness. All around me my fellow Chipmunks waited for the starting gun.

"It's a perfect night for the treasure hunt, eh, men?" The swagger stick slapped smartly for punctuation. Beavers and Chipmunks shifted expectantly. "As you doubtless know, the treasure hunt is our yearly competition between the Chipmunks and the Beavers. And the Chipmunk or Beaver who unearths the concealed Sacred Golden Tomahawk of Chief Chungacong will bring eternal honor to his lodge. All members of his lodge will receive the Camp Nobba-WaWa-Nockee Woodsman Award. My wife, Mrs. Bullard herself, designed this handsome badge. The winners will deserve their award for their valiant performance in the deep woods!"

A current of fear zipped up and down my spine as he said "the deep woods."

"Now, Captain Crabtree, issue the secret envelopes. And good luck to you all, men."

The colonel saluted Crappo, who led his crew of lieutenants around the circle. The envelopes glowed dead white in the blackness of the night. Each lodge had elected one kid who would accept the envelope and act as leader, a purely honorary title, since leadership was not a strong point among the Chipmunks. We had elected Schwartz to represent Mole Lodge.

"Stupe! Get out there! Do something!" whispered Flick from somewhere back in the crowd. Schwartz, beads of sweat popping out on his forehead, lurched forward. The Tank handed him the envelope.

"Give 'em hell, kid!" Biggie slapped Schwartz on the top of his beanie with a tooth-rattling smack and passed on to the next lodge leader.

We knew the rules, which said that we couldn't open the envelope until the signal. After that, every lodge was on its own, and the one to come back with the Sacred Golden Tomahawk was the winner. Each lodge had been supplied with an official Boy Scout flashlight to help us follow the clues in the envelope–clues that would carry us, in the dead of night, through the wilderness and straight to the treasure. Lieutenant Kneecamp (better known as "Peecamp") tossed a bundle of branches onto the fire. It roared and crackled, sending sparks shooting off into the blackness.

"Ready, boys? Remember, play the game well." Colonel Bullard's hand shot skyward. He clutched a gleaming silver automatic.

"ONE!"

Schwartz sniffed loudly.

"TWO!"

Jake Brannigan, across the circle, crouched like a sprinter.

"THREE!"

BANG!

The circle dissolved into a maelstrom of stumbling kids. The Beavers, with the craftiness of veterans, immediately melted into the darkness and were gone. Then Jaguar Lodge fled whooping off and disappeared into the woods. Schwartz stood there tearing frantically at the envelope.

"Come on, Schwartz! What the hell's in that thing?" somebody yelled. In his frantic haste, Schwartz ripped the envelope down the middle, tearing the clue into two neat halves that fluttered to the ground. Struggling to turn on the flashlight, I felt my thumbnail split back to the knuckle. Bodies hurtled past us. Schwartz and the fat Chipmunk scurried about in the blackness on their hands and knees, looking for the torn clue.

"Gimme some light!" Schwartz grunted. I felt his hand grasping my Keds.

"Leggo my foot!"

"Shut up!"

The light glared forth. Quickly we scooped up the two halves of paper. Schwartz squinted at the typewritten sheet and began to read:

" 'Into the dark . . .

This is no lark . . ? What the heck's a lark?" he asked.

One of the Moles answered, "Some kind of bird. Come on!"

" 'Due north by the wall . . .

Past Honest Abe's work . . .

You cannot shirk . . .

Straight o'er and up Everest . . .

'Neath the oldest one . . .

Only the squirrel knows? "

"Is that all there is?" asked Kissel.

"That's it."

We looked blankly at each other.

"Which way is north?" I asked.

"That way." Flick pointed past the chapel.

"Let's go!"

We charged up the path. Almost immediately, the blackness was so total that I had the sensation of running upside down on the ceiling of a black room. The others clumped and crashed around me.

"Hold it, Schwartz!" There was something wrong with the flashlight. It kept going off and on.

"My shoe came off!" wailed Flick. "Where's the light?"

We found his shoe and got it back on.

Mole Lodge was beginning to fall apart.

We examined the note again.

"What's this 'wall' stuff?" Schwartz croaked.

"I don't know," someone said.

"Well, let's go north till we hit it."

That seemed like a good idea.

"Where's north?"

"Why don't we look for some moss?"

"Moss?"

"Yeah, moss. It always points north."

We scrounged around in the poison ivy, looking for moss on a tree trunk.

"Hey, you guys, here's some!" Flick sang out excitedly. Sure enough, he had found moss at the base of an oak tree.

"It goes all the way around!" Another theory shot to hell.

"Well, it's kinda thick on this side."

We charged off once again, crashing through the dense underbrush. Branches slashed at my face; brambles and sharp twigs gouged and ripped. I began to feel a deep, mounting fear. I had no idea where we were or what would happen next. Schwartz, who was thrashing around ahead of me, was now carrying the light. I could hear Flick fall heavily from time to time behind us.

Up ahead, the flashlight suddenly vanished, along with Schwartz. A second later, the ground disappeared beneath me; I was in free-fall. I clawed at the air, then hit hard, rolled over and over down a steep hill, and finally hit Schwartz with a grunt. Other bodies landed on top of us, squirming and writhing. Mole Lodge lay in a heap at the bottom of a ravine. Scratched, bruised, scared, we huddled next to a huge ghostly boulder. The flashlight still worked, but it was growing dimmer. The silence of the woods was total. We spoke in hoarse whispers.

"What do we do now?"

Nobody answered.

Finally: "Where's Skunk?"

For the first time, I noticed that the fat Chipmunk was no longer with us.

"He musta gone back to the lodge," Flick whispered.

"He's probably back there eatin' malted-milk balls." I felt a twinge of envy.

Schwartz switched off the light to save the batteries. Once again we huddled in the darkness.

Crack! Crunch! Oh, my God! Something was coming at us.

"Turn on the light, Schwartz!" Flick squeaked.

The light flared on, its beam quivering in Schwartz's hand. There, in the feeble ray, stood Jake Brannigan. Behind him a couple of other Beavers lurked, dark blobs against the trees. Brannigan flashed a crooked smile.

"You little stupes are makin' enough goddamn noise in the weeds here to scare the crap out of every raccoon within fifty miles. Right, boys?"

His toadies guffawed behind him. Now we're gonna get it, I thought. This is it! Mole Lodge is about to be annihilated by the Brannigan Gang. I inched backward.

"Hey, Dan," he said over his shoulder, "tell these boobs who's gonna win that golden hatchet."

Dan snorted derisively, spitting out a long stream of dark brown fluid.

Jake's look of scorn softened for a moment in what might pass in another man for pity.

"You guys lost? Lemme look at yer goddamn clue." He grabbed the pieces from Schwartz's hand. I was surprised he could read.

"I'll give you dumb kids a break. This 'Honest Abe' crap must be about that rail fence up thataway." He pointed up the ravine. "Now, get outa our way."

We did not have to be told twice. Mole Lodge galloped up the ravine. The last sound we heard was Jake's dry cackle; and then we were alone.

"Boy, that was kinda nice of him, helpin' us out like that," said Flick.

"Sure was," I answered, too relieved at having been spared to question Jake's unaccountable fit of compassion.

We struggled against vines, falling rocks, and tangled undergrowth. And a few minutes later, sure enough, there was a fence. It stood ahead of us, gray and sagging.

Schwartz darted under the top rail. I followed. Close behind me came Flick and the other Mole Lodgers. It was even darker here than back in the ravine. We inched along the fence blindly, gropingly. The ground seemed to be rising steeply. We struggled upward, each wrapped in his own fear. Camp Nobba-WaWa-Nockee seemed millions of miles away. There was only us and the blackness. Our flashlight had faded to a birthday-candle glow. We clung together in a tiny knot. Schwartz held the light, futilely pointing it ahead. I was just pulling an angry thistle off my knee when Schwartz, close by, sucked in his breath hard and sharp. The sound he made was like no sound I had ever heard anyone make before–a kind of rushing, gurgling gasp.

There, in the glow of our flashlight, loomed a huge, monstrous live Thing!

"Bruuuuuuuuufffff!" it snorted.

"EEEEEEEEEEEEEEEEEEEEEEEEEYYYYYYYYYYYYAAAAAAAAAAAAA!" I heard a deafening scream. It was me!

Flick shot back past me like a cannon ball, moving with maniacal speed, sobbing rhythmically. I felt the ground pounding beneath my shoes. Schwartz kept pace with me in a curious clawing scrabble. He was running, pushing himself forward with whatever touched the ground–his head, his knees, his elbows, and occasionally his feet. He yelled hysterically over and over: "THE THING! THE THING! THE THING!"

As the cry was taken up by other voices in the darkness, I heard crashings ahead, to the left, to the right, behind, all around me. I ran even faster.

Flick gasped between sobs, "Jake done it! Jake done it! He sent us to the Thing!" Even as I faced certain death, I realized that Jake Brannigan had planned it all.

I heard muffled thuds as bodies collided with tree trunks. Sweat and tears poured down my face. My eyes burned. My head throbbed. My lungs were ready to burst. I pained from a million cuts and bruises. Ahead, I became dimly aware of a faint glow. My knee crashed against a tree. I ricocheted off a stump. I hardly felt it. I got up and ran on.

Suddenly, it was all over, like some nightmare that ends with a pail of water in the face. We broke into a clearing at blessed Nobba-WaWa-Nockee. I never thought I'd see it again. All around me, battered and torn Chipmunks, their eyes rolling wildly, pursued relentlessly by the Thing, popped out of the woods. Even a few hysterical Beavers raced by. We were safe. Miraculously, though it was covered with mud and stickers, I still had my Chipmunk hat on.

Old Leather Ass stood there glaring at us, his face grim in the flickering light from the campfire.

"This is a sorry spectacle! What's this nonsense about a Thing? What Thing? There's nothing in those woods but the gentle creatures of the forest–right, Crabtree?"

Crabtree nodded, but you could tell he wasn't sure.

"This is the first year in the history of Nobba-WaWa-Nockee that no lodge has returned with the Sacred Golden Tomahawk. I am appalled at the craven behavior–"

"Excuse me, Colonel Bullard, sir. I beg to differ, sir."

From somewhere off to my right, a reedy voice broke in. The

colonel, who was not accustomed to interruptions, slapped his thigh angrily with his swagger stick.

"What's that?"

"Excuse me, Colonel, sir. Is this your sacred golden hatchet?" The voice was drenched with sarcasm.

A figure stepped out into the circle of firelight. Great Scott! It was Skunk! His Nobba-WaWa-Nockee T-shirt was crisp, his green beanie square on his head, his thick glasses gleaming brightly. He held something in his hand.

"By George, that certainly is the Sacred Golden Tomahawk. SPLENDID!"

"Thank you, sir. When my fellow members of Mole Lodge childishly panicked, I simply took matters into my own hands. It was quite interesting, actually, although ordinarily these idiotic games bore me."

The camp was in an uproar. Mole Lodge had come through!

That night, back in our snug cabin, covered with iodine and Band-Aids, Schwartz sidled up to Skunkie and asked him where he had found it.

"In the Longlodge, of course, in the case where it's kept on display all year round. It was simple deduction that they'd try to mislead us into believing the tomahawk was buried somewhere in the woods, rather than right here in camp in plain sight of everyone. The clues led me straight to it. If any of you had ever bothered to read Poe's 'The Purloined Letter' . . ."

We didn't know whether to put him on our shoulders or throw him into the lake.

The next Saturday, our last morning in camp, was bright with golden sunshine, turning the lake into a billion flashing diamonds. After our last breakfast, the Chipmunks and Beavers, in two platoons, assembled on the tennis court. Colonel Bullard addressed us:

"You Chipmunks have come through magnificently. And now for the moment we have all awaited. There have been good times and difficult times, but we have come through it with clean bodies, clean minds, and stout hearts. I now pronounce you, with the power vested in me by the Great Spirit of Chungacong, full and honored members of the Sacred Clan of BEAVERS."

The ex-Chipmunks cheered and, in the hallowed tradition of Nobba-WaWa-Nockee, flung our hated Chipmunk caps into the air. A storm of green beanies rose over the tennis court.

A moment later I zipped up my crisp new blue Beaver jacket with its golden emblem bright over my heart. We sauntered back toward Mole Lodge, over the gravel path, past the administration building. We had three hours to kill until the buses picked us up and took us back to civilization. There they came now, wheezing up the rutted road. I saw a row of pale, staring faces all wearing bright new green Chipmunk beanies. Casually, we swaggered past the rec hall. Someone nudged me.

"Lookit that buncha babies." It was my fellow Beaver, Jake Brannigan.

"How 'bout that short little twerp?" I barked cruelly. "Let's throw him in the crapper."

"Nah," Jake answered, spitting between his teeth. "That's too good for the little bastard. How 'bout a cow flop in his soup?"

"Not bad, Jake," I answered, as we set out for the nearest meadow. "These kids are gettin' worse every year."

"Let's throw him in the crapper!"

"...a cow flop in his soup."

How's that for Utopia, gang? Did you notice that the little buggers immediately began torturing the incoming rookies just as they had been harassed in their day?

True, true, the minute one generation discovers the first wrinkle, it relentlessly attacks the upcoming generation as being callow, lacking in morals of any sort, hopelessly dumb. Going back to the days when men squatted in caves, eating clams, it has been so. I can just see a barrel-chested Neanderthal glaring across his flickering fire at a skulking teen-age Neanderthal and grunting:

"Get off your lazy ass. You never do anything around the cave. You kids don't know what it was like when I was your age. Why, we..."

The line in my lane of the tunnel began to move again, slowly, tentatively. I laughed out loud, picturing the scene in the cave. I could almost smell the charred bones of elk, the same dampness of this god damned tunnel.

I stuck my head out of the window and yelled at the next generation, ahead in their Charger.

"Move it, you dumb boobs. Get your thumbs out!" I was carry-ing on an ancient tradition.

We ground to a halt. My mind searched for another idea to worry, to play with. Boredom was setting in. I examined the inte-rior of my car minutely. The headliner, the sun visor, my little world of gauges and locked doors, sealed in a bathysphere under the mysterious waters. How many hours of my life had I spent alone in this metal cocoon, my only companion a fevered imagi-nation?

Marcel Proust Meets the New Jersey Tailgater, and Survives

"Marcel Proust, the great French Impressionist writer, had a cork-lined room built so that he could write in absolute concen-tration. This cork-lined room cut out all sounds from the outside world so that he could concentrate and relive his past, which he put into his finely detailed works."

The pasty-faced TV professor cleared his throat nervously and blinked at the camera with a noticeably spasmodic ticlike wink. He cleared his throat again, and continued—his voice crackly like dry onionskin paper that's been left in the sun too long.

"On the other hand, Balzac found it necessary to have heavy curtains hung over the windows and doors of his study. He wrote late at night, by the light of a candle. He said he had to do this to concentrate, to get away from the world."

The Prof glanced frantically off to someone or something to his right, just out of camera range. Apparently, he was getting a cue. I leaned forward sleepily. It isn't often I see "Morning Classics," an educational college course–type program that comes on the screen either so late or so early–depending on your point of view–that hardly anybody ever sees it, except maybe the professor's wife and a few video freaks who see everything, including the test patterns.

"Er . . ." he stammered in confusion.

"Er . . . that is, I'll be back tomorrow with . . ."

He was abruptly cut off the screen and replaced with a sixty-second plug for Girl Scout cookies. Poor Prof, I thought, he just ain't used to picking up his cues. So the whole point, if he had any, of his lecture went down the drain with the Girl Scout cookies and the morning news, which replaced him.

I fixed some instant coffee and as dawn was breaking somewhere out over the dark Atlantic I got to thinking of old Marcel Proust in his cork-lined room and Balzac scratching away with a quill pen with all those curtains hanging around him, at two in the morning. I sipped a bit of the lukewarm coffee and thought maybe I ought to build a cork-lined room, or hang black curtains over the window like those old-time writers did. I poured more coffee, and then it hit me—

Of course! I do have the equivalent of a cork-lined, black-curtain-draped concentration chamber, cut off from the rest of the world. My car!

I wonder how many guys there are in this world who actually find that the only time in the whole hectic day when they are away from phone calls, mysterious visitations, constant meetings, endless talks, are those few daily private times that they spend absolutely alone in their cars. A lone driver has no family, no job, no age—he is just an individual bit of human protoplasm humming through space. The mind drifts like some rudderless sailboat over the murky sea of consciousness. One part of you expertly, using some inbuilt secret mind-computer, steers the machine, calculating accurately all the changing vectors of speed, light, other traffic, road conditions, that go to make up fast driving. In fact, after you've put in enough hours behind the wheel under all kinds of conditions, you never even think about it any more. You just do it. All the while, that other part of your mind drifts around dreamily, dredging up wild

thoughts, long-forgotten memories, and fragments of old disap-
pointments. Proust had his cork-lined room; I have my vinyl-
lined GT.

Take the other day. I'm battling it out with all the other sweating lonesome travelers on Jersey's Route 22, which like all the
Route 22s of America has a surreal landscape which makes anything by Salvador Dali look like Norman Rockwell: Dairy Queens,
McDonald's, instant seat cover palaces, a pizza joint that calls itself the Leaning Tower of Pizza that actually does lean, a gas station which for some reason has a forty-foot-high plastic North
Woodsman swinging a motor-driven ax twenty-four hours a day,
his face the color of an overripe watermelon, Gino's, Colonel
Sanders, the works, all laced together with an unbelievable spi-
derweb of high tension wires, phone wires, wire wires, and miles
of neon tubing. My mind is just idling away at maybe one-tenth
throttle, thinking of nothing, when I glance up and see in my
rearview mirror that one of Jersey's folk artists has zeroed in
on me.

Jersey natives have made a fine creative art form of tailgating.
I could see in the mirror that I was in the clutches of a real master. I speeded up. He clung to my rear deck like a shadow. I
dodged around a bus, figuring I'd scrape him off like a barnacle.
No way. I shifted lanes. He moved with me like Earl Campbell following a blocker. He edged closer and closer to my rear bumper.
We were hurtling along Route 22 at the usual cruise speed of that
55 mph limit artery—75 plus. I slowed up, figuring that no true
tailgater ever resists an opportunity to pass anything. There are
guys who look upon all traffic as an endless obstacle to be passed.
This is your average tailgater.

He wasn't buying it. I slowed up; he slowed up. I quickly
switched lanes and made a fast feint toward the asphalt parking
lot of a Carvel ice cream joint, figuring he'd get mouse-trapped
into thinking I was stopping by for a quick Banana Boat. He clung
to my rear deck like a Band-Aid. He was good, in fact, one of the
best I'd ever seen. He was so close now that his face filled my en-

tire rearview mirror. I couldn't even see the hood or the grille of his car. I noticed that he had nicked himself while shaving. There was a piece of toilet paper plastered on his steel-blue chin. He was also eating a Big Mac casually as we screamed along, locked in mortal combat.

Suddenly I became aware that something was blotting out the gray Jersey sky inches from my own grille. I had fallen for the oldest tailgater trick in the book. He had maneuvered me behind a giant flatbed truck, and there was no escape. I darted tentatively to my left, hoping to pass. The tailgater hemmed me in. I tried the right. No way. A Greyhound bus was in that lane. Inches separating us, we whistled along. My mind, operating full-bore, like Proust's or Balzac's, flashed visions of shattering glass, screaming metal, and I wondered briefly whether there was anything to this heaven and hell business.

The flatbed was now four or five feet ahead of my front bumper. Its load towered above me for what looked like two or three stories. I began to enjoy the scene. I could see the truck driver's face, pale and harassed, looking at me in his rearview mirror. He was muttering. A row of discount shoe stores flashed by us in a blur. I was so close to the flatbed that I began to examine its load minutely. My God, I thought, Proust never came up with a neater bit of irony in his life.

The load, stacked twenty-deep, consisted of a giant pile of flattened automobiles, each one maybe eight inches thick, crushed like so many sardine cans under a cosmic steam roller. I had a brief image of me and my car joining them and looking exactly like all the rest. The tailgater behind me was now impassively sucking at what looked like a sixty-four-ounce family-size bottle of Pepsi.

It was then that my mind really took off. Here we were, sealed in our own little noisy, smelly projectiles, hurtling over the landscape toward . . . what? I could see the crushed cars ahead of me creaking and groaning as if in mortal fear of the fiery fate that lay ahead for them in some distant foreign blast furnace. My God, I thought, they still have their paint on.

I began to recognize the makes. There was a seven-inch-high '57 Mercury, robin's egg blue. Above it, a '61 Plymouth Fury, thinner than a blueberry pancake at a cut-rate diner. It was sand beige. Then came a sad, peeling, forest green Nash Ambassador of indeterminate year. My mind flashed a brief headline on its beaded screen: Unknown Driver Killed By '51 Studebaker. Like a news story flashed in light bulbs that march around the tops of Times Square buildings, the story went on:

Driver annihilated when a '51 Studebaker that had been in a junk yard for twelve years and hadn't been driven since 1959 leaped off a flatbed truck to engage itself in its final fiery traffic crash.

The news item disappeared from my mind as the three of us howled through an overpass that echoed and boomed to the roar of the traffic. I peered ahead at the crushed cars. Tattered bumper stickers still clung to the hulks, a veritable cross section of ancient causes: LBJ–ALL THE WAY, I LIKE IKE, IMPEACH EARL WARREN, BAN THE BOMB, FREE THE PUEBLO.

My God, I thought, "Free The Pueblo." I could hardly even remember what that was all about, but that smashed Buick Skylark remembered.

Way up near the top was a twisted, battered bumper from what looked like what was left of a moribund Dodge Charger. A torn sticker read WARNING–I BRAKE FOR ANIMALS. I thought dreamily, Poor bastard, after all that braking for chipmunks and box turtles somebody didn't brake for HIM. My mind thinks like that when I'm locked in my Proustian vinyl-lined GT, away from the cares and hubbub of everyday life with its phone calls and its feckless excursions and alarms.

I glanced in my rearview mirror. Blue Jowls, steady as a rock, was dogging me even closer. He seemed to have his front wheels up on my rear deck and was riding piggyback. He was also picking his teeth with what looked like a Boy Scout knife. I could clearly see the Scout insignia on its black bone handle. I continued reading the sad signs and pennants on the departed cars ahead of me.

Halfway up the pile, a canary-yellow Coronet had what looked like crude letters taped to its rusted bumper. They were made of faded red Day-Glo tape. I peered into the haze of blue diesel exhaust that was roaring over me from the truck. The letters spelled two names: WALT on the driver's side of the bumper, EMILY on the passenger side. Between them was a jagged, half-obliterated heart, pierced by a childish Day-Glo arrow.

Walt, I thought, poor Walt, where are you today? Somehow I felt a deep, sorrowful compassion for Walt, and Emily too. I saw that bright sunny day; that long-awaited day when they stood in the showroom taking the keys to their beautiful new Coronet. My mind conjured Walt up as being rather short, a bit beefy, but with a friendly sort of dumb face. His dark hair was cut in a bristly crew cut, the height of fashion for the day. His head looked a little like a furry bowling ball. Emily was thin and wore sagging blue shorts of the Montgomery Ward type, and she wore her hair in a Debbie Reynolds ponytail. I saw them together, polishing the Dodge on long summer weekends, Walt industriously working the Simoniz rag while Emily did the chrome. I had a brief vision of Walt making one of the endless payments on the Coronet at some sort of grilled window like they have in loan offices. He had lost a little hair and had gotten a little fatter, but you could tell it was still Walt all right. Through the window of the loan office I caught a glimpse of Emily waiting patiently in the car. There were now two kids jumping up and down on the back seat of the car. They both appeared to be boys, but it was hard to tell in all that diesel smoke coming back at me from the truck ahead. Emily looked even thinner, and her hair was put up in a pile of pink plastic curlers. The Coronet had lost two of its hubcaps, the chrome was rusting, and there wasn't much left of that bright canary-yellow paint.

I glanced again in my rearview mirror. My tailgater was now jogging up and down, his eyes glazed, his mouth hanging slackly in the manner of tailgating rock fiends.

Walt, I thought, where are you today, Walt? Are you and Emily still together? Has one of the kids been busted for Possession? Walt, do you know that your Coronet, after all these years, is still roaring along Route 22? It will be tonight in the hold of a tramp freighter sailing out of the port of Newark, Walt, a ship called, maybe, the *Funky Maru*, manned by a polyglot crew of cutthroats. Walt, your Coronet may come back to you someday in the form of a 105 mm shell.

My mind dreamily moved on. Suddenly my tailgater whistled off 22 onto the Garden State Parkway exit. He was still sucking at his Pepsi bottle. I saw him fasten himself to the back of a Mustang II.

I shifted to the left and passed the flatbed and its load of memory-laden carcasses. The mind does great things in our vinyl-lined GTs. Proust would have understood. Maybe even Balzac, for that matter.

God, I love cars. Now, I know that this is something that you're just not supposed to say these days, but there it is. We all have our faults. Sometimes I lie in the sack and run through my mind the images of all the cars I've owned in my life. I wish I could say that I thought about all the beautiful women I've known, but they tend to blend together. Not the cars.

The women, though . . . There was Daphne. And Wanda. I had a brief, fleeting image of her gleaming glasses and hint of malocclusion. Women, the whipped cream on the cake. Maybe they're the cake itself.

I fiddled nervously with the air-intake vent. I wonder if women have any idea what they do to men? I glanced at the grimy tiled tunnel wall next to me, hazy images of women I have known drifting in and out of my mind, forever the same age, never changing. Where are they now? PTA members? Library patrons? Shopping cart pushers? No, not Daphne, never!

Without warning, a mysterious white pinched face appeared out of my Mammoth Cave of a subconscious. She seemed to be at a distance, moving. She waved nervously, and disappeared back into

*the blackness. Who was she? I didn't recognize her, yet I remem-
bered her. My mind groped for a clue.*

*Another face appeared, a young man; thin, big Adam's-apple. I
grunted to myself. "Yes, of course, yes."*

That girl. The pickup truck. And poor lost Ernie.

The Marathon Run of
Lonesome Ernie,
the Arkansas Traveler

The troop train had been underway for about three hours when the
saga of Ernie began. You don't use a word like "saga" lightly, if you
have any sense, but what happened to me and Gasser and Ernie is
sure as hell a saga. At least, certainly, what happened to Ernie.

Without warning, Company K, our little band of nearsighted,
solder-burned Radar "experts," had been rousted out of the sack
at three o'clock in the morning, two full hours before reveille,
given a quick short-arm, issued new carbines and combat field
equipment, and had been told to fall out into the company street
when Sergeant Kowalski blew his goddamn whistle. Stunned, we
milled about under the yellow light bulbs of our icy barracks.
Some laughed hysterically; others wept silently. A few hunched
over their footlockers, using stubby pencils to make last-minute
finishing touches to their wills.

Me, I just slumped half-asleep on the bunk, full field pack on
my back, tin hat squashing my head down to my shoulder blades,
and waited for the worst.

"Well, gentlemen, as my father always said, it's wise to get a
good early start on a trip. That way you avoid traffic and . . ."

"Zynzmeister, will you fuck the hell off!" Gasser yelled from
his upper bunk where he was busily stuffing his legendary store
of candy bars, especially Milky Ways and Powerhouses, into his
gas mask.

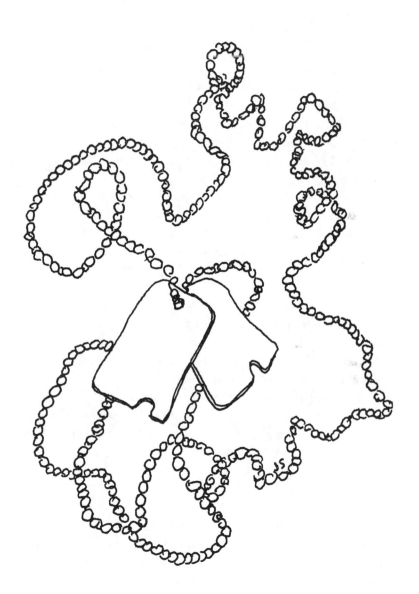

"Gasser," Zynzmeister said in his cool way, "a good brisk spin in the open air will do wonders for you. Take you out of your rut. New sights, new scenes, new people, new . . ."

"Zynzmeister, will you please, just this once, blow it out your goddamn manure chute." Gasser went back to stuffing candy bars.

"Ah, it is always thus. Coarse language is eternally the last refuge of the barren and infertile mind." Zynzmeister, our resident George Bernard Shaw, hefted his barracks bags with casual elegance amid the barracks uproar.

Corporal Elkins, our company driver and disappointed ex-air cadet, peered at me from under his tin hat.

"I told you that staff sergeant I met at Headquarters Company was not bullshitting. All you guys laughed, god dammit. Now look who's laughing."

"Elkins, I do not recall laughing at any rumors around here recently," I answered, "except the one that Edwards came up with that Kowalski has only one ball."

"Yeah, lemme tell you, we're liable to all get our asses shot off."

Several heads encased in tin helmets raised up at this. Elkins had come out with what we all secretly were thinking.

"The first goddamn guys they go for are the poor fuckin' Radar slobs." Elkins spit nervously into a butt can.

"Ironically, that is true, Elkins. In spite of the fact that our SCR 585 rarely works and when it does continually gives us false and misleading information. For that reason, gentlemen, I believe that Company K is merely a decoy to draw out enemy fire, much in the manner that a wooden duck decoy, while looking like a duck, is a clever device used to . . ."

Whistles blew in the frigid dark streets of the company, cutting off Zynzmeister in mid smart-ass crack. Clinking and clanking with damn near a hundred pounds of lethal equipment apiece, we jostled sullenly out the door of our barracks forever.

First Sergeant Kowalski, wearing his Signal Corps mackinaw, tin hat, gas mask, and, in spite of the pitch-dark night, his green air corps sunglasses, stalked back and forth restlessly in the company street.

"All right, you mens, get your asses in gear. Let's move it."

He carried, of course, his damn clipboard. He was trailed by Corporal Scroggins, a red-faced lout from Hazard, Kentucky, who had been imported from the Infantry in order to help Kowalski impose a little military discipline on our effete rabble of Signal Corps intelligentsia. Lieutenant Cherry, our company commander, sat quietly in his jeep in front of the Orderly Room. Off to the west, in the direction of the Motor Pool, the low angry rumble of an approaching truck convoy meant to each one of us only one thing. Scroggins blew his whistle. We lined up automatically in our usual four ragged lines: Gasser to my right, Edwards to my left, Zynzmeister behind me.

"At ease."

Kowalski himself sounded a bit subdued. We fell silent except for the faint clank and creak of equipment.

"You guys probably have noticed the fact you been issued new carbines. And also you been issued new field gear. And also it is three ayem, which is two hours before reveille. Now, many of you are probably askin' what is this all about? Am I correct?"

All around me in the blackness there was a restless rattle of carbines and a faint shuffling of feet. Kowalski was always a great one for the rhetorical question. He also had a notable talent for belaboring the obvious.

"Lieutenant Cherry will now give you the dope on what's gonna happen. You mens listen good. I don't wanna have no dumbhead comin' up to me after this formation and askin' no stupid questions. I got enough on my hands now without answerin' no stupid questions."

Kowalski paused for a long significant moment in order to let his broadside sink in.

"Atten-HUT!"

All around me were the familiar sounds of the company

coming to what it liked to call "Attention," which meant a slight shifting of the feet, a look of fierce concentration in the eye, and a faint pulling in of the stomach muscles.

"At ease."

We relaxed. "At ease" in the Army does not mean what it means in civilian life. It means primarily "Shut up and listen." Lieutenant Cherry casually eased himself out of the company jeep and languidly took his position in front of Kowalski, who stared stonily ahead of him.

"Gen'lmen." Lieutenant Cherry's voice had soft, rich southern overtones. His steel-rimmed glasses picked up a glint of light from the mess hall.

"Company K is about to embark on a great adventure."

His voice trailed off as he stared upward into the night sky. The sinister rumble of the approaching convoy grew louder and louder. The lieutenant calmly looked up and down the ranks of Company K. A hand rested on each hip, his legs spread wide out. I felt the faint whistle of the ice-cold winter wind under the brim of my helmet.

"We are shipping."

Gasser, in the gloom next to me, quietly cleared his throat. The lieutenant went on:

"This is not a maneuver, nor is it an exercise. We have received orders to be transported at oh-four-hundred as of this date to an undisclosed point, from which point we will be further transported by aircraft to an undisclosed destination. I have no information other than the following details."

Kowalski handed the lieutenant his clipboard. Edwards, to my left, muttered "balls." The lieutenant glanced at a fluttering sheet of paper on the clipboard.

"In a few minutes we will move out by truck convoy to the train siding at Area Two."

Area Two was about fifteen miles away in a remote, mysterious part of the camp that was enclosed by high wire fences. No one ever came back from Area Two. He continued:

"At that point we will assign each of you a shipment number. At my command you will file into the troop train which will be waiting for us. We will do this with a minimum of lost motion. As of this moment, Company K is on full alert, which means you will not move an inch out of the company area and will remain on this spot until the convoy arrives."

Somewhere I heard the muttered voice of Elkins: "Oh, God Almighty, I knew it!"

"This troop train will be sealed, since we are part of a highly secure troop movement. There will be no intermingling with other units, which will be assigned to their own cars on the train. On the train itself, you will be allowed to choose your seats, but after that you will remain in that seat as much as possible. A few of you may be assigned work details while on the train. If you are, I will notify you. Sergeant Kowalski has notified me that all your GI insurance forms are in order, that your medical records are up to date, and that for once you all successfully passed this morning's short-arm. I am pleased. I add my personal 'good luck' to the entire company."

He handed his clipboard back to the sergeant just as the first rumbling troop carrier lumbered into the company street.

From behind me in the darkness I heard the voice of an unknown terror-stricken Radar man mutter: "Christ, for one'st I wish I had the clap."

There was an answering ripple of tense tittering. Company K at long last stood silent and ready for come-what-may.

BRRRRROOOOOMMM . . . BRRRROOOOOOOMMM . . . BRRRRRRROOOOOOOM.

A pair of baleful, glaring headlights rounded the corner at the end of the company street, where the road ran between the Day Room and our fragrant mess hall, scene of so many painful events and unforgettable meals. In the blackness, the first truck in the convoy lurched to a halt, its engine burbling angrily. Another roared around the corner and formed up behind the first. One after another they came. Whistles blew. Scroggins and

Kowalski yelled orders. Squad after squad peeled off at a dog-trot and piled into the black, menacing vehicles. The usual Company K give-and-take of Quit shovin', you son of a bitch, Up yours, TS Mack, and Blow it out your ass was, in this grim predawn moment, notably absent.

My squad—Gasser, Zynzmeister, Elkins, and the rest—trotted woodenly to the rear of the third truck in line. We huddled side by side in the darkness on the hard wooden seats. I peered out the rear of the truck as the troop carrier slowly began to move with that malevolent suppressed thunder of all military trucks, with their special mufflers and oversized transmissions. The smell of GIs on the move seeped through the cold black air; sweat, gun grease, cartridge webbing, gas mask rubber, and, of course, fear. We rumbled past Barracks 903-T, now standing silent and empty, its yellow light bulbs gleaming sullenly on lonely butt cans. On our left, the doors of the silent Supply Room yawned blackly. Even the Supply Room hangers-on had been loaded into trucks like the rest of us.

"And so our happy band of warriors take leave of their old familiar haunts and . . ."

"Will you stuff a sock in it, Zynzmeister!"

Someone lit a cigarette. Gasser unpeeled a Baby Ruth bar.

"Y'know, I never thought I'd miss this dump, but already I . . ."

Elkins interrupted me instinctively, as he had for the past two years:

"Boy, when I think that you guys all laughed at me."

"Gentlemen, let us all satisfy Elkins for once by according him a round of laughter. All together now, men. Let's hear those guffaws."

The squad guffawed hollowly in unison in the rumbling, noisy darkness.

"Okay, you guys, you just wait."

Someone hummed tunelessly Elkins' beloved Air Force song:

"Off we go, into the wild blue . . ."

"Screw you."

"Clever, Elkins. The perfect riposte." Zynzmeister needled Elkins. The two were great friends, and their friendship consisted of Zynzmeister using Elkins the way a basketball uses a bounding board.

The convoy droned on through what remained of the night, past the rifle range, the Motor Pool, the BOQ, and the Number One Service Club. The squad now rode in silence. It was beginning to sink in that we really were leaving and that we'd probably never see this place again.

Finally, the convoy crept through the gates of the high tough chicken-wire fence that surrounded Area Two. A red and white sign gleamed in the headlights:

RESTRICTED AREA. NO PERSONNEL BEYOND THIS POINT WITHOUT SPECIAL PROVOST MARSHAL CLEARANCE.

Two MPs stood with rifles in the port position as Company K growled by to its uncertain fate. We passed a few dark buildings and a couple of dimly lighted offices. The convoy finally lurched to a halt. Whistles blew, and we poured out onto the gravel road.

For the first time we saw It—a long black string of railroad cars that stretched off into the night fore and aft. A dozen floodlights lit up the scene like a stage set. A grasshopper would have had trouble getting out of the area without attracting seven MP's. Any thoughts of sneaking away into the night disappeared instantly. Under the glare, our uniforms looked unnaturally green and the scratches on our helmets showed up like scars on a fish belly. Our faces, normally tanned, looked milky and tinged with bluish beards. I glanced at Edwards. He looked about twelve under his pile of field equipment. Even Zynzmeister was silent.

We assembled into our usual company formation. Being Radar, ours was a small company, little more than a swollen platoon. Lined up next to the train sidings under the floods, we looked curiously small and sad.

Lieutenant Cherry, flanked by two alien officers, a major and a captain, both bearing large yellow envelopes and thick folders, gave us our instructions in his molasses-and-grits voice:

"At ease, men. This is Major Willoughby, our troop train commander."

Major Willoughby, a sagging billowing man with the face of a pregnant basset, smiled briefly from amid his jowls. His pisscutter hat, square on his head, was pulled down low so that his two pendulous ears swung out to either side like fleshy barn doors. On his rumpled sleeve was sewn, carelessly, the patch of the Transportation Corps. It was a patch few of us had ever seen. He had the look of an old-time railroad man whose life revolved around timetables, green eye shields, cigar butts, and traveling salesmen.

"This is Captain Carruthers, the Deputy Commander." Carruthers was thin, dapper, and had a worried look on his pinched white face.

"Captain Carruthers is responsible for the safe arrival of every man on this train. He has assigned each one of you an individual number and he will personally check each of you off and on at the embarkation point and the point of debarkation. I cannot stress enough the importance of remaining in your seats as much as possible while en route."

Someone coughed behind me in that phony way you cough when the medical officer is giving you a short-arm. I knew what he was thinking. Apparently, so did Cherry.

"There is a latrine at the end of every car. You will ask your squad leader's permission to use it, in order to avoid crowding and confusion. We will leave our car only for meals, and then in the order of your transit numbers. At my command we will file into the car by squads. Each of you will give your name, rank, and serial number and will be handed a card bearing your transit number. Do not lose this. You will then immediately board the train and select a seat. You will do this with a minimum of bitching and seat changing."

He paused. From way off in the distance came a blast of the locomotive's horn: short, impatient. Lieutenant Cherry glanced at his watch. It was precisely 0400. Kowalski, at Lieutenant Cherry's nod, bellowed:

"Atten-HUT! First Squad in column, right face, Move out."

First Squad, ahead of us, clanked forward in single file toward the open door of our car. For the first time I noticed that the car appeared to be painted a dull green color and on its side was its name: *The Georgia Peach*. My squad moved forward. Up ahead of me, on either side of the metal train steps, were the major and the captain, checking off names and handing out cards. One by one, Company K disappeared into the *The Georgia Peach*. I half-expected someone to scream at the last instant:

"NO, NO! I CAN'T GO. I FORGOT MY CLOTHES AT THE DRY CLEANERS!" or to unsling his carbine and scream:

"YOU'LL NEVER TAKE ME ALIVE. COME AND GET ME, YOU RATFINK ARMY BASTARDS!"

But no. Like sheep following their leader, one by one, we silently went over the cliff. Major Willoughby stared into my face with moist brown pouch-lined eyes. I barked out my name, rank, and serial number. For a long moment he gazed at his clipboard. I had one wild moment of hope.

He can't find my name! My name ain't there! Whoopee!

"Ah yes, here we are." Major Willoughby's voice sounded like the rumble of steam in a friendly old overheated boiler. When you're around locomotives long enough you begin to sound like one. He shuffled through a stack of cards and finally handed me mine. It was small, blue, and to the point. My name, rank, and serial number were typed at the top above the decisive black numbers. They stood out bold and aggressive: 316. The major rumbled:

"Have a good trip, son."

I mounted the step and entered the car. Already it seemed that half the seats were taken. I moved down the aisle and found an empty. I unhooked my heavy field pack and hung it on the rack made of piping which was above the seat, hanging my helmet and carbine next to the pack. I took off my gas mask and flung it up on the rack. Finally, at least a half-ton lighter, I slipped into the seat next to the window. It was hard, and seemed to be covered in material made from old hairbrushes, scratchy and unyielding. Amid the hullabaloo as the rest of Company K found its seats all around me, I examined the car.

Lit by dim overhead lights, it had been stripped of anything resembling civilian comfort. The windows were sealed with black, tightly stretched canvas. Ahead of me, Zynzmeister addressed the throng:

"You will notice the deluxe accommodations which are a featured part of our holiday tours. Our guide will describe the scenic wonders as we roll . . ."

Gasser, who had sat down next to me, laughed his irritating braying laugh.

"Hey, Zynzmeister," he yelled, "hey, Zynzmeister."

Zynzmeister was busily stowing his gear above his seat. With casual elegance he turned.

"Already I am being paged. Ah, I am pleased that you have decided to come with us, Gasser, on our mystery tour."

"What's your number, Zynzmeister?" Gasser yelled from beside me.

"Ah . . . I believe I have been designated number three eighty-four." Zynzmeister waved his card in the air.

"Boy, don't tell me," Gasser yelled above the din, "they gave you just an ordinary number, like the rest of us slobs?"

Zynzmeister smiled benignly. "Of course not, Gasser. Three eighty-four is an old Zynzmeister family number. It is the street number of our family mansion on Chicago's posh North Lake Shore Drive. It is also, coincidentally, the berth number that the Zynzmeisters were issued on the *Mayflower*, so naturally . . ."

He was drowned out by a roar of Company K–style badinage, which ran heavily to Bullshit, What a lot of crap, and Some guys are so full of it that their eyes are turning brown. Zynzmeister waved to his fans and eased himself into his seat.

After that, things happened very quickly. Lieutenant Cherry strode up the center aisle with his clipboard, glancing at each seat as he went. His face was expressionless, almost as though nothing unusual was happening, that in fact he spent his life embarking into the unknown. Kowalski struggled with Goldberg's bloated, overweight barracks bags. Golberg, in spite of the fact that we all carried, theoretically, the same equipment, had managed as he always did to make his barracks bag fatter and bulkier than anyone else's. He was the only one in the company who had gained weight in our mess hall. He had found a home in the Army.

"What the hell you got in here, Goldberg? It feels like you got eight bowling balls in here."

Gasser leaned over and whispered in my ear, "I'll bet he's got his wife in that B bag."

Goldberg, a newlywed, and one of the few Company K members who was married, had managed to take his wife Sylvia wherever we were shipped. It was rumored that she even managed to go over the Obstacle Course with him one day.

There was a shudder and a couple of heavy thumps and the troop train began to move. We heard the sound of distant train whistles as we picked up speed. I have since seen countless movies on late TV that purport to show a troop train. None were remotely like the real thing; no guitars, no crap games, no scared GIs writing a last letter to their loved ones, no exchanging of photos of "sweethearts" and wives. Our car rolled along with just a minor mutter of restrained conversation. Gasser dozed off next to me, and I read a Raymond Chandler which I had picked up at the PX. Edwards leaned over the seat in front of me and said:

"I hear we're being shipped to Georgia. Fort Benning."

"Come on. They don't give you new carbines to go to Fort Benning. And whoever heard of a Radar company going there anyway?"

Edwards shook his head. "Well, that's what I heard."

"Yeah?" I continued. "Well, keep me informed on the next one you hear."

Kowalski stalked up and down the car, checking equipment and answering questions here and there. Occasionally someone got up and asked permission of the corporal to go to the toilet. We squeaked and rumbled on. Not a sliver of light from the outside world, where it now must be broad daylight, entered *The Georgia Peach*. We could just as well be taking a train through hell, which some of us suspected we were. I stuck the copy of *Farewell, My Lovely* into the crack between the seat and the wall next to me. Gasser's head lolled against my shoulder. I opened up my shirt to let in a little air. It was hot as hell in *The Georgia Peach*.

I had just begun to drop off into the great dark sea of sleep when someone shook me roughly. I glanced up in a daze, at first not quite remembering where I was. I was confused for a moment because the barracks seemed to be swaying. It was Lieutenant Cherry smiling down at me. I sat up to attention instantly, since in the past the lieutenant had rarely addressed me personally, and then never by name, calling me "Soldier" and "You there." Gasser was also sitting bolt upright next to me. The lieutenant addressed us both.

"You two guys have drawn KP. Every company on the train provides three men for KP. You guys and Ernie drew the tickets. You'll be on duty twenty-four hours—four on, four off—any questions?"

Gasser and I in unison muttered: "Nosir."

Good Christ Almighty! I thought, KP on a goddamn troop train! Everybody else will be laying around on their butts, sleeping and goofing off, and me and Gasser and Ernie will be on the goddamn Pots and Pans. God dammit to hell!

"By the way," Cherry went on, "I will guarantee you will not pull KP again for a minimum of sixty days. Okay? Put on your fatigues, leave all your gear here, and take off. The chow car is eight cars ahead. Now get moving."

Lieutenant Cherry moved on down the car to give Ernie his bad news.

Ernie was a tall, thin Iowan with a pale, tired-looking face. I only knew him slightly, since he was an antenna specialist and I was a Keyer man, along with Gasser and the rest of my platoon. Antenna men always had sad faces, since they spent a lot of their time clinging to a mast a couple of hundred feet in the air, where occasionally they would meet their sudden end. We had lost two in one day when some fool–we never discovered who–had hit a switch and rotated the disk while they were aloft tuning it. The damn thing flung them out into space like a kid's slingshot hurling ball bearings. Ernie just missed being one of them. He was about ten feet below them on the mast when it happened.

The only other squad that carried the weight of doom on their shoulders were the Power Supply men. Twenty-five thousand volts at up to two amps is damn near enough juice to ionize the whole city of Hackensack. One day when a couple of safety interlocks failed to function, one of the Power Supply men went up in a puff of light purple smoke, leaving behind only the remains of a charred dog tag and half of a seared canteen.

Keyer men were considered the dilettantes of Company K. We were also the company's intellectual elite, since the keyer was by far the most complex component to maintain, and its inherent instability lent credence to our image as Bohemian, unpredictable artists. Our keyer unit, which was wired with secret dynamite charges for immediate detonation in case of enemy capture, was the heart of our radar.

Silently, Gasser began to pull on his fatigues. I did likewise, making sure that I was putting on my crap fatigues. Every experienced soldier always keeps one pair of clean, reasonably decent fatigues for casual wear around the company area. The other pair is used for crap details such as Latrine Orderly or KP. This suit is often impregnated with everything from chicken guts to sheep dung, which is used to fertilize the lawn around the Officers' Club. This suit is mean, rancid, and gamy beyond civilian understanding.

At last Gasser and I stood up in our fragrant work uniforms. Ernie came up from the far end of the car. Wordlessly, the three of us moved down the center aisle, little realizing at the time that we had begun a saga that was eventually to be a legend throughout the entire Signal Corps.

Gasser led the way. I followed; Ernie trailed behind. As we moved up the aisle, three or four of our peers emitted faint chicken-clucking sounds, the universal GI signal that says roughly: The Army has done it again. Another indignity has been heaped upon the defenseless enlisted man's head. I find this amusing, since it has not happened to me, at least this time. My clucking denotes both sympathy and faint scorn since you were dumb enough to get caught in the Army Crap Detail net. Cluck cluck cluck.

The chicken has to be one of nature's most maligned creatures, being a universal symbol of cowardice as well as petty harassment and general measliness. My heart goes out to the chicken. What has the chicken done to deserve this reputation? Is the chicken more cowardly than, say, the mole or the gopher? It is one of those unanswerable questions. Even the chicken's daily provender is looked upon with scorn and derision. "Chicken feed" aptly describes most of our salaries. I have never heard anyone term his paycheck "goat meal" or "squirrel food," always "chicken feed."

These murky thoughts drifted through my GI brain as we went up the aisle toward the chow car. We went through car after car filled with alien soldiers wearing mysterious patches. Gasser muttered over his shoulder:

"Christ, did you get a load of those Paratroopers back there? What in the hell are we heading for?"

The same thought had occurred to me when we went through one car filled with wiry, mean-looking GIs wearing gleaming jump boots and the kind of expressions that you see at three o'clock in the morning on the faces of the birds in poolrooms and all-night diners. They all wore crazy patches that looked like a smear of blood with a mailed fist clenching a length of chain emerging right at you. Behind me, Ernie added his two bits:

"I swear that must have been a company of Mafia hit men. Did you see that captain?"

Their CO, sprawled at the head of the car, looked like a carnivorous orangutan dressed in skintight fatigues with a trench knife at his waist.

"I'm sure as hell glad they're on our side," I chirped, stepping over a pile of gas masks.

"Don't be too sure, buddy," Gasser answered without looking back. One thing that really got to me was that this captain wore a single set of captain's bars on his fatigue collar. They were painted a dull, lethal black. You just don't see outfits like that in the late late movies.

Eventually we arrived at the chow car. Actually, it was two chow cars; one for cooking, the other for serving. The feeding facilities on a troop train are not exactly in the civilian elegant dining car tradition. Since there were two or three thousand soldiers aboard, they were fed like hogs at the trough. It was all very functional. The serving car had a long stainless-steel table that ran the entire length of the car itself. At intervals there were holes a couple of feet in diameter cut in the gleaming steel, and huge thirty-two-gallon garbage cans filled with GI food were lowered into the holes. Only the tops showed. Mashed potatoes in one, creamed chipped beef in another, soggy string beans, and at the far end "Dessert," garbage cans filled with cherry Jell-O or runny fruit salad. The soldiers to be fed moved in an endless line through the car, carrying their mess kits. Sweating KPs on the other side of the steel table ladled out the glop. It was a messy job, messy and hot and hypnotic. In the next car the cooks and a team of KPs toiled away, brewing up oatmeal, meatloaves, and stewed squash in a bath of searing heat that would have done a sauna proud. Since there were so many on the train, the feeding went on almost without a break. When one part of the endless line had returned to its car after breakfast, another part of the line was ready for lunch. The instant Gasser and Ernie and I arrived, the mess sergeant, a sweaty tech wearing a white apron and a crew cut, put us to work.

"You guys from that Signal Corps bunch, right?"

Gasser grunted.

"Okay, grab them aprons. And you"—he nodded to me—"you're on gravy. And you, get down there on them peas. And you, you're on Harvard beets."

I was gravy, Ernie was peas, and Gasser was Harvard beets. Seconds later I began ladling. Now, on a swaying troop train there is a real trick to ladling gravy into lurching mess kits filled with ice cream and salmon loaf and chopped cucumbers. The job leaves a lot of room for artistic interpretations. Hour after hour faceless yardbirds jostled past amid the din of complaints and muffled cursings. There were sudden wild bursts of laughter. Through it all, the mess sergeant kept yelling mechanically:

"Keep it movin'. God dammit, keep it movin'. God dammit, keep it movin'. Hey you, this ain't no Schrafft's or nothin'. If you don't like what you get, dump it in the can at the end of the car, but don't hold up the damn line. God dammit."

I have often since wondered what became of that poor, driven mess sergeant. No ribbons, no applause, only an endless belt of hungry, wooden faces year after year. He must have had one of the most realistic views of mankind of anyone around. Like some keeper in the cosmic zoo of humanity where it is always Feeding Time, which is not at all the same as Dining Time or Lunch Time. He presided over his steaming feeding trough with a wild look of dogged persistence in his eye and a leather voice prodding the herd on.

"Keep movin', God dammit, keep movin'. Come on, you guys, let's have more mashed potatoes out here. Change them cans quick. Hey, quit spillin' that coffee all over the damn floor. Get a goddamn mop, fer Chrissake, stupid. Let's go, let's go. Keep movin'."

Time became all jumbled as I hunched over my vast tub of dark brown, steaming gravy. My wrist ached from ladling,

ladling, ladling. After a couple of hours in the heat, the sergeant told us to strip down to our shorts and GI shoes. It was a little relief, but not much. Steam rose in swirling clouds from the boiling hot food; sweat dropped from my dog tags and into the gravy. Who cared? A little sweat never hurt anyone. I toiled on. Gasser wielded his beet ladle with dash and élan. Ernie was switched from peas to string beans. Other KPs from time to time emerged in pairs from the cooking car, struggling on the slippery floor, carrying giant cans of soup or gravy or scrambled eggs. As one tub was emptied, another was immediately lowered into the slot.

I quickly discovered that the gravy ladle was highly controversial, since gravy has to be handled with skill, not to mention restraint. Too much wrist on the ladle and some poor joker's whole meal was swimming in brown glue; ice cream, fruit salad, and all. I grew hard and unyielding, impervious to the steady torrent of abuse that was heaped upon me. I ladled gravy mechanically, with no prejudice or favoritism. After all, when you're feeding half the U. S. Army on a thundering troop train there is no place for faint heart or even mere civility.

"No gravy, please. Hey you, NO GRAVY!" meant absolutely nothing to me as I ladled on hour after hour.

At long intervals the line would peter out to a faint trickle and the exhausted sergeant would holler out:

"O.K., you guys. Take a ten-minute break. You're doin' a great job, yessir, a great job. If you want any apples or ice cream or anything, just grab 'em but don't leave the car."

An endless supply of food is the quickest way to kill an appetite. One day there will be some hotshot doctor who will write a diet book based on that fact. Put any fatty in a room with tons of ice cream, mashed potatoes, and chocolate cake, with butterscotch malted coming out of the faucets, and within five hours the fatty will not be able to stand the sight of food.

I squatted down on a packing case behind the counter, my legs stiff from all the standing, my ladle hand sore and tired, my forearms and elbows itching from dried gravy. Ever since that hellish twenty-four hours of KP I have never again touched gravy in any form. Gasser sat with his head hanging low around his knees, blood-red beet juice dripping from his hairy chest. He looked like a major casualty that had taken an 88 shell right in the gut. Ernie leaned back against the side of the swaying car, his legs outstretched, straddling his string-bean tub, his eyes closed. The ten minutes flashed by in milliseconds.

"Here they come again, you guys. Keep it movin', come on, quit stragglin'. God dammit, this ain't no Schrafft's."

I tried ladling with my left hand for a while to ease my aching wrist and elbow. I was rapidly developing a severe case of Gravy Ladle Tendonitis, which occasionally still troubles me. Unfortunately, with my left hand I was gravying more shoes than potatoes and had to switch back. I tried the overhand motion; side-arm. The complaints rose and fell like the beating of an angry surf on an unyielding rocky shore.

From time to time through the surrealistic blur of the endless line I would spot a familiar face as Company K went by. They were no longer my friends, just more links in a chain that went round and round.

As the three of us toiled on along with other KPs from other units, the outside world ceased to exist. Was it day, was it night? Was it winter, was it summer? What year was it? Do they still have years? What country were we in? Were we in any country? Had we died and were we now toiling in purgatory, struggling hopelessly for redemption? Who am I? What is my name?

I ladled on and on. During one of our breaks, Gasser, chewing on a piece of celery, ambled over, trailing beet juice, to where the sergeant was moodily checking a tub of purple Kool-Aid, known to the troops as the Purple Death.

"Hey, Sarge, when do we get our four hours off?" The sergeant glanced up from the tub of inky fluid in which floated two tiny chunks of ice about the size of golf balls. He was stirring it with a huge, long-handled wooden paddle.

"Huh? What'd you say?" He wiped the sweat from his brow with his left hand and flicked it into the Kool-Aid.

"When do we get our four hours off?"

"What four hours off?" The sergeant barked a dry, hard, yapping laugh. "Jeez, what the hell are they sending me now? I ain't had four hours off since last November."

Gasser chewed angrily on his celery. "Our lieutenant informed us that we would have four hours on and four hours off and that . . ."

The sergeant shook his head slowly in the incredible wonder that anyone could believe such a transparent fairy tale. Gasser got the message. So did we.

Ernie, slumped next to me, was slowly drinking a canteen cup of cold milk.

"Boy, I'll say one thing about this job. You sure get thirsty. Boy, do you get thirsty."

"Yeah. It's all this sweating," I said, running my hand over my chest like a squeegee, pushing a wave of sweat ahead of it. My dog tags dripped steadily. Ernie nodded.

"Boy, I never sweated so much in my life."

The humidity in the car from all the steam, the moving bodies, and the fact that the ventilation system had gone out during the second year of Lincoln's administration, made the chow car about as comfortable as the inside of a catcher's mitt during the second half of a doubleheader in July.

"Well," I yawned, stretching my aching back, "it's a great way to lose weight."

"What weight?" Ernie said as he gulped his milk. Ernie was the only guy I have ever known standing six feet six and wearing size fifteen shoes who wore a shirt with a thirteen and a half collar and had a twenty-seven-inch waist. Ernie was so skinny that if he stood sideways in the wind, he made a high, whistling sound. He looked like the guy in those ads in the back pages of *Boy's Life* captioned: Are you a 98 lb. weakling? The guy that gets the sand kicked in his face. One time on a twenty-mile march, Goldberg hollered out:

"Hey, Ernie, will you please march over on the other side of the platoon? I keep hearin' your bones rattle and I get out of step."

The platoon laughed at that, and so did Ernie, who was a good guy, although very quiet. Few of us at the time would have guessed at the fate that lay ahead of him.

He raised his long, white, boy face—he looked a little like a nineteen-year-old Uncle Sam with no beard—and repeated:

"Boy, I'm so damn thirsty I could could drink some of your crummy gravy."

"Don't worry, Ernie," I said, "we only got about fifteen hours to go and we'll be home free."

I tried to pump as much sarcasm into my voice as I could manage without getting into trouble with the sergeant, who was listening to our exchange of pleasantries. The clank of many feet approaching cut short whatever Ernie was going to say. We went back into the trenches.

From time to time during the long hours I was switched to Jell-O, which I found was even trickier, if possible, than gravy. For one thing, it bounces around on the ladle and occasionally takes on a life of its own. GI Jell-O ranges in consistency from golf ball rubbery to a kind of oozy reddish gruel, and you never know what kind you're going to get on any given ladle scoop. I learned to play the windage, rolling my Jell-O scoop from side to side in the manner of a Cessna 150 approaching a narrow grass runway in high, gusty crosswinds.

Your GI mess kit folds open like a clam and has a treacherous metal handle which can operate, or nonoperate, at its own will. Half of the clam shell is a shallow oval-shaped compartment. The other side, of equal size and also oval, has raised divisions which theoretically separate the Jell-O from the mashed potatoes or the beets from the ice cream. Like most theories, the actuality was very different. For one thing, the metal of the mess kit transmits heat better than platinum wire carries electric current. A dollop of steaming mashed rutabagas in one compartment instantly turns the mess kit into an efficient hotplate. Ice cream ladled into another compartment instantly melts and is heated to the consistency of lukewarm pea soup, which is often what it tastes like after the peas have slopped over into the ice cream and the fish gravy has oozed over from the big dish. So naturally, all such old-fashioned concepts as specific tastes and conventional meal sequences are totally irrelevant when you're dining tastefully out of a red-hot mess kit. For one thing, you usually eat your dessert first in the futile hope of getting at just a little unmelted ice cream before it's too late.

Over the years I became quite fond of some specific mixtures. For example, vanilla ice cream goes surprisingly well when mixed with mashed salmon loaf. The ice cream makes a kind of sweetish coolish salmon salad out of it, a little like drugstore tuna salad. If the ice cream is chocolate, however, or maybe tutti-frutti, you've got problems.

Goldberg, the leading Company K chow hound, had a simple solution. He'd just take his big metal GI spoon and immediately mix everything in his mess kit together, forming a heavy brownish-pinkish paste in which floated chunks of, say, fried liver or maybe a pork chop or two, and just spoon it down between gulps of Kool-Aid or GI coffee or whatever we had to drink. It was all gone in maybe thirty or forty seconds. Goldberg would let out a shuddering belch and get back on the chow line for another go-round.

There were others, perhaps more fastidious, who would eat only one thing per serving, going through the line first for turnips, which they would devour, then getting back in the line for the steamed cauliflower, then finally, after three or four trips through the line, topping it off with the Jell-O or the canned pineapple.

Then there were those, and Gasser was a leading member of this group, who lived entirely on Butterfinger bars. It's hard to say which group was right. I'll say one thing. A stretch in any one of the Armed Forces is a sure cure for what my aunt Clara always called "picky" eaters. It's not that GI food wasn't good. It was, in fact, better than most guys regularly got at home. It just had a tendency to get all mixed up and run together, so that in the end being picky was even more stupid in the Army than it is in real life. The Army is also a sure cure for what is called "light sleepers." After the first ninety days among the dogfaces you can sleep standing up, sitting down, going to the john, firing a rifle, making love, or swimming underwater with a pack on your back. In all my four years I never once ran into an insomniac. Insomnia is a civilian luxury, like credit cards and neurotic mistresses.

It must have been about the tenth or fifteenth hour that I became conscious, dimly through the hullabaloo and the scorching heat, that somebody in my immediate vicinity was snoring fitfully. Every time I glanced around it stopped. Who the hell was it? Again the snoring commenced. After fifteen or twenty minutes of this irritating phlegmy sound, I realized that it was me. It has been said that the human mind is capable of only one act at any given instant, but I can't see how this can be since on numerous occasions I have found myself soundly asleep and still doing other things.

As I ladled on, flipping Jell-O over my left shoulder occasionally, for luck, I thought of these things. An extended stretch of KP is good for your philosophical side. The mind wanders aimlessly to and fro like a blind earthworm burrowing in total darkness amid buried tree roots and dead snails. There is a certain basic soul-satisfaction in low down, mindless menial labor. The body completely takes over. A mess kit swims into view; your arm flips Jell-O at it without thought or understanding. The pores are open. Your entire physical being is now functioning without a controlling mind, like the heart and the liver, which go about their work without conscious control.

Down the long line of KPs ladles rose and fell, feet in heavy GI boots clanked by. Gravy, mashed potatoes, turnips, beets, scrambled eggs, all became one. Once a voice snapped me out of my restful reverie.

"How'r y'all makin' it?"

I glanced up from the brown sea of gravy, or Jell-O, or whatever I was scooping at the time.

"Uh . . . what? You talking to me?"

It was Lieutenant Cherry.

"Uh . . . yeah, I guess so. Sir."

"Just thought I'd drop by. See how you guys were makin' out."

The steam clouded up the lieutenant's glasses. Even his gleaming silver bars were misty. He moved down past Gasser, who waved at him with his ladle, and we toiled on.

During the next break, one of the other KPs, a short Mexican Pfc from an Engineering company joined our little group. His name was Gomez and he had the smell of Regular Army about him, crafty and laconic.

"Hey, Gomez," Gasser said between mouthfuls of powdered scrambled eggs, "what do you guys do in your outfit?"

"We're Engineers."

Gomez was one of those guys whom you have to prod continually to get anything at all out of.

"Yeah, but what do you *do*?" Gasser kept on prodding.

"What the hell do you think we do? What do you think the Engineers do?"

Gasser thought about this solemnly for a moment. Finally Ernie chipped in with his two cents:

"I almost got assigned to the Engineers out of Basic. But I got the Signal Corps instead."

Gomez, sensing a slur, shot back: "Well, y'can't win 'em all. Some guys are lucky; other guys are just dumb."

We rocked back and forth on our haunches in the steady rumbling silence for a while, until Gasser, swabbing out his mess kit with a chunk of bread, continued our listless investigation of the life and times of Pfc Gomez, Engineer Corps, USA.

"Gomez, I don't like to pry but I am very curious about what your unit does. Now take me and my sweaty friends here. We are in Radar. By that I mean we are in a unit that gets no promotions, no stripes whatsoever. We just get a lot of shocks, and fool around with soldering irons and crap like that. And . . ."

Gasser knew what he was doing. Radar men were universally looked upon by the great mass of real soldiers about the same way that the Detroit Lions evaluated George Plimpton.

"Shee-it," Gomez said, "don't tell me about Radar. I got a cousin in it, a goddamn fairy. He has to squat to piss."

Ernie cleared his throat and counterattacked: "Listen, Gomez, we had nine guys in the hospital last month alone, all with the clap."

Gomez picked his teeth casually with a kitchen match. "Probably give it to each other," he muttered.

God, I thought, would I like to turn Zynzmeister loose on this bird.

"Okay, you guys, let's get movin'. Here they come." The sergeant banged a spoon loudly on the stainless steel as once again the devouring swarm of human locusts engulfed us, eating everything in their path, leaving behind desolation and bread crusts.

By now all of us had broken through that mysterious invisible pane of glass that separates dog fatigue from what is called "the second wind." A curious elation, a lightheaded sense of infinite boundless strength filled me. I whistled "Three Blind Mice" over and over as I maniacally ladled my beloved gravy. Me, the Gravy King.

> *"Three blind mice, see how they run . . .*
> *Three blind mice, see . . ."*

For the first time in my life I really looked at gravy. In the Hemingway sense, gravy was true and real. My gravy was the most beautiful gravy ever seen on this planet, brown as the rich delta land of the Mississippi basin; life-bringer, source of primal energy. How lovely was my gravy. It made such sensual, swirling patterns as it dripped down over the snowy mashed potatoes and engulfed the golden pound cake with its rich tide of life force. I wondered why no one had ever seen this glory before. Was I on the verge of an original discovery involving gravy as the universal healer, a healer which could bind mankind together once they had discovered that the one thing that they had in common was my lovely, lovely gravy? Maybe I should wander the earth, bearing the glad tidings. *Salvation through gravy. Gravy is love. God created gravy, hence gravy is the Word of God. More gravy, more gravy is what we all need!*

Yes, it is such thoughts as these that surface when the mind sags with fatigue and reason flees.

"Hey, you on the gravy."

It was the mess sergeant yelling from the other end of the car.

"Yes?" I heard myself replying. "I am the Gravy King."

"Not any more you're not, Mack. You and your buddies are going into the other car to take over Pots and Pans. Now get movin', let's keep it movin'."

With sorrow in my heart I laid down my trusty gravy ladle and the three of us, trailing sweat, struggled into the next car. It was like leaving purgatory and entering hell. Murky, writhing figures, moaning piteously, stirred great vats of bubbling food. Others squatted in the muck, peeling great mounds of reeking onions. The heat was so enormous that I could actually hear it, a low pulsating hum. A buck sergeant wearing skintight fatigues cut off just below the hips herded the three of us through the uproar to the far end of the car. Three guys armed with hoses spewing scalding water and cakes of taffy-brown GI soap capable of dissolving fingernails at thirty paces and long-handled GI brushes struggled to clean what looked like four or five hundred GI pots. The buck hollered at the three:

"You guys are relieved. Get back to the other car, on the double. You're gonna relieve these guys on the serving line."

The three pot-scrubbers, all with the look in their eyes of damned souls out for a dip in the River Styx, dropped their brushes and swabs and without a sound rushed out of hell, un-expectedly pardoned.

"Oh, Mother of God," Gasser mumbled as two sweating GIs appeared carrying more dirty pots, which they hurled on top of the pile.

Thus began a period of my existence which has haunted me to this day. From time to time, when driving late at night, my car radio will inadvertently pick up Fundamentalist preachers who thunder warnings of mankind's approaching doom and hold out promises of indescribable hells. I clutch the wheel in sudden fear, because I have been there.

The oatmeal pots are the worst. GI oatmeal is cooked in huge vats which become lined with thick burnt-concrete encrustations of immovable oatmeal matter. Oatmeal is even worse than pow-dered egg scabs, which are matched only by the vats used to con-coct mutton stew.

Through the long hours Ernie, Gasser, and myself struggled against the tide of endless pots. The GI soap had shriveled my hands into tiny crab-claws, and my body was now beyond sweat. Even Gasser had fallen silent. Ernie, poor Ernie, had entered the last and crucial phase of his approaching ordeal.

Curious thing about the truly deadening menial tasks: great stretches of time pass almost instantly. When you approach the animal state you also begin to lose the one characteristic that sets us apart from the rest of the earth's creatures, the blessed (or cursed) sense of Time. Anthropologists tell us that truly primitive man had no sense, to speak of, of the passing moments. The more civilized one becomes, the more conscious and fearful of the pas-sage of time. Maybe that's why the simple peasants live to enor-mous ages of a hundred and thirty years or more, while astronauts and nuclear physicists die in their forties. To the three of us, amid the scalding water and searing soap, there was no Time.

It is for this reason that I cannot honestly say how long our trial lasted. For all I know, it might have been a century or two. Maybe ten minutes. But I guess it to be more on the order of forty

years. It ended suddenly and totally without warning. The buck
brought in three more victims, and we were sprung.

Like our predecessors, like hunted rats, we scurried out, back
to the serving car, which now seemed incredibly cool and civilized. The car stood empty for the first time. Only the mess sergeant, alone, lounged casually against his stainless-steel rack,
smoking a Camel. All that remained of the torrent of food was a
simple aluminum colander piled high with apples. The sergeant
blew a thin stream of Camel smoke through his nostrils as he
smiled in benevolence upon us.

"You guys did good, real good. You kept 'em movin'. How 'bout
an apple?"

I grabbed an apple with my crab-claw and bit into its heavenly
crisp coolness, its glorious moistness, its . . .

It was at that moment that I became a lifelong apple worshiper.
I have often thought since of becoming the founder of the First
Church of the Revealed Apple.

We milled a bit, chomping on the McIntoshes.

"You guys can go back to your company any time you want
now. If you'd like to hang around here and cool off, be my guests.
And remember, you ain't gonna pull KP for at least sixty days.
How does that grab ya?"

The three of us, dressed only in our brown GI shorts, heavy GI
shoes, and salt-encrusted dog tags, were flooded, each of us, with
a sense of release. We had done a rotten, miserable, mountainous, incredibly rugged job and battled on until it was actually finished. "Hey, one of you guys help me with this goddamn door.
The bastard sticks."

The sergeant was struggling with a vast sliding panel that
formed part of the wall of the car. Gasser grabbed the handle and
the two of them slid the door back. A torrent of fresh air poured
into the car, flushing out the old cauliflower smells and the
aroma of countless mess kits and gamy socks.

"Would you look at that!" Gasser cheered. "The world is still
there."

Ernie hitched up his sweaty underwear shorts higher on his bony hips and the three of us surged to the door to watch the countryside roll by. The air was crisp and cool, yet tinged with a faint balminess. Hazy purple hills rolled on the horizon. Short scrub pines raced past the open door. The four of us, including the sergeant, were the only people on this sealed train—with the exception of the engineer and maybe his fireman—who were looking out at the beautiful world. The sergeant chain-lit another Camel.

"Any of you guys want a cigarette?" He waved his pack in the air. None of us smoked.

"Look, I ain't supposed to open this door except to air out the car, so if anyone asks you, that's what I was doin'."

I bit into my third apple and gazed up at the fleecy white clouds and the deep blue sky. The train was riding on a high raised track. The rough gravel walls of the embankment slanted steeply down to the fields below. A two-lane concrete road paralleled the track as it ran through farm fields and patches of pines. We were moving at a fair clip.

"Hey, Sergeant," Ernie asked, "where the hell are we? What state is this?"

We had been on the road for what seemed an eternity. The sergeant peered out at the landscape.

"Well"—he paused and took a deep drag—"if you was to ask me, I'd guess that we was someplace in Arkansas. Now that's just an educated guess."

"Arkansas!" Gasser said, and edged toward the door to get a closer look. "That's the last place I'd a'guessed."

The three of us watched a battered old pickup truck loaded with bushel baskets roll along for a while below us. The pale face of a girl peered up at us. A man in faded overalls and a railroad engineer's cap sat next to her, driving and puffing on a short fat cigar. We rode side by side for many seconds. She gazed at us; we gazed back. I waved. She glanced quickly at the mean-looking driver and then back at us. She waved timidly, as though she were afraid he might see her.

"Gee, that's a real Arkansas girl." Ernie sat down on the floor of the car with his legs hanging over the edge in the breeze.

"That's the first Arkansas person I have ever seen." Gasser and I sat beside him. Now all three of us had our legs hanging out over the racing roadbed. The girl in the truck glanced uneasily at the driver. She looked maybe thirteen or fourteen.

"Hey, do you think they are real hillbillies?" Gasser asked with great wonder and curiosity in his voice. He was from the West Coast, where hillbillies were something seen only in Ma and Pa Kettle films.

She continued to stare up at us. The old truck trailed blue smoke as it roared along. The three of us, who had not seen a female human being for many months, found her incredibly magnetic. Her long black hair trailed in the wind and billowed around her pale sharp features.

"You think that guy drivin' the Dodge is her father?" Gasser asked rhetorically. The sergeant, a man of the world, one who had seen all of life stream past the open doors of his mess car, said in his flat voice:

"Ten to one that's her husband."

"Ah, come on, you're kidding." Ernie found it hard to believe.

"Listen, you guys, in these hills it ain't nothin' for a fifty-year-old man to marry a twelve-year-old chick. What they say is, around here, 'If she's big enough she's old enough.' A virgin in these parts is any girl that can outrun her brothers." He flipped the butt end of his Camel neatly over our heads and out into the wind.

Silently the three of us watched the truck as it suddenly turned left into a gravel road lined with scraggly pines. It disappeared behind us in a cloud of dust. Ernie craned his neck out further into the slipstream to catch a last glimpse of the disappearing Dodge.

"Y'know, she was kind of cute," he said to no one in particular.

"Yep. She sure was, son." The sergeant was in a thoughtful expansive mood. "They all are in these hills. Eatin' all that fatback and grits must do som-pin to 'em. Lemme tell you one thing, and you listen. Don't you ever say nothin' like that 'she's cute' business around any of the men in these hills."

Gasser looked up from his rapt contemplation of the speeding gravel.

"What do you mean?"

"Every one of these shitkickers carries a double-barrel twelve-gauge Sears Roebuck shotgun in his pickup, for just that purpose alone. I'll bet that bastard would have blasted you quicker'n a skunk. He wouldn't think twice about it. Any sheriff around here'd probably give him a medal for doin' it."

"Hey, you guys, we're slowing up." I had noticed that gradually the train had been losing speed. The embankment was even higher here than it had been further back. The concrete road looked miles below us. I looked forward. Ahead, the long sealed train curved gently to the left like a great metal snake. Big green hills, vast vacant fields, and a few scraggly shacks trickled away to the horizon. There was some sort of trestle with lights and tanks a half-mile or so ahead of the train.

The sergeant looked over my shoulder to see what was going on. "We're probably stoppin' to take on another crew, or some water or som-pin."

Gradually, the train eased to a stop. For the first time in hours we did not sway. There was no rumble of trucks on the roadbed. We all sat in silence. The three of us sitting on the door sill, our legs hanging out over the gravel, enjoyed the bucolic scene. Birds twittered; a distant frog croaked. In the bright blue sky high above, a couple of chicken buzzards slowly circled.

At that precise instant events were set in motion that none of us would ever forget. It was Gasser who lit the fuse. Leaning forward so that his head extended far out into the soft, winy Arkansas air, he said:

"Do you guys see what I see?"

Ernie and I craned forward and looked in the direction Gasser had indicated. Down below us, far below us, was a dilapidated beaten-up old shack by the side of the concrete road. It looked like one of those countless roadside hovels that you see throughout the land on the back roads of America which appear to be made entirely of rusting Coca-Cola signs. It was deep in weeds and oil drums, but above it, swinging from a sagging iron crossbar, was a sign that bore one magic word:

BEER

There are few words that mean more under certain circumstances. All the thirst, the hungering insatiable throat-parching thirst earned during our sweaty backbreaking twenty-four hours of KP engulfed the three of us like a tidal wave of desire. Gasser, his tongue hanging out, dramatically gasped:

"Beer! Oh, God Almighty, what I wouldn't give for just one ice-cold, foamy, lip-smacking beer!"

Through the window of the shack we could see, dimly, a couple of red-necked natives happily hoisting away.

"Listen, you guys, I'm goin' forward to the can. You can leave for your company any time you care to. I'll see you guys around."

The sergeant disappeared from our lives forever. We were alone. Authority had gone to the can. The devil took over. I leaped to my feet.

"Listen, I got a couple of bucks in my fatigue jacket hanging right over there back of the table. I am prepared to buy if one of you is prepared to go and get it."

I scurried over to my fatigues and quickly brought back the two bucks. Already I could taste that heavenly elixir: ice cold and brimming with life. Beer! Real, non-GI, genuine beer!

Ernie looked at Gasser; Gasser looked at Ernie. We were one in our insane desire for a brew.

"Okay, you guys," I hissed, "guess how many fingers I'm holding up."

Gasser barked: "Two."

Ernie, his voice trembling with emotion, said: "Uh . . . one." He had sealed his fate. It was the last word we ever heard him utter.

"You're it, baby," I cheered, and handed him the two bucks. "Get as much as you can for this," I added.

Ernie grabbed the money and leaped lightly over the edge and down the steep gravel slope, his feet churning. He half-slid, half-ran down the long incline. We could hear the disappearing sounds of tiny gravel avalanches as he headed toward the shack. Ernie, like the two of us, was wearing only his sweat-stained brown GI underwear shorts, his GI shoes, and dog tags.

"Oh, man, I can taste that Schlitz already!" Gasser thumped on the floor in excitement with his right fist. "Yay, beer!" he cheered.

Below us, Ernie had entered the shack. We caught glimpses of his naked back through the window as the transaction was under way. Heads bobbed. Ernie glanced up at us and smiled broadly.

Seconds ticked by and then, without warning, the faint voices of shouting trainmen drifted back to us from far forward. At first I did not grasp their significance.

It has been wisely said many times that all of us are given clear warnings of disaster, but few of us bother to read the signs. Gasser peered toward the rear of the train.

"Jesus," he mumbled, "I never realized how long this bastard was."

The train stretched behind us almost to infinity, all the windows sealed against prying eyes, lurking enemies.

Time hung suspended amid the faint chirpings of crickets and the distant cawing of crows. Ernie's head reappeared briefly in the window. He held up a large paper sack in triumph. And then it happened.

eeeeeeeeeeeeeeeeeeeeeeee . . .

Like the distant wail of an avenging banshee, our sealed troop train shuddered a long menacing evil creak as it slowly began to move. I grabbed Gasser's arm.

"Gasser! We're moving!"

Gasser wordlessly leaned out to see if Ernie was on his way. The gravel inched slowly past our hanging feet. We were barely moving. Gasser soundlessly waved his arms, hoping that Ernie would get the message. We couldn't yell because at least fifty officers would have heard and known that we had done the one thing beyond all law, namely illegally leaving a top-security sealed troop movement. That's firing squad stuff.

Suddenly Ernie appeared at the side of the shack. He looked smaller, shorter, as he struggled through the weeds, carrying his precious sack of beer. At first he didn't seem to notice that the train was moving. Gasser and I both waved frantically. Already the train was gathering momentum.

"Oh, my God," Gasser gasped. "Oh, my God! Ernie!"

Ernie broke into a frantic run. Through the quiet air we could hear the distant clank of beer bottles and the thud-thud-thud of his GI shoes. He angled upward along the steep incline, slipping and sliding as he ran.

"Ah, he's got it made," Gasser said with relief as Ernie drew nearer and nearer.

At first it really did look like there was no problem. Ernie pounded toward us, his right arm cradling the bag of beer like a halfback lugging a football. The train moved faster and faster, but Ernie was closing the gap. Then he hit a patch of loose shale. He slid down the side of the bank, his legs churning.

Gasser, clinging to the back edge of the car, extended his hand far out into the breeze.

"Ernie! Grab my hand! ERNIE!"

Ernie's eyes rolled wildly as he struggled on. His left hand reached high, his fingers within inches of Gasser's grasping mitt.

The engine of our train let go a long, moaning blast. I sometimes hear this in my sleep, ringing hollow and lost, like a death knell.

I grabbed Gasser's knees to hold him in the car. "I'll hold your legs, Gasser," I grunted. "Grab him!"

Gasser leaned even further out over the racing gravel. I braced my feet on the floor, fear clutching my gut like an octopus. Gasser kept saying over and over again: "Oh, Jesus Christ, oh, Jesus Christ, Christ Almighty . . ."

Peering between Gasser's straining legs I saw Ernie's contorted exhausted face, his legs pounding weaker and weaker.

clink-clink-clink-clink-clink-clink . . .

The sound of his dog tags jingled with each painful stride.

. . . clink-clink-clink.

And then all three of us knew it. He was not going to make it.

Ernie was gone. But he pounded on, dropping further and further behind. He had become a tiny distant stick-man, naked and alone. He still clung to the beer.

The mess car was now swaying and rocking along at almost full speed. We both gazed outward at Ernie's tiny figure, still hopelessly striding along down on the sad two-lane country road. The sun was going down over the distant hills. The sky had purpled.

As the faint clink-clink-clink-clink of Ernie's dog tags receded forever into limbo, both Gasser and I knew without exchanging a word that we had been part of a historic moment. At the time, naturally, we didn't realize that the Legend of Ernie would grow and grow until every enlisted man in the Signal Corps knew his name and would tell the story of the GI who was lost from the sealed troop train. Some, naturally, don't believe he ever existed. After all, as a people we Americans prefer to believe that all heroic figures were frauds and shams. But I was there. I knew Ernie.

The train rounded a great bend. We entered the gloom of a high Arkansas valley. Gasser got to his feet. I followed. Without a word we donned our fatigues and headed back to Company K, men bearing a fear and a grief that few know in their lifetime.

As we inched our way through car after car, amid seas of alien troops, we held our own counsel. Back in *The Georgia Peach*, Company K lay sprawled, travel-stained by the long trip. Listless eyes gazed at us as we went back to our seats. I eased myself down into the scratchy mohair. Gasser glanced up and down the car before taking his seat. He whispered:

"Play it cool. Don't tell 'em a goddamn thing."

We sat, and for a moment we both feigned sleep. Lieutenant Cherry loomed over us.

"The mess sergeant tells me you guys did a real fine job, and I want you to know I'm proud of you, y'hear?"

He patted Gasser's shoulder and moved on back toward the rear of the car where Ernie had once sat. Seconds later he returned.

"Hey, you guys, where's Ernie?"

"Uh . . ." I beamed up at the lieutenant, wearing my Innocent face, the one that had gotten me out of endless hassles in the past. "Uh . . . gee, Lieutenant . . . hehheh . . . I don't know. I guess he . . ."

Gasser chimed in, his voice sounding as phony as a latex fourteen-dollar bill:

"He must be in the latrine. Yeah, he must be in the latrine, Lieutenant, sir."

"Fellows, the latrines have been locked up for over an hour for cleaning."

The lieutenant, sensing trouble the way all good officers can, leaned forward and peered deeply into both of our souls, his silver bars gleaming with all the weight of the U. S. Congress behind them.

"Where. Is. Ernie?"

He waited, a long, pregnant wait. I knew it was no use. I felt Gasser sag in the seat next to me.

"Lieutenant," I said. "Lieutenant, we lost Ernie."

Lieutenant Cherry's face aged ten years; his skin the parchment white of an old man. His glasses glinted in the yellow light of *The Georgia Peach.*

"You lost Ernie?"

Dumbly, we both stared up at him, terror-stricken. He repeated his plaint, his primal query:

"You lost ERNIE?"

Gasser, his voice sobbing a little like the air coming out of a deflating birthday balloon, squeaked:

"You see, Lieutenant, he . . . this . . . ah . . . that is, we . . . there was this stop and . . . we all wanted a beer, and there was this place, and . . ."

His voice cracked, his sentences were broken and incoherent.

Suddenly Lieutenant Cherry leaned lower. His voice came in a hush:

"Listen, you two," he whispered tensely, "don't you ever say a word to anyone about this. Do you realize I'll have to sign a Statement of Charges if this gets out? It's bad enough if you wreck a jeep, but to lose a Pfc from a sealed troop train!"

He paused, his eyes gleaming through his GI glasses.

"Don't you mention a word of this. I'll fix it somehow through Headquarters."

He disappeared, his shoulders hunched with care. We never heard another word of Ernie in Company K. No one ever mentioned his name again.

There are times when I awake at 3 A.M. from a fitful sleep hearing the clink-clink-clink of poor Ernie's dog tags. Ernie, lost forever in Arkansas, wearing only his GI underwear, forever AWOL, a fugitive from a sealed troop train. Is he out there yet, a haggard wraith living on berries and dead frogs? A fearful outcast? Does he know the war is over? That all wars are past?

The clink-clink-clink of Ernie's dog tags says nothing.

I stared unseeing through my bug-spotted windshield, lost in a labyrinthine reverie, seeing the faces of the soldiers I had known from that star-crossed company of military maladroit misfits, a true Company of Fools. Elkins. Gasser. Nye, of the steel-trap mind, doing humiliating push-ups in the scorching sun while the duty corporal . . . what was his name? Barney? Bernie? No, BENNY. Travers. Yes, that was the bastard's name. And poor Nye passing out from the heat, and never talking much afterward. And Goldwater. Jesus Christ, Goldwater, the bullshitter, who got four-foot-long kosher salamis sent from home while all we got was busted cookies, and Warner, Pfc Warner, who never got promoted above that one measly little stripe in spite of his 165 IQ and his ability to play whole symphonies, including the horn parts, on the piano by ear. And the captain from The Citadel, who cried because somebody busted the mirror in the cigarette machine.

A roaring van pulled up alongside me in the right-hand lane. A bearded primitive, shirtless, hunched over the wheel. It hit me: I'll bet Ernie never saw a van. All the other lost ones would never have suspected what a mad world we now live in.

I've always wondered why no real literature of The Road ever came out of America, a country that for at least three quarters of the twentieth century has lived on its turnpikes and toll roads. Maybe that's why so much of Country music is valid poetry of our time: "The Interstate Is a'Comin' Through My Outhouse," "White Line Fever," "The Carroll County Accident." This stuff gets to the core of it.

I imagined a future sociologist lecturing on various aspects of The Car to future classes.

Sociology 101
(Hip Division)

Today, class, we are going to take up the brief study of one of the true curiosities of late twentieth-century American life, a sub-strata of the population which I shall herein designate as The Van Culture. There has not been much written about this in literature; hence I feel strongly that it is time to put it down for the record, a whole way of life that has evolved, quietly, without notice of the more official sociologists and compulsive categorizers of the American scene. It revolves around that homely product of automotive technology known generically as The Van.

The Van Culture, loosely speaking, is an offshoot of an earlier culture which I hereby designate the VW People. They bear little if any resemblance to The Camper Crowd, although there are some superficial, very superficial, points of resemblance. Obviously, their vehicles have some similarities, such as unwieldiness, bulk, and a marked tendency to flip in any crosswind hitting more than 20 mph in gusts. Also, both types of vehicle can be used for sleeping purposes and for lugging large crowds over the landscape. After that, the resemblances cease.

The Winnebago or Camper Crowd tends to be dedicated family types, somewhat overweight, highly conservative politically, extremely fertile, and usually middle-aged, regardless of their chronological age. They read the *Readers' Digest, Field & Stream, The American Legion Monthly, TV Guide*, and can be heard any time of the day or night endlessly blabbing back and forth over their beloved CB radios, using such terms as "Code Seven," "Ten-Four," etc., picked up by watching "Adam 12" in reruns, one of their all-time favorite TV shows.

On the other hand, The Van People tend to be heavily bearded, dedicated lifetime subscribers to *Rolling Stone*, compulsive consumers of granola, and they often pride themselves on making their own yoghurt. Their social habits tend to a distinct aversion to marriage unless it is performed by a guru or a Navaho shaman standing knee-deep in the waters of Gitchee-Goomie while the assembled company bays in concert to the moon, evoking the Great Wolf God, which is guaranteed to bestow eternal happiness and good vibes forever.

In spite of the fact that a considerable number of them are now rapidly approaching their fifties, they remain forever nineteen. As for their political views, when they bother to vote at all they will cast their ballot for any black on the ticket, or, if no black is running, a woman. Their perfect candidate for any office would be a black woman, and ideally a black homosexual woman who once worked in the lettuce fields and has a strong dash of Cheyenne blood in her veins.

At this point, class, I feel it necessary to point out that I—personally—am making no value judgments, merely describing for the record some of the more significant movements of our time, the last quarter of the twentieth century.

Both groups, The Van Culture and The Camper Crowd, seem to enjoy plastering their respective vehicles with various bits of propaganda material designed to prove, apparently, to the world at large that the souls and hearts of the inmates of said vehicle are in the right place. It is in the actual contents, philosophically speaking, of the messages that the sharp divergence of the two cultures can be seen. The Camper Crowd is forever proclaiming proudly its married togetherness: The Murchisons; Al & Frieda

Bugleblast; Betty, Bob, Ronnie, Bonnie, Donnie, and Rover. This is often accompanied by a frank admission of their home base, regardless of how dismal it may be. Kalamazoo, Michigan, Jackson, Mississippi, Teaneck, New Jersey, Frankfurt, Indiana, seem to be among the more popular locales. This is often accompanied in large block letters by the proud CB call sign: KFU 9768, apparently the assumption being that passing mobs of like persuasion would care to communicate, instantly, with Al and Frieda and presumably Bonnie Jean and Rover. They also enjoy proclaiming publicly their never-ending cheerfulness; displaying such bumper stickers as: Have a Good Day, Have You Tried Smiling? and often Christ Is the Answer or Honk If You Love Jesus.

On the political side, their stickers usually radiate suspicion of the world at large and often downright paranoia: Fight Godless Communism, Gun Control Laws Mean Only Criminals Have Guns, People Kill; Not Guns, and that all-time favorite America– Love It or Leave It.

On the other hand, The Van People are fond of plastering their equipment with such goodies as: Danger–I Brake for Animals (apparently on the assumption that the mean old Others are endlessly and maliciously bashing their cars into goats, pigs, elderly St. Bernards, draft horses, mud turtles, and other lowly creatures with which we share this planet), Have You Thanked a Green Plant Today? Boycott Lettuce (Grapes, California Tomatoes, Kohlrabi), War Is Bad for Children and Other Living Things, and No Nukes! They, like their Camper brethren, feel compelled to advertise their political views through the medium of decals and stickers: Anderson–the Only Choice, Ban Hand Guns, Third World Power (Woman Power, Gay Power, Indian Power, Chicano Power, Granola Power).

The Van Culture shares with The Camper Crowd a compulsion to advertise its interpersonal relationships, although in a very different fashion. While The Camper Crowd seems to be very specific (Al & Frieda & the Kids), The Van Culture deals only in generalities (Love) (Peace), although just whom it loves or

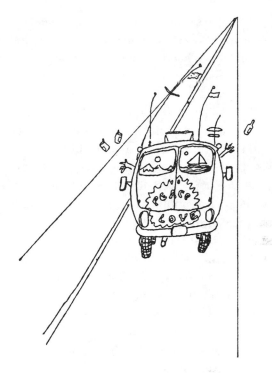

whom it is at peace with is never, ever specified (. . . I gotta keep my options open, baby).

The Van Culture appears to be, at least publicly, highly conscious of our environment. At any rate, that's what its signs say: Don't Pollute, Ecology Is for People and Dogs and Everybody, Honor Earth, Return the Earth to the People, No Nukes! These last seem to assume that vans don't pollute while Pintos do, and that the diet Dr. Pepper that The Van Culture is forever swilling comes in more ecologically compatible cans than the Pabst Blue Ribbon that The Camper Crowd tends to guzzle.

Both groups have one overwhelming trait in common—they share intense self-approval. If I were less kind I would use the word "smug," but since I'm a very kind person and am always considerate of the feelings of others and bear a total love for my fellow man (I should say fellow "person"), naturally, I cannot use this word. Future social historians, I firmly believe, are going to study the various strata in our society and their significance to the time by standards other than the old-fashioned class divisions such as economic, educational, racial, and ethnic.

All these lines are blurring rapidly, while such new social divisions as The Camper Crowd and The Van Culture are becoming more sharply defined. Incidentally, there is a newly emergent subgroup under The Van Culture that could be called The Used School Bus Tribe. I wonder what would happen to the drug traffic here in the United States if all vans magically disappeared in one puff of smoke. It is a little-known but highly significant fact that a vast percentage of quick drug buys are made out of vans. It truly could be said that a pusher who drives a van is, in fact, a Wheeler Dealer. This twist that the van has taken is somewhat ironic, since back in the early days of this type of vehicle it was first touted to the public with ads showing cool, well-educated mommies, social science majors all, obviously well-heeled suburbanites, vanning a crowd of well-scrubbed kids, off to the Little League, or camp, or whatever. Daddy taught Economics at a local junior college, wore thick glasses, religiously read the *New Republic*, and cherished his membership in the Adlai Stevenson I'm Proud I'm an Egghead club. These same apple-cheeked kids grew up to push smack out of an identical van from a parking lot outside a shopping center in Fort Lauderdale. This has nice overtones of the Theater of the Absurd.

On the other hand, The Camper Crowd has seen its beloved conveyance put to other than clean-limbed, nature-loving purposes. For example, a notorious string of Mafia-controlled bordellos operated very successfully (and in fact still do) out of a string of true Recreational Vehicles, complete with red plush interiors, brass spittoons, and in at least one case, a four-channel tape deck specializing in Turn-of-the-Century Whorehouse Piano.

The driving styles of both sects are as opposed as their philosophies. The Camper Crowd seems to be totally oblivious of any other machine on the road, ponderously rumbling with tank-like stolidity right down the exact middle of the turnpike. I have seen three hundred cars held up for hours by two or three strategically placed campers.

Naturally, there are exceptions in both groups and you'll occasionally see a lunatic Winnebago driver careening along at eighty-five plus, reminding you of nothing so much as a runaway Cape Cod house on wheels with a baboon at the tiller, but generally The Camper Crowd's driving style is as conservative as its politics.

In contrast, The Van Culture mostly drives its badly sprung, unstable, underbraked, high center of gravity, overloaded hulks as though they were so many Porsches. In fact, recently in a Howard Johnson on the Jersey Turnpike I got into a rap with a Jersey state cop who spends the days of his life patrolling the infamous NJP.

COP: Boy, I sure need this cup of coffee.

ME: How come?

COP: Me and my partner just pulled another crowd of van freaks outta the burning wreckage.

ME: Great Scott! Was it bad?

COP: Bad? You shoulda seen it. Even their designer jeans was on fire. One guy had an Afro that was burnin' so that LaGuardia coulda used it as a landing beacon.

ME: Holy smokes!

COP: That ain't funny. Not funny at all.

ME: I'm sorry. I didn't mean it that way. It's just a figure of speech. You say they were driving a van?

COP: Well, it was before they pranged it. Naturally, there was about fifteen or twenty kids in the back sleepin' off something, and the boob that was drivin' musta been going ninety-five.

ME: Ninety-five?

COP: Buddy, all van freaks drive 'em flat out. They love to tailgate. Don't ask me why, they just do. This one had *Ecology Is a Gas* written all over the sides in spray paint. Also a picture of the Grand Canyon at sunset.

ME: Gee, that's too bad. How many fatalities?

COP: Are you kiddin'? Ain't you ever heard the old saying "God protects drunks and heads"?

ME: Well, I'll be damned.

COP: It looked like there was at least thirty of them, staggering around in the bushes with their T-shirts on fire, hollering, "Far out," "Dynamite." Me and Al hosed 'em down with CO_2. For once they didn't kill nobody in another car, like that kind usually does. They just got caught in a mean crosswind doin' ninety-five and that old van went airborne and just left the road, hopped a culvert, and that was all she wrote. She flipped over a couple times and them heads spilled outta her like two pounds of dried beans leavin' a one-pound plastic baggie.

ME: Wow!

COP: Yeah, you can say that. I got one word of advice. Watch out for them vans. They love to tailgate, y'hear?

He got up, paid for his coffee, and left.

It was after this discussion that I got to thinking about the whole new Van Culture and all the good things it's brought to America; a new sense of togetherness for one. By the very nature of the van it tends to create crowds, and this can have, ultimately, a profound effect on our social structure, perhaps bringing together human beings after the splintering of the family group during the latter days of the seventies.

In fact, it's already happening. The Charles Manson family was carted around over the landscape by its guru in a succession of vans, stolen and otherwise. The old Spahn ranch was never without a half-dozen vans liberally larded with *Peace* signs and *Love* stickers, all gassed up and ready to go out on another exciting hit. In fact, several of the murders attributed to the Family were over disputed ownership of vans. Manson also utilized a used school bus, seats removed, carpeted with old rugs, to house his bevy of love-conscious females before they finally settled down to good solid family life at the ranch. In one sense, Manson was a true social innovator.

So there you have it, class. Today's discussion of The Van Culture. I don't find it necessary to remind you that questions about this subject will appear on the blue book exam at the end of this semester.

I've done a lot of writing over the years about cars. I really do believe that in many ways, automobiles are one of the very few universal realities of American life in our century, like the horse was to people before 1900.

The horse. My mind greedily grasped at a new thought. I glanced in the mirror. The guy behind me seemed to have fallen asleep.

I play these little games when in cars alone, or in reception rooms waiting for Mr. Big to summon me. Sort of like Twenty Questions: the words that the horse has contributed to our language: Put on the feed bag, Horse feathers, Put out to pasture, Horse of another color, stop Horsing around.

I chuckled. That's what I'm doing, horsing around. How come the car hasn't done the same thing? Hmmm. That's certainly a Chevy of another color. He's going out to suck on the old gas pump.

Not bad. I remembered one madly self-destructive moment I perpetrated as a writer. I banged on the steering wheel. Why the hell do I always do these things?

General Motors publishes a magazine called Friends. *It is a cheery, well-produced, colorful little monthly that, I guess, goes to people who buy Chevys. Maybe the name* Friends *means that if you buy a Chevy, you're one of their friends.*

Anyway, in all innocence, they asked me to do a piece. So what did I do?

Lemons on the Grass, Alas

Well, I had my semi-annual lunch the other day with my friend Howard. Howard and I shared KP together in the Army, and there's something about pulling KP with a guy that draws you together. Howard works at a small but highly respected public relations agency known on Madison Avenue as "B&W." Actually, their full name is Bugle and Weakfish, but "B&W" has more snap to it.

I found him in the gloom of the elegant bar of Les Miserables du Frite, a French watering hole frequented exclusively by expense account types. Actual money–dollars and quarters and stuff–hasn't been seen in Les Miserables du Frite since the Truman administration. Howard was staring gloomily into his triple Wild Turkey on the rocks. I eased onto the stool beside him.

"Hi." I greeted him coolly, as is the practice in these expense account joints, since everyone pretends he is at a business meeting and not a social whoopee. You never know when the bartender may be an undercover agent for the IRS.

"How are you, Old Sport?" I asked over my daiquiri.

"Rotten," he muttered. "I mean rotten. This has been one hell of a day." He took a deep slug of his Wild Turkey, making his eyes water. I could see he really was in a foul mood.

"Well, what's up, Howard?"

"Did you by any chance read the damn automobile want ads in the *Times* this morning? The Classic & Foreign section?" He angrily chomped at a pretzel.

"Why no, Howard, I can't say that I did. What's the flap?"

He instantly whipped a tattered clipping out of his jacket pocket, glared at it, and barked:

"Let me read you this: 'Sixteen-thousand-dollar Lemon for sale: 1979 Anaconda XGD Super-Wasp, retailing for thirty-one thousand plus available now at above price. Will supply buyer with twenty-four free bottles of Excedrin, which he will need, plus long list of Anaconda Super-Wasp dealers who claim they cannot fix this magnificent Lemon. No dealers please.' "

He slammed the clipping down on the bar in anger. "God knows how many people read that this morning! The phone's been ringing from all over the country, and I may lose the damned account, just because of this horse's backside, whoever he is!"

There was a long, pregnant pause, and all I could think of to say was: "Gee, Howie, I'm sorry. I didn't know you had the Anaconda account."

Howard snorted and laughed a bitter, creaking laugh. "Are you kidding? I never had a car account in my life. Wouldn't touch 'em." He swirled his drink with a swizzle stick like a man poking at a nest of hooded cobras.

"Well, then, what's all the flap?" I asked.

"I am the number-one man on the NLGA account, brother, the big honcho, and I can tell you the fat is truly in the fire!"

"N-L-G-A?" I asked. "Isn't that one of those new basketball leagues?"

"Look, buddy"—Howard sounded very serious—"I am in no mood for funnies, not today. The NLGA, for your information, is the National Lemon Growers Association, and I can tell you, the lemon industry has had it up to here with all this bad-mouthing lemons. Every time some fatheaded car company turns out a bummer, what does everyone call it? A lemon! Why a lemon, I ask you? Why not a cantaloupe, or a banana? For my money, bananas are a hell of a lot funnier than lemons. And you notice they use the word 'lemon' as a put-down? If something is bad, it's a lemon, meaning, of course lemons are bad."

Howard paused for breath. His face was getting a bit purple. His neck muscles were bulging.

"Gosh," I said soothingly, "I never thought of that, Howard. You're right. My old man used to call his Hudson 'the lemon of the century,' but until this very moment I never thought why bad cars are called lemons and not watermelons or cabbages."

Howard began speaking again in a low monotone, as one speaks in a bad dream:

"The NLGA spends millions every year trying to upgrade the lemon image, and one bird-brained ding-dong takes an ad out in the *Times* and blows it! Someday I'm just gonna quit this racket and take up fly-tying. It's not easy being a PR man for a lemon, I can tell you that."

"Oh well," I said, trying to calm troubled waters, "what the hell, we all have our troubles, Howard."

He thought about this for a moment and then answered in a thoughtful tone, "Yes, that is true. Have you ever heard of the BNAs?"

"No. Is that a new wonder drug?"

Howard chuckled. "BNA stands for Bad News Accounts. It's a little group of us account men who have really bad accounts. We meet every Friday after work at Michael's Pub and get drunk together. Misery loves company, and every one of us, to get in the group, has to have a really bad news account. Me, I got lemons."

We ordered another round of drinks and, to be polite, I asked him, "What are some of the other BNA's? I mean, what kind of accounts are they?"

"Well," Howard said, "there's old Pres Schuyler for example. Prescott Schuyler III. Dartmouth. You'd think he had the world tied up in a blue ribbon with silver filigree bells on it. Y'know what? He represents the ABA."

"Come on, Howie," I interrupted, "now I know they're a basketball crowd."

"Not Pres's ABA," Howard snorted. "He represents the American Baloney Alliance. This is the national association of baloney makers, and let me tell you, Schuyler is fighting an uphill battle with that one. Everywhere you turn, somebody is hollering at somebody else: 'That's a bunch of baloney,' or 'What a lot of baloney that is, you fathead.' Always bad-mouthing baloney. Nobody ever says, 'What you just said is liverwurst, or salami, or olive pimento loaf.' It's always baloney that gets put down. They do it on TV! Kojak is always saying to some drug pusher, 'That's baloney. Now gimme the real dope.' One day Schuyler's gonna kill himself. He can't get anyone to say a good word for baloney."

"Frankly, Howard," I said, "I'll never use those phrases again myself. Are there others?"

"Yep. How 'bout poor Herbie Morrison and the TBPA? That's a real bad one."

"TBPA?" I asked.

"Turkey Breeders' Protective Association. Every time a real stinkeroo opens on Broadway, what do they call it? A turkey! Why not a duck? For my money, a duck is a damn sight funnier than a turkey. Or maybe an ostrich. No, it's always a turkey! Burt Reynolds' last three pictures almost killed poor Herb. It was turkey-turkey-turkey, night and day. Sometimes he comes to our meetings and just sits in the corner and cries." Howard brushed away a tear.

"Well, how do you fight this thing?" I asked.

"Well," Howard went on pensively, "we try everything. For example, we spent about a quarter of a million tracking down just how this damn lemon business began. And we found out that it all started with some dumb clodhopper named Bergen W. Clutterback, who was a dirt-track racer in Kalamazoo, Michigan. He sold plows on the side. Well, in 1903 he got beat by six laps in a ten-lap race at the Kalamazoo Fair. He was driving an Ajax-Kavanaugh Kangaroo. After the race, the press quoted him as saying: 'This dang pile of junk ain't got no more spunk than a three-cent sour lemon.' The phrase caught on, and ever since, bad news cars are invariably lemons. We tried to counteract it by releasing press blurbs to the effect that Clutterback never saw a

lemon in his life, and furthermore, was quite possibly a blood relative of Clayton L. Clutterback, Jr., a notorious checkkiter and
confidence man from West Pumphandle, Kentucky, and hence a
man not to be trusted in any way. Not a single damn car magazine ever carried the story! And why? Because they like to call
cars lemons, that's why! It sure as hell beats me. We elected a National Lemon Queen, and do you think that Johnny Carson interviewed her? Are you kidding? We had a forty-six-page *Lemon
Lovers' Cookbook* published. It cost a bundle. In six months it
sold a hundred and forty-eight copies. And now this damn want
ad in the *Times*!"

I cleared my throat and made another game attempt to cheer
up my friend. "Well, Howard, it's true that you and the lemon
people, and the baloney and the turkey guys, are fighting an uphill battle. But there must be plenty of people who have it worse
than you."

The bartender brought us another round and set another dish
of pretzels down in front of Howard.

"Yeah," he muttered, "I suppose that's true. Lemons ain't so
bad, I suppose. It could be a lot worse. Every time I have a really
rotten day I remind myself of what happened to poor old Sylvester
Snead. Over at Y&R. You probably read about it. It happened
three, maybe four months ago, but already it seems like years
back. He was one of the nicest guys I ever knew."

"Yeah," I interrupted, "I think I read something about him.
Sylvester Snead. A *Times* obit, am I right?"

"Yep"–Howard's voice sounded sad and a little tired–"went off
the George Washington Bridge at high noon. Just couldn't take it
any more. He was the founder of the BNAs. Old Sylvester began
the club, and I can tell you we all miss him. And since he's gone,
it ain't the same without him. He had the worst account of all.
Had the account for seven years, longer than anybody in history."

Howard moodily dipped into the pretzels. Hesitantly, I asked,
"What was his account?"

"The ICM. That's what killed him! I wake up nights in a cold sweat, afraid they're gonna assign that damn account to me. The ICM is one of our top accounts, but I—personally—would just as soon have a good case of leprosy. Lemons are bad enough!"

"ICM . . " I mused. "Don't they make some kind of computers or something?"

Howard rolled his ice cubes angrily. "Buddy, if they did, Sylvester would still be with us today, telling his rotten jokes and playing handball. ICM does not make computers, not by a long shot."

"Okay, Howard, let's have it," I said. "ICM means what?"

Howard, with his inborn sense of dramatics working at full blast, intoned: "International Crock Manufacturers."

"My God!" I gasped. "Poor Sylvester!"

"Now you know what some guys have to face." Howard wearily sipped the last of his drink. "Sylvester spent his life fighting the phrase 'It's a crock! A crock of what? Well, both you and I know. Nobody ever says, 'It's a cup,' or 'It's a galvanized pail.' No, it's always a crock, and it finally killed poor old Sylvester. And one day lemons are gonna get me."

My agent nearly killed me for that one. In fact, she said that she would much rather handle a writer who is a drunken bum than one who deliberately bites the hand that feeds him. Madness, all is madness. What could I say to her, that if I had been born in India I would have been one of those guys who spends his life stretched out on a bed of nails, peering up at the sun? Actually, I did tell her that. She did not laugh. Neither did the editor of Friends *magazine. I had lost my only friend at Chevrolet.*

The little electric car that runs on the track along the wall of the tunnel whipped past me, driven by a tired-looking cop wearing a crash helmet. He was heading toward the front of the line, and the trouble that had brought on the blinking yellow light.

"Christ," I muttered, "what a job. Being a cop and spending your life in the goddamn tunnel." Do they still have eyes, or are they like those fish that live in the caves?

I studied the tile wall of the tunnel next to me. No graffiti. Must be the only public wall in any city in America that doesn't have illiterate crap scrawled all over it by the barbaric horde.

Strange thing, this tunnel. You go through it all your life, and you hardly ever think of it. I remember watching a 4 A.M. movie in a hotel room, and it turned out to be about a bunch of tough guys building the tunnel. It was called Sand Hogs or something, and Victor McLaglen had his shirt off all the time and was covered with sweat. Truly heroic. How come they don't make movies about stuff like that any more, about guys that really do things? The world has been overrun by a niggling, scurrying pack of Al Pacinos, Woody Allens, and Dustin Hoffmans.

I hunched in my steaming car, musing on and on into further, more alien destructive areas. How about a movie about the guys who built the Verrazano Bridge? That's a hell of a thing. I suppose today the only movie you could sell would be a bunch of guys blowing up the Verrazano Bridge, led by Lee Marvin and his gang of crazies. Well, we live in self-destructive times, and I'm right in there with the rest, right? With that "Lemons" piece.

Four or five cars in my line began honking angrily. This wait was getting to us.

A giant New Jersey commuter bus in the other lane stopped. I felt a row of commuter eyes peering down into my lap. It had a four-color advertising sign emblazoned on its side, plugging an elegant English gin, tropical shores, sparkling seas, and waving palm trees. I studied the scene. A gin and tonic would taste good down here in the bowels of the pyramids. I gazed hungrily at the gin ad. The beach scene looked far more real than anything down here. Probably was. The commercials today are more real than the products. Means transcending ends.

If this goddamn tunnel collapsed with all of us down here, a thousand years from now they'd dig up the bus and there would be that picture. I imagined the art director of the agency in conference with the gin guys; endless hassling over the second palm tree from the right, and whether the girl should wear sandals or not. I had been there. New York, the commercial capital of the world, like Paris used to be the art capital.

The cardboard water sparkled, the trees rustled silently, and the crystal bottle of gin looked cold and remote.

The Lost Civilization
of Deli

The expedition had been working the site, with minimal success, for some time. Tempers were frayed. Even the most civilized and erudite members of the party were nipping at one another. The rains, alternating with the searing heat, had worn down all of them. That and, of course, the looming sense of failure. None of them, in spite of earlier optimism, had the vaguest idea that they were about to make a strike that would rival, and indeed surpass, the discovery of the fabled Rosetta Stone of millennia past.

Little was known of the area where the expedition was working. The few facts, only partially substantiated, were that thousands of years or more in the opaque past a great city had flourished on the site. The area had been under the sea for centuries during the last Ice Age and had only re-emerged in recent geological times.

There was much dispute and there were many theories about what this settlement had once been called. A few hints were available to scholars who could decipher and understand the scarce archeological references, which were all in an ancient, dead language. It had been fairly well established that the site had been known as the Big Apple, which led to a theory, since it was known that apple referred to some sort of fruit, that the place had been devoted to agriculture. A small but vocal element of academics, admittedly unorthodox in their views, had recently unearthed a reference or two among the fragmentary records of the past to something called Fun City. The translation of the word *city* was sure, meaning a large, organized gathering of creatures, but a battle was still raging over the meaning of the word *fun*. Some felt that it was used in reference to a religion of the time. Others scoffed, maintaining that the civilization being studied had no discernible

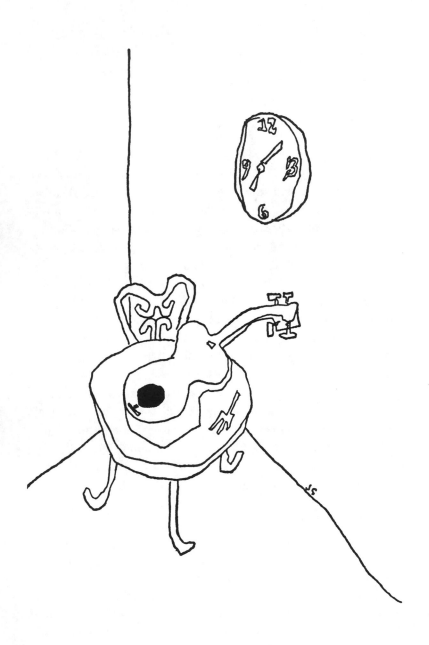

religion and hence "Fun" was just a meaningless proper name of no significance. Then, of course, there had been the discovery of that curious, deeply buried monolith that read QUEENS PLAZA IND, which, according to a recent treatise, pointed to the conclusion that the settlement had been some sort of matriarchy, if in fact there had been any form of government at all.

But to the members of this expedition, all such views were merely speculative. What was real was the mud, the boredom, and the lack of rest. The leader had considered closing out the operation and in fact had already begun to compose in his mind the message that he would send back to headquarters informing those in control of his decision, when the big strike occurred, a find that was to open up the truth of this ancient lost civilization in all its bizarre romantic glory and barbaric splendor, far more revealing than any of the poor fables and tepid myths these peoples had left behind, which they called Art and Literature. These childish scrawls had dealt mainly with the endless pursuit of something they termed sex, or even more curious, self-fulfillment. Little was ever mentioned about the actual life, the day-to-day existence of the bygone times. But today's epic discovery would change all that.

Like many significant finds, this strike came about as a result of a fortuitous accident, deep in the tunnel that had so far yielded nothing but disappointing bits and pieces of incomplete artifacts, although one curious, perhaps meaningful minor find had been made. A number of small plates bearing the enigmatic inscription IBM Selectric had surfaced. According to the leading technicians, these plates had apparently been attached to some kind of machine, although its use was not known.

The machines themselves had long since largely disintegrated. Only a few cogs and wheels had survived the millennia. One small container made of an unknown flexible substance had been found. It bore the inscription DANNON YOGURT, which was obviously the proper name of a long-dead native who had used this receptacle for some purpose or other as yet not established. Other digs had unearthed quantities of these containers, which indicated that YOGURT was a very numerous tribe, rivaled only by one that appeared to be called DELI and a third named, enigmatically, CHOCK FULL O' NUTS.

A brace had given way, causing a large section of the tunnel wall to collapse, partly blocking the passageway. Members of the expedition quickly moved to clear away the mud and other debris. Suddenly they beheld a sight that none of them would ever forget. A great gray metal vault gleamed dully under the lights. The leader was summoned immediately. The very air was charged with excitement as he peered at the mysterious discovery. A small label attached to the front bore the inscrutable letters BBD&O and, in smaller script, TV 60 SEC COMMERCIALS.

With a sense of scientific history being made, the cabinet, after being suitably measured and photographed, was carefully opened. The interior revealed row upon row of reels wound with a sort of film. The lowermost compartment contained, in absolutely perfectly preserved condition, a device that was obviously to be used in conjunction with the mysterious reels. The party was jubilant, but even in their joy they had little appreciation as yet of their stupendous find.

Months later, in the laboratory, all the work and disappointment paid off. A new, startling vision of this ancient extinct civilization burst upon the scholars and scientists like a thunderbolt. For months there had been intensive research into the connection between the mysterious machine and the reels, and at long last, through a series of keen deductions, it had been found that the device had been used to project images from the reels so that they could be viewed. A carefully selected group of high-level personages had assembled for the first viewing of some of the reels. The lights were dimmed. There was absolute silence as each observer waited for a true vision of the past. Then there came a whirring sound from the rear of the room. Ancient symbols flashed on the screen: X-X-X-8-7-6-5-4-3-2-1.

And then it happened. A spectacular scene so stupefying in its effect as to boggle the mind blazed forth before them. A dozen figures dressed in colorful, crisp uniforms danced and cavorted wildly, their teeth flashing, their footwork remarkable. High above them, gleaming in the brilliant sunlight, were two Olympian golden arches. As they danced, their rhythmic chant, pulsing with primitive vigor and abandon, boomed deafeningly:

> *"We do it all for yoo hoo hoo . . .*
> *We do it all for yoo hoo hoo!"*

The scene quickly changed and a manic, wild crowd of natives, who appeared to be arranged in family groupings of various colors, their teeth sparkling, eyeballs rolling, consumed vast quantities of mysterious round, spongy objects. The dancers in their uniforms reappeared, intoning: "We do it all for yoo hoo hoo!" The family members, many of whom appeared to be immature, or possibly a subspecies, grew more agitated as they ate voraciously. The arches suddenly reappeared, then darkness.

The observers sat in stunned silence. Then pandemonium broke loose. The leading scholar of them all lurched upright. His voice shaking with emotion, he blurted, "Nothing we have studied even hinted at what they were really like! None of their famous authors or artists even suggested anything like this!" He sat shaking with emotion, unable to speak further.

"More! More!" they shouted. No longer was this a solemn gathering of minds.

"More! More!"

Again the machine whirred in the darkness. The numbers came and went. Another horde of celebrants appeared, if anything even more manic and wildly contorting than the previous tribe. They seemed to be at the seaside, on a sandy beach, dressed in outlandish pagan costumes of staggering immodesty. They leaped about madly, striking balls with extreme childish delight. Again a deafening chorus intoned another chant:

> *"Join the Pepsi Generation, come alive, come alive!"*

A sudden close-up of one crazed native caught him frantically sucking at some sort of small urn, or container. His frenzy increased as he was joined by a female, also sucking a similar container.

"Come alive, come alive...
Join the Pepsi Generation..."

The sea crashed noisily as the scene ended.

One of the scholars hissed in the stunned silence, "Is it possible that it was a whole damn civilization that worshiped food?"

Another voice cut in: "Don't jump to conclusions. We haven't even scratched the surface."

A third: "I wonder what Pep-see was."

A fourth: "What about those arches? Now, that's significant."

The leader spoke: "Easy now, let's not get excited. The only thing sure is that these things they call 'commercials' are far more important than anything else they ever did. By the way, I agree with you about the arches."

Another voice, choked with emotion: "Those dancers were young females. Maybe a variation on the old Vestal Virgins cult. This is incredible! I can't stand it!"

The leader cut in hastily: "Settle down, all of you. Let's not go off the deep end. One thing is obvious, to me at least. Every theory we've ever held about this curious civilization is now under question. Let's bring a semblance of order to this meeting. First off, I'm going to assign you and, yes, you too"—he indicated two of the more solemn scholars—"to come up with some kind of theory, or a rational explanation, if possible, of what the word *commercial* meant. What were they trying to do? Perhaps these were recorded messages directed at us."

The two scholars nodded solemnly as they began taking notes.

"And you, over there. Your assignment is to decipher BBD and O. Was it, perhaps, a religious order? It'll be a tough one to crack, but it may be the key. While you're at it, if any of you have any ideas about this 'Tee-Vee' business, I want them in writing. That phrase, as you know, has appeared over and over in other digs."

"Sir?" a youngish, eager-looking scholar interjected.

"Yes?"

"Respectfully, sir, a monograph was recently published by Sponlak Seven in which he suggested that for the purposes of scholarship we apply the official designation of the Tee-Vee Culture to this tribe. Do you–"

The leader interrupted, "Yes, yes I read it, of course. He may be right, but those golden arches may change things. We'll just have to wait and see. All right, have you got that next spool ready?"

A voice from the darkness at the rear of the room mumbled, "I think so. This crazy machine is a bugger to work."

The leader cut him off. "Let's be tolerant. Remember, we're dealing with a people of very minimal technical skills."

The lights dimmed, the machine whirred, the mystic symbols marched again across the screen, followed by a brief second or two of blackness. Then the screen was filled with a great mass of silvery, gleaming metal, some sort of massive grille. The scene widened to show a large, gaudily painted wheeled machine covered with strips of silvery material. Again a native family group cavorted around it, their eyes gleaming with emotion. The dominant male ran his hands lovingly over the machine as a chorus chanted:

"Hot dogs, apple pie, and Chevrolet . . ."

A large, furry animal leaped about, making guttural barking noises. Smaller natives, apparently the young, opened and closed metal hatches, emitting squeals that possibly denoted pleasure.

"Yes, America, Chevy's done it again."

The voice boomed, the chorus chanted:

"Hot dogs, apple pie, and Chevrolet . . ."

as the little band of ancients entered the machine, finally joined by the mysterious fuzzy animal, still busily issuing its ugly barking sounds. The dominant male, now strapped in the machine, appeared to be holding some kind of large hoop, attached to it, in his hands.

"Hot dogs and apple pie . . ."

The screen went dark.

The lights came up in the room to show a very pensive group of researchers. Someone in the rear finally broke the silence:

"Well, no arches in that one, that's for sure."

Another voice picked up the theme: "It's that furry thing that scares me. Do any of you know what language it was speaking?"

A third asked, "That machine? What savage use of colors! They certainly weren't inhibited. I'm very impressed by their childlike exuberance, and—"

"Just wait a minute," the leader broke in. "That machine, as you call it, has appeared often in what fragmentary images have survived from that time. I frankly believe it wasn't a machine at all but a habitation of some sort. They apparently lived in those."

"Uh . . . sir?" the young scholar timidly asked. "Is it possible, sir, that Chev-vee, or its variation Chev-ro-lay, was the name they gave to one of their benevolent gods? In what we have just seen, he appears to have given them something, for which they are grateful."

"That's the trouble with you radicals," the leader said, "always jumping on every bandwagon that comes around. That's an interesting thought, and I don't want to inhibit you, but they also had other quasi gods. Don't forget, we're dealing with a highly superstitious culture."

He glanced around expectantly, encouraging discussion.

"What were those hatches and that furry thing? Is it possible that he was their leader? Perhaps they were enslaved by—"

The leader imperiously motioned for silence. "Save all this for later, when we get down to specifics."

He stood, facing the team. "I want none of this released. You hear me? Do not speak to anyone outside this room about anything you have seen. As you no doubt already suspect from what little we have examined today, there will be enormous repercussions. The religious questions alone are staggering. Reputations built over a lifetime of study and toil will, I repeat, will come crashing down."

He glanced meaningfully around the room. They sat silently, and yet it was obvious that they were seething with excitement. From somewhere a hoarse whisper: "Apple pie . . . apple pie. My God, do you know what that could mean?"

Several nodded pensively. The leader gestured again for silence.

"There, see what I mean? Let's just try to remember that we are scientists."

Refreshments were brought in. Little groups of excited researchers gathered in corners, discussing the incredible visions they had just watched. One, who had said little up to now, spoke to his comrades.

"I never thought I'd live to see anything like this. It's as if we were privileged to watch the Romans in their daily lives, or the barbaric Huns at play. I tell you, this is a turning point, a . . ."

"Shhhh," his friend hissed, "back to work."

They took their seats as the leader returned to the room, his face grave, yet with a hint about him of tightly controlled elation. After the group had quieted down, he spoke.

"I have been in communication with the Supreme Foundationman. Naturally, I did not go into details, because of the sensitive nature of some of the things we have witnessed today." A sly smile creased his face. "I don't have to tell you what this will mean for next year's funds."

There were a few muffled cheers from the rear. The leader continued: "As you know, you were carefully selected from among the world's experts for your specific knowledge of the dead language we are hearing today for the first time spoken by those who actually used it. We are a chosen few. Before we continue viewing, are there any questions?"

A hand was raised.

"Yes?"

"Ah . . . it's not exactly a question, sir. But as you know, some time back I published a monograph on the symbol 'Y & R,' which I proved conclusively stood for the words *young* and *rubicam*, and–"

The leader cut in: "What's your point?"

The speaker continued nervously: "Well, sir, we know the word *young* means 'an immature state,' but *rubicam* has been more difficult. I believe it is a misspelling of a legendary river, which was also called Rubi-con. Perhaps, using my methodology applied to 'B B D & O,' I could conceivably–"

The leader interrupted again. "Are you suggesting that there might be a connection between Y & R and these B B D & O symbols?"

"Er . . . just possibly, sir. I note that bits of material bearing the Y & R symbol were found in the vicinity of this recent dig. There might just possibly be some parallels. And . . ."

The leader motioned for silence. He appeared deep in thought for a moment. "Hmmm. Possibly. Just possibly. But these people seem to have had hundreds of cults bearing indecipherable, symbolic names. We know of NCR, RCA, TRW, NBC, and who knows how many others? I'll leave that sort of study to the dusty ones who spend their lives working puzzles leading nowhere. But never let it be said that I stood in the way of research. So if you want to play around with the idea, go ahead. It's an interesting thought. Anyone else?"

No one volunteered.

"Well, then, let's push on."

The lights dimmed. They leaned forward, some scarcely breathing. Whirrr. Clackety-clack-clack. A muffled curse from the rear of the room. The leader's voice boomed out: "What's the trouble?"

"I'm sorry," the voice replied, laced with exasperation. "This thing got all unwound from the spool and is tangled up . . ."

The lights came back up. More muffled swearing. The leader stared at the ceiling, feigning great boredom. A few laughed. Most were afraid to.

"Sir, I think I've got it. Those old-timers must have had some trouble with this dumb monster."

Whirr. Darkness fell: 5-4-3-2-1-BEEP.

Seven multicolored furred and bewhiskered tiny monsters danced on the screen.

"Meow meow meow meow meow meow meow meow . . ."

A large, lumpy female appeared, dancing in unison with one of the furry creatures. Together, they sang:

"Purina Cat Chow . . .
Chow chow chow!"

Excited shouts and muffled screams echoed throughout the room. The leader leaped to his feet.

"Turn that thing off!"

"Purina Cat Chow . . .
Chow chow chow!
Purina Cat Chow . . .
Meow meow meow meow meow meow meow meow . . ."

The leader faced the rear and bellowed, "Are you sure you have that thing hooked up right? This is incredible!"

"Yes, sir. I can't help what–"

The leader barked an order. "Put that one aside for special study."

The room bristled with excitement. The leader asked what was obviously a rhetorical question.

"Now what in the world was that!"

The eager young scholar piped, "That creature was what they

called a cat. The ancient Egyptians had them, too. In fact, they worshiped them."

The leader, lost in thought, muttered, "Meow. Does anyone here know the meaning of that? Mee-yow."

There was no reply.

"Hmmm. We may have to rethink some of our theories on their language. There's a lot we don't know. It's obvious."

The technician called out from the rear, "I have another one threaded on this thing, sir. Should I run it?"

The leader grunted in affirmation. He leaned to his left and whispered to his trusted lieutenant. "You realize that this could mean my directorship, at last. I can tell you now that I was worried toward the end of the dig that it was just another dry hole, but I always knew that there just had to be something of importance in the Madison Ah-vay Littoral. I just knew it. It had to be."

He glanced to the rear, where the operator was struggling with the machine. His lieutenant politely asked, "Why do they call that area Madison Ah-vay?"

The leader, always delighted to show his superior erudition, went on expansively. "Canmut Nine's first dig years ago came across a plaque or shield of some sort bearing that name in the area, and you know how he was. He immediately gave the dig that name, whether it was significant or not."

The assistant leaned forward thoughtfully. "Does Madison Ah-vay mean anything?"

"Yes, I suppose it does. Canmut at least thought so. Madison was the name of one of their early patriots or generals, and Ah-vay is a Latin word meaning prayer or sacred song. If Canmut was right, the area might well have been a sacred place of leaders. Or perhaps of high priests."

His lieutenant, now thoroughly interested, asked, "You mean it's possible that these 'commercials,' as we call them, could be some sort of Scripture, or–"

"Shhhh." The leader motioned for silence. "Never give away your theories for free, especially in this crowd."

3-2-1-BEEP. A magnificent pastoral scene burst upon them: green trees, grass, but above all another wildly enthusiastic group of celebrants, young and old. At the center a rapidly revolving device bearing mysterious wooden animals, upon which many of the young were seated. Pennants and banners flew. This curious scene was accompanied by loud pagan music. There was revealed, high over them all, another revolving device gleaming in the sunshine. It resembled a vast spinning container bearing the likeness of a benevolent white-bearded ancient. The voice boomed:

"When Mother needs a rest, give her a day off. Go to the Colonel's!"

A group appeared bearing containers exactly like the one in the sky, but miniature. They began devouring the contents, while looking upward in rapt adoration at the bearded ancient's image.

"The Colonel's eleven secret ingredients make it finger-lickin' good . . ."

A chorus, accompanied by native drums, screamed:

"FINGER-LICKIN', FINGER-LICKIN', FINGER-LICKIN' GOOD!"

The scene disappeared.
"Wonderful!"
"Incredible!"
"What style they had!"
Various disjointed phrases echoed around the room. The leader's lieutenant hissed into his ear, "You could be right. That revolving icon must have been one of their major priests!"

The leader, impassive, his face stony, nodded imperceptibly. "Shhh. Don't tip your hand."

The technician, who seemed to have gotten the hang of the primitive machine, almost immediately announced that he had another spool ready for action.

5-4-3-2-1-BEEP. An interior of a colorful repository of some sort appeared, row upon row of shelves adorned with gaudy cubes. Three females in bizarre costumes moved into the foreground. They were pushing spidery, wire-like contrivances filled with more cubes.

The three of them stopped and reverently picked up some mysterious white circular rolls. Their eyes glazed in ecstasy. They fondled the rolls. A stern male arrived, clad in a white uniform. He resembled a guard, or perhaps an officer of some kind—definitely a figure invested with authority.

"Ladies, *please* don't squeeze the Charmin!"

The three females continued to fondle the rolls, with even more intensity. The guard, overcome by emotion, himself began to squeeze a pair. One female piped: "I just can't help it, Mr. Whipple."

Nervously the guard squeezed even harder.

"See, Mr. Whipple, Charmin's so squeezably soft!"

The scene concluded with all four of them fondling the rolls in high excitement.

As the lights came back on, there was a barely suppressed roar of conversation in the room. The leader stood and cut through the hubbub with his voice of command.

"All right, that's more than enough for our first session. Tomorrow I want to hear some of your theories on what we've seen. Remember, no leaks. I repeat, we must not allow any of this to get into the wrong hands. Get some rest. We'll see you on the morrow."

He and his lieutenant moved toward the exit. As they left the chamber, the leader, his voice low and shaking with emotion, said, "We are right. Now it's clear to me. Those tightly rolled white scrolls . . . they were worshiping! Are you ready for a cosmic theory?"

They both glanced around conspiratorially as they moved toward their conveyance.

"Yes, yes. What is it, sir?"

The leader muttered almost to himself, "If we can find out what was on those Charmins, or what they were used for, I believe we would know what their civilization was all about, what they believed in. Do you follow?"

The lieutenant gasped, "By Karnak, you could just be right. Yes, you could just be right!"

In high triumph they moved off.

Ah, Mr. Whipple, with that sissy mustache and those funny little glasses, running around squeezing Charmin. I wondered how many shoppers secretly began squeezing toilet paper after that ad campaign, just to stay up with the crowd. Once, there was a commercial for Alka-Seltzer where the bride cooked up a heart-shaped meatloaf. Not long afterward I myself was served a heart-shaped meatloaf by a smiling, toothsome wench. Life imitates art again.

I chuckled, remembering squirting Heinz catsup on the heart, which gave it a distinct religious overtone. Like the time my grandmother served a cake molded like a lamb, with coconut wool, for Easter. She whacked off the head and served it to me with vanilla ice cream, which caused me to wake up screaming for years afterward and ultimately caused my conversion to zealous atheism in my teens.

So my fevered thoughts ran, in my endless odyssey through the Lincoln Tunnel, jammed wall-to-wall with Detroit iron of various marques and vintages. Oh, I've had my share of tunnel adventures. It isn't always dull. Like the time late at night, with little traffic, I was racing along free as a breeze when I happened to glance in my rearview mirror. The guy directly behind me at that very instant,

just as I was looking at him, had the whole front end of his car col-
lapse, with a giant roar and a blood-curdling scream of metal on
metal.

I had a brief clear view of their astounded faces as the car, a
new model, incidentally, slid along on its gut. They had the look
of those people you see in old, grainy black-and-white pictures of
travelers on the deck of a sinking ocean liner, or that moment in a
Laurel and Hardy film when Hardy discovers that the grand pi-
ano is rolling down the stairs toward him and somehow a horse
had gotten atop it and is going along for the ride. Or maybe that
golden moment when you were a kid and you tried out your new
shipment of Sneezing Powder from Johnson Smith in Racine, Wis-
consin. Along with a new bird-call whistle and a device for throw-
ing your voice into trunks ("Help, help, let me out!"). The look of
startled disbelief, like you've truly been had.

The Whole Fun
Catalog of 1929

"TRAGEDIES OF THE WHITE SLAVES–
TAKEN FROM ACTUAL LIFE!
FOR GOD SAKE, DO SOMETHING!"

Countless red-necked, raw-boned farm boys licked their lips in
lustful righteousness as they addressed an envelope, using a
chewed, stubby, penny pencil, to Johnson Smith & Co., Racine,
Wisconsin. They were ordering #1375 from the "Big Book," or
"*The* Catalog." In a few weeks they would have in their horny
hands two hundred pages of some of the ripest outhouse reading
this side of *The Police Gazette.*

Johnson Smith & Co. is and was as totally American as apple
pie; far more so in fact, since they do make apple pie most places
in the civilized world. Only America could have produced John-

son Smith. There is nothing else in the world like it. Johnson Smith is to Man's darker side what Sears Roebuck represents to the clean-limbed, soil-tilling righteous side. It is a rich compost heap of exploding cigars, celluloid false teeth, anarchist "stink" bombs ("more fun than a Limburger cheese"). The Johnson Smith catalog is a magnificent, smudgy thumbprint of a totally lusty, vibrant, alive, crude post-frontier society, a society that was, and in some ways still remains, an exotic mixture of moralistic piety and violent, primitive humor. It is impossible to find a single dull page, primarily because life in America in the early days of the twentieth century was not dull; it was hard, a constant struggle, and almost completely lacking in creature comfort. The simplest activity was, to use a popular phrase of the day, "fraught with danger." For example, the "Young America Safety Hammer Revolver" is described as "very popular with cyclists." Apparently, to the reader of the day, no explanation was necessary. The mind boggles at the unknown horrors that a "cyclist" daily faced. The same item is also described as "excellent for ladies' use." It is just this sort of thing that makes the Johnson Smith catalog zippier reading than any James Bond fiction. It is hard to believe at this date that the writers of the catalog were dealing with real life of the time. I don't recall ever meeting a "lady" who carried a .32 caliber automatic in her handbag ("for immediate use").

Along the same lines, in the description of the "Automatic Break-open Target Revolver" ("it hits the mark!") is the following come-on: "You never know when War may come, or you may find yourself dependent upon your skill in shooting for a meal of game." Can you imagine the same in, let us say, an Abercrombie & Fitch catalog?

The thing that immediately gets you about the Johnson Smith world is its naked, unashamed realism. It reflects a world in which humor involves the "Squirt Ring" ("an attractive-looking diamond that cannot fail to be the center of attraction. The observer experiences a very great surprise") or the classic "Itching Powder" ("thoroughly enjoyable—the intense discomfiture of your victims is highly amusing"). It was the era of the "Pig Bladder" and W. C. Fields, and subtlety was somehow foreign and feminine.

As history, the Johnson Smith catalog is far more revealing than many of the voluminous, self-conscious products of historians. For example, the ten-cent "Bootlegger Cigar" says more about the days of Prohibition than anything I've ever read on the period: "An exact imitation of a real cigar, which consists of a glass tube with a cork in the end. It is really a well-designed flask that can be used to carry any liquid refreshment." And they weren't talking about Orange Crush or Pepsi-Cola. The immediate image, of course, is of a man (how about W.C. himself?) walking around with a glass cigar in his mouth filled with sour mash bourbon.

Another almost extinct phase of the American scene is fully documented. It is a classic list of emblems of an American phenomenon that flourished in small towns from just after the Civil War through the early thirties: the Lodge, the Brotherhood, the secret society. In a day when men had to band together for one reason or another, mainly social, these institutions were really the focal point of life in many a hamlet. Men wore badges proudly and without self-consciousness.

For example, the "Panama Canal" medallion stated to the world that the wearer had worked on the famous canal. This item, which today would bring big money from Americana museums, sold for twenty-five cents through Johnson Smith. The plumber, the plasterer, the bricklayer, the blacksmith, and the carpenter all had badges to be hung proudly from watch chains. Where now are the men who wore in honor the Brotherhood of Streetcar Trainmen badge?

For just a quarter a member could also get a watch that proclaimed to everyone that he was in the Sons of Veterans. Veterans of What? The Civil War? The Spanish-American War? The War of the Roses? They never said. Are there any chapters still flourishing? You can see their proud escutcheon in the catalog and probably nowhere else.

Johnson Smith was also the Bible of the go-getting entrepreneur, always alert for new opportunities offering "untold riches." "Make big money stamping key chains," advised the catalog, or "Raise mushrooms in your own 'Mystery Mushroom Garden,'" an avocation which "has earned several dollars a week for satisfied users."

Every live wire, life-of-the-party in those days had a complete repertory of parlor tricks. Totally equipped by Johnson Smith & Co., of Racine, Wisconsin, he was prepared to conquer every social gathering with the sheer audacity of his wit and with the legerdemain he displayed. You needed at least a steamer trunk, apparently, to bring your equipment to a party, because "Diminishing Billiard Ball," "The Handkerchief Vanisher" ("practically undetectable; never fails"), "The Mesmerized Penny" ("defies the law of gravitation"), and "The Mysterious King Tut Trick" were merely basic equipment. The truly dedicated social climber would need the "Spirit Medium Ring" as well as the expensive but effective "Mysterious Chalice." This was obviously a time when people provided much of their own entertainment and did not or could not rely on the movies, television, or the canned humor of the stand-up comic. For this reason the joke books which filled several pages of the catalog were popular and highly functional. *One Thousand Choice Conundrums and Riddles* was one such smash seller. It featured such boffolas as:

MAN: *Why don't you help me find my collar button?*
FRIEND: *I would, but it always gives me the Creeps!*

This crusher must have panicked them from Kalamazoo to Keokuk, and for only a dime you got 999 more, "enough to last you for years!" And that was the unvarnished truth! Some of those jokes are still kicking around, and writers are earning Big Money selling them to comics who apparently never read the Johnson Smith & Co. catalog. If you have any doubts about this, read a couple of these joke books, and then watch television for a month. Furthermore, the timelessness of the Johnson Smith catalog is not restricted to its gag books. For example, the Ouija board, invented by a Baltimore man as a parlor trick, is selling in greater numbers today than it did when it was introduced and distributed by Johnson Smith.

The chatty quality of the unknown caption writers is also unique and seems to emanate from a single, crotchety yet ribald human being. On the one hand he cozies up to the reader, nudges him in the ribs, and says: "Here's your chance, boys. Put on one of these Bunged-up Eye disguises. The effect as you enter the room is most bewildering. Real fun!" On the other hand, he thunders from his soapbox in tones of outraged virtue: "Your heart will burn and you will wonder how such awful things can be, and you will feel like others that you must become a crusader and go out and fight and tell others and warn against the danger." He is exhorting us to buy *From Dance Hall to White Slavery–The World's Greatest Tragedy* ("an absolute steal at 35¢").

It is this eerily personal style that sets the tone of this great volume of human desires and vanities. A very necessary and ubiquitous ingredient of the catalog is the consistently provocative illustrations, again the work of anonymous, humble artists who probably never signed a picture in their lives. For example, the grotesque drawing illustrating "Joke Teeth with Tongue" foreshadowed the best of the later surrealists. The man's startled yet strangely evil expression as he displays his seven-inch rubber tongue and his gleaming celluloid false teeth is enough to make us wonder what it's all about! On the same page is another fine, unsigned work illustrating "The Enormous Vibrating Eye," obviously the work of an artist of another school. He, nevertheless, perfectly catches the raffish cloddishness of a man who would wear such a monstrosity. The cap he wears in the drawing betrays a touch of sheer genius. Physical infirmities also abound in the Johnson Smith humor world. "The Swollen Thumb" is a good example, incidentally illustrated nicely with a pair of rubes peering dolefully at a giant, bulbous thumb.

Apparently another sure-fire laugh-getter was the substitution of phony items for commonplace objects. Most of them were made of soap and were "guaranteed to liven up any party." A real wit could spark up his friendly gatherings with soap cheese ("it might fool even the mice") and soap biscuits ("a few of these mixed in with a dish of regular crackers will really start the fun"). You bet, especially after a couple of martinis!

Soap gumdrops, soap cigars, soap pickles, soap chocolates,

and even a bar of soap soap that dyed its user an indelible blue made life exciting for the friends of a Johnson Smith addict. There is no record of the number of murders, assault and battery cases, and simple divorces that this single line of Johnson Smith specialties provoked. A man wearing an enormous vibrating eye feeding his wife and kids soap pickles is a commonplace still life in the world of Johnson Smith.

Everything, or almost everything, came by mail in the early twentieth century. The mailman was often the only link between the great outside world and a largely rural America. Mail order catalogs had an irresistible appeal to simple folk who rarely saw more than a crossroads general store. During the days just before World War I, few homes were without the Sears Roebuck, Montgomery Ward, and Johnson Smith & Co. catalogs, especially if there were boys in the family. The Johnson Smith catalog was predominantly male in its appeal and was not all fun and games. In fact, the catalog had a kind of Horatio Alger upward-and-onward appeal to the young man of the period. He could order correspondence lessons from Johnson Smith in everything from playing the ukulele to *New and Simplified Methods of Mimicry, Whistling and Imitation* to *Polish, Self-Taught.* In a day when education beyond the fifth grade was a rarity, these self-help courses represented serious educational opportunity to people who often studied by kerosene lamps.

The constant drive for financial success, which has played such an important role in creating the character of America, is well documented throughout the Johnson Smith catalog. One example is *The Book of Great Secrets: One Thousand Ways of Getting Rich!* ("To persons who work hard for a living and then don't get it, we have a few plain words to say. Every person wants to make money and wants to make it fast and easy. This book will tell them how.") For only a quarter this fantastic volume outlined moneymaking schemes ranging all the way from home recipes for Holland gin and to corn cures to a formula for treating "various diseases to which horses are subject." It would be interesting to know the number of people who read this volume and then went on to fame and fortune using the Johnson Smith tested formula for making "Eye Water" or "Tomato Catsup."

To the superstitious and the basically ignorant, attaining wealth has often seemed to be a matter of either luck or secret, sinister, mystic knowledge. Johnson Smith stood ready to provide the struggling clod with the hidden key. If he couldn't make it as an honest veterinarian or plumber he could at least master hypnotism and gain his ends by treachery. The pamphlet *Mysteries of Clairvoyance* is only one example of numerous appeals that Johnson Smith made to the superstitious side of rustic America:

> *"How to make yourself a perfect operator. This work lifts the curtain and tells what some books only hint at."*

> *"Discover Thebes and find out where the plunder is hidden."*

> *"To see the issue of all 'Pools,' whether in stocks or financial matters. Be the MASTER."*

> *"This book should be kept under lock and key. You don't want everyone to be as wise as yourself."*

All of this for only a thin dime.

The mixture of primitive mysticism and modern technology is one of the things that makes the Johnson Smith catalog so endlessly fascinating. Its pages are jammed full of appeals to every human vice and fear. Cupidity, nobility, lust, piety—all are given equal space, and significantly there is never a sense of embarrassment or shame anywhere. Violence is taken for granted in almost every form of activity. "Emergencies" are continually encountered on every hand. Johnson Smith was pre-eminent in the field of providing personal tools of mayhem for the righteous. Nowhere is it hinted that the bad guys could, just as easily as the good, mail in their quarters for the "Silent Defender" or

"Aluminum Gloves." These case-hardened lightweight knuckle-dusters are described as "very useful in an emergency." The buyer was advised to "buy one for each hand."

On the very next page we are tempted with the "Spring Steel Patent Telescopic Police Club," "the most reliable arm for self-defense." It was designed to be telescoped for concealment and could be carried in the hand without being noticed. When an "emergency" arose, this is what happened according to the caption writer: "Your adversary is caught quite unprepared and is landed a stinging blow of a totally unexpected nature, rendering him completely helpless." Since this little beauty was made of spring steel, the writer was probably understating the case. The warning "Do not mistake this club with weak imitations" is well taken. Many items displayed in the catalog carry similar advice. Apparently there were unscrupulous "imitators" everywhere dealing in spurious exploding cigars, sneezing powder, hand grenades, and horse liniment. Since Johnson Smith always sold the real thing, there was a sense of security which went with a mailed order to Racine, Wisconsin. And there was something to it. In the glory days of the company, mail order flimflams were everywhere. Every magazine was filled with appeals to the unwary. Fifty cents sent off to an important-sounding address in Chicago most often brought nothing in return. Johnson Smith stood like a rock of integrity in the midst of this sneaky landscape.

Johnson Smith also recognized something that only began to appear in more sophisticated advertising circles years later: that advertising must be entertaining in itself, whether or not the customer buys. They knew that if he read the catalog for sheer enjoyment eventually something would grab him. Throughout the catalog, usually at the bottom of the page, little gratis knee-slappers were thrown in.

LAWYER: *You say your wife attacked you with a death-dealing weapon. What was it?*

LITTLE TOD: *A fly swatter.*

As feeble as this joke was, it made no attempt to sell. It was just there, like the dozens sprinkled throughout the catalog like raisins in rice pudding.

There was one thing in the catalog more than any other that became identified with the company. It was sent everywhere and probably became as much of a classic in the field of vulgarity as any practical joke ever created. Johnson Smith introduced this zinger to the waiting populace, which immediately embraced it wherever yahoos proliferated and low buffoonery flourished. In fact, it sets the tone of the entire Johnson Smith catalog.

The first time it appeared in the catalog few suspected that it would attain such timeless significance. Even today, one hears references to its unfailing success at achieving hilarity and bringing cringing embarrassment to its victims. There are few alive who have not heard of it, yet many have never actually seen one. Johnson Smith & Co., now of Detroit, Michigan, still carries a full line, and if you'd care to order one, they would be delighted to comply.

"The Whoopee Cushion" says it all. Here is what Johnson Smith has to say about their classic:

The Whoopee Cushion or Poo-Poo Cushion as it is sometimes called is made of rubber. It is inflated in much the same manner as an ordinary rubber balloon and then placed on a chair. When the victim unsuspectingly sits upon the cushion, it gives forth noises that can be better imagined than described.

The accompanying illustration leaves nothing to the imagination.

Today this catalog is just a very funny coffee-table curiosity, because we are still too close to the life and times it describes. In two hundred years it will be a truly significant historical and social document. It might well be the Rosetta Stone of American culture.

You know what I'd like to do? It suddenly hit me. Some time when I'm coming through here late at night, and there are no cars behind me or ahead of me, I'm going to stop, jump out with a paint brush and a can of black paint, and paint a huge, jagged crack right down the side of that tile wall. The next son of a bitch that comes through is going to flee the tunnel screaming, "The tunnel cracked, the tunnel cracked!" like the mob in Thurber's story about the day the dam broke in Columbus, Ohio.

"The tunnel cracked, help, help, flee for your lives!" I wonder why they call practical jokes "practical"? That's the one thing they aren't.

The line moved arthritically. Number 69, in the Charger, had fallen asleep, his head lolling back and forth on the cushions of the Dodge, a sorry crew of Scarlet Knights indeed; shaggy and tired from a weekend in the Eighth Street fleshpots. I studied each of them as we rolled slowly forward: a lumpish lot. Only divine intervention would get them their Rutgers diplomas, from what I could see. But then, you never can tell about God, and the academic world, I mused, remembering what Aunt Florence used to say:

"If God had not wanted us to have meatloaf, then we wouldn't have meatloaf."

Yes, God does work in mysterious ways. Take that time back in Pittinger's class.

Lost at C

A wave of numbness surged through my body with stunning force. At last I knew what it felt like to be sitting with that brass hat on your skull with those straps around your ankles as the warden pulls the big switch. Out of the corner of my eye I caught the glint of Mr. Pittinger's horn-rims and the ice-blue ray from his left eye. As the giant baroque equation loomed on the blackboard, my life unreeled before my eyes in the classic manner of the final moments of mortal existence. I was finished. Done. It had all come to this. Somehow I had always known it would.

It all started in first grade at the Warren G. Harding School, where I was one among a rabble of sweaty, wrestling, peanut-butter-and-jelly sandwich eaters. But it was not until the end of the third month of school that I became dimly aware of a curse that would follow me throughout my life. Along with Martin Perlmutter, Schwartz, Chester Woczniewski, Helen Weathers, and poor old Zynzmeister, I was a member of the Alphabetical Ghetto, forever doomed by the fateful first letter of our last names to squat restlessly, hopelessly, at the very end of every line known to man, fearfully aware that whatever the authorities were passing out, they would run out of goodies by the time they got to us.

Medical science has finally begun to realize that those of us at the end of the alphabet live shorter lives, sweat more, and are far jumpier than those in the B's and E's and even the M's and L's. People at the tail end of the alphabet grow up accepting the fact that everybody else comes first. The Warren G. Harding School

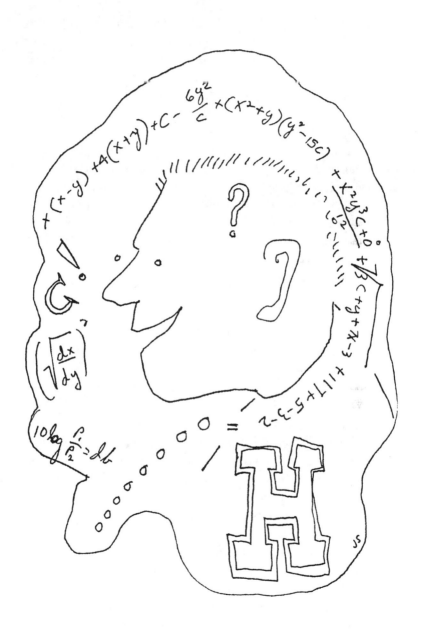

had an almost mystic belief in the alphabet; if you were a P, you sat behind every O, regardless of myopia.

Me and Schwartz and Woczniewski sat so far back in the classroom that the blackboard was only a vague rumor to us. Miss Shields was a shifting figure in the haze on the distant horizon, her voice a faint but ominous drone, punctuated by squeaking chalk. Within a short time we became adept at reading the inflection, if not the content, of those far-off sounds, sensing instantly when danger was looming. Danger meant simply being called on. Kids in the front of the classroom didn't know the meaning of danger. Ace test-takers, they loved nothing more than to display their immense knowledge by waving their hands frantically even before questions were asked. Today, when I think of the classrooms of my youth, I see a forest of waving hands between me and the teacher. They were the smart-asses who went on to become corporation presidents, TV talk-show hosts, and owners of cabin cruisers. *Cars*on, *Cav*ett, Steve *All*en, *Cron*kite, *Don*ahue—there isn't a goddamn Woczniewski in the lot. Every one of those bastards grew up never doubting that he was destined to be at the head of the class, with the rest of the mob, the Schwartzes, the Zynzmeisters, forever in the *Lumpenworld* of the audience.

We in the back of the classroom trod a rockier and far more dangerous path. Since we could neither hear nor see, we had only one course open if we were going to pass. The key was never to be called on. It was imperative never to be caught out in the open, if possible not to be seen at all. Each of us evolved his own methods of survival. Fat Helen Weathers could sweat at will, surrounding herself with a faint hazy cloud so that Miss Shields could never quite see her in focus, believing that Helen was just a thumb-smudge on her glasses. Perlmutter had a thin pale beaky face that you could not remember even while you were looking at it. He didn't have to hide. No teacher ever remembered his name or whether he was even there. He'd sit for hours without moving a muscle, as anonymous as a pale hat rack. He was a born cost accountant.

One day during an oral quiz, however–always a dangerous time for all of us–Perlmutter displayed the true stuff of champions. Miss Shields unaccountably called on him during an incomprehensible discussion involving the principal parts of speech, which seemed to be called "participles" or something like that. It was a discussion, naturally, only vaguely heard back in the ghetto. We thought Perlmutter was finished, but we had underestimated him. Without missing a beat, his face turned bright purple, his eyes bulged like a pair of overripe grapes, his neck throbbed, and a spectacular geyser of blood gushed from both nostrils.

"This is terrible!" Miss Shields cried, scooping him up in her arms and rushing him to the nurse's office, where he was excused from school for the rest of the day. She never called on him again.

Schwartz, short, squat, built like a fireplug, would slowly scrunch down in his seat until only the top fringe of his crew cut could be seen, level with his desk. As for Zynzmeister, a strict Catholic, he sat so far behind even us that he spent his entire school career jammed up against the cabinet in the rear of the room where worn erasers, pickled biology specimens, and moldering lunches were stored; Zynzmeister, destined to go through life listed on the last page of every telephone directory. God only knows how he saw the rest of mankind in his troubled imagination; probably as an endless line snaking to the cosmic horizon, with poor Zynzmeister, shuffling from foot to foot, the very last person at the end of the Big Parade. His defense was religion; divine intervention. The click of his beads as they were counted kept up a steady castanet beat during Miss Shields's distant cluckings. It seemed to work.

My salvation was simple, yet deceptively difficult. I moved like a snake, bobbing and weaving, shifting my body from side to side, dropping a shoulder here, shifting my neck a few degrees to the right there, always keeping a line of kids between me and the teacher's eagle eye. I blessed the Beehive hairdo when it became popular. I would have loved the Afro.

For those rare but inevitable occasions–say, during a chicken-pox epidemic–when the ranks in the rows ahead were too thin to provide adequate cover, I practiced the vacant-eyeball ploy, which has since become a popular device for junior executives the world over who cannot afford to be nailed by their seniors in sales conferences and other perilous situations. The vacant eye-ball appears to be looking attentively but, in fact, sees nothing. It is a blank mirror of anonymity. I learned early in the game that if they don't catch your eye, they don't call on you. Combined with a fixed facial expression of deadpan alertness–neither too dead-pan nor too alert–this technique has been known to render its practitioner virtually invisible.

The third, and possibly most important, tactic of classroom survival is thought control. When danger looms, it is necessary to repeat silently, with intense concentration, the hypnotic com-mand Don't call on me, Don't call on me, Don't call on me, send-ing out invisible waves of powerful thought energy until the teacher's mind is mysteriously clouded. After endless hours of re-hearsal before the mirror in the bathroom, I had developed a fourth and final gambit–my Cute Look: shy, boyish, a smile of such disarming cuddliness as to be lethal. I flashed it, of course, only with great caution, during comparatively safe periods in the classroom–upon entering and leaving–and at lunch, recess, I would warm teachers when their guard was down.

Those of us in the back rows learned quickly that grades are handed out not on the basis of actual accomplishment but by in-tuitive feel. At that crucial moment when Miss Shields sat down to fill out my report card, I knew that my Cute Look would pop into her mind when my name appeared before her. Since she had nothing else to go on–other than catch-as-catch-can test answers gleaned from my shirt cuff or the blue book of the kid ahead of me—it was only natural for her to put down a B, which is all I ever wanted out of life.

So it was that I weaved and bobbed, truckled and beamed my way through grade after grade at Warren G. Harding School. Perlmutter, Schwartz, Woczniewski, Helen Weathers, and I, as well as poor old Zynzmeister, sat on shore as the deepening river of education flowed by us unheard, unseen. Once in a great while, of course, a teacher would raise her voice above the usual bleat, or a transient air current would carry an isolated phrase or maybe even a full sentence all the way back to our little band, and this would often precipitate labored intellectual debates.

Like the day we clearly caught the word *marsupial*. We knew it had something to do with animals, since Miss Robinette had pulled down a chart on which we could barely make out drawings of what could not have been people, unless they were down on all fours. After school that afternoon, Schwartz and Chester and I were kicking a Carnation can down an alley when a large police dog with one ear missing roared out from between two garages after a tomcat that must have weighed thirty pounds. The dog's name was Ratso and he was owned by the postman, Mr. L. D. Johnson, who, I guess, kept him at home so that he could bite their postman when he delivered mail to their house.

"Boy, I'd like to see old Rat go after one a them marsupials," said Chester.

"They lay eggs," Schwartz stated with satisfaction. He had a way of saying things like that as though he had been the first to discover them, or at least had confirmed them through independent research.

"You mean like ducks?" I asked. My hungry mind was questing for more knowledge.

"Do they quack, too?" Chester asked.

"How should I know?" said Schwartz, looking disgusted. "I ain't no mind reader."

Thus the subject of marsupials was closed forever. They were never mentioned again in class, at least as far as I know, and to this day my entire knowledge of marsupials consists of what Schwartz told us about them.

I can truthfully say that in all the years of my struggle through grade school at Warren G. Harding, I actually learned one true fact about the great world. For some reason, a mysterious vagary of acoustics perhaps, a complete sentence arrived back at our little ghetto headquarters one day:

"Bolivia exports tin."

That is the sum total of my grade school education. I grabbed that fact like a drowning man clinging to a bobbing 2×4 in a trackless ocean. It has been endlessly useful ever since. At cocktail parties I silently bide my time, nibbling cashews and sipping my martini thoughtfully, and then, in a lull of the conversation, I drop my bomb: "But all of you have ignored the tin economy of Bolivia, a crucial point." I saunter away as though in search of more intellectual companions, leaving behind a covey of stunned new admirers. Some men have achieved cabinet rank on the basis of one such fact.

Warren G. Harding was widely known, during the dark ages when I was attending it, for being an "advanced" school, and actual tests were very rare. This worked in beautifully with our survival techniques and made it possible for me and my band of fellow ignoramuses to slide by year after year undetected. Although, of course, we didn't know it at the time, we were part of the pioneering advance wave of generation upon generation of total illiterates that have been spawned by "progressive" education.

At home, grade by grade, my reputation slowly grew until I was considered a truly superior intellect. This is one of the great American myths. It has persisted for ages–the unfailing belief that every generation is brighter, taller, more beautiful, than the one before it–in spite of obvious evidence to the contrary. Naturally, I did everything I could to encourage my old man in this belief. I must admit that I, too, firmly believed it. Every generation does, until, inevitably, the walls come tumbling down.

"Boy, kids today sure are a lot smarter than we was when we was kids. Why, at his age I hardly knew nothin'." The old man, sitting at the kitchen table with a can of Blatz in his mitt, was talking to my uncle Carl, who kept shoving his upper plate back into his mouth. He had gotten his false teeth from the Relief, and he was proud of them.

"Tell your uncle Carl about Bolivia," the old man ordered.

"Why, certainly," I said confidently. It was a command performance I had given many times before. "Bolivia exports tin."

My father, his jaw slack with amazement, turned to Uncle Carl and said in a low, emotional voice, "See what I mean? Kids nowadays know everything. Didja hear that, Carl? Bolivia exports tin!"

"Geez." Uncle Carl's teeth clicked back into place. "When I was a kid they didn't even have Bolivia! Boy!"

They both nodded in silent humility, and went back to guzzling beer. Coolly, I made my exit through the back door, lugging a Kraft-American-cheese-and-jelly sandwich. Another triumph!

The years passed, punctuated by occasional tight squeaks, but my true identity as a faker was never really in danger of exposure. Finally the big day came. On a glorious sun-drenched morning when even the red clouds of rusty blast-furnace dust glowed in spring beauty, Graduation Day arrived. I had made it. Dressed in our scratchy Sunday clothes, we were herded, along with parents, uncles, aunts, and a few scattered cousins, into the gym.

The despised glee club sang the Warren G. Harding fight song, accompanied by Miss Bundy, the kindergarten teacher, on the piano, her crinkly straw-colored hair bobbing up and down with every beat, her huge bottom enveloping the piano stool. Then a famous local undertaker and Chevrolet dealer delivered a mind-numbing oration on how his generation was passing the torch of civilization from its faltering hands into our youthful energetic and idealistic hands. Naturally, we were seated alphabetically, and we in the rear caught only a few disjointed phrases.

Schwartz, sweating profusely in his new sports coat, whispered, "What's all that stuff about torches? I didn't get no torch."

"They must have given them to the front of the class," I answered. Little did I realize how right I was.

But I got my diploma. It was official. I was a graduate. Clasping my sacred scroll there on the stage–while those even farther below me in the alphabet filed up to receive theirs–I found myself growing wise and dignified, a person of substance, well equipped to carry torches, to best foes, to identify the parts of speech, including gerunds, to draw from memory the sinister confluence of the Tigris and the Euphrates.

At last we were free. Warren G. Harding and its warm embrace, its easy ways, stood forever behind us. On our way home the old man, his clean white shirt crackling with starch, said: "Whaddaya say we celebrate by pickin' up some ice cream at the Igloo?"

Ecstatic, I sat in the back seat of the Olds with my kid brother, clutching the precious document on which–though I didn't discover it till later–my name had been misspelled, in Old English lettering.

That summer sped by in a blur of sun and gentle showers that made the outfields fragrant with clover and sweet William. In September I would be a full-fledged high school kid. Guys in high school had always seemed to be remote, godlike creatures who drove cars, wore thick sweaters with letters on them, and hung around Big Bill's Drive-in. What actually happened in high school was never mentioned, at least among those of us in the R's and the Y's. A few rumors, of course, had filtered down to us, and they only added to our sense of rising excitement about the new life that was about to begin.

The first omen of evil struck early in September, just a few days before school was to open. I came home covered with scratches and mosquito bites from a great day out in the weeds and walked right into it.

"There's some mail for you," my mother grunted to me as she struggled out the screen door with a huge bag of garbage that was dripping coffee grounds onto the linoleum.

"Mail? For me?" I was surprised, since I received very little mail except for an occasional announcement from the International Crime Detection Institute of East St. Louis, Illinois, informing me that I was frittering away my life when I could be "Earning Big Money Spotting Crooks."

I ripped open the envelope and found a printed form stating that high school registration and classes for freshmen would begin next Monday, and that I was assigned to Miss Snyder, to whom I would report at 8:30 A.M. Period.

"Hey, Schwartz," I barked into the phone, "didja get yer card?"

"Yeah!"

"What's this registration stuff?"

"I don't know!" Schwartz shouted to be heard over the uproar of his mother screaming at his kid brother, Douglas. "I guess that's where you pick the teachers and the classes and stuff you want to take!"

"Yeah!" I hollered back. Ah, the dreams of youth.

Registration day dawned windy, with a flat silver sun gleaming through the haze from the steel plant. Schwartz, Flick, Chester, and a whole crowd of us rode the bus to high school. No one had ever taken a bus to Harding. We all got there our own way, the girls strolling down the sidewalk, the boys scurrying up alleys, through vacant lots, over fences, past dogs, chickens, sprinklers, and one maniacal goose that from time to time rushed out of its yard and ripped a chunk from somebody's corduroys. Catching a bus on the corner was a whole new thing. I sat in the back, amid the din, my guts in an uproar of excitement. High school!

We carried rulers, fountain pens, erasers—a full arsenal of equipment for use on the battlefields of higher learning. Schwartz had a T square made of red plastic and a matching compass, God knows what for. I clutched the brown-and-white fake-marble Parker automatic pencil that my aunt Glen had given me upon graduation from eighth grade. And inside the front of my three-ring notebook, which had green imitation-leather covers, I had pasted a picture of an Indianapolis Kurtis-Kraft racer. I was ready for anything. In keeping with the gravity of the occasion, I was wearing my electric-blue sports coat and my silver tie with its red hand-painted snail, both stars in my wardrobe. The bus was heavily scented with Lucky Tiger hair oil, since every male aboard had gotten a haircut for the big day.

I had lain in bed making plans the night before. I would grab the front seat in every class and listen to every word. No longer would I duck and dodge behind a screen of kids. That was all behind me. Mentally I crouched at the mark, waiting for the starter's gun to send me flying down the track ahead of the pack. If others could actually learn, so could I. It was going to be a whole new ball game, a clean slate, a new start. I was the victim of another American myth, namely that things can actually change for the better, that if you try hard enough you can transform the lead of your crummy self into some golden ideal. Countless billions are spent yearly in our blessed country on diets guaranteed to peel suet off in seconds, books that promise incredible sexual bliss, and others promising stupendous riches and happiness to those who can master the Seven Golden Rules contained therein. Alas.

The bus rolled up before nirvana and we piled out, some on the run yelling hysterically, others ashen-faced and stiff-legged with terror. A few pretended that it was like any other bus ride. The school loomed over us like the walls of the Grand Canyon. Made of dull red brick, it stretched out to either horizon. Thousands of kids milled around the outside, waiting for the doors to open. Girls bigger than my aunt Clara towered over me, and they had bumps in their sweaters like the ladies that Gene Autry sang to at the Saturday matinees. A blind torrent of fear washed over me. For a while, I had been one of the truly big men at Warren G. Harding and now I was nothing. Clinging to my lunch bag with a sweaty hand, I hunted frantically for a familiar face, but Schwartz and Flick and the others had been swallowed up.

BRRRRR-INNNGGGG! I was carried forward on the crest of

the horde as it surged in through the huge front doors. Great
staircases with rivers of kids streamed in all directions. My card
read REPORT TO ROOM 220. Kids all around me hollered and
laughed back and forth. They all seemed to know one another. I
had never felt so alone. Figuring astutely that Room 220 had to be
on the second floor, I joined the torrent raging upward. The second floor looked even vaster than the first. The halls stretched so
far in both directions that I couldn't see the ends. Lockers banged
and I smelled, for the first time, that indescribable high school
building aroma, a rich fragrance made up of thousands of bodies,
floor wax, chalk, leftover tuna fish sandwiches, chlorine from the
swimming pool, disinfectant from the johns, and fermenting
jockstraps from the gym.

I tried to read the numbers on doors as I was swept onward
like a salmon in the spawning season: 205, 207, 214, 218–220! My
home room, where I was to spend four hellish years of my life. A
gaunt, razor-sharp teacher sat at a gray steel and formica desk;
silver gray hair, glistening rimless glasses, gray mannish wool
suit; even her face was gray. Miss Snyder, my home room teacher.

I sensed immediately that she wasn't going to be a pushover
for my Cute Look, but I turned it on anyway, at full candle power.
She peered at me coldly through her rimless glasses.

"Your card, please," she snapped in a crackling, flat voice. I
handed it over. She glanced at it, glanced up at me, registering my
face in the rogue's gallery of her mind. I could almost hear the
shutters clicking.

"Take that seat there back of Rukowski. He's the one in the
purple sweater."

I walked down between the aisles of alien faces to my seat. It
was, of course, in the next-to-the-last row. It would be mine for
the next four years. Ahead of me loomed Rukowski, a giant
mountain of flesh over which had been stretched a purple jersey
covered with chevrons, the number 76, and a row of stripes. Later
I learned that Rukowski had been an all-state tackle for the past
six years and was the bulwark of one of the toughest defensive

lines in seven states. He was a good man to sit behind. I peered around the room. I was the only delegate to Room 220 from Warren G. Harding.

Miss Snyder stood at the blackboard and hurled the first harpoon of the season: "You freshmen who are with us today are already enrolled for the courses you will be required to take. Here are your program cards." She dealt out 3×5-inch blue cards, which were handed back to the freshmen. Each card was neatly lined into eight periods, and after each period was the name of a teacher, a subject, and a classroom. One period was labeled LUNCH, another STUDY, and so on. Every minute of my day was laid out for me. So much for my dreams of freedom.

"Freshmen, this is your first day in high school. You are no longer in grade school. If you work hard, you will do well. If you don't, you will regret it. You are here to learn. You are not here to play. Remember this and remember it well: *What you do here will follow you all through life.*" She paused dramatically. In the hushed silence, I could hear Rukowski wheezing ahead of me. None of this, of course, affected him. Anyone who could block the way he could block would have no trouble getting through life.

"Your first class will begin in five minutes. Any questions?" No one raised a hand.

I sat there, pawing in the chute, anxious to begin my glorious career of learning. No more would I fake my way. A new era was about to begin. The bell rang. The starting gate slammed open.

I had thundered a couple of hundred feet through the hall with the mob before it hit me that I had no idea where the hell I was supposed to go. As the crowd surged around me, I struggled to read my program card. All I could make out was Room 127. I had only a minute to make it, so I battled my way down a flight of stairs. Then: 101, 105, 109, 112, 117–127, just in time. Already the classroom was three-quarters filled. Ahead of me, running interference, was Rukowski, trying his luck at this course, I later learned, for the third time in as many semesters. Getting his shoulder into it, he bulled his way through the door, buffeting aside a herd of spindly little freshmen. It was Schwartz, good old Schwartz, and Flick and Chester and Helen Weathers. My old gang! Even poor old Zynzmeister. Whatever it was, I would not have to go through it alone.

"Hi, Schwartz!"

Schwartz smiled wanly. And Helen Weathers giggled—until she saw, at the same moment I did, a tall, square man standing motionless at the blackboard. He had a grim blue jaw and short, kinky black crew-cut hair. His eyes were tiny ball bearings behind glasses with thick black rims. He wore a dark, boxy suit that looked like it was made of black sandpaper. The bell rang and the door closed behind us. I joined the crowd around his desk who were putting registration cards into a box. I did likewise.

"All right. Settle down. Let's get organized." The man's voice had a cutting rasp to it, like a steel file working on concrete. "We sit alphabetically in this class. A's up here in front to my right. Get going."

I trudged behind Schwartz and Helen Weathers toward the dim recesses in the back of the classroom. Well, at least I'd be among friends. It was about a quarter of a mile to the front of the room, but I sat bolt upright in my seat, my iron determination intact. No more faking it.

"Class, my name is Mr. Pittinger." He was the first male teacher I had ever had. Warren G. Harding was peopled entirely by motherly ladies like Mrs. Bailey and Miss Shields. Mr. Pittinger was a whole new ball game. And I still had no idea what he taught. I would soon find out.

"If you work in this class, you'll have no trouble. If you don't, I promise you nothing."

I leaned forward at my desk, scribbling madly in my notebook: *class my name is mr. pittinger if you work you will have no trouble if you dont i promise you nothing . . .*

I figured if you wrote everything down there'd be no trouble. Every classroom of my life had been filled with girls on the Honor Roll who endlessly wrote in mysterious notebooks, even when nothing seemed to be going on. I never knew what the hell they were writing, so I took no chances. I figured I'd write everything.

"Braaghk." Mr. Pittinger cleared his gravelly throat.

braaaghk, I scribbled, *brummph.* You never know, I thought, it might appear on the exam.

He turned, picked up a piece of chalk, and began to scrawl huge block letters on the blackboard.

A-L—the chalk squeaked decisively—G-E-B-R-A. I copied each letter exactly as he'd written it.

"That is the subject of this course," he barked.

Algebra? What the hell is that?

"Algebra is the mathematics of abstract numbers."

I gulped as I wrote this down.

"I will now illustrate."

Pittinger printed a huge Y on the blackboard and below it an enormous X. I doggedly followed suit in my notebook. He then put equal signs next to the X and the Y.

"If Y equals five and X equals two, what does the following mean?"

He wrote out: X+Y=?

Black fear seized my vitals. How could you add Xs and Ys? I had enough trouble with nines and sevens!

Already the crowd in front of the room were waving their hands to answer Pittinger's question. The class wasn't thirty seconds old and I was already six weeks behind. I sank lower in my seat, a faint buzzing in my ears. Instinctively I began to weave. I knew it was all over. Out of the corner of my eye I saw that Schwartz, next to me, had hunched lower and begun to emit a high, thin whimpering sound. Helen Weathers had flung up a thin spray of sweat. Chester's skin had changed to the color of the cupboards in the back of the room. And from behind me I could hear the faint, steady click of Zynzmeister's rosary.

Second by second, minute by minute, eon by eon that first algebra class droned on. I couldn't catch another word that was said, and by the time Mr. Pittinger wrote the second equation on the board, I was bobbing and weaving like a cobra and sending out high-voltage thought rays. A tiny molten knot of stark terror hissed and simmered in the pit of my stomach. I realized that for the first time in my school life, I had run into something that was completely opaque and unlearnable, and there was no way to fake it.

Don't call on me, Don't call on me, Don't call on me . . .

That night I ate my meatloaf and red cabbage in sober silence as the family yapped on, still living back in the days when I was known to all of them as the smartest little son of a bitch to ever set foot on Cleveland Street.

"Boy, look at the stuff kids study these days," the old man said with wonder as he hefted my algebra textbook in his bowling hand and riffled through the pages.

"What's all this X and Y stuff?" he asked.

"Yeah, well, it ain't much," I muttered as coolly as I could, trying to recapture some of the old élan.

"Whaddaya mean, ain't much?" His eyes glowed with pride at the idea that his kid had mastered algebra in only one day.

"Abstract mathematics, that's all it is."

The old man knew he'd been totally outclassed. Even my mother stopped stirring the gravy for a few seconds. My kid brother continued to pound away at the little bbs of Ovaltine that floated around on the top of his milk.

That night sleep did not come easily. In fact, it was only the first of many storm-tossed nights to come as, algebra class by algebra class, my terror grew. All my other subjects—history, English, social studies—were a total breeze. My years of experience in fakery came into full flower. In social studies, for example, the more you hoked it up, the better the grades. On those rare occasions when asked a question, I would stand slowly, with an open yet troubled look playing over my thoughtful countenance.

"Mr. Harris, sir," I would drawl hesitantly, as though attempting to unravel the perplexity of the ages, "I guess it depends on how you view it—objectively, which, naturally, is too simple, or subjectively, in which case many factors such as a changing environment must be taken into consideration, and . . ." I would trail off.

Mr. Harris, with a snort of pleasure, would bellow: "RIGHT! There are many diverse elements, which . . ." After which he was good for at least a forty-minute solo.

History was more of the same, and English was almost embarrassingly easy as, day after day, Miss McCullough preened and congratulated herself before our class. All she needed was a little ass-kissing and there was no limit to her applause. I often felt she regretted that an A+ was the highest grade she could hand out to one who loved her as sincerely and selflessly as I did.

Every morning at eight-thirty-five, however, was another story. I marched with leaden feet and quaking bowels into Mr. Pittinger's torture chamber. By the sixth week I knew, without the shadow of a doubt, that after all these years of dodging and grinning, I was going to fail. Fail! No B, no gentleman's C—Fail. F. The big one: my own Scarlet Letter. Branded on my forehead—F, for Fuckup.

There was no question whatever. True, Pittinger had not yet been able to catch me out in the open, since I was using every trick of the trade. But I knew that one day, inevitably, the icy hand of truth would rip off my shoddy façade and expose me for all the world to see.

Pittinger was of the new school, meaning he believed that kids, theoretically motivated by an insatiable thirst for knowledge, would devour algebra in large chunks, making the final examination only a formality. He graded on performance in class and total grasp of the subject, capped off at the end of the term with an exam of brain-crushing difficulty from which he had the option of excusing those who rated A+ on classroom performance. Since I had no classroom performance, my doom was sealed.

Schwartz, too, had noticeably shrunken. Even fat Helen had developed deep hollows under her eyes, while Chester had almost completely disappeared. And Zynzmeister had taken to nibbling Communion wafers in class.

Christmas came and went in tortured gaiety. My kid brother played happily with his Terry and the Pirates Dragon Lady Detector as I looked on with the sad indulgence of a withered old man whose youth had passed. As for my own presents, what good did it do to have a new first baseman's mitt when my life was over? How innocent they are, I thought as I watched my family trim the tree and scurry about wrapping packages. Before long, they will know. They will loathe me. I will be driven from this warm circle. It was about this time that I began to fear—or perhaps hope—that I would never live to be twenty-one, that I would die of some exotic debilitating disease. Then they'd be sorry. This fantasy alternated with an even better fantasy that if I did reach twenty-one, I would be blind and hobble about with a white cane. Then they'd really be sorry.

Not that I'd given up without a struggle. For weeks, in the privacy of my cell at home, safe from prying eyes, I continued trying to actually learn something about algebra. After a brief mental pep rally—This is simple. If Esther Jane Alberry can understand it, any fool can do it. All you gotta do is think. THINK! Reason it out!—I would sit down and open my textbook. Within minutes, I would break out in a clammy sweat and sink into a funk of nonunderstanding, a state so naked in its despair and self-contempt that it was soon replaced by a mood of defiant truculence. Schwartz and I took to laughing contemptuously at those boobs and brown-noses up front who took it all so seriously.

The first hints of spring began to appear. Birds twittered, buds unfurled. But men on death row are impervious to such intimations of life quickening and reborn. The only sign of the new season that I noticed was Mr. Pittinger changing from a heavy scratchy black suit into a lighter-weight scratchy black suit.

"Well, it won't be long. You gonna get a job this summer?" my old man asked me one day as he bent over the hood of the Olds, giving the fourth-hand paint job its ritual spring coat of Simoniz.

"Maybe. I dunno," I muttered. It wouldn't be long, indeed. Then he'd know. Everybody would know that I knew less about algebra than Ralph, Mrs. Gammie's big Airedale, who liked to pee on my mother's irises.

Mr. Pittinger had informed us that the final exam, covering a year's work in algebra, would be given on Friday of the following week. One more week of stardom on Cleveland Street. Ever since my devastating rejoinder at the dinner table about abstract mathematics, my stock had been the hottest in the neighborhood. My opinions were solicited on financial matters, world affairs, even the infield problems of the Chicago White Sox. The bigger they are, the harder they fall. Even Ralph would have more respect than I deserved. At least he didn't pretend to be anything but what he was—a copious and talented pee-er.

Wednesday, two days before the end, arrived like any other spring day. A faint breeze drifted from the south, bringing with it hints of long summer afternoons to come, of swung bats, of nights in the lilac bushes. But not for such as me. I stumped into algebra class feeling distinctly like the last soul aboard the *Titanic* as she was about to plunge to the bottom. The smart-asses were already in their seats, laughing merrily, the goddamn A's and B's and C's and even the M's. I took my seat in the back, among the rest of the condemned. Schwartz sat down sullenly and began his usual moan. Helen Weathers squatted toadlike, drenched in sweat. The class began, Pittinger's chalk squeaked, hands waved. The sun filtered in through the venetian blinds. A tennis ball pocked back and forth over a net somewhere. Faintly, the high clear voices of the girls' glee club sang, "Can you bake a cherry pie, charming Billy?" Birds twittered.

My knot of fear, by now an old friend, sputtered in my gut. In the past week, it had grown to roughly the size of a two-dollar watermelon. True, I had avoided being called on even once the entire year, but it was a hollow victory and I knew it. Minute after minute inched slowly by as I ducked and dodged, Pittinger firing question after question at the class. Glancing at my Pluto watch, which I had been given for Christmas, I noted with deep relief that less than two minutes remained before the bell.

It was then that I made my fatal mistake, the mistake that all guerrilla fighters eventually make—I lost my concentration. For years, every fiber of my being, every instant in every class, had been directed solely at survival. On this fateful Wednesday, lulled by the sun, by the gentle sound of the tennis ball, by the steady drone of Pittinger's voice, by the fact that there were just two minutes to go, my mind slowly drifted off into a golden haze. A tiny mote of dust floated down through a slanting ray of sunshine. I watched it in its slow, undulating flight, like some microscopic silver bird.

"You're the apple of my eye, darling Billy . . . I can bake a cherry pie . . ."

A rich maple syrup warmth filled my being. Out of the faint distance, I heard a deadly rasp, the faint honking of disaster.

For a stunned split second, I thought I'd been jabbed with an electric cattle prod. Pittinger's voice, loud and commanding, was pronouncing my name. He was calling on ME! Oh, my God! With a goddamn minute to go, he had nailed me. I heard Schwartz bleat a high, quavering cry, a primal scream. I knew what it meant: If they got him, the greatest master of them all, there's no hope for ANY of us!

As I stood slowly at my seat, frantically bidding for time, I saw a great puddle forming around Helen Weathers. It wasn't all sweat. Chester had sunk to the floor beneath his desk, and behind me Zynzmeister's beads were clattering so loudly I could hardly hear his Hail Marys.

"Come to the board, please. Give us the value of C in this equation."

In a stupor of wrenching fear, I felt my legs clumping up the aisle. On all sides the blank faces stared. At the board—totally unfamiliar territory to me—I stared at the first equation I had ever seen up close. It was well over a yard and a half long, lacerated by mysterious crooked lines and fractions in parentheses, with miniature twos and threes hovering above the whole thing like tiny barnacles. Xs and Ys were jumbled in crazy abandon. At the very end of this unholy mess was a tiny equal sign. And on the other side of the equal sign was a zero. Zero! All this crap adds up to nothing! Jesus Christ! My mind reeled at the very sight of this barbed-wire entanglement of mysterious symbols.

Pittinger stood to one side, arms folded, wearing an expression that said, At last I've nailed the little bastard! He had been playing with me all the time. He knew!

I glanced back at the class. It was one of the truly educational moments of my life. The entire mob, including Schwartz, Chester, and even Zynzmeister, were grinning happily, licking their chops with joyous expectation of my imminent crucifixion. I learned then that when true disaster strikes, we have no friends. And there's nothing a phony loves more in this world than to see another phony get what's coming to him.

"The value of C, please," rapped Pittinger.

The equation blurred before my eyes. The value of C. Where the hell was it? What did a C look like, anyway? Or an A or a B, for that matter. I had forgotten the alphabet.

"C, please."

I spotted a single letter C buried deep in the writhing melange of Ys and Xs and umlauts and plus signs, brackets, and God knows what all. One tiny C. A torrent of sweat raged down my spinal column. My jockey shorts were soaked and sodden with the sweat and stink of execution. Being a true guerrilla from years of the alphabetical ghetto, I showed no outward sign of panic, my face stony; unyielding. You live by the gun, you die by the gun.

"C, please." Pittinger moodily scratched at his granite chin with thumb and forefinger, his blue beard rasping nastily.

"Oh my darling Billy boy, you're the apple of my eye . . ."

Somewhere birds twittered on, tennis racquet met tennis ball. My moment had finally arrived.

Now, I have to explain that for years I had been the leader of the atheistic free-thinkers of Warren G. Harding School, scoffers all at the Sunday School miracles taught at the Presbyterian church; unbelievers.

That miracle stuff is for old ladies, all that walking on water and birds flying around with loaves of bread in their beaks. Who can believe that crap?

Now, I am not so sure. Ever since that day in Pittinger's algebra class I have had an uneasy suspicion that maybe something mysterious is going on somewhere.

As I stood and stonily gazed at the enigmatic Egyptian hieroglyphics of that fateful equation, from somewhere, someplace beyond the blue horizon, it came to me, out of the mist. I heard my voice say clearly, firmly, with decision:

"C . . . is equal to three."

Pittinger staggered back; his glasses jolted down to the tip of his nose.

"How the hell did you know?!" he bellowed hoarsely, his snap-on bow tie popping loose in the excitement.

The class was in an uproar. I caught a glimpse of Schwartz, his face pale with shock. I had caught one on the fat part of the bat. It was a true miracle. I had walked on water.

Instantly, the old instincts took over. In a cool, level voice I answered Pittinger's rhetorical question.

"Sir, I used empirical means."

He paled visibly and clung to the chalk trough for support. On cue, the bell rang out. The class was over. With a swiftness born of long experience, I was out of the room even before the echo of the bell had ceased. The guerrilla's code is always hit and run. A legend had been born.

That afternoon, as I sauntered home from school, feeling at least twelve and a half feet tall, Schwartz skulked next to me, silent, moody, kicking at passing frogs. I rubbed salt deep into his wound and sprinkled a little pepper on for good measure. Across the street, admiring clusters of girls pointed out the Algebra King as he strolled by. I heard Eileen Akers' silvery voice clearly: "There he goes. He doesn't say much in class, but when he does he makes it count." I nodded coolly toward my fans. A ripple of applause went up. I autographed a few algebra books and walked on, tall and straight in the sun. Deep down I knew that this was but a fleeting moment of glory, that when I faced the blue book exam it would be all over, but I enjoyed it while I had it.

With the benign air of a baron bestowing largess upon a wretched serf, I offered to buy Schwartz a Fudgesicle at the Igloo. He refused with a snarl.

"Why, Schwartz, what seems to be troubling you?" I asked with irony, vigorously working the salt shaker.

"You phony son of a bitch. You know what you can do with your goddamn Fudgesicle."

"Me, a phony? Why would you say an unkind thing like that?"

He spat viciously into a tulip bed. "You phony bastard. You studied!"

Inevitably, those of us who are gifted must leave those less fortunate behind in the race of life. I knew that, and Schwartz knew it. Once again I had lapped him and was moving away from the field, if only for a moment.

The next morning, Thursday, I swaggered into algebra class with head high. Even Jack Morton, the biggest smart-ass in the class, said hello as I walked in. Mr. Pittinger, his eyes glowing with admiration, smiled warmly at me.

"Hi, Pit," I said with a casual flip of the hand. We abstract mathematicians have an unspoken bond. Naturally, I was not called on during that period. After all, I had proved myself beyond any doubt.

After class, beaming at me with the intimacy of a fellow quadratic equation zealot, Mr. Pittinger asked me to stay on for a few moments.

"All my life I have heard about the born mathematical genius. It is a well-documented thing. They come along once in a while, but I never thought I'd meet one, least of all in a class of mine. Did you always have this ability?"

"Well . . ." I smiled modestly.

"Look, it would be pointless for you to waste time on our little test tomorrow. Would you help me grade the papers instead?"

"Gosh, Pit, I was looking forward to taking it, but if you really need me, I'll be glad to help." It was a master stroke.

"I'd appreciate it. I need somebody who really knows his stuff, and most of these kids are faking it."

The following afternoon, together, we graded the papers of my peers. I hate to tell you what, in all honesty, I had to do to Schwartz when I marked his pitiful travesty. I showed no mercy. After all, algebra is an absolute science and there can be no margin for kindness in matters of the mind.

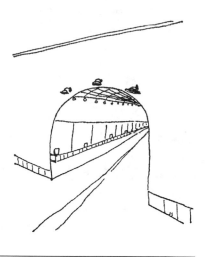

I smiled my thin, crafty Sidney Greenstreet smile, admiring it in the rearview mirror.

"Yep, you pulled it off, you snake in the grass . . . heh, heh." It ain't luck. It's like Lippy Durocher said: "There ain't no such thing as breaks. Winners make their own breaks."

I peered into the gloom ahead, rich with burned Exxon. Some days you grease right through this bastard; others, it's forever. This is one of the mean ones–bad. A Jack Daniel's night.

A warning buzzer which I had never heard before sounded off under the hood. Now what the hell? Mysteriously, it stopped, but my life around cars of all types had taught me one thing: Nothing bad ever really goes away.

In desperation for something to do, I flicked on the radio. Still nothing. Well, you don't get anything in the tunnel anyway these days. I remember a few years back, maybe in the early sixties, they had a radio station inside the tunnel. It just came in all over the dial, playing music, with a happy voice giving you facts about how long the tunnel was, when they built it, how many cars go through. Really exciting stuff, but at least it was a human voice and not a warning buzzer. Gone, all gone, with other graces of *human existence in these dark days of advancing barbarism and approaching ice ages.*

Ice ages—I wonder if the tunnel will get clogged with ice when it comes, and a few last commuters will get frozen down here for all time like those Mammoths in Siberia? Or like that ancient Irishman they dug up a couple of years ago, perfectly preserved in a peat bog. He was sitting in his canoe, still wearing his socks. They say that even though he was three thousand years old, he had that smart-ass look on his Irish map like all the Third Avenue Irishmen I ever knew, including Breslin.

Tough, boy. That's what they are. Or at least loud. I turned over mossy rocks in my memory, rummaging around looking for tough Irishmen I had heard of. Why? Well, that's the kind of thing you do in traffic jams. The late Mayor Daley, a true Mick. Used to say, "Gimme a dozen Irish cops and I'll clean up this crummy neighborhood."

Out of the blue, it came to me, the toughest Irishman I ever personally ran into, who didn't look tough, but when the test came, he was there. I knew his kid from high school. What was his name? Leggett, of course, Mr. Leggett. Tougher than a cob.

Ellsworth Leggett and the Great Ice Cream War

As I drove my rental car over the cracked and potholed surface of what had once been the main drag of my home town, I felt a bit like an invisible alien from another planet. First of all, it was the car itself; anonymous, sexless, of no known make. Perhaps it was a Hertz Deluxe, or maybe an Avis. It was hard to tell: cheap, cigar-scarred naugahyde seats, a Taiwanese radio that emitted only a crackling hum; it was a far cry from the proud, gleaming chariot I had floated down this very street during my lusty youth.

My old man's Pontiac Silver Streak 8 with its three yards of gracefully tapering obsidian black hood, its glorious Italian marble steering wheel with gleaming, spidery chromium spokes—a steering wheel that could well hang on the walls of the Museum of Modern Art—its low, menacing purring classic Straight 8 engine, bore as much resemblance to this eighty-five-dollar-a-day tin can as the *Queen Mary* does to a plastic Boston whaler.

Past the boarded-up, graffiti-splattered ruins of what had once been elegant shops and petite tearooms, past burnt-out hulks of erstwhile department stores, I had the disturbing sensation of being a Pompeian suddenly restored to life and being treated to a tourist jaunt through the ruins of old Pompeii. I had an instantaneous feverish image of the leering Italian spiv who had collared me as I alighted from the bus one day outside tourist Pompeii. As he hissed into my ear: "Cocka-balla, Cocka-balla. Maka dem laugh at home," he furtively displayed his wares: key rings carved crudely to resemble swollen, erectile male genitalia made of the actual alabaster that his far-distant ancestors had used to create "David" and "The Pietà." At the time I had thought, God, Rome really *has* fallen, but now I knew that our time, too, had come.

My home town in industrial northern Indiana stood craggy and sharp against the grayish mud-colored skies of the Region. Even the seemingly immutable steel mills looked sullenly deserted and were decaying into rust. Never a town to be confused with Palm Beach or Beverly Hills, Hohman resembled a vast, endless lake-side junkyard that had been created by that mysterious obscene wrecking ball known as Time.

Summoned back from civilization to attend the funeral of a distant relative, I felt curiously alone, as though surrounded by lurking, unfriendly natives speaking mysterious tongues and worshiping alien gods.

"How would Norman Rockwell have handled this?" I muttered as I lurched past a row of decaying porn shops and "Adult" theaters, one of which bore a crude, hand-lettered sign reading: TOPLESS MUD WRESTLING! LIVE! XXX RATING!

It was the very site on which once the proud Parthenon theater had reposed, named after the Parthenon itself of ancient Athens. It had been famous for its elegant lobby and its graceful Fred Astaire movies. Now, TOPLESS MUD WRESTLING and dealers in greasy film cartridges shot in the cellars of Caracas. Where Clark Gable was once the King, Linda Lovelace now reigned.

I fiddled with the knob of my rented alleged radio. A few whistles and the distant sound of someone singing "Bringing in the Sheaves" was all I could manage. I flipped the bastard off and concentrated on the potholes.

A giant dump truck roared past me, flinging bits of gravel and what appeared to be molten tar over my windshield. I struggled for control in his wake. His tailgate bore a sticker that read THE CHICAGO CUBS SUCK. I felt a note of reassurance that at least some things hadn't changed. This was White Sox country for sure, where the fans followed a ball team as ragged-assed as they were and as cosmically defeated. The White Sox, who once, in my salad days, had actually advertised in the Classified section of the Chicago *Tribune* for a third baseman, they were that desperate. Four thousand out-of-work hod carriers and steel workers showed up for the audition, which was by far the largest crowd the Sox had drawn in ten years. Oh well.

Heavy diesel fumes rolled in my window. I frantically tried to crank it up, but naturally the handle came off in my hand. I flung it under the seat with a snarl, there to join the handle from the other door and an empty Pabst Blue Ribbon can thoughtfully left for me by the previous renter.

Out of the gloom rose the great bulk of my beloved former high school. My God, there it was! It was like meeting a totally unexpected old friend strolling through the streets of Bombay.

> *"Hoh-man, we'll fight for you . . .*
> *Pur-ple vic-tree is our hu-ue.*
> *Vic-to-ree is ever ours*
> *As . . ."*

I croaked the words of the "Wildcat Victory Song" as the great building loomed against the sky, untouched by time. It was all there, even the weedy athletic field with its paint-peeling goalposts where I had once played the role of an intrepid defensive lineman and where I had irrevocably shattered the ligaments of my left knee, which now began to throb sympathetically as we passed the old battlefield.

Ghostly voices of my teachers of that golden time moaned in my subconscious: Miss Bryfogel, her high, thin bleat intoning facts about Bull Run and Appomattox, Miss McCullough's birdlike chirp squeaking something about gerunds or whatever they were, old red-faced Huffine, our coach, barking, "I don't want to kick no asses, but . . ."

I clutched at the plastic steering wheel in a cold sweat. Old fears never really die. The long winter days I had spent in this red brick mausoleum, its echoing halls, clanging lockers, its aromatic gym and cafeteria, scented forever with the aroma of salmon loaf and canned peas. The roar of thousands of students surging up and down the stairways. My peers, now scattered to the four winds and more by the tides of life. Wars and presidents had come and gone. Do they all remember Miss Bryfogel, Miss McCullough, the salmon loaf? And do they remember . . . ?

Great Scott! If it's possible to reel in an Avis (We Try Harder) Rent-a-Car, I reeled. It was still there, exactly as it had been in my days as a Wildcat lineman, as a ceaseless unsuccessful pursuer of Daphne Bigelow, the belle of the junior class; the shrine where Schwartz and Flick and I had squandered many a hard-earned quarter. Untouched! Unchanged!

Now squatting defensively in the shadow cast by a majestic Burger King, still gleaming snow-white, topped by a gigantic concrete Rainbow three-dip ice cream cone was—THE IGLOO.

The Igloo! My God, I can't believe it. Still in business, still spreading tooth cavities among the young—the Igloo. The home of the greatest malted milk ever created by the hand of man!

So ran my feverish thoughts as I smartly cut across traffic, dodged a lounging drug pusher, and pulled into the very parking slot where eons ago I had moored the Silver Streak Pontiac.

Drawn to the Igloo by forces too immense to comprehend, I eased out of the car and headed for the same old glass door through which my generation had passed, the door that Flick had once shattered while attempting to kick Schwartz in the ass, an act which sent us on the lam for weeks and was the cause of an investigation that eventually involved the police (but they never got us)—the door through which I had once escorted Daphne on a disastrous double date centuries before.

The Igloo was not a candy store, not a hangout. No, it was purely and functionally a place that made and sold ice cream. There were no booths, jukeboxes, all the other semi-mythic appurtenances of the traditional American kid high school hangout. You went to the Igloo for one thing alone—ice cream. Ice cream such as must be served in the ice cream parlors of heaven: rich, creamy, many-flavored, and made on the premises. It did not come out of machines, squirted out like toothpaste. No, the Igloo dealt in serious ice cream.

In keeping with its high purpose, its interior had all the charm of the inside of a Kelvinator refrigerator; a long white formica counter, a bank of deep ice cream drums set in stainless steel, ladled out by hand with gleaming chromium scoops. The Igloo was as clean and functional as a paring knife.

In my day, it was presided over by Mr. Igloo himself, a small, worried-looking man who was never called anything but "Mr. Leggett." His life was devoted to ice cream the way a Jesuit focuses in on the nature of good and evil. Mr. Leggett was never known to wield a scoop himself. No, his troop of disciplined dedicated high school students handled the job, clad in sparkling aprons and Igloo helmets. They were the Praetorian Guard of tutti-frutti and rocky road.

I really can't say why I did it, since I have long subscribed to Tom Wolfe (the First) and his seminal dicta that "You can't go home again," but, flying in the face of good sense, I pushed open the heavy glass door. A wave of achingly familiar ancient aromas poured over me. Ice cream joints have a distinctive smell, a kind of vague, sweetish/sour that is as uniquely American as a Fenway Park hot dog.

Great Scott, it's shrunk! That measly little formica counter, those spindly stools. But, by God, it's all here!

A few acne-riddled youths were squatting at the far end of the counter. One wore a faded purple T-shirt imprinted with a giant insolent finger and bearing the inscription UP YOURS. I eased myself gingerly onto one of the familiar stools with its red imitation-leather padding. Of course, it had been slashed several times and its cotton guts were oozing outward, indicating that the ancient roving tribe of Vandals had left their mark, their universal barbaric yawp of pure malevolence.

The heavy-jowled, white-aproned citizen behind the counter bellowed out at the acne victims:

"Look, you birds, tone it down or I'll kick your butts right out of here."

He swabbed a wet rag over the counter, glaring with the tired eye of a man whose life is truly spent at the end of his rope. There was something vaguely familiar about him. He wore a plastic igloo on his head, a white half-cantaloupe of imitation snow complete to the tunnel doorway, which extended out over his bulbous nose as a visor.

The same stupid hat. I wonder if that's the very one that Junior Kissel tried to steal one day and damn near got his arm broke. It can't be.

"Come on, Al. How 'bout a free scoop of marshmallow brickle?"

"Look, you punk, I'll give you a free scoop right where you don't want it, y'hear?"

He turned and moved toward me. I was about to enjoy, once again, the blessed fruits of the Igloo. The Igloo, a historic battleground fabled in local song and folklore, the site of one of the first decisive skirmishes of modern times between individual man and the faceless corporation. Agincourt, Waterloo, Omaha Beach—the Igloo.

"What'll you have, buddy?"

His gray bb eyes peered out from under his festive igloo as he glared down at me with the customary truclence which is in this day and age standard treatment given to the rank and file. Our eyes met. He wavered. In a low voice, I greeted him.

"Al, make it the regular."

I allowed a thin, ironic smile to play over my handsome, craggy features. For a long, pregnant moment our stares locked.

"Jesus," he hissed, "what the hell you doin' here?"

"The regular, Al."

"That'll be a dip of pineapple and a dip of Dutch chocolate on a sugar cone, right?"

"Right, Al. I'm glad to see that you have not forgotten the tastes of a true connoisseur."

"Look, buddy, you were here during the Great War. How could I forget?"

"Yes, Al, I was. Those punks down at the end of the counter couldn't imagine anything like it, right?"

Al chuckled as he scooped deep into his ice cream vats. "Yep. But they heard of it. They teach 'em about it at the high school, in history."

"God, that sure was something . . ."

It had all begun on a steamy hot day in July. It was a Friday, and there were none who suspected that this nondescript day would go down in legend. It was hot, really hot, as only Indiana can get when the sun hangs like a molten ball in the brass-colored skies, the air so thick that the clothes poles and drooping trees shimmered in your vision. The low, heavy bank of perpetual smoke from the steel mills ringed the horizon, and the air was ripe with the million rotting-egg smells of the refineries. Cicadas screamed, their cries dying out in exhaustion.

We were playing a listless game of softball, just swatting the ball around and tossing it back and forth, not a real game but the kind you play when there's nothing much else to do.

"Come on, Schwartz. Quit hitting 'em in the stickers." Flick gingerly poked around in the weeds, trying to find the ball amid the miserable sand burrs that made life in Indiana such a joy. These burrs are mean little buggers. They fester the skin and work their way up through the marrow of the bones, and they cover the sandy soil of Indiana like scratchy fur on a yellow Airedale. Flick casually tossed the ball to Schwartz, who was knocking out the flies for us to shag. He scooped it up and yelled in pain.

"Ow! God dammit, Flick, take the stickers off the ball before you throw it!"

He dropped the bat and began surgery on his injured mitt.

And so the game went, if you could call it a game. An airplane droned painfully overhead, chopping through the thick atmosphere on its way toward Chicago. Half the county was out of work. They're always having things called "slumps," but the current one had gone on for years. The White Sox were in seventh place, forty-three games behind the Yankees. They were trailed only by the St. Louis Browns, but by a mere half-game. As Charles Dickens put it, it was not the best of times, nor was it the worst of times, but something sure as hell was about to happen.

"Boy, am I thirsty. Wow. My tongue is hanging down around my knees. Boy, do I need a drink. Gaaahhh!" Kissel clutched at his throat and reeled around in the weeds, pretending that he was dying. Schwartz slammed a fast hopper at him and caught him neatly in the gut as he staggered about.

"Come on, Kissel, quit horsing around," I yelled. Kissel was the worst ballplayer for miles around. He tried to make up for it by clowning, but he wasn't very good at that either. Kissel picked up the ball and awkwardly tossed it into the stickers back of Schwartz.

"Y'throw like a girl, Kissel," Schwartz hollered.

This was, of course, a maximum insult.

"Hey, Kissel, you're horsin' around, you go after the ball in the stickers." Flick sailed a rock in the general direction of Kissel, who was now groveling in the dust pretending that he was dying of thirst. Schwartz fished the ball out of the sand burrs with the end of the bat and began golfing it around without picking it up, since it now looked like a porcupine about to strike. The field we were using was a semi-abandoned city ball park with a rickety chicken-wire backstop and barely discernible base lines.

Thirst is a contagious disease. Kissel had started it; now all of our tongues were hanging out. Schwartz picked up a rock and said, "Let's see if we can open the spigot." The spigot was a mysterious pipe that stuck out of the ground a couple of inches, back of third base just outside the foul line. It had caused many a swollen ankle, and had never been known to be turned on.

Schwartz banged on it with the bat, first on one side and then the other.

"Come on, Schwartz, you're tightening it." Flick tried to grab the bat away from him. "You gotta hit it on the other side."

"How do you know so much?" Schwartz snarled. "You ain't my boss."

We gathered around the faucet, some kicking, Kissel hammering with a derelict chunk of grandstand. Schwartz whacked it again with the Louisville Slugger, putting his back into it.

S S S S S S S S S S S!

A silver spray of liquid arced fanlike into the air. We jumped back.

"Boy, you got it, Schwartz!" Kissel leaped on the faucet and wrapped his mouth around the pipe, gulping frantically. He came up for air and again the crescent of water sprayed over us.

"Oh, boy, is that good! Wow!" Kissel's dripping face was contorted in ecstasy. Flick fell onto the faucet and gulped greedily. Each in his turn filled up our tanks.

Five minutes later, our stomachs taut and sloshing, we wandered listlessly toward the far end of the field. Without a word being said, the game was over. Contentment had us in its silky, comforting grip.

"Hey, there's Clarence." Schwartz waved the bat toward the chicken-wire fence. "Hey, Clarence, is there gonna be a ball game here tomorrow?" Flick hollered out.

Clarence "worked for the city." He was sort of in charge of the park, but he never came around much, spending most of his time at the Bluebird testing the Pabst Blue Ribbon to be sure it came up to city health standards. Clarence wore coveralls and drove a pickup truck with the seal of the city on its door, so he was a celebrity among the kids who hung around in the park.

"Hey, you guys, was you guys foolin' around with that spigot over there?"

"Why, no, of course not, Clarence, what gave you that idea? Why, we were just having a bit of infield practice." Flick, the resident smart-ass, was back at his trade.

"Come on, I saw you guys drinkin' out of that spigot. Lookit, it's still squirtin'."

"C'mon, Clarence, we were thirsty. It's really hot today." I tried pure reason as a last resort. After all, there was no telling what Clarence could do, since he was Official.

"Well"–Clarence shot a stream of tobacco juice into the stickers–"don't come around and ask me for no sympathy when you start throwin' up and heavin' all over the place."

"What do you mean?" Kissel squeaked. His mother was a legendary hypochondriac who carried a shopping bag full of pills with her wherever she went. It was rumored that she sprayed Kissel himself with Lysol three times a day, and she had a deadly fear of something she called "germs."

Clarence threw his shovel into the back of the city pickup and clanged the tailgate shut.

"Just don't say I didn't warn you." He squirted more juice into the weeds.

"Come on, Clarence, stop the kidding." Flick looked a little worried.

"I ain't kiddin'." Clarence blew his nose loudly into a blue-and-white bandanna. "That ain't city water. That stuff is pumped right out of the river. It's supposed to be used just for waterin' the grass. There's a sign over there on the tool shack, if you wanna know. That stuff'll kill you."

Water out of the river! The river that moldered and festered its smelly way through the Region was so gooey and full of dead snakes that it wasn't water at all, just a kind of brown ooze. Every chemical factory for miles around dumped stuff into it. It once caught fire, and the Fire Department had to come and squirt water into it to put it out.

Clarence climbed into the cab and started the engine.

"Don't come cryin' around to me when you're dead." He laughed nastily and roared off down the street, trailing a cloud of stickers and tobacco juice.

There was a long moment of tremulous silence, broken only by the distant sound of someone beating a carpet.

"He's kiddin'. He's always sayin' that kind of stuff." Schwartz had a funny sound in his voice.

"Yeah" was all I could think to say.

Flick kicked his tennis shoe against a curb. "He got tobacco juice on my new laces."

"Listen, you guys, don't tell my mother. She'd go crazy. She won't even let me drink out of the hose. She says there's rubber in the hose and it could stop up your kidneys or something. Boy, she's gonna kill me."

Schwartz laughed. "How could she kill you if you're already dead from drinkin' that water? When you're layin' there in the kitchen, turning green, and she comes in there and starts hollerin', and you're layin' there . . ."

Schwartz, as was true of all of us, was always ready with the needle.

"Look, you guys, this ain't funny. I never heard of anybody drinking water out of that crummy river. That ain't even water!"

Kissel spoke the truth. It was sobering. The sun was hanging low over the flat plains of Illinois to the west. Many a pioneer forefather had passed on into the Great Happy Hunting Grounds from drinking at the wrong water hole. All of us had seen enough cowboy movies to know what could happen.

"It was your idea, Flick," I mumbled through the sweat.

"What do you mean, my idea! It was Kissel started all of it. Rollin' around in the dirt like a nut, with your tongue hangin' out. It was Kissel!"

"I got a right to roll around in the dirt. It's a free country. I never even knew that spigot was there." Kissel was the color of a dirty dishrag with fear.

"You started hitting it with the bat, Schwartz," I said, giving him a shove.

Schwartz, as the guilty always have, took the offensive. "Nobody forced y' to drink it. I ain't your boss. You hit it too, Flick, with that board!"

We trudged on through the stifling heat. The first mosquitoes were coming on duty. A ragged sparrow flew by on his way to the city dump. Each of us carried his own private knot of fear that the end had come. We had many such terrors in our lives. For instance, it was well known that if you licked the point of an indelible pencil, thus purpling your tongue, there was no hope. Or, it was fully recognized by the best medical authorities among the kids that a sure way to commit suicide in a particularly nasty manner was to swallow a wad of bubble gum, which would "cause your guts to stick together." Naturally, it was believed that eating too much candy caused you to "get worms," which, while not fatal, was certainly serious. There were hundreds of these mortal dangers that we believed in, and I must admit that even today I'm very careful around indelible pencils and bubble gum. We all had heard of the kid who once cut open a golf ball, which had, of course, exploded, blowing up his neighborhood. Then there was the two-aspirins-and-a-swig-of-Coca-Cola, which was guaranteed to make you drunker than a skunk. It goes without saying that drinking a tank full of river water had to be, at the very least, fatal.

We were listlessly shuffling in the general direction of our various houses. Instinctively, the way a herd of Guernsey cows heads for the barn at twilight, kids in the flatlands of Indiana mosey barnward at suppertime.

"Y'know, that water tasted kinda funny." Schwartz juicily shot a wad of bubble gum at a passing brown-and-white rat terrier that was innocently going about his job of knocking over garbage cans and rooting among the coffee grounds. "Sorta like rusty iron, or something."

The rat terrier glared indignantly at Schwartz, his feelings clearly hurt. Even rat terriers have some pride.

"Well, stupid, that spigot was rusty iron. You dummies don't believe that jerk Clarence, do you?"

"Nah."

"Nah."

"Nah."

We all joined in the loud chorus of denial, about as phony as a set of mail order celluloid false teeth.

"Tasted kinda oily, too," Schwartz said, licking his lips noisily to recapture the rich bouquet of tap water.

"That won't hurt you, fathead," Flick snorted, flipping a bottle cap toward a passing Studebaker. "My grandpa drinks kerosene when he gets a cold. Never hurt him, and he's about two hundred years old. He oughta know something."

"Kerosene!" Kissel was astounded. "He drinks kerosene? Like the kind you get at the Shell station, and they use in lanterns?"

"Yup. He drinks it right out of our lantern that we keep in the basement in case the lights go out."

"Boy!" Schwartz was impressed. "I'll bet he don't smoke no cigars after he does that. That'd cure his cold!"

"No, smart-ass. He chews tobacco. Chewin' tobacco is why he's lived so long, he says. That and drinkin' kerosene." Flick concluded the medical seminar by emitting a low, musical burp.

We split up at Ace's Rack'n Q Poolroom and headed to our various comforting nests. The river water was never mentioned again. Since nobody died, it's a good bet that Clarence was giving us the business. Ever since, though, I never drink out of freelance faucets. You never know.

I drifted in through the kitchen door.

"Don't slam the screen," my mother said absently, the way you intone something that you've said a million times before, until you don't even know that you're saying it. My kid brother was under the kitchen table, pushing a small green dump truck around on the linoleum.

"Rrraahhhr, raaaahhhr." He made a mean, nasty little sound, something like a dentist's drill digging into a root canal.

"Eeeeeiiinnnggggg . . . raaaahhhhr."

"Will you cut that out, Randy. You're getting on my nerves. Now go get washed up for supper."

"Eeeeeiiinnnnggg . . . awwwwrrrrr . . ."

She clanged open the oven door to inspect her meatloaf. The kitchen was even hotter than the outdoors, if possible. Our white plastic AC/DC radio, with its cracked cabinet and its heavy 60-cycle hum, droned atop the refrigerator.

> *"When the DEEP purple falls . . .*
> *Over SLEEpy garden WALLS . . ."*

Life was rich and full.

I headed for the bathroom and sloshed some Mercurochrome on a punctured thumb knuckle, after extracting the malevolent sticker spine with my teeth.

"Your father's home, your father's home!"

I heard the distant roar of the family Pontiac out in the driveway. The old man always revved up the engine a couple of times before he switched the key off. "Blows out the carbon," he always said after the operation. I strolled into the kitchen, licking my aching thumb.

"You cut yourself?" My mother stirred a little salt into the canned peas that were heating on the stove.

"Nah, just a sticker."

"LOST in a DEEEP purple DREAM . . ."

"Would you turn that darn radio off? It makes your father mad." My mother glanced over her shoulder at me, rattling the aluminum rheostats she wore in her hair. I flipped off the little AC/DC beauty in mid-dream. It let out a squawk and expired, after a final blast of phlegmy hum.

The screen door slammed open. The old man lurched into the kitchen, his tie at half-mast, his face bathed in sweat. Without a word he rushed to the refrigerator, wrenched the door open, and rummaged frantically among the wilted lettuce, the horseradish jars, the oleo cartons.

"Aha! I knew there was one little sweetheart left." His mitt clutched a can of Blatz. Flinging his suit jacket over the back of his chair, he sank down at the kitchen table, popped the can, took a big slug of beer, all in one fluid motion.

"Goddamn traffic."

He took another quick gulp.

"Whew, boy. Hot as the hinges of hell."

Over by the stove, my mother stirred the mashed potatoes.

"Was it hot at the office today?"

"Ha! Don't ask. Those crummy cheapskates. You'd think a five-dollar electric fan would break the bastards. Boy, what a bunch of cheapskates. Zudock brought his own fan from home, but it blew a fuse. Crummy cheapskates."

He shook the Blatz vigorously to give it a head.

"Mrs. Kissel had to borrow some ice cubes today. Their refrigerator caught on fire."

"No kidding? Sorry I missed it." The old man finished off his beer. He flipped the can neatly into the garbage bag next to the stove.

"Hey, dog-collar, how'd the Sox do today?"

"The Indians beat 'em six to three. They got five runs in the ninth."

I was expected to have the daily ball scores for the old man when he got home from work. It was almost always bad news. He was a lifelong White Sox fan, which, of course, only made him more frustrated than a normal person. Year after year it was not only failure, but also humiliation. I went on:

"Yankees beat the Athletics fifteen to two."

The old man unbuttoned his shirt while the sweat dripped from his chin.

"Goddamn Yankees."

"Supper's ready, supper's ready, supper's ready," my mother sang out gaily, bravely trying to change the subject. She knew from long, mean experience that once the old man got on the subject of the Yankees the whole evening was shot. Her meatloaves were famous even among such notoriously picky meatloaf connoisseurs as my aunt Clara, who had made a life's work of not liking anything.

We began supper, as it was always called in the Midwest in those days, since dinner was a meal that was served only on Sunday afternoons, as in "Sunday dinner," and was somewhat ceremonial. Supper was what you ate at night, after work.

"Pass the catsup." The old man hammered at the bottom of the Heinz bottle. A great gout of his favorite gourmet treat gushed over the peas.

"Mrs. Kissel threw the dishwater on it."

I looked up from my plate and asked: "On what?"

"She had to get the hose," my mother continued as she served the mashed potatoes. "Sit up, Randy. You can't eat under the table like that."

"Threw the dishwater on what?" the old man barked. At least he had forgotten the Yankees.

"The refrigerator. It caught on fire. Mrs. Van Hoose was visiting her. They were eating bridge mix at the time."

So the conversation went; labyrinthine, almost Byzantine in its complexity, as the kitchen grew hotter and hotter. Sometimes in Indiana, perversely, the heat grows as the sun disappears and night takes over.

The old man leaned back in his chair and luxuriously lit one of his beloved Luckies.

"How 'bout taking the car and going out for a ride?"

My mother, who was putting the dishes into the sink, said, "That'd be nice."

" 'Ray, h'ray!" Randy, who had once again sullenly refused to eat, came to life.

"Going for a ride" was a big thing in those days. Whenever the old man suggested such a debauch, he was in a good mood.

We trooped out into the Pontiac amid the soft, primal hum of a billion mosquitoes. Fireflies winked around the garage. A few crickets chirped doggedly in the steamy humidity.

We always sat in the same seats in the Pontiac; the old man behind the wheel, of course, my mother next to him, directly behind her Randy, who began kicking the seat ahead of him with his tennis shoes, and me behind the king of the house.

—Brooommm, Brroommm . . .

He gunned the mighty Eight.

"Listen to that power."

Bar-ROOOOM.

The Pontiac was the very center of the old man's existence. It had replaced his equally beloved Olds, and like an Arab chieftain tends to his horses, the old man meticulously curried and groomed his cars.

"Randy, would you stop kicking that seat! How many times have I told you not to do that?" My mother swatted a neat backhand in the direction of the kid brother.

"Awwwwww." He scrunched down in his seat.

"What did you say? Don't you give me any back talk." He shut up, for the time being.

This seat-kicking business was an old battle between Randy and my mother.

The old man backed the car effortlessly out of the driveway and whipped neatly out onto the road. Although none of us knew it at the time, the wheels of great adventure were set in motion.

This night would live in the memory of thousands, and would become one of the great legends of the Region.

The sun had finally set after the lingering Indiana twilight.

–SPLAT!

Some giant furry flying creature splattered its guts out over the windshield.

"Goddamn bugs."

The old man spoke with no rancor, since bugs were a natural part of Indiana summer life and he, for one, accepted them.

"Why don't you turn on the windshield wipers?" My mother was always giving the old man little helpful hints.

"Jeez, how stupid can you get? It'd smear that stuff all over the windshield."

It was before the days of automatic windshield squirters, so viewing the world through bug juice was as natural as breathing.

"There goes Mr. Kissel, there goes Mr. Kissel," Randy sang, thumping the seat back with his Keds.

"What a snootful! How ya doin', Kissel?" The old man waved cheerily out the window at Kissel, who was staggering homeward from his nightly celebration at the Bluebird. He blearily peered at us, waving shakily, after which he fell heavily into a privet hedge.

The old man laughed sardonically. "He's really tanked up tonight. He ain't feelin' no pain."

"Poor Mrs. Kissel," my mother said as she peered gloomily out her window at the passing scene.

"Wait'll Kissel finds out the refrigerator caught on fire." The old man laughed even more uproariously. The thought made me laugh, too. Naturally, Randy joined in.

"I fail to see the humor of that," my mother said in a hurt voice. The old man didn't answer; he just snickered on into the night. She gave him a mean look.

"Mrs. Van Hoose tried to put it out with a rug beater."

The old man shook his head in mock amazement.

"Oh, Jesus," was all he said.

Ever since that night I have had occasional fleeting visions, usually just before I fall asleep, of Mrs. Van Hoose banging away at a Kelvinator refrigerator with her mouth full of bridge mix, while the flames shot out the freezer compartment, and Mrs. Kissel flinging dishwater over the whole scene.

The hot summer air poured into the car windows like a flood of overheated oil. We drove past the ball park where I had spent the listless afternoon.

"I see they're sprinkling the grass," my mother observed, her spirits bouncing back after her brief sorrowful reverie over Mrs. Kissel's failed life.

Sure enough, out there in the gloom I could see our faucet still squirting its fan of deadly river water into the night.

"Christ Almighty, no wonder our taxes are so high. Sprinklin' the stickers." The old man was always spotting evidences of further idiocy on the part of "stupid politicians," all designed to increase the bite on the taxpayer.

The twin devils of his existence, "stupid politicians" and the "cheapskates" at the office, formed at least 95 percent of the conversation when he and his buddies got together at, say, the bowling alley.

"Jeez, look at those dummies, sprinklin' the stickers!"

I kept my mouth shut.

"I gotta wee-wee," Randy piped in his most irritating voice. There was something about just stepping into the car that apparently was a powerful, irresistible stimulant to his bladder.

"You'll just have to wait till we get home." My mother had been handling the wee-wee problem for years. Like most mothers, much of her life was spent in mopping up wee-wee left behind by everything from kids to turtles.

"But I gotta go!"

"You'll just have to hold it."

"Eeeeaaagghhh," he whined nasally, making a sound that he had perfected since tothood. He had one of the most effective nasty whines of his generation.

"Will you knock off that damn whining!!" The old man's voice was rich with warning. "You heard what your mother said. Now cut out the whining."

That did it. It was before the days of Dr. Spock and the age of the mollycoddled moppet riding roughshod over his parents. The old man was the possessor of a lethal backhand, and he did not hesitate to use it when the occasion arose.

We rolled on, chattering away, enjoying the ride. We passed my old man's favorite signboard, a giant, multicolored creation, brightly lit, starring an enormous, well-endowed bull, advertising Bull Durham. It bore the legend, under the bull, HER HERO. My mother modestly averted her gaze.

The old man lit up one of his Luckies. He coughed fitfully.

"Hey, I got an idea . . ." he wheezed, blowing smoke out of his nostrils. "How 'bout us going down and watching the mill for a while?"

" 'Ray, 'ray!" Randy cheered.

"Watching the mill" was a special treat known only to the residents of the Region. On hot nights, people would drive to the lakefront and park in the velvet blackness near the shore to watch the flickering Vesuvius fireworks of the blast furnace and the rolling mills across the dark waters. Cherry-red ingots and sepia-shaded orange glowing sprays of sparks flung high in the air by the Bessemer converters made a truly beautiful and even spectacular sight as the hissing colors were reflected in the black waters of Lake Michigan. It had a curious hypnotic effect, since the mill was far enough away so that no sound came over the water, but the darkness and the lake somehow magnified the colors in the eerie light. It was a sight genuinely worth seeing. Heavy industry has a very distinct beauty all its own; mighty forces at work with the unearthly radiance of distant volcanoes.

"Boy, ain't that somethin'?" The old man's voice was edged with awe as the orange light played over our faces in the dark car.

The Pontiac was only one of a silent fleet bearing beauty

lovers, all enjoying the colors, the mysterious majesty of barely controlled explosions, and the heat.

The smell of the lake was part of it, of course. Lake Michigan, that great, sullen, dangerous, beautiful body of water is, in mid-summer, like a primitive reptilian animal in heat. For miles inland on such nights, the natives can "smell the lake." It makes them restless, on edge; dangerous. Tonight was no exception. Maybe it was that damn lake that caused it all, but who's to know?

We sat for a while in the blackness.

"Randy, go out and wee-wee now beside the car."

My mother unerringly knew how to shatter a magic moment.

"I don't have to wee-wee," he whined.

Of course, I thought, one day the old man's gonna kill that kid. And he deserves it.

"I thought you had to go."

My mother hung in there.

". . . Nahhh."

The old man's head swiveled in the darkness, and he turned the Ray on the kid.

"Look, you, if you don't go now and I hear one more word about wee-wee tonight, you're gonna feel it, y'hear?"

Randy mumbled something from deep in his seat.

"Whaat was that? Are you giving me back talk?"

Silence. As Hemingway would have put it, the wee-wee question was well and truly settled. For tonight.

We sat for a few moments more, enjoying the fireworks, when the old man laid a true goodie on us, one that led, in the end, to our part in one of the great dramas of our time.

"Gang"–he paused dramatically–"what would you say if I drove you down and treated everybody to triple-dip ice cream cones at the Igloo?"

"H'ray, 'ray!"

"Whoopee!"

"H'ray!"

He started the engine, backed the Pontiac out of its slot, and we happily headed south toward the Igloo and destiny. The troops were assembling for the Great Ice Cream War.

Behind us, the sky glowed red over the immense steel mills. Not until I had left the Region as a semi-adult did I realize that not everywhere was the northern sky a flickering line of orange and crimson, a perpetual man-made sunset.

The old man flipped the switch on the Motorola, with its dial that matched the speedometer and the gas gauge of the Pontiac.

> *"When the DEEEEP purple FALLS*
> *Over SLEEpy GARden WALLS..."*

My mother began to hum along with the syrupy saxophones. "What a stupid song. Jesus, I hate that song."

> *"LOST in a deep PURple DREEEAM..."*

"I kind of like it. I think it's nice."

She was a known Bing Crosby disciple, while the old man shared with Ring Lardner a total scorn of any form of popular music.

"What the hell's a deep purple dream, for Chrissake?" he snorted, blowing smoke at the Motorola.

> *"Over SLEEpy Garden WALLS..."*

She sang on, the incorrigible sentimentalist who all her days believed completely in the verses on greeting cards.

"Anybody who has deep purple dreams oughta get his head examined."

The old man was forever recommending that people "have their heads examined." Perversely, he scorned all forms of psychoanalysis.

The song ended. On came the commercial.

> *"Pepsi-Cola hits the spot...*
> *Twelve full ounces, that's a lot...*
> *Twice as much for a nickel, too...*

PEPsi-Cola is the drink for you.
Nickel nickel nickel nickel..."

Randy loudly joined in the chorus:

"NICKEL NICKEL NICKEL NICKEL..."

He was one of the first kids to know the lyrics of all commercials ever aired, the forerunner of today's tot who loves Ronald McDonald far more than his own uncle.

"I wonder why all this traffic is out." The old man squinted through the windshield. Ahead, a line of cars that were heading in the same direction as we were.

"I wonder if there's a game or something at the high school. Hey, paper clip," he hollered back at me, "is there a game or something?"

"Nah. School's out. They don't have games in the summer."

"I wonder what the hell it is."

"Maybe they're going to the Dart Ball tournament at the Presbyterian church."

My mother played something called "dart ball" with Mrs. Kissel and her gaggle of buddies.

"Five hundred cars heading for dart ball? No way."

The old man stepped on the gas to keep up with the horde of Fords and Chevys and Hudsons hurrying through the night.

It was right about then that we all became aware of a kind of tension in the air: excitement, an electric tautness. We raced through the night, as other dark sedans joined the stream from side streets and driveways. I caught glimpses of staring eyes in their black interiors.

"What the hell's goin' on?" The old man hunched over his wheel. Randy whimpered softly, sliding down deeper in his seat.

The temperature throughout the evening had been creeping up degree by degree, and now must have been well over a hundred, with humidity to match. There was no wind, just a thick, redolent blanket of spongy, overheated air. The fireflies had long since turned off their lanterns, while only the mosquito horde stayed on duty.

A battered Buick thundered past. It appeared to be packed with silent people. We rocked in their wake.

"Look at that nut. Goin' like stink! What the hell's goin' on?"

Ahead, the distant glow of the "business" section of town dimly lit up the sky.

"Hey, would you look at that? Look at all those people!"

I waved toward a clot of running figures thundering over the dark sidewalk to our left. They were heading in the same direction as the cars. They ran with a maniacal intensity; men, women, kids, old ladies. Occasionally one would stumble and fall, only to rise immediately and struggle forward.

"Does this look like a dart ball crowd to you?" the old man cracked, spinning the butt of his Lucky out into the night.

A white ambulance screamed by, its red crosses catching the light from the passing neon signs.

"Holy smokes!" The old man fed the gas to the Silver Streak. He was a dedicated Disaster fan, and the sight of a hurrying ambulance drew him like honey draws a grizzly bear.

"Be careful!" My mother clutched the dashboard. "I don't like this!" Her aluminum hair curlers rattled nervously.

Silently, the old man whipped the Pontiac faster and faster. He was in his element. Ahead and behind us, a long line of vehicles roared in an unbroken, maniacal stream: pickup trucks, cars, a couple of old, broken-down school buses, anything that could move.

"Boy, must be somethin' big!" the old man hissed over the roar of the Straight 8 engine. At the time, he did not realize just how big the "somethin'" was.

The lights of town were drawing nearer. We passed some cars that had broken down in the race. They were empty; their occupants had charged ahead on foot. Even my mother was now caught up in the excitement.

"I wonder what it could be?" She leaned forward over the

dashboard, her aluminum rheostats clicking against the glass as she stared ahead toward the action.

The heat, which seemed to have grown even more intense, rolled in through the Pontiac's windows.

"Jesus, it's hot. That old tutti-frutti is going to hit the spot." The old man spun the wheel neatly, avoiding a stalled Nash, its hood open, great plumes of steam rising from its tortured, overheated engine.

About four blocks from the Igloo, it became obvious that whatever was going on up ahead, the traffic was snarled, blocking the streets. If we were going to get any ice cream, we'd have to park and hoof it.

"Watch out the back," the old man barked as he backed briskly into a parking spot so tiny that only a truly expert wheel man could manage it.

"One pass. How d'ya like that? Let's hear those cheers." The old man loved showing off.

" 'Ray, 'Ray!" Randy thumped the back of the seat happily with his Keds. " 'Ray, 'ray!"

We piled out of the car.

"Must be a hundred and ten," the old man muttered as he locked the Pontiac. Now that we had stopped driving, the night closed in with its mosquitoes and heat.

"My, there certainly are a lot of people out tonight."

My mother fanned her face listlessly with her sweaty hand. We trudged toward the Igloo, joining the surging throng, still unaware of the history that was in the making.

It was then that a tiny ray of light, a hint of what was up, occurred. A heavy-set lout in his late teens thundered by, his T-shirt drenched in sweat.

"Hey, what the hell's going on?" the old man shouted.

Without turning his head, his eyes staring wildly, the lout yelled, "Ice cream war, ice cream war, ice cream war!"

He disappeared down the street.

". . . ice cream war!"

"What the hell?" The old man's Lucky sent off angry sparks. "Ice cream war? What the hell?"

His jaw dropped at the sight of an elderly lady hurrying toward us against the flow of the surging crowd. She carried in her arms at least a dozen juicily dripping triple-dip ice cream cones.

"How much?" A thick man wearing a railroad engineer's cap and blue suspenders shouted at her as she struggled bravely with her ice cream cones. One shot out of the pack and landed squashily at her feet.

"Oh my, oh my . . ." Her voice cracked.

"How MUCH?"

She didn't answer, since she seemed to be crying. From somewhere behind us, a voice squawked:

"They're running out, they're running out!"

There are always the Rumor Mongers.

Two kids came toward us carrying between them what looked like a washtub full of ice cream cones.

"HOW MUCH?" Engineer Cap yelled.

"Twelve cents," the lead kid sang out happily. "Twelve cents apiece. Triple dip!"

"Oh, my God," the old man hissed, "it's an ice cream war. Triple-dip cones twelve cents apiece. Let's go!" He broke into a full run. My mother gamely struggled to keep up, clattering along on her high heels.

The crowd grew thicker as we neared the Igloo. At last we rounded the corner, and there before our eyes was the whole spectacular history-making panorama.

The main drag, brightly lit by high, overhead street lights, had the sharp unreality of a movie set. A long, unruly line snaked down one side of the street for a couple of blocks and ended at the Igloo. Several police cars, their red lights flashing, roamed up and down the street, their bullhorns blaring, vainly trying to keep the mob from going berserk.

"Wouldja look at that!" The old man gazed out over Armageddon. Up ahead, the Igloo, all lights blazing, was a frenzy of activity. On its glass front, a great sign painted in whitewash read: 12¢ TRIPLE-DIP!

"There's Mr. Leggett," I said.

"Who?" My mother stood on her tiptoes.

"Mr. Leggett. He owns the Igloo."

"I'll be damned" was all the old man said.

The crowd roared as a line of ice cream cone bearers poured out of the Igloo, carrying their loot, the ice cream dripping down their elbows.

"It's the Happy Cow! That's what's doin' it!" The old man pointed ahead excitedly. Sure enough, there it was, every bit as brightly lit as the Igloo, and right across the street.

A couple of weeks back, a new ice cream joint had opened up, operated by a vast conglomerate, a corporate giant known as Gordon's Milk, a company which owned everything from airlines to sardine packers.

The Happy Cow, known in the ads as "Tessie," was a smiling bovine who wore flowered aprons and had a husband, a henpecked bull known as "Toby." Cast in concrete, she beamed malevolently across the street toward the Igloo. Tessie and Toby were sent out by the corporate tarantula to put the poor little Igloo, and Mr. Leggett, out of business. Newspaper ads appeared, proclaiming that Tessie was now open for business, featuring a huge picture of her, one cloven hoof clutching an ice cream dipper, the other holding aloft a sign which read: TOBY SAYS OUR PRICE CAN'T BE BEAT.

The radio was inundated with commercials which began:

Mooooo . . .
I'm Tessie, the Happy Cow.
Ho, Ho, Ho . . .
I want you all to try my Creamery-rich ice cream . . .
At low, low prices. Moooooo!
(DING-DONG, DING-DONG, Ding-dong–a cowbell clanked.)

At first no one paid much attention, but then the word got out that triple-dip ice cream cones were going for twenty cents at the Happy Cow, while right across the street the Igloo was charging a quarter. Naturally, ice cream maniacs poured in to Tessie's. For a couple of weeks the Igloo languished, empty and forlorn, while business roared just across the street.

"Holy Christ, Mr. Leggett is taking on Tessie, the Happy Cow!"

My old man was delighted, since another of his constant gripes was those nameless entities that he called "The Big Boys," who he believed were behind every conceivable event from the electing of presidents to the humiliation of the White Sox. He was always saying things like: "You don't think The Big Boys are gonna stand for the White Sox winning the pennant! Are you kiddin'?"

And now he was delighted to see that Mr. Leggett was challenging his hated enemies.

Mr. Leggett's brave 12¢ gleamed out in the night, his defiant warning to the encroaching world of conglomerates. The word spread like Bangkok flu. People surged out of the darkness, from across state lines, to take advantage of this incredible bonanza.

Far ahead I could see Leggett's toiling team of countermen dispensing triple-dippers as fast as they could. In front of the store, Mr. Leggett himself, his dignity unruffled, stared out across the teaming street at his hated rival.

For the first time since its doors had opened, the Happy Cow was totally devoid of a single customer. The Manager, a gray-faced, nameless minion of "The Big Boys," known only as "The Manager," paced nervously inside the brightly lit store. His corps of soda jerks, each wearing a set of plastic cow horns on his head, stood idle, their dippers dry and motionless.

The long line that snaked its way to the door of the Igloo was swelling moment by moment as ice cream bargain-hunters arrived by the thousands. Out there in the stifling heat, neighbor was phoning neighbor; striplings on Elgin bicycles were racing about the streets, crying the news. The Paul Revere tradition is not dead in America. The combination of boredom, heat, mosquitoes, "the slump," and now this incredible bonanza had ignited the populace. They were going crazy.

"Hey, what's he doing?" I called out.

"Who? What? Who?" My old man was in the grip of the frenzy His eyeballs rolled wildly.

"The Manager. The Manager of the Happy Cow. What's he doing?"

Inside the brightly lit, gaily colored store, The Manager was on the telephone, which was behind the counter. We could see that he was talking fast and waving his free arm frantically. He hung up the phone, leaped to his feet, and rushed through the EMPLOYEES ONLY door of the store. Seconds later, he popped out, carrying a bucket and a large paint brush. Even in this heat, he was wearing his corporate gray flannel suit. He rushed out of the store, and with bold, slashing strokes of his paint brush, he took up Mr. Leggett's gauntlet:

10¢ 3-DIP!

This drama was played out under the brilliant lights of the street, before a vast audience. The throng, like a single living animal, let out a great sigh. For a millisecond or two nothing happened; then, with a powerful, thundering rush, the blocks-long human centipede roared across the street in a giant, crashing wave, to line up before the Happy Cow. The looming concrete Tessie atop the store beamed evilly across the street at poor Mr. Leggett, who was suddenly left alone in his deserted shop.

We were borne across the street in the mob like corks on a tidal wave.

"My shoe, my shoe!" My mother clung weakly to the old man's shoulder. "My shoe!"

"Ten cents. My God, ten cents for a triple-dip!" The old man was quick to shift allegiance to the side of the best deal. I guess it was at that moment that I learned one of the great lessons of my life: that everyone has his price. If the Mr. Leggetts of the world can't meet it, too bad.

"My shoe! I lost my shoe." She listed heavily to port, since she was now wearing only one high-heeled pump.

Ahead, we could see the troops in the Happy Cow scooping frantically, their yellow horns bobbing in excitement as the mob surged in for their ten-cent triple-dips. The Manager, smiling thinly, stood in front of the store, urging them on with short, barking commands.

The police had been reinforced. Motorcycle cops on their Harleys, lights winking, droned up and down the street, trying to keep order.

We had moved steadily closer to the doors of the Happy Cow. Satisfied customers were surging past us, bearing the greatest ice cream buy ever seen in Hohman. You could hear them licking and slurping; smell the butterscotch walnut, the chocolate ripple as they went by. You could almost taste it.

Elbows jammed into my ribs from behind. The crush was immense. My old man's face was covered with sweat, his eyes gleaming with excitement.

"Smell that marshmallow chocolate chip!"

Across the street at the lonely Igloo, Mr. Leggett silently observed the sickening scene of his ex-customers and friends, who had deserted him like rats leaving the *Titanic*. From somewhere near the distant end of the line, the crowd began to sing "MOOOOOO, MOOOOOO . . ." in homage to Tessie's radio commercials. There was a roar of applause.

I guess it was that, those damnable Moos, that got Mr. Leggett. Moving like a shot, he disappeared into the Igloo and reappeared almost in the same movement. He quickly scrubbed off his enormous 12 and with a dramatic flourish of his dripping whitewash brush, scrawled "7," a vast, defiant 7 gleaming out into the night.

For a moment or two, the crowd was caught off guard, but not for long. Again, the great tidal wave of humanity crashed and thundered across the street. Screams and goatlike grunts of pleasure echoed from building to building. A policeman swinging a rubber truncheon was swept under by the wave and disappeared beneath the avalanche. Someone kicked me heavily in the kidney, but I hardly felt a thing. My kid brother bobbed somewhere below me. I could hear him squeaking in terror, but it was every man for himself.

"Shut up and hang on!" I yelled. He clung to my belt.

Once again, the brave band of Igloo troops, their plastic helmets glowing, dished out a stream of magnificent triple-dip cones. Mr. Leggett operated the cash register as the slurping, licking, sucking, crazed ice cream eaters lurched past him.

From outside, we could see that Mr. Leggett's dramatic move had ignited even those who already carried cones. They were forming up in the distant darkness for seconds, maybe thirds.

"By Christ, I never seen anything like it. Good old Leggett!" The old man, true to the tradition of his sort, had instantly forgotten his defection and was now back in the fold, cheering loudly.

The Happy Cow was a somber sight: empty, inert, showing a few signs of the battle. Broken cones littered the sidewalks, and ice cream dripped from its walls, but nary a customer. Again, The Manager spoke frantically into his phone. Later, there were those who said he was crying.

Someone in the mob yelled, "IG-loo, IG-loo, 'ray, 'ray, 'ray!" The crowd raggedly took up the chant, amid applause and whistles. The lines were definitely being drawn.

Seven cents, triple-dip ice cream cones, I thought, seven CENTS! Who could believe it?

"Hey, Flick," I yelled. I had spotted Flick going by, eating two cones at once; one a brilliant cascade of banana, raspberry royale, and maple walnut, the other a splendid mountain of rocky road, pistachio, and vanilla—a sight to bring tears to the eyes of any ice cream nut.

"Hey, Flick, how 'bout a little river water to wash it down?" I yelled.

He laughed, sending a spray of pistachio juice into the mob.

"River water? What do you mean, river water?" my mother asked. She was now carrying her remaining shoe.

"Nothin'," I grunted, "I was just kiddin'."

"My God!" The guy in the engineer's cap and suspenders, who was still just ahead of us in the line, lurched sideways as he struggled to cross the street again. I looked over at the Happy Cow, and couldn't believe my eyes.

3¢ 3-DIP!

The Manager flicked his whitewash brush insolently toward the Igloo. Mr. Leggett, his mouth hanging open in astonishment, his eyes staring at the incredible "3¢," seemed to shrink as the ungrateful herd charged out of his store. The immense, writhing human bullwhip thundered over Hohman Avenue, leaving in its wake shoes, a few broken crutches, smashed eyeglasses, the impedimentia of total war.

The mood had changed dramatically from a sort of carnival gaiety to a grim, lurching, slit-eyed rapacity. Even my mother had a hawklike look on her face that I had never seen before. My kid brother snarled angrily. The old man hitched up his pants and stood in a slight crouch, his eyes slatey gray.

Three-cent triple-dip ice cream cones, went through my mind, THREE CENTS! Where will it ever end?

None of us in that vast throng were aware that the final act of war was fast approaching.

Ice cream cones of all shapes, sizes, and colors were emerging from the Happy Cow, in an unbroken stream. The Manager coolly lounged under his death-defying "3." He knew that there was no way that Mr. Leggett could top that one.

In the silent Igloo, Mr. Leggett appeared to be huddling with his troops. Several helmets were cracked. One soda jerk wore a rough bandage on his shoulder. I recognized Al Symenski, a senior from my home room.

We were now not more than ten or fifteen feet from our ice cream cones. We were so close to the battlefield that we could hear the clatter and bang, the squish squish of the corporation ice cream scoops doing their deadly work.

"Mooooo, Mooooo, Moooo," echoed up and down the main street as the crowd applauded wildly the concept of a three-cent triple-dip cone.

We all knew, instinctively, that this was a once-in-a-lifetime thing.

"He's finished," the old man laughed as he watched Mr. Leggett addressing his troops. We, all of us, were about to witness the single greatest act of human courage that most of us would ever see.

High above us, the towering concrete Tessie had taken on an air of triumph. Her eyes, lit by blue winking light bulbs, gloated over the fallen Igloo. Mr. Leggett, his shoulders square, his face without expression, strode through his glass doors. He was carrying his paint brush. Quickly swabbing away the "7," he fired his last shot.

F-R-

"Oh no!" the old man staggered against the bird in the engineer's cap. They clung together. The crowd had fallen totally, eerily silent. It was like watching an execution by hanging.

F-R-E-

Somewhere a siren wailed as one of the wounded was carried off the battlefield. Before he could finish the last letter "E," the multitude had grasped Mr. Leggett's atom bomb. Mindless as an express train, dangerous as a maddened bull, the colossal, primitive animals who had once been human beings, with families, mortgages, used cars, and bad eyes, bellowed and stampeded in for the kill.

Free! Triple-dip ice cream cones! All you want! The floodgates were opened. I saw my friend Al slam backward against the door of a freezer, his dipper loaded with rum raisin. Mr. Leggett stood quietly, his cash register now useless. After all, how can you ring up a free triple-dip cone?

We were inside the Igloo now, amid the piglike grunts of the wallowing mob, the floors slippery with a rich patina of Dutch chocolate, cherry ripple, and strawberry sherbet. Mr. Leggett's troops bravely dipped like automatons. No longer did flavors matter, or even cones. Balls of ice cream were dipped into clutching hands. It was a sickening scene of total debauch.

Across the street, The Manager hung up the phone, his face grim; ashen. He appeared to have aged a decade or more. He took a long, defeated stare at the roistering Igloo.

"FREE! FREE! FREE!" the mob screamed in the stifling heat.

It was all over in moments. The lights went out in the Happy Cow; the doors were silently shuttered. The blue bulbs in Tessie's eyes flickered weakly to darkness.

For the rest of the night, Mr. Leggett and his brave band ladled out triple-dip cones until there was no more. The great primitive beast, now once again uncles and cousins, kids and old aunties, faded into the darkness. The Great Ice Cream War was over, but it would be remembered forever in the town, a story passed from generation to generation.

The Happy Cow closed its doors two days later, never to reappear in the neighborhood. Mr. Leggett, a valiant warrior, never mentioned his stirring victory. In the tradition of all true heroes, he was a modest, silent man.

Al loomed over me, an immense triple-dip masterpiece dripping in his paw.

"That was some night. My shoulder still aches," Al chuckled as I took my first delicious lick of Igloo ice cream. It was as good as ever.

"Yep," Al went on, "I used one of the old scoops from them days on that cone. Look at the size of that ball! The scoops we use today are like Ping-Pong balls, but for an old veteran of the Great War, who was really there, nothin's too good."

Like two ancient survivors of Bull Run, we were both lost for a moment in silent reverie.

"Yep, Mr. Leggett's been gone for years," Al said, "retired to St. Pete, plays shuffleboard every day. They tell me he ain't been beaten in sixteen years."

"That sounds like him." I took a lick of the rich Dutch chocolate. "Al, did he ever have a first name? He was always 'Mr. Leggett.' "

"Yep." Al swabbed at the counter with his rag. "Ellsworth. Ellsworth Leggett. Worked for him till the day he retired, and fifteen minutes before he left the place for the last time he said, 'Al, you can call me Ellsworth.' "

"Ellsworth Leggett. Ellsworth." I rolled the name over my tongue. "Got a good classical ring to it. A name that means business."

Al laughed and raised aloft his gleaming dipper. "Here's to Ellsworth Leggett, the man who beat Tessie, the Happy Cow, at her own game."

"I'll buy that." I licked a bit of pineapple off my Omega.

Some customers came in, laughing and hooting. Al moved to serve them. I rose to leave. It was getting late.

"How much for the triple-dipper, Al?" I called out. Al, smiling under his gleaming Igloo helmet, said: "Are you kiddin'? The same price you paid for the last one I made for you."

I went through the doors and back to my rented tin can. It was growing dark. The first mosquitoes had shown up, but the ice cream tasted fine.

The tunnel made its final jog. I knew that only a few hundred yards of struggling machinery stood between me and the open air, the sky, the sun.

"Price wars," I muttered. "It's hard to believe they really had them."

The Shell station passed out NFL shot glasses, Mobil featured steak knives.

"Holy Moley."

Those feckless undergraduates ahead in that smoking heap probably never heard of a price war, and would laugh if you told them that the Amoco station gave away free tea trays, for God's sake. Tea trays!

Another thought hit me. They charge you a buck fifty for going through this Tunnel of Love. The least they could do is put in a few trap doors that opened up, with skeletons rattling or spooky skulls or something to give you a little extra fun for the ride. Turn the job over to the Disney Company and people would line up for hours just to go through the tunnel. They do anyway. But at least they wouldn't hurl obscenities at the lady collecting the toll.

Ah, you mad impetuous dreamer with a rose in your teeth. I

was getting sullen and moody, as I often did at the end of a bad day, with the car reading 200 degrees on the Fahrenheit scale. I sang a few snatches of my old high school fight song. It didn't help. I tried my favorite Chevy commercial:

> "We go together, in the good old USA . . .
> Baseball, hot dogs, apple pie . . .
> and CHEVROLET!"

The poor Pilgrim behind me was being held prisoner in a tired Impala that had what looked like cold sores around its grille. I hummed tunelessly. The light had changed subtly. The end of the tunnel was not far away.

In a low, cracking voice I sang:

> "When Johnny comes marching home again . . .
> Hurrah, hurrah.
> We'll give him a hearty welcome then . . .
> Hurrah, hurrah.
> The men will cheer, the boys will shout . . .
> The ladies, they will all turn out,
> And we'll all feel gay . . .
> When Johnny comes marching home."

The Barbi Doll
Celebrates
New Year's

There was nothing to do now but just sit and wait for the whistles to blow, signaling the end of our army careers. The last minutes of a whole era in my life were slowly ticking away. A short, fat Pfc sat on a bunk across the aisle from us. He plucked continuously and nervously at imaginary lint on the GI blanket.

"You guys gonna re-up?"

His high, quavering voice didn't fit his solid, potlike body. He wore the pale blue braid of the Infantry and the look in the eye of a man who had seen a lot of things that he wished he hadn't.

"Nah," I answered. It hadn't even occurred to me to re-enlist. The question surprised me.

"I think I'm gonna," the Pfc said to no one in particular, and went back to plucking at the lint.

Whistles blew. We stampeded through the door and out into the cold for the last formation many of us would ever stand, a formation I had pictured in my mind a thousand times, through countless boring, mosquito-ridden, heat-rashed nights of the endless past. This was it! Already I could feel civilian life seeping into my being, a rising note of excitement. My God, I was getting out! From now on life was going to be so unbelievably great that already I could hardly stand it.

We formed a neat column of twos, with the professional cool of veteran soldiers. A captain wearing the insignia of the Quartermaster Corps stood next to the master sergeant, who now cradled in his arms a stack of large, pale yellow folders. Every last one of us riveted our eyes on that treasure trove of precious papers. The captain calmly began reading names: last name, comma, first name, comma–initial, comma, rank, comma, army serial number. As each name was called the man stepped forward through the frigid air, and the sergeant handed him his papers.

At last my name was called. I lurched forward, feeling as though I were floating over the ground. I felt the cold surface of the yellow folder in my hand, floated back into formation. Then everything seemed to happen fast, in a jerky way, like the shutter of a camera.

The captain spoke: "Misters, I am pleased to be the first to call you 'Mister.' As of now, you are no longer under obligation to the United States Army."

He said this in a kind of official voice. He then went on, and his voice changed somehow:

"Well, that's it, you guys. There's bus tickets and stuff to get you home in those envelopes. Have a ball. I wish I was getting out with you."

A ragged cheer broke out in the platoon.

"Well, that's it, as the captain said," Gasser lit a cigarette. "Now for the Brave New World. We are reborn. We shall walk forever in shining glory and beauty." He laughed sardonically and headed down the company street. I never saw Gasser again.

Company K was now part of history. We had no proud, tattered regimental banner, no unit citations. All I had left to remind me of Company K, 3162nd Signal Air Warning Battalion was a pair of wire cutters I had stolen and which were now weighing down my back pocket and digging me sharply in the rump.

I squatted on my bunk and loosened my scratchy GI tie. My B-bag was packed and ready to go, stuffed with worn suntans, an old pair of trusty PX shower clogs, an extra pair of GI shoes, a couple of sad souvenirs; a moldering compost heap of stained letters, petrified cookie crumbs, buttons, broken combs, extra stripes, a faded field jacket, and all the rest of the effluvia that sinks to the bottom of every soldier's barracks bag, no matter what the war or army.

Zynzmeister was carefully folding a shirt on the next bunk.

"Do you realize, gentlemen, that a whole new life has begun?"

Zynzmeister, Company K's resident philosopher, was still getting in his licks.

"Yes, it is an awesome thought."

He neatly folded a tie and tucked it inside the shirt.

"I hope you are absorbing everything about you, since this is a historical occasion."

He paused dramatically. Faintly, in my mind, I could hear the sardonic voice of Gasser, who right about now would be saying, "Road apples!"

"You know, Zynzmeister, I miss Gasser," I said, scraping some snow off my shoes with a tent peg.

"Never fear for Gasser," Zynzmeister laughed, beginning to pack away his library, which had mystified Company K for many years. The reading material, by and large, in our late company ran heavily to tattered magazines composed largely of photographs of poorly clad young ladies, all extraordinarily developed in the mammary regions. Gasser once said you could tell a lot about a man by whether he called them "boobs," "tits," or "bosoms."

"Zynzmeister, do you remember the night Lieutenant Cherry blew his stack over Elkins and all those guys from the Motor Pool fighting it out over Ava Gardner's boobs?"

"Yes, I certainly do recall that deplorable incident. In fact, it will remain one of my fondest memories of Company K. Truly typical of the festive times that we all will cherish in years to come. Yes, I would certainly classify that night as a Golden Memory. Had I been Gasser, I would have vulgarly referred to it as a 'Golden Mammary.' But I'm glad I do not have that kind of mind. No, indeed."

"Why do you think Cherry got so mad?"

"I have often wondered about that myself," Zynzmeister answered, briskly tightening the drawstrings on his barracks bag. "I believe it stemmed from one important fact." He paused to straighten his tie.

"Yeah? What was that?" I asked.

"It is my belief that Lieutenant Cherry was a desperate man, and on the night of the Bazoom Caper, became a bit overheated."

I had never thought of Lieutenant Cherry as particularly desperate. Chicken, yes. Desperate?

"How do you mean, 'desperate'?" I asked, as the wind rattled the eaves of the barracks and the unfamiliar, alien GIs with their strange patches and foreign braid nervously paced and twitched all around us.

"It is obvious," Zynzmeister continued as he carefully sat on the edge of his bunk so as not to blunt the crease of his ODs. "Consider, he was a company commander. Usually an exalted position. But Lieutenant Cherry commanded Company K."

"Yeah. I never thought of it that way."

We both sat for a while staring reflectively into our mutual past. Zynzmeister had opened up new vistas again. I mulled it over. It had been bad enough being in Company K, but commanding Company K must have been a special hell

"Yes, there were times when I felt profoundly moved by the plight of our brave lieutenant. The night of the Tumult Over the Tits was certainly one of them."

He carefully straightened his garrison cap, hoisted his barracks bag with the practiced ease of an old soldier, and stuck out his free hand.

"Well, old friend, my comrade in arms, this is truly it."

"Yeah, Zynzmeister."

We shook hands.

"We have survived, which is a lot more than many have done." He shifted his B-bag to his other hand. "Have a good life. May your soldering iron always be hot," he laughed. "My transport awaits."

"Good luck, Zynzmeister."

"Be careful," he laughed again, and disappeared out the door. I knew I would never see him again, either. We had been through a lot together. Now it had all disappeared like smoke.

Fifteen minutes later I was in the Greyhound station, with a one-way ticket, waiting for the bus to take me up north through the frozen cornfields and the icy used-car lots of midwinter Indiana. To kill time before my bus left, I hoisted up my bags and drifted in to the coffee shop. A waitress in a yellow apron came over and slid a menu to me, a sheet of faded blue mimeographed goodies featuring salmon loaf, a veal cutlet with tomato sauce, and pig-in-the-blanket, Indiana-style. The menu was encased in cracked and scratched celluloid.

"What'll you have, sol'jer?" she asked, staring vacantly over my head at a plastic Santa Claus that hung from a Pabst Blue Ribbon clock on the wall behind me.

"Cheeseburger and coffee."

"You want cream inna coffee, sol'jer?"

"Black. And I'm not in the Army."

"You're what?" she asked, sticking her pencil into her shellacked blond hair.

"I'm not in the Army."

"Howcome you're wearin' that uniform?"

"I've been discharged."

"You honest ain't in the Army?" She peered at me suspiciously.

"Nope. I've been sprung."

"Tough luck, buddy," she said, smiling evilly, showing a faint glint of a gold tooth. "That means you ain't entitled to our serviceman's free cuppa coffee. You gotta pay like everybody else, mister."

"Oh."

It was all I could think of to say. Civilian life was starting off great.

Eventually the bus roared into the station, trailing clouds of blue diesel smoke. I got a seat near the back, over one of the wheels, naturally. The bus was packed with people going wherever people keep going on Greyhounds. A blue-jowled customer in a stiff black suit, wearing a white shirt with dirt on the collar, sat next to me, taking up both armrests. I squeezed next to the window, thinking, Dammit, it's always my luck.

Every time I ride on a bus some old lady or a guy who sells bird cages by mail gets the seat next to me. No matter what I do. I concentrate every time some girl comes down the aisle, trying to lure her to sit next to me, but it never works.

"Care for a smoke, soldier?" Blue Jowls snapped out a pack of Camels. They always smoke Camels.

"No, thanks," I answered, staring out at the gray, frozen Indiana skies as we barreled north along Route 41 toward my new golden life, the Yellow Brick Road to the Emerald City.

As we pulled out of town, a bullet-riddled sign flapped in the icy wind—COME BACK SOON—LION'S CLUB. I settled deep into my seat and felt a slow, rising wave of excitement banging and crashing around in my guts. Home! A new life! I'm out!

I dozed off in the sweaty half-sleep that you sometimes have in buses and planes. We droned on and on and on. Twilight came and went. The villages became towns, then cities. I slept fitfully.

"Let's go, buddy. End of the line."

I woke in a daze. The bus driver rousted a drunken sailor out of a front seat, his blue pea coat covered with a verminous green, lumpy substance. We were the last passengers. The swabbie carried a yellow envelope, too.

Out on the street I pulled my collar up against my old enemy, the Indiana wind, and set out for home. I sniffed the air, the familiar, fragrant, sickening aromatic air of home, redolent of blast furnace fumes, the noxious gases of innumerable refineries, the pungent yet titillating overtones of the Grasselli Chemical Works, subtly blended with the exhalations of Lake Michigan, its frozen, clammy, detergent-laden waters.

Ah, how familiar. How warm. Home is more than just a place, a geographical location, a house. It is light, it is sound, it is smell. I breathed in deeply the rich compost of life-giving poisonous vapor and trudged on into the night. For three years I had not walked this ground. I had grown from callow, feckless youth to hard-jawed, flat-bellied, iron-muscled man. With Company K I had roamed the earth. Now, like all returning warriors throughout history, I had come back to claim my own. The wind screamed through the ropes of my barracks bag, down my spine, around my bent form as I carried it on my back for the last time.

In the darkness I passed a familiar house, half-hidden behind luxurious shrubs. My God, yes! Daphne Bigelow! Beautiful Daphne. Daphne, the Daphne of my dreams. A sick feeling hit me deep in the gut as I remembered the night I had disastrously struck out with Daphne. I straightened up, walking proudly in the darkness, my campaign ribbons digging deep into my chest. She should see me now. By God, she should see me now, my skin bronzed by endless tropical days, pockmarked by endless tropical nights fighting endless tropical mosquitoes and heat rash. I was no longer the sweaty yap who had made such a horse's ass of himself in the long-ago. It's a whole new ball game, I exulted.

My eyes were watery from the cold. I battled on past laundries and bowling alleys, past the little candy store where as a loose-limbed stripling I had bought a sinister top. I tacked into the wind and around a bleak corner, and there before me lay the Warren G. Harding School. In the blackness of the playground I almost saw the dark, moving shadows of Farkas and Grover Dill, of Schwartz and Flick, of me playing a ghostly game of softball.

I slogged on past my alma mater, past my infanthood, past the scenes of my most humiliating traumas, into the Future. I felt thirty feet tall; free, strong, magnificent.

At last I walked up the sidewalk of my childhood home, banked high on either side with midwinter Indiana snow. I could see our old garage faintly outlined against the dull cherry-red, the purplish skies of the steel mills off to the north.

Home at last. Easing my barracks bag off my aching shoulder, I straightened up my cap and rang the bell. It hit me suddenly that this was the first time I had ever rung the doorbell of my own home. I glanced at the radium hands on my PX watch, which I had been allowed to buy, as a bona fide GI, at only seven dollars over the price ordinarily charged to mere civilians. It read exactly 2:34 A.M. It was at that instant, that minute, that my new life truly began.

"Who's there?"

I heard the weak, quavery voice of my mother coming from behind the locked door.

"It's me, Ma."

Dead silence. My mother had always been afraid that something was going to come and Get Her out of the dark, and she probably figured that it had now arrived.

"IT'S ME, MA!" I hollered again, louder, in a voice more fitting to a returned warrior still dressed in his armor. I heard faintly a muffled squeak, and the clankings and bangings, the clinkings of chains, latches, and locks being manipulated.

Silence, and then: "I can't get it open."

Nothing had changed. That door had been sticking since before I was born, and I knew exactly what to do. I gave it a swift kick at the lower left corner, at the same time hurling my right shoulder forward and simultaneously giving it a blow with my left knee. It never failed. The door swung open.

Instantly, I was engulfed in the totally familiar smell of my own family nest. Every home has its own distinctive aroma, which reflects the diet, the skin condition, the personal habits, the state of deterioration of the sofa, of the specific family that is holed up in that particular cubicle. Meatloaf, red cabbage, the old daybed, moldy tires in the basement, my mother's Chinese red chenille bathrobe, which faintly breathed out the myriad aromatics of countless breakfasts past, swept over me.

"Ma!" I blurted. "It's me. I'm home!"

My mother, faintly luminous in the reflected glow of the street light, peered sleepily at me, her hair festooned with aluminum rheostats. For an instant I was sorry that I had not sent a telegram or something letting them know I was coming home. I figured the surprise would really be great. But I had the distinct impression that my mother looked a little like Ebenezer Scrooge seeing the ghost of old Marley rattling his chains.

"What are you doing home?"

"I'm home, Ma. I'm out. Lemme get the hell out of this wind."

"Don't use such bad language."

"Jesus, I'm freezing my ass off!"

I squeezed into the living room, dragging my barracks bag behind me. She closed the door, struggling against the howling Indiana gale. Stumbling into the kitchen, I flipped on the light and sank down at the kitchen table, the old white enamel kitchen table.

My mother seemed stunned to see me squatting in the kitchen, wearing a snowy GI overcoat, loaded down with equipment and speaking a strange tongue. Everything seemed totally unreal, yet so completely familiar, but somehow smaller, more worn.

"When do you have to go back?"

She stood by the sink, plucking nervously at her bathrobe. Obviously I was as unreal to her as she was to me. Three years is a long time.

"I don't have to go back. I'm out."

"Out of what?"

She turned on the hot water in the sink and instinctively began to swab the cupboard top with a damp Brillo pad.

"Out of the Army. I'm done. I paid my dues."

"You mean you're home for good? Is that what you mean?"

"Yep. Home for good. Got any salami in the icebox?"

I unbuttoned my GI overcoat, pretending not to notice her glistening eyes. Our family never was much for crying, and when someone did, you weren't supposed to notice.

"I think there's some summer sausage left. You mean you never have to go back? Never?"

"Never, Mom."

She busied herself with buttering bread and pouring milk.

"WHAT THE HELL'S GOING ON OUT THERE?"

A familiar bellow boomed out through the house. It was the old man.

"HOLY CHRIST! MY GOD ALMIGHTY! I'll break my leg one night!"

Ever since my twelfth year, when the family invested in a Carole Lombard-style chromium-and-glass coffee table, the old man had regularly crashed into it in the dark. He had more lumps on his shins than a second-string goalie for the Chicago Blackhawks. He lurched into the light in the kitchen, his long johns flapping.

"Howcome y'didn't let us know you were coming?" he hollered while rubbing his shin.

"Figured I'd surprise you."

"Boy, you could have given your mother a heart attack. When y'gotta go back?"

"I'm out."

I dropped my bomb in the same quiet voice that John Wayne always used in moments of cool.

"Well, I'll be damned. You're really out?"

He belted me on the shoulder, spilling my milk all over the table.

"Hey, bring me a beer."

He always accompanied big moments in his life with a beer, winter or summer. Beer for him spoke the language of Joy.

"Heard from Randy lately?" I asked.

My kid brother was also in the Army, forty million light-years removed around the globe.

"Yep. Got a letter from him last week. Got a case of heat rash." He banged me on the arm. "It sure is good to have you back."

The old man took a drag of his Blatz. His stomach rumbled distantly.

"Yep, it sure is good to be here. Yep, it sure is."

"You've grown," my mother said faintly from near the stove. "You're so brown . . ."

"Yep" was all I could think of to say. I had dreamed of this moment for three years, off and on, this instant of reunion. Now here it was, and all I could think to say was "yep," "nope," and to chew on a summer sausage sandwich. I was overcome by a great weariness. For the past two weeks we had stood reveille at 5:30 A.M. at the Separation Center; countless formations punctuated by mysterious whistles in the night, and now it was catching up with me.

"What's the matter? You look sick."

My mother hovered over me nervously, patting my shoulder tentatively as though touching a mysterious visitor from an unknown planet.

"I guess I'm tired, Ma. Just tired."

"You better hit the hay. Seven o'clock comes early." The old man laughed. It was his eternally repeated joke. He had said that every day for as long as I could remember. He never got up at 7 A.M. in his life.

"Yep. It sure does," I answered.

I got up wearily, went through the dining room into the old familiar bathroom. The sink seemed far lower than it had when I left; the tub was so small. I looked in the mirror. A heavy stubble had emerged since my distant 5:30 A.M. shave four lifetimes ago, when I was still in the Army. My GI tie had twisted slightly under my OD collar. The Signal Corps crossed flags glinted back at me from the mirror. I took off my overseas cap with its orange-and-white braid and tossed it in the tub, doused some water on my face, and slowly began to undress.

"I've got your pajamas," my mother called through the bathroom door.

Five minutes later I was in my childhood sack, back in the bedroom where my fielder's mitt moldered in the closet and my ice skates rusted under the bureau. Instantly, I tumbled into blackness.

For a minute or two I couldn't figure out where the hell I was. It was morning; I knew that. But where the hell was I? For the past three years I had gazed up into the dark gloom of tents and barracks' ceilings. I couldn't figure out what all those roses and birds were on the walls. A moment of terror hit me, figuring that any minute now the MPs would burst in and drag me out of this whorehouse.

I smelled bacon and heard the whooping and splashing that my old man always made in the john. I leaped out of bed. I was free! Free! Waves of ecstasy roared through every fiber of my being. Never again would Sergeant Kowalski tell me to get the lead out of my ass as he had every morning for years; never again would I have to watch Elkins, our company driver, slurp his soggy Wheaties down like a demented pig. Never again would I pull another shit detail and find myself wallowing around in the grease trap or pulling Latrine Orderly on the weekend and doing nothing but swabbing out crappers.

I pulled on my olive-drab GI shorts, opened my barracks bag, and took out my PX clogs. Dog tags rattling, I wandered out into the kitchen to begin my first civilian day.

The old man was sprawled out at the kitchen table, reading the sports page of the *Tribune*. My mother hunched over the stove, stirring the Cream of Wheat. I sat down at my usual spot.

"Son of a bitch," the old man muttered, peering at the paper, "I can't figure out what the hell them dumb bunnies in the front office are thinking."

"White Sox make another bad trade?" I asked.

"Boy, they got nothin' but morons in the front office."

It was as if the three years hadn't passed. Every year the White Sox systematically traded away all their talent for an endless succession of little skinny scurrying infielders with many-syllabled names and low batting averages. Every year the old man roared at breakfast with each new outrage.

"What's that stuff on your back?" my mother asked timidly.

"Heat rash." I scratched under my arms.

"What are those things on your neck?"

"Dog tags, Mom."

"Oh? What are they for?"

"Well, it's like sort of a dog license. If a dog gets lost they can tell who he is by looking at his dog tag. And if you get blown up or something, they can find out who you were, if they can find 'em."

"Oh."

She sprinkled brown sugar on my Cream of Wheat, something Banjo Butt, our mess sergeant, never did. I looked around the kitchen at the weak sun streaming through the windows.

"I'll bet you're gonna have a wild time New Year's Eve this year," the old man laughed as he folded up the paper.

"New Year's Eve?"

I had forgotten. New Year's Eve was two days away. In the excitement of coming home, I had even forgotten what time of year it was. New Year's Eve! The beginning of a new time. Jesus, yes, I gotta get a date for New Year's. I'm gonna really swing wide and high.

"Gee, that's right, Dad. I better get myself a date."

"Well, I'll tell you what. You can have the car. After all, you don't come home from the Army every day."

"Fuckin' A right!"

For one brief flashing blue instant I had the sensation that a grenade had gone off in the kitchen. There was a high, faint ringing in my ears. Everything seemed frozen in place; my mother's wide staring eyes, my father's astounded gaping jaw.

Just this exact situation had been a standard running joke in Company K since my days in Basic, the GI home on his first leave calling loudly for the fucking mashed potatoes. My God Almighty! It had happened to me!

Slowly the smoke cleared and the wounded and dying lay about me. I weakly reached out for my spoon and numbly ladled in Cream of Wheat. The old man rose to his feet and said:

"Well, I gotta get off to work. I'll see ya when I get home, sol'jer."

He went out the back door. I could hear him laughing on his way to the garage.

"Well, I guess I'll get dressed and go out. It sure is great to be back."

I lamely tried to rally. When you've really laid a monster egg the best thing to do is pretend nothing has happened.

"What are you going to do today?" my mother asked in a strained voice as she cleaned away the breakfast wreckage.

"Well, I guess I'll just go out and fool around. Walk around and take a look at things."

I got up and stretched nonchalantly, still staggered by my spectacular gaffe. I wondered how Gasser was doing back home in his kitchen, and what Zynzmeister was having for breakfast.

I pulled on my OD trousers, took a clean suntan shirt out of my barracks bag, and began to dress. Ten minutes later I was wandering aimlessly up Main Street, looking for action.

It was cold as hell, but I didn't mind. I was home. I was grown up. I had the world by the ass. My back pocket was full of GI discharge cash. There was nothing I couldn't do.

I stopped in at the drugstore, squatted on the stool at the fountain where I'd frittered away the better part of my teens, and ordered a lemon Coke from the waitress. I didn't remember her from the old days.

"Where's Janie?" I asked as she swabbed away at some glasses.

"Janie who?"

"Janie. The girl who works behind the counter. The redhead. Janie . . . uh . . . Hutchinson."

"You sure you got the right place, soldier?" She eyed me narrowly. It was an eerie feeling. What the hell was going on? This was our drugstore, me and Schwartz and Flick. We were the stars here.

Old Doc Millard, the pharmacist, came puttering out of the back and spotted me.

"Is there anything I can do for you, soldier?"

"It's me, Doc. Don't you remember me?"

He wiped his hands on his white uniform coat and peered myopically at me through his glasses.

"Why, of course. When did you get back? Well, by George, I certainly do remember you. By George, of course. Um . . . uh . . . you're . . ?"

It was obvious he didn't remember me from Adam. He went back into his den. I finished my Coke and left as fast as I could.

I strolled aimlessly up the street, past Friendly Fred's used-car lot, its stiff plastic pennants flapping in the icy breeze, the mass of assembled used clunkers huddling together like a herd of aged buffalo against the cold.

Rounding the corner, I headed toward George's Bowling Alley and ran smack into a girl. In fact, we almost banged heads. As I ducked right to let her pass, she ducked left and for an instant or two we carried on that idiotic ballet of shifting from foot to foot, making sounds like "oops," "sorry," "heh heh." After the third or fourth duck-and-feint, I recognized her.

"Barbi!"

"Excuse me?" She seemed surprised.

"Barbara. Aren't you Barbara ... uh ... Barbara Jean Dorthoffer?"

She backed off warily. "Why, yes. Do I know you?"

"Don't you remember me? We were in Chemistry class together and ..."

She gave me a long, hard look, and brightened as virtuous girls will when they feel danger has passed.

"Why, yes ... Ralph. Ralph ... Parker."

She remembered me! Move in for the kill. New Year's Eve!

"Yeah, boy, remember the time Mr. Harris' apron caught on fire, and Alex Jossway blew up the sink, and ..."

"Now I remember you"–she laughed an elfin, tinkling laugh–"of course. You're the one who had the date with Daphne Bigelow and ..." She tittered again.

"Good old Daphne," I said, playing it cool.

"You've changed," she said softly, her long, rich, curved lashes fluttering in the breeze, her sparkling crystal-blue eyes dancing. "Really changed."

"Well, you know how it is," I answered, casually touching the bill of my garrison cap so that the sun would flash more brilliantly on its golden eagle. "A guy gets around, you know."

"How long are you home for?" Her voice was musical and trilling, like distant fairy flutes.

"I'm out."

She was even cuter than I had remembered. Schwartz had once described Barbara Jean Dorthoffer for all time:

"... she reminds me of Debbie Reynolds' kid sister."

Under her picture in the yearbook was: Captain of the Cheerleaders, Secretary of the Girls' Figure Skating Club, President of the Home Ec Club, lead in the Senior play "Seven Keys to Bald

Pate," State Champion Twirler, Alto saxophone player in the band.

Naturally, she was continually surrounded by an admiring horde of fans. Now here she was, actually talking to me and looking me right in the eye. At least as much of her eye as I could see under her elfin little pom-pom cap with its white, fluffy earmuffs. By God, she was cute as a button.

"Really?" she smiled. "I'll bet you're excited."

She didn't know the half of it.

"Barbi, uh ... well ... uh ..."

"Yes?"

A milk truck roared by, drenching us in a sheet of gray slush. I should have recognized the omen for what it was.

"Uh ... do you have anything on for New Year's? Like a date, or a party or something?"

She hesitated for a long pregnant instant, and then said softly and slowly, "Yes, I do have a date. My Scout troop is putting on a Cookie Dance down at the church. But I don't think they'll miss me. Yes, I'd love a date."

I wrapped up the details cleanly and quickly. I didn't want to louse up by talking too much, or flopping around in my usual style.

That night at home I wolfed down my slab of meatloaf with its accompanying red cabbage with zest.

"I got the car simonized today at the garage," the old man said. "I figured you might want it for New Year's. Just got the plugs changed. You got a date?"

"Yes," I said slowly, setting the old man and my mother up for their second shock of the day, "I've got a date with Barbara Dorthoffer."

The old man carefully set his can of Blatz down. "Barbara Dorthoffer?" he muttered. "You mean Reverend Dorthoffer's daughter? The one that's always heading the Red Cross and all that stuff? You got a date with a preacher's daughter?"

"Correct. She's really cute."

My mother, who had read the famous Dorthoffer name many times in the paper connected with every conceivable Good Work, and a few that they'd invented themselves, smoothed her apron as though the reverend himself was about to come through the kitchen door.

"Why, that's nice. That's very nice."

"Oh, sure. We've been friends for a long time," I lied. "We used to hang around together in high school."

"Reverend Dorthoffer . . ." the old man mused. "He's the bird that tried to close up all the taverns. The guy that got the mayor kicked out." He nodded his head slowly from side to side, lost in thought, contemplating a sad world with all the taverns shuttered.

"I'm glad you're going out with a nice girl. Just watch your language when you're with her."

"What are y'gonna do? See the New Year in playing dominos and making fudge?" My father looked forward to New Year's as the absolutely greatest holiday of the year. It was on New Year's that he always performed his famous Snake Dance, blew horns, and wore lampshades pulled down over his ears.

He had a point. It hadn't occurred to me. What were we going to do on New Year's Eve? After all, you didn't just go down to a movie and have a cheeseburger afterward on New Year's Eve.

I got up from the kitchen table and went into the living room for the evening paper. Let's see, I thought, riffling through the amusement pages of the *Sun Times*. They were filled with ads for special New Year's Eve midnight shows, most of them showing a naked lady wearing a high silk hat, surrounded by bubbles, with little musical notes running up and down the sides and tiny smudgy cocktail glasses dotted here and there.

One ad caught my eye: *See the New Year in in Style. Dance to the sophisticated rhythms of Lester Lanin on the elegant dance floor of the Ambassador Starlight Roof. Make your reservation now for a truly memorable New Year's Eve. Beverages, and sump-*

tuous dining, to the music of Lester Lanin and his incomparable orchestra.

Aha! That was it! What the hell, you can't take it with you. I wanted this night, of all nights, to be perfect. I was going to enter the New Year with style, grace, and elegance, the way my new life was going to be. I rushed to the phone, in keeping with the decisive New Me.

The last day of the year sped by in a frenzy of preparation. I got a haircut. I bought some new Jockey shorts. By nine o'clock that night I was ready.

"Just watch out for those New Year's drunks, if you're heading toward Chicago. Them Illinois drivers are crazy, all of them."

My father, in the tradition of all good Americans, firmly believed that all drivers from adjoining states were the true menace of the road.

I eased myself out into the cold of the back porch and struggled through the snow to the garage where the polished Olds 88 was waiting. The temperature in the last hours of the year was down to around ten degrees, and everything was so still that I could hear freight trains slamming together over at the roundhouse two miles away.

I backed out of the drive and pulled the Oldsmobile out into the hard, ice-rutted street. I noticed the old man had invested in a set of crackling-new Scotch plaid seatcovers. Letting me have the car for New Year's Eve was, for him, the final statement of fatherly love. It meant he would spend the big night sitting around in Zudock's basement, playing pinochle and eating Polish pickles.

The Allstates crackled and popped over the snowy, icy street. I felt light and airy, like a Signal Corps weather balloon in my civilian clothes. I drove under a swinging arch of red-and-green Christmas tree lights across Hohman Avenue in front of Goldberg's. They still had their Christmas window going full blast. I checked the heater and a nice puff of warm air billowed into the car. Everything was going right.

I eased past the stark Gothic whiteness of the Reverend

Dorthoffer's church with its grim spire reaching up into the flickering darkness, the muttering hell-fire of the distant Open Hearths touching the night clouds with subtle magentas and oranges. The reverend lived in the white frame rectory next door, surrounded by black winter trees and heavy snowdrifts.

Pulling into the driveway, I hopped out of the Olds–and dropped the car keys into the snow. Digging my hands deep into the grimy drift, I scraped around in the darkness for the goddamn key ring. My coat sleeves inched up to my elbows as I frantically tried to locate it. Ah! I grabbed something icy and pulled it out of the snow. It was a frozen dog turd.

Just at that instant the front door opened. The scene was suddenly brilliantly lit. There I was, crouched over, blinded by the light, caught totally off guard.

"WHO'S THERE?" a voice from the wide, glass-paneled doorway boomed. "WHAT DO YOU THINK YOU'RE DOING THERE?"

For once I was totally without words.

"JUST WHAT ARE YOU DOING OUT THERE, SIR?" the voice persisted.

It was then that I realized that I was standing in a full spotlight, holding a frozen dog turd in my right hand. From the size of it, he must have been bigger than the Hound of the Baskervilles.

"Is Barbara ready?" I asked, casually dropping the disgusting frozen object back into the snowdrift.

"Barbara?" The voice repeated on a rising note of incredulity, "You're here for Barbara?"

"Yes. Tell her I'm here."

The door closed silently and I was left in total darkness. Immediately I dropped to my knees and began sifting the crud for the goddamn keys. I turned up gum wads, cigar butts, bottle caps, but no keys. Oh, for Chrissake! What the hell am I going to do now? Yeah, the old man always tapes a spare set of keys under the left rear fender. Yeah!

I darted around the rear of the Olds, giving my shin a nasty shot on a bumper guard. A quick trickle of red-hot blood gushed down through my natty Argyles. I put my hand under the left rear fender. Nothing! I reached in deeper amid shock absorbers, axles. Oil dripped down my wrist. What's this? A sodden lump next to one of the body braces. I ripped it out. The old man had not failed me. A pair of greasy keys rested in the palm of my hand, amid crumbs of dog turd. I dashed around to the front of the car, straightening up my coat as best I could.

The front door swung open. There stood Barbi Jean Dorthoffer, Debbie Reynolds' kid sister, the rosy, cuddly, All-American baton twirler, the preacher's daughter.

We spun out of the driveway toward the wide world, toward the quiet dignified elegance of the Ambassador Starlight Roof.

"Where are we going?" Barbi asked in her little-girl voice.

"Oh, just a little place I know." It was a line I'd picked up from David Niven movies. "I think we'll have fun; you might find it interesting," I said, allowing the words to ooze out in a silken purr.

"You know . . ." She stopped in mid-sentence.

"Yes?" I coaxed. "Go on."

The faint perfume of violets or taffy apples or buttercups filled the Olds. I felt deep stirrings, primal stirrings down in the depths of my being.

"You're . . . not like I remember you from Chem lab."

I casually guided the Olds with my left hand, using masterful flicks of the wrist to spin past slower, stodgier vehicles piloted by ordinary cloddish mortals. We skimmed into the night. My mind raced: Remember, she is a fragile bird on the wing. Don't, for Chrissake, blow it!

The clock on the dashboard read just after ten. We had entered the last hours of the old year. In a few fleeting minutes, the New Year would be rung in. My new life would truly begin at the stroke of Midnight. I would take her in my arms; kiss her softly, gently.

At that moment we were driving through a truly barbaric

neighborhood, shoddy stores punctuated by pizza joints and bookie parlors, with an occasional poolroom to brighten the block. I stepped on the gas to get through this miserable, sordid slice of the world. Obscenities were scrawled on every wall.

I neatly avoided a reeling drunk, who waved blearily as we passed. I felt embarrassed that Barbi should witness such a spectacle.

"Would you like the heat turned up a bit? How 'bout some music on the old radio?"

We had slowed for a stoplight. The drunk happily relieved himself against a lamppost, in full view of whoever cared to watch.

"Say, isn't that an interesting Army-Navy Surplus store over there?" I pointed across the street to somehow head off Barbi's seeing the sordid exhibition. The bum started to sing loudly.

The light changed. I whipped across the intersection. ". . . across this land of ours people are celebrating the New Year. We salute the men of our Armed Forces who are returning home, and tonight, here in New York . . ."

I flipped the dial, looking for music.

"Oh," Barbi squeaked, "isn't that a cute little place?"

"Uh . . . where, what? What place?" My windshield was icing up. I peered into the gloom of the dingy street.

"Over there."

I spotted a flickering neon sign in the shape of a red champagne glass. Blue neon bubbles rose from the glass.

KIT KAT KLUB KIT KAT KLUB KIT KAT KLUB—it flicked on and off.

"I have a wonderful idea." Barbi clutched my arm. "What do you say we drop in, just for fun?"

"But . . . we have a reservation, and . . ."

"Oh, just for a drink. Come on. It looks like such a cute place."

What the hell, why not? A quick drink to give Barbi Jean a glimpse of the sordid underbelly of Life, and then on to the Starlight Roof. Why not?

I quickly parked the car behind an abandoned pickup truck, which had been stripped down to the bare bones.

Inside the Kit Kat Klub was darker than a bat's groin, the air a thick compost of stale beer, cigar smoke, ripely fermenting urinals. The stench rocked me back on my heels.

"Barbi, are you sure that we . . ?"

She grabbed my arm and hauled me in. "Come on, don't be a poop."

Well, here goes nothing. I went in over the horns. My eyes focused in the gloom. There was a horseshoe bar. A trio: bass, tenor sax, piano, worked in the darkness on a high stand behind the bar. All three musicians wore black shades. All around the horseshoe, drinkers hunched in the gloom. Barbi led the way eagerly. We squeezed onto two empty stools, jammed in between drinkers like slices of pastrami in a Coney Island sandwich. The band roared into "Perdido."

"Hey, look who's here," the bartender, also sporting black shades, yelled over the uproar. He strolled toward us.

"What'll you have, Barbi?"

"The regular, of course, baby."

"Comin' right up." The bartender flipped glasses and bottles around like a juggler.

The regular! What the hell is this? The regular?

I glanced around to see who he was talking to. It couldn't be us. I hadn't been in a dive as mean as this since the night Gasser, Elkins, and I had spent a hellish time in Pearl's Bamboo Hut in Lodi, New Jersey.

"What're you having, buddy?" the bartender tossed over his shoulder. No doubt about it. He was talking to me!

"Bourbon. Bourbon and water. On ice."

"Comin' at ya," he hollered.

More clanking and banging as the bass player switched to guitar for the second chorus.

The bartender leaned his hawklike face over the bar as he laid the bourbon in front of me and ceremoniously passed a tall thin glass that looked like a test tube over to Barbi.

"One regular, and one bourbon."

He flipped out a Zippo lighter and whipped it quickly over the test tube. A blue flame flared to life.

What the hell is that? A regular?

Barbi leaned forward, kissed the bartender lightly on the cheek. "How are they hanging, Vinnie?" She kissed him again.

How are they hanging? How are what hanging, for Chrissake!

"Ah, you win some, you lose some. You know how it is, Barb." He turned and faced the band. "Hey, Zoot, look who popped in." He extended his hand out with his finger pointed comically down at Barbi's tousled Prom Queen head. The bass player shoved his shades up on his forehead for a second and kept right on playing without missing a beat.

"Hey, man, good to catch you."

Barbi blew him a kiss. She inhaled deeply the fumes of the flaming test tube.

"Ahhh," she sighed sensuously.

"Barbi, I've never seen them fix a regular quite like that."

She squeezed my arm lovingly. "It's a Pousse Café au Vinnie."

Something banged heavily into my side. I turned to my left. "Oh, excuse me, I . . ."

"Hey, honey, y'gotta light?"

I recoiled slightly as the woman on the next stool leaned drunkenly against me. Her watery eyes swam blearily in the gloom, her lips painted a neon red. She wore a pink, lacy blouse that was too young for a twelve-year-old.

"Y'gotta light, handsome?" Her voice slurred as she knocked over my bourbon.

"Oops. 'Scuse me."

The icy bourbon dripped off the bar, soaking my freshly cleaned suit.

"C'mon, Vera, straighten up or it's out on your ass," Vinnie barked. He rapped sharply on the bar with a ten-inch piece of rubber hose. Vera reeled back, spinning off her stool and sitting down heavily, behind me. She shrieked with laughter.

Holy Christ, what the hell is this I'm in?

I reached down to help Vera up off the floor. She appeared to be sleeping. Barbi laughed.

"Isn't this fun?" She sipped her regular.

"Yeah. Sure is." I tried to recover. "Really an interesting place."

"Sorry about that, buddy." Vinnie shoved a fresh drink toward me. "She don't mean no harm." He suddenly leaned forward and whispered into my ear, "Owner's wife."

He went down the bar, rapping his rubber hose to show the flag. Somewhere in the gloom behind me, a scuffle broke out and subsided. The band had disappeared.

"What's in that thing you're drinking, Barbi?" I tried to make conversation. I've never been good at Bar talk, a special category of time-wasting. Some make a life's work of it.

She held her glass up to the dim light provided by a brightly lit framed scene advertising Old Jeeter Ozark Bourbon. The scene was a little boy peeing into a moving electronic stream.

"You see, there are seven colors"–Barbi carefully turned the glass to show off the drink–"each one is a different liqueur. Plus Vinnie's secret ingredient."

"Who's your friend, Barb-O?"

We turned. The bass player leaned over us intimately.

Barbi introduced me to Zoot, who apparently had no last name.

"When's the last time you seen Jimmy?" he asked, his eyes opaque behind his impenetrable shades. "I hear he got busted."

I hunched over my bourbon.

"Don't worry about Jimmy." Barbi tossed off her Vinnie Spectacular. She coyly raised her empty glass.

"Another little drinkie poo?"

I waved down to Vinnie, who quickly supplied us with two more. I laid a twenty on the bar. Vinnie scooped it up and disappeared. I stood up.

"I'll be right back, Barbi. Men's room."

She didn't answer, being busy inhaling fumes from her flaming Pousse Café au Vinnie, her eyes closed in ecstasy. I headed toward the rear of the cave, through the throng, my suit stinking of bourbon, my head beginning to throb from the noise, the smoke, and the thought of Jimmy getting busted. I had the brief sensation of being on a three-day pass in Hoboken.

The restroom doors were marked SETTERS and POINTERS, in true Kit Kat Klub style. I shoved the POINTERS door open. A heavy wave of urinal disinfectant engulfed me. I began to relieve myself.

"Are you cruising, honey?" A tall guy in a velvet suit was washing his hands and smiling at me over the urinal divider.

"Wrong number, Mac," I barked, zipping up my zipper decisively.

"Well, you don't have to get huffy about it," he sniffed.

I plunged back into the club, crouching low, my old Infantry skirmish line move. A sailor reeled into me, splashing beer all over my coat.

"Out of the way, fuckhead," I clipped, giving him an elbow over the kidney.

A giant moth-eaten moose head hung over the bar, an obscene red balloon extending from its mouth like some grotesque swollen tongue. It bore the legend HAPPY NEW YEAR ONE AND ALL. The moose wore a fireman's hat.

I stepped over Vera, who slept peacefully amid the feet.

"How're you doing, Barbi?"

There were two more empty test tubes in front of her. I tried to open the conversation again, yelling over the din of the band, who were back in the saddle. My eyeballs felt like raw sores from the smoke. My throat ached from yelling. Bowling balls careened around the inside of my skull.

"What have you been doing since we graduated?"

She didn't answer, but stared sullenly into her drink.

"Yep, those sure were good old days, back in high school. Remember the time that Wilbur Duckworth, the drum major, was spinning his baton and . . ."

"Oh, will you shut up, for Chrissake." She began to cry softly.

"What's the matter, Barbi? Did I . . . ?"

"She needs another drink, buddy." Vinnie shoved another flamer at her. She blew out the fire and sucked the drink down greedily. Her hair hung limply over her forehead, her eye makeup streaked down over her cheeks.

"Barbi? Oh, Barbi? It's getting late. Maybe we . . ."

I held up my wristwatch. It read eleven-thirty-five.

"Our reservation at the Starlight Roof is . . ."

"I wanna drink," she muttered, "order me a drink. I wanna nother drink."

I waved my hand. "Vinnie, oh, Vinnie. Another regular for the young lady, Vinnie."

"I had it already made, buddy." He moved down the aisle behind the bar as if born to it.

Somebody nudged me from behind.

"In case you change your mind, honey." I knew that epicene voice. I turned and he slipped me a matchbook.

"My number's inside." He slinked away, his hips swaying. My head throbbed even harder. Was this the brave new world I had been dreaming of all those years in Company K?

I took a hefty belt of Kit Kat Klub bar bourbon. It hissed down my throat. My eyes watered, but I needed that drink.

Something tugged at my foot. I looked down. It was Vera, with a broad smile on her doughy face.

"Yes, Vera?" I asked as politely as I could under the circumstances.

"Happy New Year. Happy New Year . . ."

She snoozed off.

"Oh, for God's sakes, Barbi. It's getting later, and we'd better . . ."

"Poor Jimmy," she sobbed, "busted again. Poor Jimmy . . ."

I stared up at the moose. His swollen tongue drooped in the fetid air. Zoot swayed behind his bass as the band worked its way through the Dizzy Gillespie fake book.

Watch out for women who know the musicians, and kiss bartenders. I had just created a Life Principle.

"Hit you again?" Vinnie held up the bourbon bottle.

"I wanna nother drink . . ." Barbi's forehead touched the bar. I flung out another twenty. Vinnie picked it up.

"That'll be thirty-two fifty," he smiled.

"Jesus!" She put away fifty bucks' worth of Pousse Café au Vinnie. They must be seven bucks a hit!

"Heh heh . . . of course, of course." I fished around in my wallet for another twenty. The roll was getting skinny, and we hadn't gotten anywhere near the Starlight Roof.

I made up my mind right then and there. I slapped a twenty down on the bar and drank off the last of my bourbon. Vinnie brought back the change, and I shoved a five spot toward him. He nodded. Barbi sat with her head lying peacefully on the bar. Vinnie laughed.

"Keep an eye on her. She can be mean when she comes to."

"Yeah," I lied, pretending that I knew all about how mean Barbara was when she came to. You don't want to sound like you're not in the club. Jimmy sure as hell knew, and Zoot, and probably Vera. Now I knew.

I stood, carefully avoiding stepping on Vera's knees.

"Let's go, cheerleader."

"I wanna drink," she muttered sleepily.

"Come on." I grabbed her under her armpits, pulled her off the stool, her legs rubbery as noodles.

"See ya, Vinnie," I hollered into the din, propping Barbi up against the wall with my shoulder. "Play good, Zoot." Zoot silently extended five, giving his cool musician's benediction.

I dragged Barbi through the crowd, past a guy wearing a paper Napoleon hat, a lady blowing a horn into a guy's ear. Someone yelled "Happy New Year!" after us as I lurched out into the icy street, half-carrying, half-dragging Barbara, who now was bent in the middle like a folding beach chair.

"Come on. Stand up."

"I wanna drink," she snarled, digging her heels into the caked snow. "Where we goin'?"

"Out, for Chrissake. Out of that hell hole."

She began to struggle. Jesus, she was strong, and with two gallons of booze in her.

"I wanna DRINK!"

"Come on!" I yanked her toward the Olds.

"I WANNA DRINK!" she shrieked, her voice echoing off the empty store fronts.

"Now come on, you've had enough." I tried my Sweet, Understanding voice.

"You son of a BITCH, if JIMMY were here he'd get me a drink!" She started to cry again. "Jimmy's busted . . ."

The cold did nothing for my headache, which was now working itself down the back of my neck. I wrenched the car door open and shoved her in. She instantly popped out.

"I'm not goin'," she giggled.

"Yes you are." I pushed her back in.

"No I'm not," she giggled again.

Oh, God, I'm going crazy. Who the hell is this broad?

I finally got the door shut, after tucking her foot in and scooping her shoe out of a snowdrift. I darted around to the other side of the Olds like a flash, before she could escape again. I swung the car out into the street, past the Kit Kat Klub, just as Vera came staggering out onto the sidewalk.

"Happy New Year, Vera!" I hollered as she sat down on the curb.

Barbara had slumped against me, her head lolling back on the seat. She hummed drowsily.

"Barbi, that was some joint. Boy oh boy, that was some joint."

"I sure could use a drink . . ." Her voice was slurry, the words slipping and sliding over one another. I flipped on the radio. The roar of an immense crowd boomed out.

"The ball has just gone down. It is now the New Year. Happy New Year, everyone, from coast to coast we bring you the celebration of New Year's in Times Square . . ."

Horns blew; whistles, bells.

> *"Should auld acquaintance be forgot . . .*
> *And never brought to miiinnd . . . ?"*

Guy Lombardo and his Royal Canadians blew in the New Year. Barbi flopped over on the seat, sound asleep.

> *". . . and days of Auld Lang Syne . . ."*

The Olds bored into the night. I knew what I had to do.

"I'm gonna be sick . . ." Barbara struggled upright. "Gonna be SICK!"

Oh no, now what? On top of everything else. Happy New Year, buddy.

"UUuurrrrrppp," she retched violently. Oh, my God, the old man's new seat covers!

Within seconds all fifteen or so of the deadly Pousse Cafés au Vinnie had erupted over us.

"And now we switch you to Chicago, and the Ambassador Starlight Roof, where Lester Lanin is ushering in the New Year. Take it away, Chicago."

The elegant crowd applauded; the tinkle of fine glassware and polite music filled the car.

God, they should have switched to the Kit Kat Klub for Zoot and the boys, and maybe a cheer or two from Vera.

"Gonna be sick again—uuuuuuurrrrRUP." Another shuddering retch, followed by more of Vinnie's regulars. She passed out, sinking to the floor amid the swill.

We arrived at the rectory at last. Staggering up the walk, I carried her as best I could, considering how slippery she was, limp as a sack of washrags. Hitting the doorbell with my elbow, I propped her up and tried the knob. The door swung open. I shoved her into the darkness. She landed with a squashy thud. I closed the door, quickly, silently.

"uuuuUUUUUUUPP!"

She was still at it. It ain't my problem now, Reverend.

I fled into the night. Seconds later I was back on the highway.

"Should auld acquaintance be forgot, and . . ."

The icy air blew in through the open window. It felt good. A New Year. My great new life was well under way.

"Judas Priest, what a gallimaufry!" I bellowed my favorite W. C. Fields quotation, from The Bank Dick, in my W. C. Fields crotchety voice as I roared out of the tunnel. I thundered up the curving ramp, taking deep, gulping swallows of air rich in hydrocarbons and the smell of burning rubber that always hangs over the Jersey meadows.

I was back in Gasser's brave new world, or was it Huxley's? Or Orwell's? Or Johnny Carson's?

Behind me, the towers of Manhattan reached high into the gathering summer twilight, touches of purple and gold. The Empire State Building, so achingly familiar, was black against the sky.

I glanced down at the temperature gauge. It was back to normal. The crowd in the Dodge Charger boomed alongside. The Scarlet Knights were heading home. My radio burst into life. It was Frank Sinatra, WNEW's Chairman of the Board, lamenting his lost "good" years.

I snapped it off.

"A very good year . . ." I sang. For forced marches in the rain, for K rations at dusk, for swabbing latrines, and plucking chickens in the mess hall. It was a very good year.

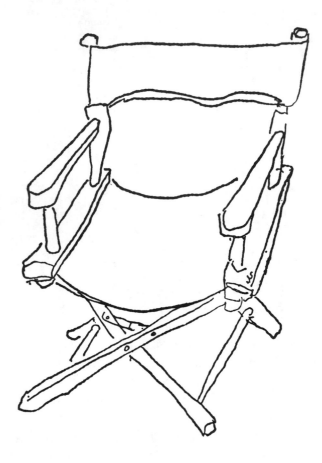

I laughed, lighting up a stale White Owl as I headed into the velvety blood-orange sunset hanging over the Jersey Turnpike.

The night wind blows softly
                    over the restless land
The smoke of time
The chalk dust of the classrooms
            of memory
To the waterbed of desire
                perchance to dream

Perchance

> *to plot*

>> *to scheme*

The selling platers struggle on

>>>> *the race never done...*

Never won.

Oh, America

Sweet Bird of Mendacity

>>> *a field of golden linemen*

>>>> *Joints of grass.*

Call me Ishmael,

> *Call me Cronkite,*

The PEQUOD is lost at C.

>> *Farewell.*

JEAN SHEPHERD
AL's GRASS SHACK BAR & GRILLE
PITCAIRN ISLAND, 1981

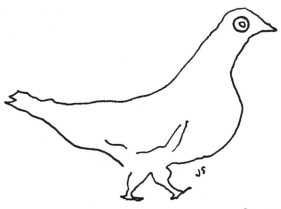

...ALAS

About the Author

For many years a cult radio and cabaret personality in New York City, Jean Shepherd was the creator of the popular film *A Christmas Story*, which is based on his books *In God We Trust, All Others Pay Cash* and *Wanda Hickey's Night of Golden Memories* and has become a holiday tradition on the Turner Network. He was also the author of *The Ferrari in the Bedroom*. He passed away in 1999.